I0721503

KILLER KISS

SAINT VIEW STRIP
BOOK 3

ELLE THORPE

Copyright © 2024 by Elle Thorpe

All rights reserved.

No part of this book may be reproduced in any form or by any electronic or mechanical means, including information storage and retrieval systems, without written permission from the author, except for the use of brief quotations in a book review.

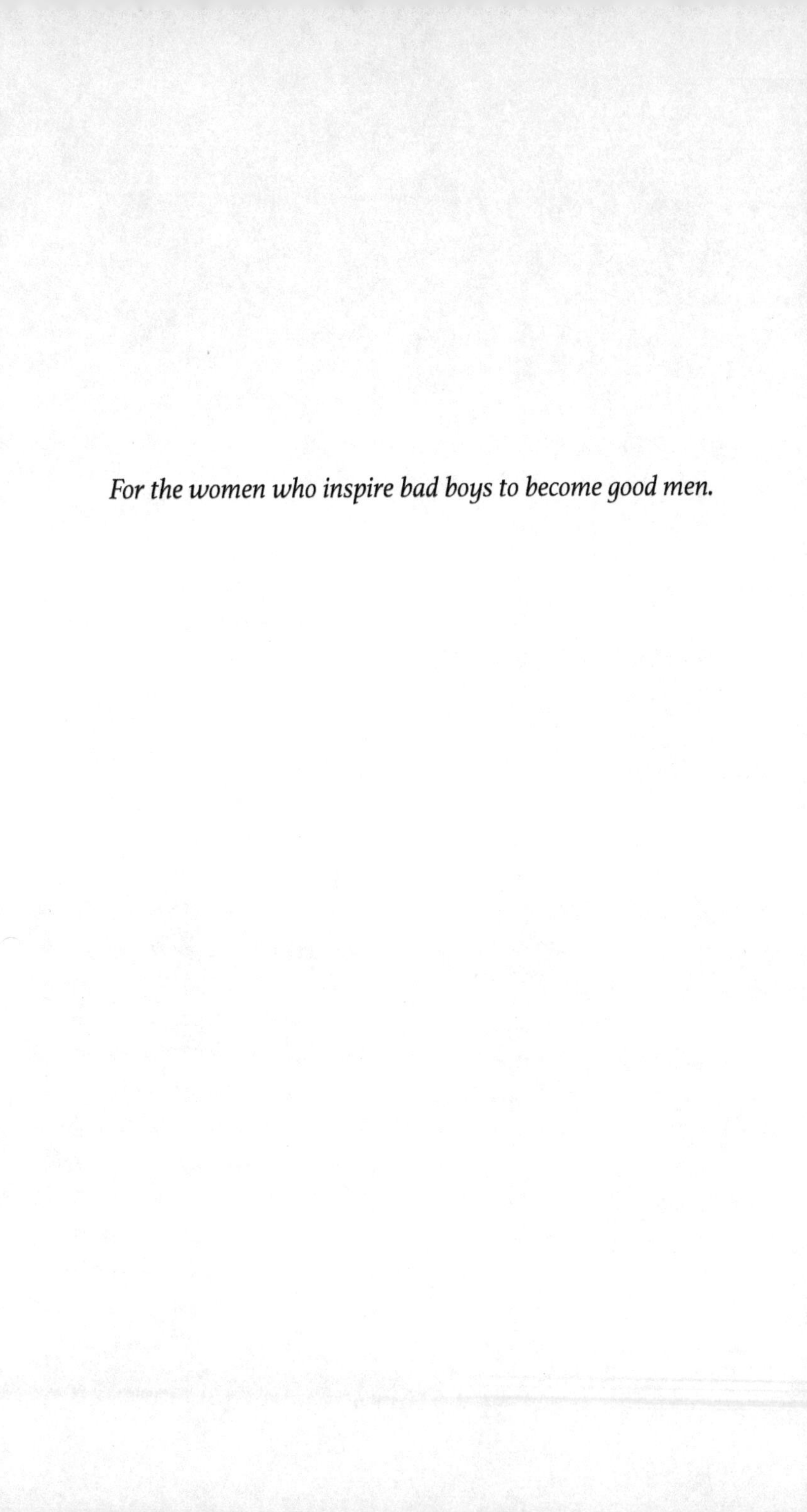

For the women who inspire bad boys to become good men.

1

OPHELIA

"*P*lease go away."

The girl's timid request was almost lost beneath the grumbling of the train hurtling along the subway.

"It's a free country, sweetheart. I ain't doing nothing but sitting next to you."

But it was clear from the man's leer and the disgusting way he looked the teenager up and down that he had other things on his mind. The car had plenty of other free seats he could have sat in. His decision to take up that particular one spoke volumes about his intentions.

The girl stood, gathering her purse close to her chest and moved to a different row.

A second later, the older man followed, stalking her like she was prey. This time he took up the spot across from her, fingers grazing across her bare knees.

She flinched away, tucking her legs to one side, and steadfastly stared out the window. Like a kid who hoped that if she couldn't see the problem, it wouldn't exist.

"Come on now, sweetheart. I just want to talk to you. Pretty little thing like you, you must have men like me talking to you all the time. You know, I'm a talent scout for movies and TV. I think you have a look casting directors would really like. My company could make you real famous."

I fought the urge to roll my eyes. The man's dirty sweatpants and falling-apart sneakers hardly screamed successful businessman.

To her credit, his attempt didn't sway the girl. She didn't so much as glance at him. She was holding it together as best she could.

But her bottom lip trembled. Her entire posture was so rigid with stress and fear it was visible to me, even from across the car.

She was barely old enough to be on the subway alone. She definitely wasn't equipped to deal with predators like this creep.

I waited for the middle-aged businessman a few seats ahead of me to stand up and say something. He probably had kids her age.

When he didn't move, I focused on the young guy who could have just stepped out from beneath the squat rack at a gym. Surely he'd noticed what was happening. He was right next to them.

There were half a dozen men between me and the scene going down who could have stepped in at any minute and told this asshole to back off and leave the girl alone.

Yet, none of them did. There was a whole lot of shifting and sinking down on their seats. Diverting their gazes to things less uncomfortable. Some took out phones and acted like being busy playing *Candy Crush* was an excuse to not call out the problem right in front of them.

The train pulled into a station, and the businessman got up, walking straight past the creep without so much as saying a word in his direction.

"Unbelievable," I muttered to myself, putting my knitting needles down on my lap. I called out to the girl. "Excuse me, Miss? There's a spare seat over here next to me."

The girl's head jerked in my direction, relief flooding her expression. She was on her feet, practically running down the center aisle before I even had time to stand up so she could get past me.

She climbed over me to sit by the window, giving me a wobbly smile. "Thank you," she whispered.

I nodded. "Anytime."

The man twisted and scowled in my direction, clearly pissed off that I'd ruined his fun.

I lowered my gaze, diverting my eyes back to my knitting.

Knit one, purl one. Knit one, purl one. I chanted the pattern over and over in my head to keep myself focused, my needles clacking together with each stitch.

Despite my best efforts, I was still well aware when he stood and moved to the seat behind us.

His hot, disgusting breath kissed the back of my neck. "I could get you a modeling contract, too, pretty lady. With those tits, and those legs...mmm."

A whimper escaped the girl next to me, and I reached over and took her hand. "Ignore him."

"I need to get off at the next stop. I'm scared he'll

follow me," she murmured, low enough I barely heard her.

I chewed that over for a second, then took out my phone to search for a number. Hitting the call button, I twisted to stare at the man behind me. "Yes, Officer?" I asked when the woman on the other end answered. "I'd like to report a man for harassment of a minor and request officers be at City Station when the three-oh-five train comes in. I believe he'll get off there to try to follow the girl."

"You're full of shit," the man accused, his bushy eyebrows drawn together in annoyance. "There's no one on the line."

Not giving his comment any attention, I paused for a moment while the woman talked, and then I nodded. "Yes, he's wearing a blue crew-neck T-shirt, gray sweat-pants, and ripped sneakers. He's bald, has a graying beard... Eyebrows like two fat caterpillars. Currently in car three."

"You stupid bitch," he hissed, clearly no longer willing to bet I was bluffing. He shoved to his feet, flipped his middle finger in my direction, and left the car through the adjoining doors.

I waited until he was out of sight, then ended the call and turned to the girl. "You'll be okay. He won't dare get off if he thinks the cops are out there waiting for him." Even if they didn't show in time, it should be enough of a threat that she could get out of the subway and away from him.

"I don't know." She twisted her fingers around each other nervously. "He seems kind of dumb."

I hid a smile. "If he does take the chance, he'll run

before the cops notice him. He's not going to be hanging around, waiting for you. But do you have someone to pick you up when we get there?"

She held her phone up to me. "I already texted my dad. He's on his way."

"Good."

The train slowed as we neared the station, and the girl put her phone away in her bag.

"Thanks again." She pushed to her feet.

I tucked my legs to one side, letting her pass by.

She shot me a small smile. "Whatever you're knitting is really pretty. I love those colors."

I beamed at her compliment. "Thank you! It's a scarf for my sister."

The girl walked away to stand with the handful of other people waiting for the doors to open, and I slid across the bench seat to sit by the window, making sure she got off okay. As I had assumed, there was no sign of the creep trying to follow her. He was probably farther down the train somewhere, trying to harass someone else.

A new crowd of passengers swarmed on and spread out in different directions, each person searching for a seat. They weren't of any interest to me, though, so I put my headphones in, hit 'play' on my app, and waited for the train to start up again.

"Fawn!"

I flinched internally at the familiar name, hearing it even over my music. On instinct, even though my gut said there was no chance, I looked around the car, hoping for a glimpse of familiar eyes and a wide, white smile.

There was no one around me but strangers. Whoever this Fawn person was, she wasn't *my* Fawn.

My Fawn was sweet and funny and kind. She was all innocent eyes with a big heart that made her the best person I knew.

My Fawn had walked out on our family years ago and begged us not to follow.

We'd agreed. Hell, my brother and I had fought for her to be able to do that, even when our parents had threatened to drag her back and punish her for her insolence.

I still knitted her things, though. Even though I knew she'd never wear them.

A shadow fell over me, and a tall, solid man stared from the aisle. His mouth moved, his lips making the shapes I recognized as my sister's name, even though I couldn't hear it over my music now that he wasn't shouting.

People had always said we were alike, even after she'd dyed her hair blonde to avoid the comparisons.

I took the little speaker from my ear. "Sorry, were you talking to me?"

He sat down hard in the empty seat beside me as the train pulled away. Recognition was written all over his face. There was no need to tell him. I was clearly not the sister he'd hoped I was.

Join the club. No one preferred me over Fawn, and I couldn't blame them. I preferred Fawn over my own company too.

Without answering my question, he doubled over, elbows to his knees, head in his hands. "Never mind. I thought you were someone else."

I watched him curiously, oddly interested in this man I'd never met before but who was clearly a part of my sister's new life. His broad shoulders filled out his T-shirt perfectly, muscled biceps showing beneath the sleeve hems. His skin still held the hint of a faded summer tan, and his dirty-blond hair fell around his face like he hadn't brushed it in days. Dark-blond stubble covered his chiseled jawline and cheeks.

Despite his unkempt appearance, there was no doubt the man was stunning. He had the high cheekbones models would give their eye teeth for, and his eyes were the bright, pale blue that could stop a girl in her tracks.

Filled with pain, but so freaking beautiful.

While my tastes normally skewed to dark hair, dark eyes, this guy was absolutely Fawn's type. She'd been falling for men like him down at the beach ever since she was thirteen years old. I'd had to run more than one of them off when they'd got too interested.

Was he her boyfriend? Or just a friend? Someone she worked with? I had no idea, because I had no clue what my sister was doing with her life. Jealousy swirled in my stomach. He was a complete stranger, and yet she hadn't pushed him away, the way she had with me.

That rejection still stung, even though I understood it.

Beside me, the man's fingers dug into the photo clenched in his hand, the edges tattered and smudged.

Shock punched through my stomach when my sister's smiling face stared out from the image. The word 'missing' printed across the top in thick, black text.

In a heartbeat, my entire world shifted on its axis.

Guilt rushed in, slamming me hard.

My parents were right. A thought I hated to admit.

I should have never let her go.

I pointed at the picture and played dumb, no idea whether this guy could be trusted. Maybe he was her friend. But there was also an awful lot of scumbags out there, like that creep who preyed on young women. Only worse, because at least he'd done it in a public place. There were other men who stole women. Trafficked them away and sold them like they were property.

"This is the woman you're searching for?" I asked him, trying to keep the shake out of my voice.

He glanced over, the expression in his eyes changing slightly. His gaze raked over my long dark hair that I'd painstakingly styled in loose curls that morning. Then shifted to my eyes.

I knew he was noticing exactly how similar my sister and I were.

I hated it. We were similar in nothing but looks. I didn't want him to think I was like her when nobody was.

Fawn was one of a kind. If she was missing…

I swallowed thickly, not wanting to think about that. I indicated the photo crinkling in the man's fingers.

He smoothed it out before handing it over to me. "Her name is Fawn. Have you seen her?"

I studied Fawn's picture before returning my gaze to his. I needed to know who he was. If my sister was missing, I was going to need to know who she'd been spending her time with, and where. "Why are you looking for her?" I asked, trying to keep my voice casual. "She your girlfriend?"

He shook his head. "No. A friend from work. She went missing a few weeks ago. We believe she's being held against her will by her ex."

My blood ran cold. A few weeks? Anything could have happened to her in that time. I ground my teeth together at the mention of her ex but kept a lid on the swirling rage building inside me, knowing I needed to get as many details out of this man as possible. "That's horrible. Where do you work?"

"Saint View Strip Club."

Oh God, no. I felt sick at the thought my sweet little sister had run from us, straight into swinging around a pole and taking her clothes off for money. I'd let myself assume she was teaching kindergarten somewhere.

But of course, that was hard without a college degree. Or a family to support you. She'd left with nothing but the clothes on her back. It had been naïve to hope she was living somewhere nice, with a good job, and surrounded by people who loved her.

Panic threatened to rise up my throat and cut off my air supply.

Stay on task, Ophelia, I reminded myself. *Get the information. Get the job done.*

Emotional responses were weak and unhelpful.

I raised an eyebrow at the man, mulling over the revelation he took his clothes off for a living. It explained the ripped body. "You're a stripper?"

He seemed too tired to lie. "Yeah. Among other things."

Curiosity piqued again, and I crossed one leg over the other. The fact he'd just dropped that sort of information like it was no big deal was interesting. I studied him, trying to work him out. "Like what?"

"I sleep with women—men, too, sometimes actually —for money."

He watched me with his guard up, his expression full of a dare for me to have an opinion on his chosen career.

I had a better poker face than that. Even if I hadn't, it wouldn't have mattered.

I had no opinion on the man's occupation, because I didn't care what strangers did in their own time.

Only what my sister was doing. Had she been doing that as well? Sleeping with men in order to make ends meet? My fingers clenched into fists. I despised the idea she'd had to endure the touch of someone she didn't care about just to make money.

When our parents had more than enough of it to go around.

The train conductor's voice crackled over the intercom. "Next station is Providence."

I glanced out the window, then back at the man. "That's my stop."

He stood to let me pass. Oddly gentlemanly of him.

I cocked my head to one side, studying him while I waited for the train to slow. In the silence, where we just stared at each other, curiosity go the better of me.

"Nice to meet you…"

"Augie," he supplied.

"Augie," I repeated back. I nodded toward the photo. "I hope you find your friend."

The train came to a stop at the underground platform of Providence Station, and I moved for the doors.

"What's your name?" he called to me as I stepped off the train.

I didn't answer. My interest in the man had passed. I already had my phone to my ear. "Vincent?"

"Try again, big sis," my brother drawled down the line.

I rolled my eyes at my sibling's alter ego. "Scythe, then. Even better. We've got a problem, brother. A big one."

Vincent or Scythe, depending on which day it was, had dissociative identity disorder, otherwise known as a split personality. So I never knew if I was going to get Vincent, his much more reserved and polite side. Or Scythe, the smart-ass lunatic with a penchant for violence.

Frankly, Scythe was probably the better option if Fawn's ex had her. I shuddered at the thought of Eddie laying a single finger on her. I'd never liked that man. He was a big part of her removing herself from our family. Not the only part. We were all guilty on that front. But he wasn't someone Fawn ever should have been involved with.

Scythe clucked his tongue. "Is this another one of your 'my favorite contestant was kicked out of *MasterChef*' dilemmas? Or is this something actually important?"

I strode through the underground. "That was you, dumbass. You called me and wailed about Sadie being eliminated for a good twenty minutes. Pretty sure you threatened to peel the skin from one of the judges if they didn't get her back."

Scythe snorted down the line. "Oh, yeah. But you have to admit, she was robbed blind."

"Scythe. Focus," I huffed.

"Fine. If it's not a reality TV issue, what's your problem?"

"Fawn's missing."

Scythe went quiet on the other end. "Missing as in the same sort of missing she's been ever since she told Mom and Dad to shove it where the sun don't shine? Or…"

"The other sort of missing. The kind with posters and milk cartons."

Scythe swore under his breath. Even though I couldn't see him, his entire vibe changed. "Where will I meet you?"

"Mom's. Tomorrow night."

There was silence on his end.

Enough for me to notice the footsteps of a man walking too close behind me. I tightened my grasp on the straps of my bag. "Scythe, I gotta go. I'll see you over there."

I ended the call before he could launch into another rant about his favorite and least favorite celebrity chefs, and tucked my phone into my purse, nudging aside my knitting so the phone could sit in its designated pocket.

Instead of following the crowd up the stairs that led to the road, I veered to the right, striding down the empty platform in the opposite direction. I kept my pace steady, even when there was a squeak of old sneakers on the cracked tiles behind me.

The man's chuckle wasn't quiet. "Look at all that long leg, practically running to get away from me."

I glanced over my shoulder, my suspicions confirmed by the leer of the creep from the train. I turned back around, quickening my pace, heading for the dark shadows engulfing the very end of the platform.

"Where you running to, pretty lady? There ain't nothing down here." He lengthened his stride, matching mine until I reached the end, the shadows swallowing us up.

I had nowhere to go. It was the end of the road. I spun around.

He closed the gap between us, grabbing my left arm roughly. "You thought you were real smart, calling the cops on me. Not so smart now, are you?"

He was probably an inch shorter than me, but I shrank away from his touch, so it seemed like he was bigger. "Please don't hurt me."

He dragged me in, so my chest hit his. He ran his nose up the side of my neck and inhaled. "Don't scream, and maybe I'll even try to make it good for you. Capiche?"

I nodded quickly, a tiny whimper escaping my mouth.

"You should have just minded your own damn business."

"I should have." I reached into my purse with my free hand, my fingers wrapping around the stainless-steel knitting needle and sliding it out of the yarn loops. I straightened to my full height and dropped the scared little mouse act. "But it really kinda pisses me off when pieces of shit like you think they can prey on helpless women."

That girl on the train had reminded me too much of Fawn.

And this guy reminded me too much of her asshole ex.

He reared back at the sudden change in my tone, the acid in my voice. "What the—"

I moved quick. The knitting needle to his jugular cut off any further attempts at words, blood spurting across my hand in the darkness as the man slumped to his knees at my feet, clutching at his neck.

I frowned at the crimson seeping beneath my nails and ruining the manicure I'd gotten earlier in the week. "Now look what you made me do." I sighed. I didn't have any of my usual cleanup supplies. My brother would say that was lazy and unprepared of me, but in my defense, I hadn't expected to be murdering someone in the subway this afternoon.

Sometimes things happened, even when you were just quietly trying to knit a scarf. Dammit. I'd have to start over again now.

The thought made me irrationally angry.

Knitting was hard.

I gripped the man's collar, wiping my fingers off on the material. Red foamed at the corners of his mouth, and he made pathetic noises that almost sounded like begging.

I leaned in closer. "What was that?"

"Help," he choked out. "I don't deserve to die."

Bitch, please. "The only place you belong is on your knees, begging me to let you live."

Not that I was going to.

I let him go, and he fell to the side, blood rapidly flowing from the well-aimed puncture wound, no longer plugged by the needle.

I'd paid good money to upgrade my plastic ones. I wasn't leaving one of my expensive metal ones sticking out of this guy's neck.

With a good nudge from my boot, the man rolled off the edge of the platform and hit the tracks below.

With a bit of luck, he'd get obliterated by the next

train that came through before anyone even noticed he was there.

I strode away, tucking my hands inside my pockets so no one would notice the blood.

I had a sister to find.

2

AUGIE

ucinda, our club DJ, had the music pumping by the time I dragged my sorry ass through the doors. Despite her best efforts, the upbeat music didn't match the vibe of the room at all. The depressing number of patrons sitting around the tables was even more pathetic than the number of times I'd scoured the streets for Fawn, only to come home empty-handed.

Eve, the owner of the club, jumped down from the stage when she noticed me. I barely registered the fact she was in nothing but a G-string. We were all so used to nudity that having a full conversation while one of us was bare-ass naked was just a regular Thursday night.

"Anything?" she asked above the music, though it was clear from her expression she knew what my answer would be.

Same thing as always.

Nothing.

Absolutely fucking zero.

I didn't mention the woman I'd seen on the train. The one with the dark hair, and long legs, whose eyes were so much like Fawn's I'd thought for a second it was her. There was no point telling that story and having Eve's hopes raised like mine had been. She didn't need that extra stab of pain I'd felt when I'd realized the woman was just another dead end.

Lyric, one of the other strippers, had once described my relationship with Fawn as fatherly. It had rung so true I hadn't been able to forget it. But if that were the case, then Eve's relationship with Fawn had been motherly. Neither of us were handling her disappearance well, and we both felt responsible for the sunshine woman who hadn't been seen in weeks. No matter what anyone said, no matter how many times the others tried to assure us, Eve and I shared pain and grief in a way nobody else did.

She squeezed my arm. "Go get ready. There are women waiting in the other room for you."

I could already tell by her lackluster tone that the other side of the club wouldn't be any more happening than this side. Which would be fine if this hadn't become the usual.

We'd gone from filling the place regularly, with tips pouring in so thick and fast I'd been able to be choosy with who I went home with afterward. My little side hustle was a good time when it was like that. I liked sex, and getting paid for it was better than slaving away at a janitor's job or some other bullshit. When the club was full, I could pick the hottest person there, someone I would have gone home with anyway, and make an extra five hundred to top up my night.

But it was a different feeling when it was desperation

that drove you into that lifestyle. I'd been there before, and it had forced me to do things I wasn't proud of.

That desperation had cost me everything.

My friends. Jobs. Self-respect.

My brother.

I couldn't blame him. I wouldn't want to be anywhere near me either.

How quickly I'd found myself back here again, knowing this shift wasn't going to bring in the tips I needed to pay for a burger, let alone the rent that was already overdue.

I loved this club and the people here, but ever since Fawn had been taken, it hadn't been the same. Eve and the others were trying, but I'd damn near given up. Without Fawn, we were all falling the fuck apart, and none of us seemed able to stop it.

I dumped my bag in the locker room, not bothering to take a shower or even glance in the mirror. What was the fucking point? Nothing I did was going to help the dark circles under my eyes or the gaunt hollows of my cheeks.

The club was too small and not soundproof enough to have two different sets of music playing across both rooms. Eve's playlist poured from the speakers in the smaller space I normally performed in, but I didn't care that it wasn't really my vibe. I barely heard it anyway. I went straight into autopilot, avoiding the stage female strippers often preferred, and walking straight into the crowd.

Or in this case, the handful of women sitting at a table in the middle.

I got why Eve and Lyric and Fawn hadn't particularly like getting down at floor height. Men were grabby bastards and would put their hands all over them if given half the chance.

But that was what I wanted. I wanted hands on me. I wanted people touching me, seeing the look in my eyes that made them feel like they were the only person in the room.

That was how you got taken home afterward.

That was how you paid the bills when you couldn't make ends meet.

Often my side of the room had a mixture of men and women, but tonight it was just the one group of ladies, who all tittered with embarrassment when I strolled over and asked how they were doing.

"We don't normally do this," one called to me. "But it's her birthday, and she needed to be taken out!"

The birthday girl's cheeks were pink, maybe from awkwardness or maybe because they'd been here a while and were several glasses in.

Her hair was long and dark, the same color as her eyes.

The same color as the woman on the train. The same color as Fawn's.

I needed a fucking drink. This day had just been one torture after another.

I took the glass from the woman's hand and downed it in one.

Her eyes widened, watching my throat bob as I swallowed. Her friends around her erupted into cheers and hollers.

I tugged the woman's chair away from the table, singling her out, separating her a little from the group. "What's your name?"

She had pretty lips, and they parted only wide enough for her to whisper, "Victoria."

I forced a smile. "Like the queen."

She nodded.

"Got a man at home, Victoria?"

She nodded.

"So what are you doing here, waiting for me to take my clothes off?" The dry, sarcastic words were out of my mouth before I could stop them.

Internally, I kicked myself. This was always my fucking problem. Saying things before I thought about it. I didn't give a shit if this woman had a husband and a dozen kids at home. I was hardly in a position to judge someone. She was about as intimidating as a field mouse, and yet here I was, being a prick to her for no reason, just because I was in a foul mood.

What I really needed to do was lay the charm on so damn thick she fell in love with me and was begging me to fuck her before the night was through.

That was how my rent would get paid.

Her mouth opened, then closed. Her eyes went glassy with unshed tears.

Ah, fuck. Was she seriously going to cry?

Good fucking work, Augie. You've reached an all-time low.

If I was going to salvage this, I needed to give her the full-blown boyfriend treatment. I cupped the side of her face and rubbed my thumb over her lips. "Don't answer that. In here, the outside world doesn't matter. Just for a few hours. Let me treat you the way he doesn't. Okay?"

Her gaze darted to her friends who were all giving her wide-eyed nods of encouragement, clearly zero loyalty to her husband. Which told me they probably didn't like him.

In my experience, two types of women came to the club. The party girls who were all happy at home but just wanted a fun night out with friends. They drank, cheered once or twice at the performers, and then went back to having fun with each other.

Those weren't the women I was interested in.

It was the ones like Victoria, who came here seeking something more. They came searching for what they weren't getting at home. Sometimes that was just someone to talk to. Sometimes it was a person to hold them.

And sometimes they came looking for a man who could blow their minds in ways their husbands were too selfish to.

I could be all three, and more.

I could be whatever I needed to be if it meant I could afford to eat that week.

As the night rolled on, a few more people entered the room, grabbing drinks from Echo at the bar and settling in to watch me dance. But it was Victoria I paid the most attention to. Even when I was giving a lap dance to one of her friends, it was Victoria whose gaze I continually sought out, even though she nervously turned away.

But by the time the club closed, and she was one of only two people left, I knew I had her. I waited for her friend to go to the bathroom and then slid into the seat she'd left empty.

"Did you have a good night?" I asked.

She nodded. "You were great."

"Thank you. So were you."

She stared down at her hands, twisting her fingers. "I didn't do anything."

"You didn't need to. I liked that you were here."

She looked up and drew in a stilted breath. "Can I tell you something?"

"Yes."

"I came here with an ulterior motive. I've seen you here before. You probably didn't notice me..."

I hadn't.

"But I heard that sometimes you do...uh, private events after your shift."

"Who'd you hear that from?"

Her eyes widened. "Oh my gosh, you don't? I'm so sorry!" She grabbed her purse so quick she knocked over a half-drunk glass of wine.

Shit. There I went, being an asshole again. I swear I didn't even mean to. It was just a force of habit.

I put my hand over hers and pulled her to her feet. With a little tug on her fingers, I drew her in and put my lips to her ears. "Get rid of your friend. I'll meet you in the parking lot."

She cleared her throat. "Um. You mean for...for..."

I leaned back and grinned at her. "Yeah, sweetheart. For that. Five hundred for the night. Your place or mine. The car. A park. Whatever you want. Let me know when I get out there."

I let go of her and walked away into the locker rooms.

The second I made it through the doorway, the smile I'd forced onto my face all night fell.

Eve was wrapped in a towel, her face scrubbed clean of makeup during her shower. She leaned on the lockers. "How'd you go tonight?"

"Dead as fuck."

She sighed. "Me, too." She cocked her head to one side. "You want to hang around for a drink? On the house. We can drown our sorrows."

"No, thanks."

"Come on, Aug. We miss you. And it's Fawn's birthday in a couple of days."

I stiffened. I didn't want to think about Fawn spending her birthday with a man who beat and tortured her. Because I knew men like Eddie. If Fawn was even still alive, she wasn't soaking in a bubble bath, being cooked nice meals, or showered with birthday gifts.

She was tied up. Hurt. Praying that one of us would walk through those damn doors and save her.

I didn't deserve to sit around the club, enjoying a drink at the end of a shift. How could I do that when everything she was going through was my fault?

I shouldered my gym bag and moved past Eve. "Not all of us are done with work for the night."

It was a low blow, and I knew it. Though sleeping with clients was strictly forbidden on the club premises, Eve had always turned a blind eye to what I did outside the club. It didn't mean she liked it though. As the owner and self-appointed mother hen, she felt responsible for those of us who worked for her.

Which was stupid. Because my bad decisions weren't her problem.

They weren't anyone's problem but my own.

She watched me sadly as I left.

In the parking lot, Victoria waited by a sleek, dark-colored car.

Huh. I thought for sure she would have chickened

out, but she talked on the phone with someone until I approached and then hastily ended the call.

"This your ride?" I asked her.

She nodded, unlocking the car, and motioning for me to take the passenger side.

I slid into the seat, noting the perfect leather and expensive interior. Shit. I should have asked for more money. I could have gotten a thousand from her. She clearly wasn't from this side of the Saint View-Providence border. The car screamed of Providence wealth.

I stewed on that while she drove us in silence, winding through the streets of the affluent town on the other side of the Saint View slums I called home. She didn't try to make conversation, and every time I did, she answered in monosyllables, so eventually I gave up.

Whatever. We didn't have to talk. I'd do what I was getting paid for and then I could leave.

Eventually, she turned off the main road and into a side street lined on both sides with thick trees. We bumped along for a minute until the lights were no longer visible behind us, then she pulled over to the side of the road. Low-hanging tree branches scratched at the roof, and I cringed at the thought she'd rather scratch up her expensive car than be seen with me.

She turned the engine off but then went back to staring straight ahead, like I wasn't even in the car.

I cleared my throat. "So I'll need the money up front."

She reached around to the back seat and grabbed her purse. With fingers that shook, she rummaged through her bag and eventually withdrew five hundred-dollar bills and passed them to me.

I took them, shoving them deep in the pocket of my

jeans and pulling out a condom at the same time, setting it down on the center console between us. She glanced at it, her eyes widening in fear.

Fucking hell. I'd been accused of being an insensitive prick more than once, and years ago, I probably wouldn't have even noticed her expression. Nor cared about it.

But I wasn't that man anymore.

"You don't have to do this, you know," I told her softly, using a tone not too many people knew I even possessed. "If this isn't what you want…"

She shook her head hard, finally looking me in the eye. "You're incredibly attractive. It's not you."

I laughed. "Don't worry about my feelings, Your Highness. I haven't got any."

Her eyebrows furrowed together. At the royal nickname or the out-and-out lie that I didn't have feelings, I wasn't sure which. But she didn't voice her questions out loud.

"I want to do this. My husband…"

"Is a piece of shit?"

She stared at me with her big eyes. "He slept with someone else, and I found out a few weeks ago." Her fingers trembled.

I realized the way she shook perhaps wasn't in fear, but with an anger she'd bottled up, now ready to explode.

"I thought I would feel better if I evened the score…"

I sat back and stared out into the dark night. "Doesn't really work like that, though, does it?"

A tear dripped down her cheek, and she brushed it away angrily. "No."

I could relate. I'd done things I could never take back, all because I was trying to make myself feel better.

It never worked for me, and it clearly wasn't working for Victoria.

I shoved my hand back in my pocket and retrieved her money. "Here."

She shook her head fiercely. "No. You take it. You deserve it."

I didn't. I'd done the bare minimum. Barely even that. I pushed the money toward her and grabbed my gym bag from the floor. "Go home. Work it out with him. Or don't. Whatever. But this isn't where you want to be tonight."

I opened the door and put one foot out onto the leaf-littered grass.

"Can I at least drive you home?"

But there was relief in her eyes already. She didn't really want to take me back to Saint View. She wanted to drive away and forget this had ever happened.

So did I. Because the longer I sat in this fucking car, the longer I felt like shit about it. It was too small and cramped, and I suddenly craved fresh air like I needed my next breath. "Don't worry about it. I could use the exercise."

She drove off so quickly I didn't have a chance to change my mind. Her tires spun on the dirt road, leaving me behind in her dust.

I was stranded in the middle of Providence without a way of getting back home. Not that I'd have that home for much longer since I would probably be evicted.

I really needed that five hundred dollars.

Fuck.

The trees around me shook as a strong breeze picked up, bringing the scent of seawater from the nearby ocean. Hoisting my bag onto my shoulder, I found my way back to the main road, which was mostly quiet at this time of night except for the occasional set of headlights that flew by, zero consideration given to the loser standing on the side of the road with his thumb sticking out.

Should have known the fancy, rich assholes in Providence wouldn't stop to help someone else out. They always had their heads shoved so far up their own asses.

Whatever. Wouldn't be the first time I'd had to walk. If I turned to the left, I'd be headed in the general direction of Saint View.

But my brother's McMansion was only a couple of streets away. Even though the whole town pissed me off with its perfect lawns and overpriced properties, without any conscious decision from me, my feet took me deeper into Providence until I was staring up at his place.

To my surprise, there were lights on in two of the upstairs windows, a soft glow spilling out from behind gauzy curtains. The walls behind were a bubble-gum pink, telling me it had to be his daughter, Luna's, bedroom.

Figures moved around behind the curtains, faces not clear from this distance but easy to assume it was my brother and his partners, probably tucking their daughter in after a bad dream.

I'd done that once or twice for Banjo after I'd gotten him out of the foster care system. He probably didn't remember because he was so young. Or maybe he'd even blocked out those years around the time he'd come to live with me.

The things he'd seen in foster care were traumatic.

But I'd been there in the middle of the night, holding him while he'd screamed. I actually hoped he'd forgotten, because I couldn't forget all the times I'd woken up in the same way but had nobody there to hold me.

Just a foster parent to scream, "Shut the fuck up!" Or one of the guys I'd buddied up with on the streets before I'd managed to secure a shitty little government-assisted house in an even shittier neighborhood.

After that, anytime I'd woken up screaming I'd quickly tried to muffle the suffocating feeling so Banjo wouldn't hear.

I wanted to go to his door now. Beg him for forgiveness. Ask to be a part of his life again.

I even took a step down the path, drawn in by the sweet family scene taking place in that upstairs window. Then I caught a glimpse of myself in the side mirror of one of their cars and remembered what I'd been about to do with that woman. She'd been about to cheat on her husband, and I would have let her, as long as I'd gotten paid.

Remembered how Banjo had looked at me when he'd told me to get out of his life.

Remembered how the last time I'd cared about someone, she'd been taken. Hurt. Maybe even left for dead.

All of that was on me.

I was the darkness that brought bad things to the doorways of good people.

I was the one who ruined everything he touched.

I turned around and headed back to Saint View, knowing that was where I belonged.

3

OPHELIA

I pulled into the driveway of my mother's house a moment after my little brother did.

Not that he was really all that little anymore. I was tall, but he still had a good few inches on me. He closed his door and came over to lean on mine while I shoved my phone and keys into my purse.

I was stalling because I didn't want to go inside. From the street, the house was beautiful. A sprawling Providence mansion with well-tended gardens and expensive vehicles in the eight-car garage.

All perfectly designed to conceal the horrors that lurked inside.

My mother being the biggest danger of them all.

Dread bubbled up in my stomach every time I came here.

Scythe stared up at the house with a deep frown between his eyebrows, his arms crossed defensively over his chest. He seemed about as thrilled as I was. If it had been for anything other than Fawn, I doubted either of us would ever come here willingly.

It was bad enough FaceTiming from across the ocean.

How I missed my apartment in Spain. I missed the beach and the people and that it was nothing like this fucking place. My family's shit had still followed me there, but not this overwhelming feeling of apprehension that swamped me now.

Not that I'd ever let my mother or even my brother know it bothered me. We didn't do that in our family. Weakness wasn't tolerated.

Just look at where being soft had gotten Fawn.

Probably fucking dead.

I poked Scythe's biceps, trying to lighten the mood. "Stop staring at Mom's house like you're going to burn it down. Not saying you can't do it. That might actually be fun, and I'll help. Bonus points if she's in it when it happens. But please, just not tonight. We have other things to discuss right now."

He drew his gaze slowly back to me, and my mistake registered.

I swore under my breath. "Vincent. Sorry. I forgot how quickly you and Scythe can switch back and forth these days."

Vincent had always been the dominant personality, only letting Scythe out to play when the messed-up world we'd been brought up in got too much. For years he'd fought to keep Scythe at bay, locked up in a prison in his mind.

Until a series of events—a stint in prison, being caught then tortured, and falling in love—had made keeping Scythe locked up an impossibility. The two switched back and forth freely now, and from what I could tell, they were both happier for it.

I loved that he'd found some joy. He'd spent way too many years being antagonized and used by our mother. He deserved some peace.

Yet here I was, dragging him right back into it.

There was nothing else for it, though, when the problem was our sister.

"How's Bliss and War and Nash?" I asked him, trying to make small talk to keep him from actually slitting our mother's throat before we got what we needed from her. "Bliss popped out your devil spawn yet?"

Vincent frowned at me as we walked as slow as humanly possible to the front door. "Don't call my child devil spawn, Ophelia. I don't like that."

I tucked my arm into his, well used to his formal, matter-of-fact manner after growing up with him. Scythe was a smart-ass who would have laughed at my teasing, but Vincent wasn't the same. "You're right," I assured him. "I'm sorry. Being around here makes me stabby."

"Do you want to borrow my knife? I have a spare."

He'd said it with the utmost seriousness. That was Vincent to a T. Quiet and serious. But scarily lethal.

I grinned up at him. "You always do. But I'm good." I patted my bag that may not have held a knife, but who needed a blade when I had knitting needles sitting right next to my favorite gun?

Some siblings made small talk about sports or their jobs. My brother and I compared weapons. It was just the way we were.

I'd maybe even missed it a bit. I'd been away for a long time, which had been my decision, but it meant I rarely got to speak freely. I was forever censoring myself, because when your new friends called you up for dinner and asked what you'd been up to, you could hardly just say, "Hey, I stabbed a guy in the jugular yesterday. Please pass the salt."

There was nothing like family for being able to be your true, authentic self.

Shame that also applied to my mother.

Her true self was despicable at the best of times.

Vincent didn't bother knocking when we got to the door. He just tapped out the security code and strolled on in like we owned the place. He shoved one hand deep in his pocket, most likely reassuring himself he had a knife at the ready.

If I hadn't already checked my own weapons, I probably would have done the same. "Mother dearest! Could you come on down here, please? The fruits of your loins —well, two of them anyway—are here to visit you."

Vincent wrinkled his nose at my word choice but didn't comment.

My mother popped her head over the upstairs railing. "My babies! I've been waiting for you!"

Despite the fact she was getting on in years, her hair graying and skin weathering from too much sun, she still moved well with soft, graceful steps. She hurried down the elegant staircase, trailing one perfectly manicured set of nails along the polished banister.

She went straight for Vincent, which was hardly surprising, since he'd always been her favorite. Couldn't blame her really. When all you valued about your children was their ability to take care of business, Vincent had always outshone me and Fawn. Not that I was a slouch in the contract killing department. I liked a good neck snap as much as the next guy. But Vincent had a darkness I'd never quite mastered.

One my mother adored because it set our family apart from others like us.

Vincent stiffened when Mom wrapped her arms around him, swaying back and forth like he was a toddler who needed comforting. She pulled back, gripping his arms to look him in the eye.

Even I saw her expression droop when she realized her affection wasn't returned. "Oh. Vincent."

One of my brother's alter egos was her favorite. Just not this one.

She turned to me, her dark eyes taking in my outfit choice and then her nose wrinkling. "Have you put on weight?" Her gaze swept over me, head to toe, lingering on my thighs and hips. "You're getting lazy."

I rolled my eyes. "So lovely to see you again too, Mother."

I was used to her constant criticisms, and even more familiar with pretending they didn't hurt. Turning away, I strode into her spacious kitchen, sucking in a breath to calm the little girl inside of me who still craved her approval.

I hated that little girl. She was so stupid. Craving something from a woman who was never going to give it.

Vincent followed me but froze the moment he stepped foot in the room. "What is that?"

Mom shoved the dark-colored gym bag in my brother's direction. "Take a peek and see. I think you'll like it."

His jaw clenched, and through gritted teeth he barked out a single syllable. "No."

But he stared at the bag like it might open and spew evil into the room at any time.

Or like he might actually want to open it.

A spiteful smile flickered at the edge of my mother's lips.

I glared at her, shoving the bag off the edge of the counter and away from my brother. It hit the kitchen tiles with a solid thump. "Don't do that. We've already had this conversation. He's not interested in your job bags. He's out and he's staying out." I glared at him. "Don't let her drag you back into her bullshit, V. You've got a family to think of."

He gave me a tiny nod, his knuckles going white from how hard he gripped the marble countertop.

"Fawn is missing," I told my mother, changing the subject and drawing her attention away from Vincent.

She squinted at me. "Fawn who?"

I gaped at her. The fact she could even say that about her own daughter was astonishing. "What is wrong with you?"

She lifted a shoulder. "Why would I care what Fawn is or isn't? That girl decided her own fate when she walked out on her family." Her gaze strayed to my brother again, a warning in her tone. "You don't do that and expect people to still care about you."

I stepped in front of him, trying to protect him from her poison.

Which, of course, meant her sharp stare landed on me instead.

As a girl, I'd shriveled under that gaze. But no longer. At least not on the outside. I threw one right back at her. "She's your daughter."

"Much to my disappointment." Mom poked at the cuticles of her nails. "Is this what you both came here for? It's boring."

She really didn't give a shit. I didn't have any kids. I shuddered at even the thought of them. They were not in my future plans. But even I had more maternal instinct than she did. We'd never been something for her to love and cherish. We were just assets. Designed and raised to be her little killers and carry on the family business, now that she and Dad were too old.

I fought to keep my anger at bay. "You knew, didn't you? That she was missing? You spiteful bitch—"

Mom flapped her hands around dismissively. "Oh, Ophelia. Stop being so dramatic. I hear things. That's my job. Which, by the way, pays for that comfortable little setup you have in Spain, and the house your brother and his...whatever...live in. Or have you forgotten that?"

His whatever? Bliss and War and Nash were his family. Not that she had any idea what that was.

"And Fawn, Mom?" I spat back at her, refusing to let her torment my siblings. "What does your job do for her? Other than push her to the brink so she's forced to disown the lot of us?"

She narrowed her eyes at me. "You're awfully quick to point fingers, Ophelia. What exactly have you done for your sister while you were lying on that beach in Spain for the past year, partying and spending my money? Clearly not protecting her."

My anger spewed over the tentative hold I'd had on it. "Oh, that's rich. I wasn't even in the country and yet it's my fault? Maybe it's your fault for trying to force her into your damn business when you know very well she was never cut out for that life."

"Not like we ever got a choice either," Vincent muttered.

He wasn't wrong.

Mom slammed her palm down on the counter. "Enough! You two are so incredibly ungrateful! Your father and I have done nothing but provide beautiful lives and opportunities for you. Look around you! Do you see all those mindless zombies out there, working nine-to-five every day like slaves? Is that what you want?" She scoffed, "You'd be a terrible hairdresser, Ophelia." She turned Vincent's way. "You think you'd cut it sitting at an office for eight hours a day?"

"I liked working at the daycare center," Vincent said quietly.

Mom rolled her eyes. "Minimum wage, Vincent. You have a family to support, don't you? Isn't that hussy of yours knocked up? You of all people should understand the sacrifices that have to be made to be a good parent."

I burst into laughter at the irony of her handing out parenting advice. "Yeah, you're a great fucking parent, Mom. Fawn hated everything about this family so much she refused to have anything to do with any of us. Vincent is so fucked up he needs an alter ego just to cope."

She glared at me. "And you? How have I fucked you up, my dear?"

"I killed someone with a knitting needle yesterday, Mom. That should probably give you an idea. I find men and sex so boring I can't have any sort of relationship.

And every job I've ever had I've been fired from when they started noticing how fucking weird I am."

"You aren't weird," Vincent told me.

I shot him a look. "Thank you, but coming from you, that's not exactly a compliment."

He didn't argue, probably because he knew I was right.

Mom pointed her bony finger at me. "You can't blame me for something you enjoy."

My mouth dropped open. My ass, I couldn't blame her. Everything I was, was because of her. "You think I was born wanting to do this? You think I *want* to enjoy killing people?"

"But you do, don't you? You both do."

I shook my head, moving away from the counter and edging toward the door. "This is messed up. I don't even know why I came here. Of course you're going to do nothing to find Fawn."

"She made her decisions. Now she has to live with the consequences."

"She's twenty-two, Mom! She's a goddamn baby!"

"What were you doing at twenty-two, Ophelia?"

I ground my teeth. At twenty-two, and for many years afterward, I'd been my mother's puppet. This was exactly why I'd left and gone overseas. Except my upbringing had followed me. Even when I hadn't wanted them, my mother's 'job bags' had been delivered to my apartment in Spain and I'd never been able to ignore them.

I'd always had to feed the beast inside me.

The beast she'd created.

Like she knew exactly what I was thinking, she nudged the bag in my direction.

Vincent's hold on his dark side was slipping. His voice lowered until it was little more than a barely held-together snarl. "We'll go to the strip club and find out what they know about Fawn. But that." He pointed to the offending bag. "I'm not having anything to do with that."

He was on the verge of breaking down and drawing a weapon. I could practically see the murder in his eyes when he glared at the woman who'd birthed us.

He strode out of the room, not waiting for me. I couldn't blame him. She brought out the worst in both of us.

Mom just waited. Watching me silently.

The battle inside me roared. The desire to tell her to go to hell versus the gaping need inside me that demanded blood.

Despite knowing better, the draw of that damn bag was too strong to ignore.

I picked it up and followed my brother.

4

OPHELIA

In the neon-pink glow of a strip club sign, my brother's alter egos switched places. It was a silent change, one that came without warning, though when Scythe slung his arm around my shoulders and drew me in to kiss the top of my head in a way Vincent never would have, I wasn't all that surprised.

Our mother was Vincent's biggest trigger. A constant battle waged inside him when she was around, with one part of him twisted up in family loyalty, the other desperate to wring her wrinkled neck.

Scythe and I stared at the front door to the strip club with its 'Closed' sign hanging from the handle. But music and dancing and laughter came from behind, a private party taking place inside.

We both headed for the back of the building without a word to each other. He shortened his strides just a touch to match mine, and we fell into an old, familiar rhythm that was oddly comforting.

"I don't know why we even bothered going to her," I

admitted to him. "It was stupid to suddenly think she would be all sweet and caring when the woman hasn't ever given a shit about any of us."

"Vincent writes lists sometimes. Of ways he could kill her."

I raised an eyebrow. "Sounds like your bad influence."

He grinned easily. "Hey, I'm Mom's favorite. I wouldn't dream of taking her to a zoo, spraying her in meat juice, pushing her into the lion enclosure, locking the door, and holding back anyone who tried to help her." His smile widened at the very thought.

It didn't matter how much time passed; I still knew my brother like the back of my hand. "You're thinking about her screams for help, aren't you?"

"They sound like angels singing."

I laughed quietly in the darkness but sobered, thinking about our sister held captive somewhere for weeks now, and all because our mother didn't even care enough to let us know.

My anger was maybe a little misplaced.

It might have been myself I was angry with more than anyone. I should have been keeping a better eye on Fawn. Watching her from a distance, even though she didn't want to see us.

Scythe nudged me, uncharacteristically quiet. "You don't have to do this, you know. If you want to go back to Spain, I'll handle it. You did me a favor, coming back here when I needed you. This one doesn't have to be on your shoulders."

But it wasn't that simple. "She's my sister. I can't just leave now I know what's happening." I kicked at a rock, and it went skittering across the dingy parking lot. "I just hate that it's her, you know? You and I? We deserve whatever happens to us. But we tried so hard to keep Fawn safe."

"If it's Eddie who has her, that isn't really Mom's fault. Fawn picked him herself."

"But our business was the reason she was around men like Eddie in the first place." Guilt flooded my system. "I should have never gone overseas. Everything was fine when I was here."

For Mom to use as her punching bag, I added silently in my head. Mom had left Fawn alone when I was here to torment instead. I'd never been able to fully protect Vincent and Scythe, from our mother or from outsiders who wanted to hurt them, but I'd done a damn sight better than Mom had. It was on her watch that he'd been arrested and locked up. It had been her who'd driven Vincent to want out of the business altogether. And it was because of her he'd been captured and tortured.

Her stupid fucking pride had prevented her from calling me even then. It had been my best friend who'd had to let me know about that one.

I'd been on the next plane out.

Scythe shook his head. "You are such a typical eldest child. You do realize my shit had nothing to do with you, or even Mom, right? Fawn... That's on both of us for not keeping a closer eye on her."

"She wanted space," I admitted. I'd thought we were doing the right thing in giving it to her. In letting her have a normal life, away from our mother's demands. I thought she'd be safe.

His eyes darkened as he flexed his fingers into fists. "We were wrong in giving it to her. She was already too deep to get out. Not just with us, and Mom, but with Eddie and his bullshit as well. We should have known he wouldn't just let her walk away, even if we did."

I hated that he was right. But there was no point dwelling on it. What was done, was done. All we could do now was try to fix the mistakes we'd made.

Because the thought of Fawn lying on a dirty floor somewhere, bound and gagged, was too much for me to comprehend. I shoved the thought out of my mind and steeled myself with determination. "We'll find her," I said to myself as much as my brother. "I'm having coffee with Jezebel tomorrow. I'll ask if she's heard anything."

Scythe made a face. "You know Mom tried to marry me off to her, right?"

I cringed. I'd heard all about that. I didn't know what our mother was thinking when she'd tried that one on for size. Jez was my best friend, had been ever since we were kids, but her and my brother would have been a recipe for disaster. She liked knives as much as he did and had no problem using one when the mood struck her. All I could think about was the two of them sitting together at a breakfast table, Scythe asking her to pass the Froot Loops and her stabbing him in the hand because she didn't like the way he held the box.

One psychopath with a penchant for violence per relationship.

Two was a crime scene waiting to happen.

Even still, a protective urge rose in me. Jez was my best friend, and I didn't want to have to choose between her and my brother. "That wasn't Jez's fault. We've known our entire lives we'd be married off to one of Mom's connections eventually. At least Jez is a good egg."

"She's completely fucking insane."

"So are you."

"Thank you. But I've got my girl. And my guy. And my... Nash. That's more than enough."

I eyed him, a tiny spark of jealousy lighting up inside me. His life was so incredibly different now. It still amazed me that Mom had even allowed it to happen. Her marriage to my father had been arranged. Jez's parents had been the same. It was just kind of the done thing in the circles we ran in. You married for position and power. Not for love. Hell, I was pretty sure my parents barely even liked each other. They were about as romantically involved as coworkers who only passed each other in the office hall on the way to the bathrooms. A polite nod was about the most intimate I'd ever seen them.

That sort of thing was normal to me. It mirrored all the relationships I'd ever had. I might have, so far, been allowed to choose my own dates, but I always picked men who were as vanilla and dull as my father, all while knowing that eventually, the man I ended up with would be chosen for me by my parents.

But Scythe and Vincent had wanted more, and Mom had somehow allowed it.

"You always were Mom's favorite," I complained. "You've always been able to do whatever you wanted."

He scoffed, "Tell Vincent that. You didn't see the shit she put him through."

"But the two of you got what you wanted in the end."

"You could stand up to her too, you know. You don't have to marry someone she picks out for you. Even Fawn woke up and backed out when Mom tried to marry her off to fucking Eddie." He cracked his knuckles again at the very mention of Fawn's ex's name.

I shrugged. "It's not like I'm doing a good job of choosing men for myself. You met Nicholas."

Scythe rolled his eyes. "Did you drown that guy in his cereal yet? Like, literally? 'Cause oh my God, that one FaceTime call I did with him made me want to put a rope around my neck and—" He made choking noises that were muffled by the music coming from inside the club.

I elbowed him. "Nicholas wasn't that bad."

Scythe stared at me. "He's worse than bad and you know it. At the risk of making myself sick because I'm talking about sex with my sister, you need someone who gets you hot. Nicholas the Noodle ain't it. Neither is settling for someone Mom picks out for you. That's a recipe for disaster."

I couldn't disagree with him. Nicholas was an American I'd met in Spain while he was working abroad for his technology firm. They'd had some big project he'd told me all about in great detail. I'd smiled and nodded and laughed, all while thinking about how much I'd rather watch paint dry than listen to another word about his boring-ass career.

But my friends all thought he was wonderful. They'd gushed about how handsome and smart and wealthy he was, and though I couldn't see the appeal, I'd figured if they'd thought he was so great, then I could at least give him a shot.

The sex had been as vanilla as his conversation. Missionary position, me flat on my back with him heaving and sweating over me. I'd had to mentally recite the national anthem in my head to keep from making faces at his expression, contorting into weird shapes as he'd moaned my name in a high-pitched wail.

I shuddered just thinking about it. I hadn't even said goodbye to him before I'd gotten on a plane to come back home, and I'd avoided his calls ever since.

Nicholas had never gotten me hot. Nor had any other man. There was none of the excitement of meeting someone new that my friends talked about. I didn't know what 'chemistry' felt like, nor had I ever had a burning desire to get naked with someone.

I liked men.

Until they opened their mouths and ruined it.

So what did it matter if I married someone Mom picked out for me?

We'd reached the back door. Scythe peered through a dirty window while I fingered what appeared to be a patched-up bullet hole. It was hardly surprising. We were deep in the heart of Saint View, which wasn't exactly known for its upper-class population.

I hated that this was where Fawn had found herself.

Hated she'd been so miserable in her life with us that this had been preferable.

"There's a lot of people inside," Scythe reported. "Mostly women. Some kids. A couple of big guys. Weird crowd for a strip club, but it's still early, so maybe they haven't opened for the night yet. They're all just hanging out."

I fought the urge to press up on my toes and peer in as well, just to see if the man from the train was inside. "Is there a blond man who looks like he should be on a runway in Paris?"

Scythe took another peek. "Yeah. Plus an older guy

and—shit. There's a dark-haired man in there who I think might be a cop."

"How would you even know that? He in a uniform?"

"No, but I'm sure I recognize him from my latest stint in prison."

I eyed him. "You want to pull the pin on this then? He could call for backup."

My brother, in typical Scythe fashion, rolled his eyes. "Don't be insulting. I'll just kill him if he tries."

That suited me just fine. "Fair enough. After you, then."

I made a grand gesture toward the door, and Scythe thumped on the heavy wood.

"Do you ever knock politely?" I asked.

"Why?" He seemed honestly confused as to why he should bother.

Sometimes it still shocked me how different Scythe and Vincent were.

The door opened, and a wall of muscle stood on the other side, fluorescent light hitting them from behind and illuminating their broad shoulders. There was an older guy who'd heaved open the door. Two younger, dark-haired men who glared at us with distrust written all over their faces. I didn't know which one Scythe thought was a cop, but I didn't get much of a chance to think about it because my gaze landed on the hot blond from the train.

His eyes widened in a mixture of surprise and recognition.

A slow tingle worked its way down my spine as his pale-blue eyes locked with mine.

I raised my head in a tiny nod of acknowledgement,

but that tingle in my spine wasn't just because the man was hot. It held a silent warning.

Men couldn't be trusted. Especially not men who looked like him. Beauty was easily used as a weapon. It was why I'd never seen my mother without a full face of makeup. It was why she hounded me about losing weight if I so much as glanced at a donut.

He had the sort of face that left other people tongue-tied and awkward. I bet he liked it. I bet he'd used it to his advantage more than once.

He'd be stupid not to.

He didn't seem stupid.

"I'm Ophelia," I said to the group but with eyes only for him. God, they were really fucking blue. "That's Vincent."

"Scythe," he corrected.

I blinked and glanced over at him. He gave me a questioning look, and I knew he was wondering why I'd used the wrong name.

I didn't even know. One minute I'd been caught up in noticing that man's eyes, the next my brain was clearly misfiring.

Disgust for myself hit me hard. I didn't fumble around men. Not even the attractive ones.

I huffed out a sigh, trying to hide my mistake. "Fine. Sorry. He's Scythe today. It's a long story."

The older guy clearly didn't give a shit. "It's a private party," he barked out at us. "We ain't open. Come back tomorrow."

He went to close the door, but Scythe stuck one heavy boot in the way and pinned the man with a glare that sent frost into the air. "I don't think we'll be doing that."

He clapped a hand on the door and pushed it open, gaze bouncing around the four men who blocked the entryway.

His gaze came to rest on the man from the train. What had he said his name was? Aaron? Austin? I swear it started with an A but I'd been so distracted.

My brother clearly wasn't concerned with the name on Train Man's birth certificate like I was. He took him in, every inch of his tall, solid frame and practically snarled out his words. "Where the fuck is my sister?"

"Who the hell is your sister?" someone asked.

"Fawn," Andre or Adam spoke up with surety in his tone, his gaze never leaving mine. "They're Fawn's siblings. I met her the other day." He pointed in my direction. "Told her I worked here, which I'm guessing is why they're here now."

At least I was memorable.

A curvy brunette gasped from across the room and came rushing forward, shoving at the broad-shouldered man who held her back. "Dammit, Josh, get out of the way." She pushed at his thick arms, but he wasn't budging. She stopped and glared at him. "They're Fawn's family. Let them in."

To my surprise, the man glanced over at us, his expression softening. "You got weapons?"

"No," Scythe and I both lied in unison.

The woman gave him a triumphant look and focused on us. "Please. Come in. We've got a ton of food. Are you hungry?"

Like it was just waiting for the mention of food, my stomach gave a pathetic growl of hunger. I could blame our mother for that. It's not like she'd offered us a meal at her place. I'd barely eaten anything all day, and the club smelled oddly delicious.

I took in the room, expecting to see half-naked bodies writhing around poles and depressed old men shoving dollar bills in G-strings. But the lights were all turned up, tasty plates of food sat half-eaten on the tables, and a group of children stood by their mothers, all staring at us with big, wide eyes.

"This is the weirdest strip club ever," I muttered. But I followed the woman, pausing distrustfully when she offered me a plate of a rich, meaty stew.

I eyed it, but Scythe had no such concerns. He reached around me and took the bowl from the woman's hands. "You snooze, you lose, big sis. That smells amazing. Thanks." He grabbed a chunk of crusty bread, dipped it into the stew, and took a bite.

The woman beamed at him, then tried again with me. "I'm Eve," she said quietly. "I own the club. Please. Sit. Have something to eat. We can talk."

"We just want to know where our sister is," I told her.

Eve nodded, placing the food on the table beside where my brother was already scarfing down the meal like he wasn't ever going to get another.

"Eat while we talk," Eve said. "We'll tell you everything we know."

"Like hell we will."

I glanced back at the deep growl from the man from the train. "Excuse me? Anthony, was it?"

"Augie," he gritted out between clenched teeth.

Pretty men like him always got pissed off when a woman forgot their name.

I wrinkled my nose, just to be a bitch. "Augie, as in

short for August?" I fought to control a laugh. He didn't look like an August.

"As in none of your business. Eat your food if you want, but we aren't telling you anything."

"Augie!" Eve admonished sharply. "I'm so sorry, he's a jackass at the best of times. Ignore him." She glared in his direction. "The rest of us do."

Scythe mumbled a complaint in Augie's direction, but his mouth was too full for anyone to understand him.

I didn't need my brother to stand up for me. I was perfectly capable of fighting my own battles. I narrowed my eyes at the big blond man. "Why exactly don't you want to tell us where my sister is?"

Those same inkling suspicions I'd had on the train that warned men weren't trustworthy sounded again. If he had nothing to hide, he'd just tell me.

But Augie gripped the edge of the table and leaned down, so we were eye to eye. "Why didn't you tell me she was your sister when we met on the train?"

I raised an eyebrow and told him the truth. "Because I don't have a clue who you are or whether you can be trusted."

"And yet you walk in here like you have any right to and expect us to trust you?"

I shrugged. "Why wouldn't you? We seem to be in agreement that I am who I say I am. But I know nothing about you, not even your real name."

Eve glanced over at him. "Augie isn't even your name?"

He ignored her, his gaze never leaving mine. "You don't need to know anything about me. I'm not the one demanding information."

I pushed slowly to my feet, the prickle of irritation I'd felt when he questioned me turning into a thorn in my damn side. I stared at him from across the table. I was no shrinking violet. I was barely a few inches shorter, but even if he'd towered over me, I'd never been one to back down. Not to a man. I'd been raised better. I'd give my mother credit for that. A seething anger rolled up my spine. "She's my sister."

"She hated you."

The venom in his words froze me to the spot. Even Scythe stopped his obnoxious chewing, his hand halfway to his mouth with another stew-soaked piece of bread.

On instinct, I shook my head. "No. She hated our mother and our family business. She didn't hate us." I gestured between my brother and I. "We let her leave."

Augie recoiled like the words personally offended him. "You *let* her leave? What the fuck kind of messed-up shit is that? She was—is—a grown-ass woman who gets to make her own decisions. You don't *let* her anything." He shook his head, staring at me like I was the scum on the bottom of his shoes. "I see why she wanted nothing to do with you."

My mouth dropped open. I could snap the man's neck if I wanted to. Pull out the gun in my purse and put a bullet through his brain. Hell, those knitting needles hadn't seen any action for a few hours. Plenty of places I could shove one of those that would be nicely painful.

What had Fawn told him about me? About our family? Surely, she hadn't told him the truth?

Yet something in his blue eyes seemed to cut right through every defense I had, like he already knew all my secrets.

I didn't like it.

It was wholly uncomfortable.

The guy was a grade-A asshole, and he could stick it where the sun didn't shine. "Come on, Scythe. There's nothing for us here. We'll find her without their help."

Scythe moaned something about not being finished with his stew and that it was the best thing he'd ever tasted, but he shut up when I glared at him.

Eve caught my arm as I turned for the door. "Wait. Don't go. What Augie isn't saying is that we've been searching for your sister every day since she was taken. We've turned over every leaf. Gone down every rabbit hole. We've spoken to everyone we can think of, and we've begged the police for help and information they refuse to give us."

There was a plea in her unspoken words. A desperation in her eyes. "Fawn came to me a long time ago, broken and battered from a life she was desperately trying to outrun. So forgive us if we aren't as forthcoming with information as you might want us to be. But you didn't even tell Augie you were her sister, so from where I'm standing, it seems like we're in a standoff."

She wasn't wrong. There was a clear line down the middle of the table, with her and Augie on one side, my brother and me on the other, both sides staring at the other with distrust in their gazes.

Except when I glanced over, Scythe wasn't actually staring at anything except his stew with some sort of love-struck puppy look that made me want to slap the back of his head.

He was lethal but also an idiot.

Eve cleared her throat and offered an olive branch.

"Come by the club this week. Hang out. Have a drink. Get to know us and let us get to know you."

Still prickly from Augie's comments, I spoke too quickly. "I don't make a habit of hanging out at strip clubs."

Augie straightened, crossing his arms over his chest and shaking his head at me. "Why? Too good for them?"

"No," I said too quickly.

Except, the answer really was kind of yes. Call me a snobby bitch if you wanted, but this place, in the middle of the Saint View slums, was about as far from my life as you could get. We'd moved around a bit, but I'd grown up with money. I'd never had to work a regular job because my mother's business made more than enough money for all of us. When I met up with friends, we went to nightclubs in Europe and ate meals in expensive restaurants.

Not that you'd know it to look at my brother, who clearly thought that stew was the best thing he'd ever tasted.

I didn't fit in here. Neither did my sister. These people weren't her family.

Eve's voice was quiet when she pushed a flyer into my hand. "I'm starting up a dance class. You should come. Let us get to know you. When we all trust each other, maybe we can actually try working together. For Fawn."

I stared down at the paper in my hand and then up again.

My gaze met Augie's.

His blue eyes were hard. Closed off. An anger burning behind them so brightly I just knew there was no way in hell this man was ever going to give me anything. He'd already made his mind up about me. I didn't know what Fawn had told him, but it clearly wasn't anything good.

The hate behind his eyes was enough to make me never want to step foot inside these walls ever again. I crumpled the flyer into a ball. "No thanks. Come on, Scythe. We'll find our sister ourselves."

5

―――――

OPHELIA

"I'm sorry, miss. But I can only give that information to family."

My first impulse was to tell the officer on the other end of the line that I could gut her like a fish if she didn't tell me everything the useless Providence Police Department knew about my sister's disappearance. But I sucked in a deep breath, kept my pace even along the sidewalk, and tried to smile through my frustration. "As I said before, I am family."

The woman sighed, clearly as frustrated with me as I was with her. "Then you should have no problem getting the information you require from your family contact."

My family what? "Who exactly is that? My mother?"

The woman's nails clacked over a typewriter. "No, it's a male relative, I believe. Augie Mitchell."

You had to be fucking kidding me.

"Are you seriously telling me you won't give me any information about my sister's case, but you will tell her random strip club coworker?"

"Miss, the occupations of family contacts are none of our concern. Mr. Mitchell has been the contact for this case ever since the woman in question went missing. In fact, he was the one to report her as such. I'm sure you understand we have a lot of ongoing cases here, and we cannot be explaining each and every update of all of them to every family member. One contact per family. Yours is Mr. Mitchell. Anything we know about the case that can be shared with the general public, he already knows, and your best bet is to get that information from him. Now, is there anything else I can help you with?"

I hit the red 'end call' button. "Fucking useless," I muttered, yanking open the door to Jezebel's florist while a tinkling bell sounded overhead.

Jez glanced up when I entered, but she was with a customer, discussing a bouquet of flowers I mostly couldn't identify. So I wandered up to the front counter, stopping to take a whiff of a fragrant bunch in a vase filled with water.

Jezebel was as tall as I was, but her hair was blond and her skin fair. She'd been the freckled, nerdy weirdo the other kids had teased at school because she was so long and lanky and awkward.

While I'd shouted at them all and threatened to flush their heads down the toilets, Jezebel had never reacted, just letting their comments slide right off her.

Or so it seemed.

I wasn't convinced she didn't see their faces every time she stuck a blade through the heart of one of her targets.

But it wasn't my place to pry into her head. I was her

friend, not her therapist. And fuck. I had enough problems of my own.

Jezebel left her customer umming and ahhing over whether to pick the red-and-white, romance-themed bunch, or the yellow-and-orange combination that reminded me of sunshine. Personally, I would have gone for the black and red ones that screamed of Jez's love for death but were, unsurprisingly, wilting away in the corner, clearly unloved by anyone but the two of us.

Jez popped herself up on a stool behind the counter. "When she's done, I'll put the 'back in five' sign up and we'll drink that coffee." She eyed the two to-go cups I'd brought in with me.

I nodded but was too impatient to wait that long to needle her for information. The fact bloody Augie Mitchell was the only person the police would talk to was really just fueling my irritation. "Have you seen Eddie around lately?"

Jez recoiled like I was a snake ready to bite her but kept her voice down, eyeing her customer. "Eddie Sinclair? Are you joking? God, no. Why would you even ask me that?"

I sighed. "Fawn's gone missing. One of her new friends mentioned Eddie's name when I asked about her. They wouldn't tell me anything more, but who else would take her?"

She started rattling off a list of names, families of targets and enemies of my mother, until I waved a hand at her. "Okay, okay. I get it. It could be anyone, but they said Eddie, and he's a good place to start."

She trailed her finger along a rose stem before

pressing her fingertip to one of the thorns. It pierced her skin, a perfect crimson droplet pooling at the site.

"Jez..."

She distractedly pressed her bleeding finger to her apron. "Sorry. No. Haven't seen Eddie in years, and I'd like to keep it that way." She shuddered with revulsion. "That guy is the worst."

My stomach churned. Jez having a visible reaction to Eddie's name was disturbing. Jez was the biggest badass I knew. She was similar to Vincent at times, with a quiet intensity that was terrifying, but she was also loyal and sweet and fearless.

The bell over the door tinkled again, and Jez stiffened beside me. I glanced over at her curiously, taking in the whites of her eyes and the knife she reached for that I knew was taped beneath the desk.

One look at Riddick standing in the doorway reminded me Jez was *almost* fearless. There was only one person she was truly scared of.

The one she shared DNA with.

Riddick spotted me at the counter with his sister, and a wide grin spread across his handsome face. "Little Ophelia. Is that you?"

I wondered if he knew how bad his acting was. It was clear he'd known I'd be here, though I didn't know how. I hadn't seen anyone following me, but Riddick was as good as they came. I wouldn't have seen him unless he wanted me to.

I glanced at Jez. "You didn't tell me he was back in town."

"I was trying to forget," she whispered back.

Riddick came over and leaned his elbows on the

countertop, propping his head up in his hands. "Didn't your parents ever teach you it's rude to whisper?"

Neither of us dared to say a word, so Riddick took that as his cue to keep on talking.

"Need to talk to Ophelia, sis. Beat it."

She stared at him, pulling her shoulders back to square off with him. "This is my shop. I'm not leaving it. I have customers."

He leaned in closer to her, his irritation at her defiance clear in his expression.

But when he spoke, his voice was as polite as an altar boy at church on a Sunday. "Oh, ma'am?" he called to the customer Jez had left pondering bouquets. "Do you like those red and white flowers?"

The woman glanced over at him and did a double take. I couldn't blame her. Riddick wasn't exactly easy on the eye. He was huge at over six and a half feet. Eyes too close together. Lips small. Thickly muscled with a face only a mother could love. Though I knew their parents were no more loving than mine.

"Oh, yes," the woman stuttered. "They're very nice."

Riddick ran his finger along the edge of the countertop. "They'd be lovely on your coffin."

The woman jerked back. "Excuse me?"

"Coffee." He pointed at the two to-go cups sitting by the cash register. "My sister here always says she loves fresh flowers on the table while she drinks her morning coffee. Such a soothing way to start the day, don't you think?"

The woman clearly didn't want to believe what she'd heard the first time around. The frown lines on her forehead melted away as she silently talked herself out of her panicked state. I sighed. People always did this. It was so rare for someone to actually be attacked completely out of the blue. More often than not, people gave you warning signs, showing their true colors.

Yet most people ignored that gut instinct that something wasn't right.

The woman laughed, picking up the red-and-white bunch and bringing them to the counter for Jez to ring up. "Oh, of course. Yes. Sorry, I thought you said something entirely different. My hearing..."

Was perfectly fine.

But that was Riddick's favorite game to play and always had been. He lived for making others uncomfortable in whatever way he could. Right now he was practically sucking in deep breaths of the concern wafting off this woman. Even I could tell she was on the verge of running out of the store with a scream bubbling up her throat.

She should. If she had any idea what the three of us did in our spare time, she'd run away and never look back.

Jez took the flowers and tried giving the woman a warm smile, but that had never really been Jezebel's forte either. The woman rolled her head back and forth, while Riddick practically salivated, watching like it was an invitation to snap it.

The bell rang again, and a young woman walked in with two friends.

Riddick's eyes lit up like light bulbs.

"Will you excuse me for one moment, please?" Jez asked her customer. Without waiting for her to agree, she grabbed my arm and Riddick's and shoved us toward the storeroom. "Stop staring at those girls like you're going to eat them alive! Whatever you need to say to Ophelia, say it in there," she hissed. "Away from my customers."

"Jez!" I complained, but she pulled the door closed behind us anyway.

Great freaking friend she was. Though I couldn't blame her. Riddick was more unpredictable than Scythe and twice as deadly because he truly didn't give a shit about anyone or anything other than himself. Young or old. Innocent or guilty. Riddick killed for the pure pleasure of getting blood beneath his nails.

And I was stuck in a shoebox of a closet with him.

At least Scythe had Vincent to keep him a little bit in check. Riddick had lost all humanity a long time ago. If he'd ever had it in the first place.

He grinned in the dim light, his smile entirely too Joker-like to be comforting. "This feels familiar. Didn't we play this game at a party once?"

I shifted back an inch, trying to put some distance between us. "Only in my nightmares."

He chuckled and clucked his tongue. "Now, now. Play nicely."

"Because you do?"

"Never, but we aren't talking about me now, are we?"

I sighed. "What do you want? Can we just get whatever this is over with so I can go on with my day, please?"

Treating him like he was my friend's annoying older brother was the only way I knew to keep him at bay.

He folded his arms over his chest and stared down at me. "Your mom tells me you have a job bag."

I froze. "Why were you talking to my mom?"

He shrugged one of his broad shoulders. "We're friends."

"Friends?" What the hell did that mean? I wrinkled my nose. "You aren't..."

He gave a deep chuckle. "Sleeping with your mom?"

I didn't confirm, and he didn't deny. Oh, vomit. It wouldn't have surprised me. My parents' relationship had always been more of a business arrangement than a romantic one. There was no love between them.

Now that I was about as uncomfortable as he could possibly make me, he continued, "Your mom wants me to help you with your job bag."

I recoiled like he'd slapped me in the face. Which frankly, he might as well have. "What on earth for?"

His finger trailed down my arm. "To hold your hand, maybe?"

"Gag me with a spoon. No thank you." The insult was out of my mouth before I could stop it. Internally, I cringed, waiting for Riddick to respond. Insulting a man like him wasn't smart for anyone, and we were in a very small space. Before I even had a chance to shout for help he could have me bleeding out, if he wanted to.

I imagined Jez opening the door to her storage room and finding me dead in a pool of my own blood, all because I was mouthy and had dared to tell her brother I found him kinda repulsive.

Damn. That would suck.

I just wanted to meet up with her for coffee.

But for once, the insult rolled off Riddick's back like he couldn't have cared less. "Fine. No hand-holding. I'm not one for public displays of affection anyway. So what's the job?"

I hadn't even opened the bag yet. I'd been too busy worrying about my sister and trying to banish thoughts of her hot coworker that kept popping into my brain at inappropriate moments.

Like right now.

Being locked in a closet with Augie might not have been so bad. At least I didn't have to worry about him slitting my throat.

Riddick snapped his fingers in front of my face. "Do you make a habit of zoning out like that? Is this why your mom thinks you can't handle a simple job by yourself?"

Scary psychopath or not, he could go to hell. I reached around him for the doorknob.

He blocked me.

I glared at him. "You aren't helping me with that job."

Quick as a snake, he had my chin between two fingers, his nails digging into my skin. He jerked my head so sharply I gave an involuntary cry of pain.

He smiled, like the sound pleased him. "I didn't ask for your permission. You need to get used to us working together. Eventually, that's how we'll do all jobs. I'll meet you tonight for the surveillance I know you're so fond of. I'll wait for your text to let me know when and where."

He leaned in, and my breath caught on a sudden burst of terror. He could snap my neck like this. I probably wouldn't even feel it. I'd be dead on the floor without it even registering.

But he only placed his lips to the top of my hair and inhaled deeply. "Just like I remember."

He walked out before I could argue, not bothering to say goodbye to his sister.

She glanced over at me from behind the counter, a worried expression in her light-colored eyes.

She didn't need to say anything.

When Riddick chose someone, the way he'd very clearly just chosen me, it always ended in death.

6

———

AUGIE

Insomnia had been a constant companion for most of my life. Foster care had ruined any hope of a consistent sleep schedule after spending too many nights too scared to even close my eyes.

Bad things happened during dark nights. Letting down your guard left you vulnerable in a way I tried real hard not to remember.

The insomnia hadn't improved any once I'd brought Banjo home. In those days, back when he was barely tall enough to see over the kitchen counter, I'd spent my nights lying awake, listening for anything that might try to hurt him in the night. I'd kept a hockey stick by my bedroom door and a gun tucked away in the top of a cupboard, ready to defend my brother against anyone who dared to try breaching the walls of the tiny home I'd tried to make for us.

It was ironic that the thing that had eventually hurt him the most was me.

My inability to sleep was why I'd taken up surfing in

the first place. The beach at five in the morning, when the surfers were all out, waiting on the best waves of the day, was the one place I could go and be sure I wouldn't be alone.

Fuck, I hated being alone.

I wasn't much for making friends. I'd never been any good at that, but there were regulars at the beach. Those crazy few who cared more about catching the perfect early morning waves than they did about sleeping until their alarm blared and they had to shuffle off to their day jobs.

I didn't even know their names, but some mornings, when sleep had evaded me altogether, sitting on my surfboard, knowing there were other people around me, was the only thing that kept me going.

Especially after Banjo had left.

I hadn't surfed in weeks now though. Punishing myself because having something good in my life didn't feel right when Fawn was missing.

But I couldn't get Ophelia off my mind. I hadn't slept in days, not since she'd stormed into my club like she owned the fucking place, and then told us all to go to hell.

Bleary-eyed, I dragged myself from my messed-up sheets and stumbled into the little bathroom on the second-floor landing of my tiny, government-owned house. The faucet spluttered when I turned it on, rusty-colored water spewing from the spout at first until it eventually ran clear.

I scooped up a handful of it and splashed it on my face, craving the cold shock.

It wasn't enough. I needed more.

Without letting myself think about it too much, I threw on some shorts and a hoodie, retrieved my board and wetsuit from the corner of my room, and headed for the stairs.

Banjo's old bedroom door was open a crack, everything he'd left behind still there, in case he ever returned for it.

His board still sat in a corner.

It had been his pride and joy once upon a time, back when he'd been a little blond-haired grommet who could barely swim, let alone ride a wave. I couldn't help but smile at the memory. I'd taught him though. I'd dragged him out there every morning until he was riding barrels with the rest of us.

I wondered if he still did that.

If he did, he wasn't surfing at the Saint View end of the beach.

And I wasn't welcome at the Providence end.

I yanked his bedroom door closed and took the stairs, two at a time, my board tucked tight beneath my arm, my wetsuit clutched in my fingers. The sun was barely up when I made it outside, but I didn't bother turning on the porch light. There was no need. I'd done this dance hundreds of other mornings and remembered it well, even if I hadn't been surfing recently.

Trying to keep quiet so I didn't wake Willa next door, I jogged across the yard and let myself out of the gate. But the car outside Willa's house stopped me in my tracks.

"Shit," I mumbled, staring at the expensive Cadillac Escalade still mostly shrouded in the gradually lightening shadows. The tire was as flat as a fucking pancake.

Nobody was driving anywhere on that thing anytime soon.

I put my board and suit down on the cracked pavement and grabbed a jack and a lug wrench from the trunk of my car. It only took a few minutes for me to get the sleek SUV raised and the wheel nuts off.

The door to Willa's house opened and closed, and a quiet gasp came from the older woman on her porch. "Jesus H Christ, Augie Mitchell. You scared the shit out of me. I thought you were some street thug stealing tires. Again."

I wiped some grease off on my hoodie. "Sorry. Tire is flat. Didn't want Lacey to be late dropping Luna off at daycare...or whatever she has on today." I shuffled the tire around, not wanting to look Willa in the eye.

Willa came to stand beside me and stared down at my handiwork. "You really don't need to do that with me, you know," she said softly. "I know you memorize everything I tell you about your brother and his family. You don't have to pretend like you don't know they stay here on Sunday nights because I insist on having some time with my son and my granddaughter."

Heat crept up the back of my neck. I was hoping she hadn't noticed. It was fucking pathetic the way I hung on her every word, just so I had an idea of what was going on in Banjo's life. Colt, Willa's son, was one of Banjo's three partners, so she had all the insider knowledge I craved.

"The invitation is always open, Augie. You're family, too, you know."

But we both knew that wasn't really true. Even if I had showed up at her place in a suit with an expensive bottle of wine in my hand, she would have been the only one pleased to see me.

Banjo, Lacey, Colt, and Rafe would have simply packed up their daughter and walked out.

Which was why I'd never taken Willa up on her offer. And why she'd never truly meant it.

She sighed into the cold morning air. "He's gotta talk to you sometime, Aug."

But he didn't. Banjo could easily go the rest of his life without forgiving me for what I'd done, and I wouldn't blame him one bit. The fact Willa still talked to me only said Banjo had never told her the full extent of everything that had happened between us. I pulled the tire off the axle with a hard tug. "I'll get this fixed up for them before they wake up. They're going to need to go to the shop and get that tire fixed."

"Thank you. I'll let them know it was you who changed it for them."

I shook my head sharply. "Please don't."

Willa sighed again but turned a blind eye when I easily picked the lock on the trunk of the car in order to get the spare out. She clicked her fingers in the air. "Oh! I was going to come over and see you later today actually. I have something for you."

I wiggled the new tire into place and glanced over my shoulder at her. "Oh yeah? What?"

She rummaged around in the pocket of her scrubs and produced a small white business card. "I got to talking to the brother of one of my patients last night. Turns out he's a private investigator. His office is in the city, but he lives out this way, in Providence."

She passed the card over to me, and I took it, smudging grease onto the corners of the pristine card.

"Bert Leddith, Private Investigator," I read from it, then passed it back to Willa. "What am I supposed to do with this?"

She pushed it back in my direction. "I thought maybe he could help you with looking for your friend, Fawn. She hasn't been found yet, has she? I still see your missing posters all around town…"

I swallowed the lump in my throat. "No. She hasn't been found."

"Talk to this guy then. I told him what I knew, and he thinks he can help you."

I hated the tiny spark of hope that lit up inside me again. I'd had too many of those, only for them all to be viciously stamped out.

"What have you got to lose, Aug?" Willa asked.

She was right. It was worth at least going and asking.

For the tiniest of seconds, I'd hoped that Fawn's brother and sister would lead to some sort of breakthrough in finding her. But Fawn had run from them for a reason. Her sister had lied to me from the very first second I'd met her. If Fawn didn't trust them, neither did I.

Willa took a sip of her coffee and ruffled my hair like I was ten years old. She was the only person in the world who I would let get away with that. I took the card back and shoved it in the pocket of my hoodie. "I'll give him a call. Thank you. Now go to work. And please don't tell them it was me who changed this tire."

Willa pointed up at the bedroom window on the second floor. "Too late for that."

Behind the glass panes, my brother watched, his dark-haired daughter perched in his arms and waving to her grandmother with a big smile on her rounded face.

Willa waved back, but Luna kept on going, her waves getting more and more insistent.

"She's waving to you, Uncle Augie."

I stiffened.

"Wave back, Aug. Smile at her and wave back."

My heart pounded in my rib cage. It was like I'd forgotten how to lift my damn hand and make the motion. My limbs felt disconnected from my body, but somehow, I managed to force my lips into a smile and waved awkwardly at the little girl.

Her grin widened.

My brother jerked away and disappeared from view, the curtains falling back into place.

That rift between us as deep and strong as ever.

7

OPHELIA

text from Riddick hit my phone at eight that night. I rolled my eyes. So much for waiting for me to text him. There was no greeting. No introduction. No explanation as to how he'd gotten my phone number, though I suspected from our earlier conversation that my mother was probably the culprit there. Did I need him to have manners? I supposed not, considering we weren't friends. But a, "Hey Ophelia. It's me, your not-so-friendly neighborhood psychopath, Riddick," might have been nice.

Instead, all I got was a single line of text that demanded I be outside the old, burned-down Providence School for Girls at eight fifteen.

I shook my head, cancelling out of the message and tossing my phone onto the dashboard. Fuck that. The target in that job bag was mine. I didn't need his help. If he wanted to ride my damn coattails, then he could wait until I was ready.

We weren't going to find anything out at the old girls' high school anyway.

Though to be fair, we probably weren't going to find out anything sitting in the parking lot at Saint View Strip either.

I clenched my fingers around the steering wheel and huffed out an annoyed breath. I'd been sitting here for a good twenty minutes, waiting for any sign of Augie on his way into work. Plenty of other people had shown up—that woman Eve and her boyfriend whose name I couldn't remember. A leggy redheaded woman who'd stopped to hug the older guy we'd met the other night. He sat at the door now, his eye on me, though he hadn't made a move from the door he guarded like there was precious cargo on the inside.

I swallowed hard. He'd looked out for those women like they were his daughters, which I was fairly sure they were not. Because wouldn't that be weird? To have your father working security at a club where you danced around naked? He cared about them, though, that much was obvious.

Must have been nice. My father was a virtual stranger. There but not there. Just a shadow of my mother, a ghost who wandered around, doing her bidding but not really participating in life beyond that.

When a dark-green, falling-to-pieces hunk of shit car rolled into the parking lot, Terry finally moved. He strode across the lot and leaned down, talking to the driver through the open window.

Augie got out a moment later, his head swiveling in my direction.

I gave him a cocky wave.

He clapped Terry on the shoulder, and the man returned to his spot, guarding the entrance.

Augie and I just stared at each other, him leaning on the side of his car, me sitting behind the wheel of mine.

Neither of us budged.

Seconds ticked by, and my leg developed an impatient bounce I couldn't seem to control. I really hoped it wasn't jiggling the car.

Augie didn't seem bothered at all. He stood there so casually, like he had all the time in the fucking world, while I had a contract killer waiting for me across town.

Riddick would fucking lose his shit if I were late. Goddammit.

I got out of the car, slammed the door, and shouted across the parking lot, "The cops won't tell me anything about their investigation on Fawn."

He lifted a shoulder in a shrug. "So you're in the same boat you were a few days ago when you didn't give a shit she was missing."

I clenched my fingers into fists. This guy was such an asshole. "Why did you tell them you were her brother? You aren't."

He pushed off the car and stalked across the lot to stand in front of me. Anger sparked behind his blue eyes. "I'm well aware. But you know what the cops told me when I reported your sister missing weeks ago? And when I called up every day after? They said they couldn't tell me anything because a family member hadn't come forward as the contact person. So I waited. I waited for someone related to her to notice she wasn't picking up calls or answering her door. See, I'd assumed that when she said she didn't want anything to do with her family, she was exaggerating. That you guys had an argument but that you actually still cared. I figured you all at least checked in on her occasionally, seeing as she was—*is*—your sister and all. I waited for one of you assholes to give a shit. When none of you did, I eventually told them I was her brother."

"You lied," I accused.

"If you'd showed up, if you'd cared about her as much as you're saying you do, I wouldn't have had to!"

There was an anger in his tone that pissed me right the fuck off. This man had no idea what we'd been through with Vincent and Scythe in the last few weeks. I hadn't deliberately lost track of Fawn. I shoved my phone in his direction. "You need to call the cops and tell them I'm the contact person from now on. All information about my sister's case needs to be reported to me."

Augie scoffed at the bright-pink phone hanging from my fingertips. "Yeah. I don't think I'm gonna do that, sweetheart."

Sweetheart? Oh, fuck no. Nobody called me that. And certainly not in the tone he'd just used. "Don't call me that."

A smile lifted the corner of his mouth. "Why not...sweetheart?"

I realized my mistake. I'd given him a weakness to needle at. I'd let him know that something bothered me. A stupid, rookie mistake I couldn't remember making in years.

I knew men. I knew how to control and manipulate them while keeping myself detached. It was one of the first things my mother had taught me, and it was a skill that came in handy when most of the people you were hired to kill were male.

Yet Augie had gotten beneath my skin in minutes. Not just tonight, but the last time I'd been here, and even that first time we'd met on the train as well.

I didn't like that he knew it too. His expression was smug, and I wanted to slap it right off his face.

Except emotional outbursts never solved anything. They just showed more weakness. "Then tell me what the cops have done."

Augie's smirk widened. "Say please."

I ground my teeth. I wasn't going to fucking beg him.

He opened the passenger-side door of my ride without asking. "All good, sweetheart. I can wait."

He slid onto the seat and picked up the job bag that had been sitting at his feet. "What's this?"

I dove inside the car so quickly I smashed my head on the doorframe. But it didn't stop me from snatching the bag from his grasp and pulling it onto my lap. "That's none of your business."

But I was too late to stop him from noticing the gun inside.

To my surprise, he didn't ask about it. He reached for my head instead.

I flinched away on instinct. "What are you doing?"

He pointed somewhere above my line of sight. "You just cut your head open."

I touched my fingers to the sore spot. "What?" Sure enough, my fingers came away sticky with blood. "Shit." I searched around the car for something to stem the flow but I kept my car neat as a pin, so there was nothing. Not so much as a stray receipt.

Augie's eyebrows were drawn together in concern. "You don't even have a Kleenex?"

"Do you?"

He scoffed, "No."

"Then why would you assume I do? I'm not sick. I don't have allergies. I'm not the mother of a snotty-nosed, dirty-fingered two-year-old." I had the scarf I was knitting for Fawn, but I wasn't about to ruin that. It had taken me hours to pick up all the stitches I'd lost when I'd used the needle as a weapon.

My head really was bleeding though. It was running down my neck in a little river of red. Dammit.

Augie pulled off his T-shirt, revealing a tight set of abs I would have drooled over if my head hadn't been suddenly throbbing like a motherfucker. Even with it, my gaze trailed involuntarily over the ridges and lines of his stomach.

"Here," he offered, holding out the shirt. "Use this."

"I'm fine."

His hand dropped to rest on the center console, and he rolled his eyes. "Just take it. You're getting blood everywhere. Jesus Christ."

I snatched the shirt from his grasp because he wasn't wrong. I was smearing blood all over anything I touched. "Shut up. It's not like it's your car. You aren't the one cleaning it." But I pressed his shirt to my wound and let it soak up some of the blood.

Augie leaned out the door and shouted to the bouncer, "Terry! Can you get us a first aid kit, please?"

"You all good?" the older man called back.

"Yeah, I'm fine, but Fawn's sister is as clumsy as she is."

My mouth dropped open at the insult. Fawn, as much as I loved her, was not the most coordinated person. It was part of what made her working at a strip club so unbelievable. I didn't even know she could dance. But then, I was beginning to realize there was a lot about my sister that she'd kept from me. That stung almost as much as my head did. "I am not clumsy," I protested.

"The way you just smashed your head says otherwise. Move the shirt. Let me see it."

I found myself doing as he'd asked. My brain pounded in protest.

He winced. "I don't know what you hit your head on that was sharp enough to cause that, but you need to get yourself to a hospital. That needs medical attention."

"No." I didn't have time for all the fuss of doctors, and them asking for ID and insurance. I didn't even want to think about what Riddick would do if I just didn't show up. I doubted anyone had ever disobeyed him before. As much as it pissed me off that he was calling the shots, it was something I was going to have to just go along with for now until I worked out some way of getting him off my back.

Augie paused, and I braced myself for a barrage of questions. But they didn't come.

He just shrugged. "You gonna let me stitch it then?"

I recoiled at the thought as Terry came back with a first aid kit and a worried-looking Eve behind him. She clapped her hand over her mouth at the sight of Augie's blood-covered shirt. Which really made the whole situation seem worse than it actually was. Head wounds bled a lot. I'd had enough of them to know that.

"Holy shit!" Eve gasped. "What happened!"

"She's fine," Augie said at the same time I claimed the same thing.

Eve slapped his shoulder. "She's not fine. She needs stitches."

"I just told her that."

Eve leaned in around Augie's shoulder and squinted at me. "He's good. Let him stitch it."

I pulled my hand away from the injury again and instantly felt a new flood of blood. "Shit," I muttered.

He was right. It wasn't closing up. It needed stitching. Or glue. I didn't have time to go to the hospital and get it done. Riddick was going to murder me. Quite possibly literally.

I gave in. "Fine. Whatever. Just do it quick. I have somewhere to be."

Augie took the first aid kit from Terry's fingers and nodded at him and Eve. "Go. There're people lining up. I've got her."

That annoying tingle down my spine came again at his words. Nobody ever *had* me. I never needed them to. I *had* myself. Relying on others only got you in situations you couldn't control.

But for the tiniest of seconds, some stupid caveman-level, damsel-in-distress bullshit liked the way those words had sounded.

"For fuck's sake," I muttered to myself. "Get a grip."

Augie easily threaded a needle with some sort of black twine and then held it up in my direction. "My grip is just fine, thanks. You gonna stay still or you gonna squeal like a baby?"

I glared at him. "Just do it."

He took my chin in his fingers, tilting my face toward him.

I flinched back sharply.

He frowned. "What just happened? The needle wasn't anywhere near you."

A cold sweat broke out across the back of my neck.

Riddick had gripped my chin like that. Not gently, the way Augie had. But he'd dug his fingers in, yanking on my head to force me into submission. Anger balled up inside me that I'd let him. I fucking hated that I was scared of him. "Nothing. I'm fine. Just...don't touch me like that."

Augie's gaze darkened, but his fingers slid across my cheek.

I found myself leaning into his touch for the tiniest of seconds, before his hand settled at the back of my neck.

"This better?" he asked. "I need to keep you steady."

His face was close to mine. Close enough for me to notice the light-blond stubble that coated his strong jawline. Close enough for me to see what looked like flecks of silver in his light-colored eyes. I nodded once, giving my consent.

The needle pierced through my skin, but I didn't cry out. I'd already embarrassed myself enough in front of this man for one night. I wouldn't add to it by not being able to handle a couple of stitches without anesthetic.

I'd suffered so much worse in the past.

His breath misted over my lips. Minty fresh. Warm, just like his fingers tangled in my hair at the nape of my neck.

Augie made small, quick stitches in my head and was finished in under a minute.

His gaze flickered to mine. "There. You're all done."

He didn't move back.

And for a moment, I didn't make him.

A car horn blared, and we both jumped a mile. It took me a second to realize I'd leaned on the horn without even noticing because I was too busy getting lost in his eyes.

Terry gave us a questioning thumbs-up, silently asking if we were okay.

If Augie was okay, I corrected silently. Terry didn't give a shit about me.

Augie flashed him a thumbs-up while I busied myself inspecting his handiwork in the rearview mirror. The stitches were incredibly tidy. Almost professional level perfect. "You a doctor by day or something?" I twisted my head side to side, but there was no angle those stitches didn't look pro.

He packed his equipment away into the first aid kit again, neatly tucking the scissors into their designated compartment. "I doubt I'd be working here if I was. My neighbor is a nurse. She taught me how to do stitches a long time ago. Between me and my brother, one of us was always coming home with some sort of injury, and we never had insurance. Unless we were bleeding out, we just dealt with it at home."

I sat back in my seat. "Your parents just let you stitch your brother up?"

"Hard for them to have an opinion when they weren't around."

He'd sounded bitter about it, but sometimes an absent parent was better than one like my mother, who knew every aspect of your business.

"Well, your neighbor taught you well. Your brother was lucky you were around."

Augie scoffed, "Not sure he'd agree with you on that one." He glanced at me quickly, like he realized he'd said too much. "Look, the cops don't have anything other than what we told them. Which was that Eddie took both Fawn and Eve, but Eve was released once Eddie realized her father was a politician. We're guessing Fawn was always the target and Eve was only taken because she was there. We guess he might have seen Eve as a bonus and tried trafficking her, but when he realized who her father was, decided he didn't want that level of publicity."

"But there was no one to make a fuss over Fawn's disappearance so he could just sneak under the radar with her," I finished for him.

"We've been making as much noise as we can. But without money or resources, we haven't had much luck. Nobody cares about a missing stripper from Saint View."

I suspected he was suddenly offering up information to distract me from the overshare of information about his own life, but I would take it.

"Okay. Well, at least I know where to start from. Thanks. We'll take it from here."

His eyebrows furrowed together. "You'll take it from here? What does that mean?"

I scraped at a dried bit of blood on my neck. "It means you tried your best with what you had. I appreciate that."

He raised one eyebrow. "But what? You have money so you can do better?"

"I never said that."

"You implied it." He shifted. "I've been out there scouring the streets for her, every damn day, for weeks."

Irritation prickled at me. "And where did that get you? I'm not trying to be an asshole, but—"

"But what I'm doing isn't good enough?"

I let out a breath. "Honestly? No. It's not."

He shook his head, his gaze sliding to the gun in my job bag.

I quickly covered it up.

He raised his eyes to meet mine. "You look so much like her. But you're nothing alike."

The words stung because the implication was clear. Fawn was good and sweet and kind. She was the sort of woman who had friends who loved her so much they put their entire lives on hold to search for her.

And I was the opposite. Apart from Jez, I didn't even have any true friends. Not ones who honestly knew me.

But that was the way it had to be. Whenever anyone got too close to me, I had to push them away. What else was I supposed to do? Just tell them that every time my mother sent me a 'care package' it was actually a request to put a bullet through some random person's brain? Or worse, that I actually liked it?

It was almost funny, thinking about the way my roommate in Spain would have run screaming from our apartment if she knew she'd slept under the same roof as a murderer every night.

I didn't want to sit here in this car with a man who found me disappointing in comparison to my sister. I already knew it. I didn't need the reminder. "Thanks for the stitches, but get out of my car, Augie."

His beautiful lips pulled into a tight scowl as he got out of the car and slammed the door. He leaned down and pinned me with a final glare through the open window. "I'm not going to stop searching for her."

But for all he portrayed the bad boy, Augie was as innocent as Fawn was. I didn't want him digging any deeper. "You don't have any idea what you're getting yourself into. Just let it go."

The words came out dark. A warning.

It was all I could do for my sister's friend. Try to keep him safe because I knew she would want me to.

Once I started poking into the past and the people in it, blood would be shed.

I didn't want Augie's to be among it.

8

OPHELIA

*R*iddick steered his truck along the beach road that ran the length of the coast connecting Saint View and Providence. The sun had only just popped up above the horizon, and the orange and gold rays it cast over the ocean should have been beautiful.

Except the man sitting next to me made everything feel dark and dangerous.

Riddick glanced over at me with a deep frown. "You aren't drinking your coffee."

"Because I told you I didn't want any," I said through gritted teeth.

"You like coffee. Drink it."

I did like it. I also didn't trust Riddick as far as I could throw him, and he'd come out of the gas station with this cup. For all I knew he'd dropped Rohypnol in it and was just waiting for me to take a sip.

I also didn't like being told what to do, and after hours and hours of this bullshit, I was over it. My patience snapped. I rolled down the window and upended the to-go cup, letting dark-brown liquid splash all over the road.

I had the pleasure of watching Riddick's jaw tense for a second before his eyes turned deadly dark.

It was enough to remind me who I was dealing with. And that poking this particular bear was a death wish. "Sorry," I muttered. "I'm not a morning person."

It had been the most boring stakeout ever, just sitting there waiting for someone to leave a building. Who did overnight shifts at an office? That was dodgy in itself, and it likely had something to do with the reason this man had a hit on him.

But the reasons behind hits and who ordered them weren't my business. We weren't told information like that, and I knew better than to ask. I didn't even want to know. The less I knew, the better.

"I like mornings when everything is fresh and clean and possibilities are endless." Riddick put his blinker on, following the target, as we had been ever since he'd emerged from his workplace a bleary-eyed and disheveled mess.

I shifted uncomfortably. "Well, that's nice for you, but I'm definitely more of a night owl."

Riddick tutted like that was the wrong choice. "Your mother didn't tell me that when I agreed to this."

I glanced at him, seeing the out I'd been hoping for. "You can watch this target during the day. I'll watch him at night. Then we can compare notes and create a plan of attack."

Whatever got me away from Riddick.

He didn't say anything, just frowned when I yawned

again. I didn't know what he expected from me after we'd been up all night. I shifted and peered out through the windshield at the now-familiar license plate of the car in front of us. JE 87 ME. I'd memorized it hours ago, while we'd been sitting outside the office building. Surveillance was always the most boring part of the job. My parents gave us a head start with the job bag, filled with as much information as they could find. But I liked to go that one step further. I liked to watch. To wait. To get to know the person and their habits before I made my move. Sometimes I did that for months, making sure I knew everything about them. Sometimes it only took a week. But never less.

Anything less was sloppy. Rushed and careless.

That wasn't how I rolled.

The Benz in front of us turned into a street, and Riddick followed, accelerating around the corner, closing the gap between the two vehicles.

"Stay back," I warned him. "You're too close. He's going to notice us."

Riddick ignored me, urging the vehicle on faster so we were practically nose to bumper with the other car.

"Riddick!" The demand was sharper this time. "Knock it off."

"I told you. I'm a morning person, and this morning seems like a good one to get this job done."

"What?" I snapped, straining forward against my seat belt to stare at him. "We aren't doing this now. It's broad daylight, we know nothing about the target—"

"We know enough."

"We don't even know who he lives with! He could

have an entire police squad camped in his kitchen for all we know."

The Benz turned into a driveway, and to my horror, Riddick did the same. "Get your mask on, Ophelia. Let's go have some fun."

"What? All these houses have security cameras, Riddick! The cops will have your license plates—"

"Please. They're stolen. How stupid do you think I am?"

The fact we were doing this with the sun shining and almost no preparation made me think the answer was 'a lot' but I didn't have time to say that. He'd already dragged his mask down and had one foot out of the truck.

There was nothing left for me to do but pull out my balaclava, hastily shove it down over my face, and follow.

Gorman Dentry shuffled papers and a briefcase into his arms as he got out of his Mercedes then turned in our direction. His mouth opened in shock when Riddick rushed him, clapping one gloved hand over his mouth so he couldn't scream and the other around his chest. Riddick squeezed his victim like he was an anaconda, cutting off his air supply, and dragged him toward the house.

I had little choice but to go after them or be left standing on Gorman's perfectly manicured lawn while Riddick did my job for me.

I ground my molars, pissed off I was being shut out of my own damn job. I was going to kill my mother for even so much as breathing a word of this in Riddick's direction. It was fucking insulting the way he was carrying on.

I scooped up a set of keys from the ground where

Gorman had dropped them and shoved one into the lock on his front door.

Gorman snapped out of his shock enough to struggle against Riddick's hold, but it was pretty pointless. Riddick was a big guy, and Gorman had the physique of a math nerd who got bullied by the jocks.

I finally found the right key, and the lock gave way, the handle twisting beneath my grasp. The three of us fell through the door, Riddick kicking it closed behind us.

I rushed around a corner, checking there was nobody else downstairs, while taking in the posh formal living room. "Who else lives here?" I hissed at Gorman while Riddick hauled him onto a couch.

Riddick moved his hand from Gorman's mouth to let him answer me, and the first thing the scared little man did was scream for help.

I rolled my eyes. "Are you happy?" I snapped at Riddick as he silenced the man again. "The whole fucking neighborhood probably heard that. Certainly, anyone who lives—"

"There's no one else here," Riddick scoffed. "Quit getting your knickers in a twist."

"Gorman?" a voice called from the top of the stairs. "Gorman, is that you?"

I glared at Riddick who didn't even have the grace to be embarrassed. He just stared at me.

"Oh," I scoffed. "I'll go get her, shall I?"

"You're the one who keeps telling me this is your kill."

Gorman whimpered pathetically while I stared daggers at Riddick. But he was right. He might have been ruining every plan I'd had for how this job would play out, but what's done was done, and now I had to think on my feet. I stomped toward the hallway and stared up at the willowy blonde halfway down the staircase.

She screamed in about the same pitch as her husband and scrambled back up.

"Why must you run?" I muttered, sprinting after her, taking the stairs two at a time. "It's too early in the morning for cardio." But nonetheless, I thanked my genetics for long legs and caught up with the woman easily. With a sharp tug, I pinned her up against the wall.

"Please don't hurt me," she begged.

"I won't if you do as I say. Understand?"

She nodded quickly.

"Good. I need tape."

"In the garage," she gasped.

Good Lord, some people were stupid. Why not say they didn't have any?

I dragged her down the stairs and left her on the couch next to her husband, who was sniveling pathetically under Riddick's quietly deadly gaze. I tried a couple of doors along the left side of the hallway, eventually finding the one that led to a neatly organized garage. A roll of duct tape hung on a pegboard. I grabbed it and returned to the living room, where the woman let me tape her mouth and wrists without so much as a complaint.

Despite my mask, the woman's big eyes felt like they could see everything beneath, and I cursed Riddick again while I taped her ankles. This was so fucking unnecessary. This woman wasn't the target. It wasn't her fault someone had a grudge because her husband was messed up in shit that was bigger than he was. If I'd been left to do this job alone, I would have waited for her to be out of the house and spared her the trauma of what was about to happen.

I glared at Riddick. "Well? Is this what you wanted? An audience? You some sort of exhibitionist?"

He shrugged. "You don't like it?"

"Do I like that we now have a witness just because you were too impatient to do your fucking job properly? No! I don't like that. Why couldn't you have just waited? She didn't fucking do anything wrong. Her name isn't mentioned anywhere in the job brief."

He cocked his head at me. "You're right. I'm sorry."

I blinked in surprise. That had been the last thing I'd expected him to say.

I was so shocked by his apology I reacted too late when he pulled a gun from the back of his jeans and shot the woman in the neck without even glancing in her direction.

I gasped, taking in the bullet hole through her throat and the wide, panicked eyes that said she felt every burning second of agony before the life seeped away and she slumped over onto her husband's shoulder.

He yelped and tried to get away from his wife's dead body.

I stared at Riddick, cursing his completely out-of-line behavior. "What the fuck!"

He grinned as he switched the gun with an attached silencer to his other hand. "What? You're the one who said you were the boss. You pointed out that I'd created a witness. Didn't your mother teach you not to leave witnesses? I know mine did."

He knew very well I'd been taught exactly the same way he had.

But that was why I did surveillance. It was why I would have never followed this man into this house, not knowing if there were others inside. What if that had been a kid who'd walked down the stairs? Would Riddick have treated them in the same way?

A chilling realization confirmed he probably would have. I turned to him, suddenly terrified that exact scenario was going to play out if a kid appeared from upstairs. I needed to get him out of here before that could happen. "Go on then. Get on with it."

"Please." Gorman desperately shook his head from side to side. "Why are you doing this?"

"Rule number one," I told Gorman idly, playing it as cool as I could. "We don't ask why. We don't care."

Riddick squeezed the trigger, and the gun sent a silent bullet straight into the man's leg.

I dove on him, muffling his scream of pain while shooting Riddick a dirty look. "What the hell? I know you're a better shot than that!"

I winced at the blood pouring from the man's thigh. He sobbed, clutching at the bullet wound uselessly. Riddick was making a mess just for the fucking sake of it.

I shoved some tape across the man's mouth and then held my hand out for the weapon. "Give me the gun."

Riddick glanced over at me. "You have your own."

"I'm well aware. But this is my target and this is my show." I wasn't letting him run it anymore.

He grinned at me. "You gonna mess him up?"

I took the gun from him. "No. I'm going to do what I was paid to do and then I'm going to go home and go to bed, because like I already told you, I'm not a freaking morning person."

The words came out strong. Sure. Just the way I'd intended.

But my gaze kept straying to the dead woman and the thought she hadn't deserved this.

I pointed the gun at Gorman's balding head.

The power it spread through my entire body was undeniable. The rush was heady, the adrenaline spiking until it coursed through my blood.

Riddick moved behind me, his voice taunting in my ear. "Go on. Have a little fun. You know you want to."

I hated that I paused. I hated he was right. That some part of me actually did want to prolong this.

That some part of me was as dark as he was.

When Riddick put his hand over mine and lowered it a few inches, I pulled the trigger.

The bullet found its mark in Gorman's shoulder.

His cry of pain was muffled by the tape, but Riddick's voice was filled with delight. "See? You liked that, didn't you?"

I didn't want to.

But I couldn't stop watching the gush of blood and the power it created inside me.

"We're the same, you and I, Ophelia. This is why we're going to be great partners. Keep going. Watch him bleed."

His lips brushed my cheek.

I froze.

When Augie had touched my cheek I'd leaned into it, craving his warmth.

When Riddick did it, my entire body cringed away from the connection, and I pulled the trigger again.

This time the bullet landed right between Gorman's eyes.

The room went silent.

Gorman's breaths ceased to exist.

Riddick stared at me, frowning because I'd wrecked his little game.

I shoved the gun at his chest. "You and I are nothing alike, Riddick. Not a fucking thing."

____

9

AUGIE

I sat outside the address on Bert Leddith's card and peered at the pretty little house. It wasn't in the most expensive part of Providence, but it was a tidy, well-kept home that looked damn sweet from where I was sitting. "Should have been a private investigator," I muttered, shoving the card Willa had given me into my pocket again. "You clearly make more money than I do."

I got out and strode up the driveway to rap my knuckles across a bright-blue painted door.

The man who opened it was a few inches shorter than me and maybe ten years older. He smiled. "Augie, right? Come on in. I've got an office just down the hall there to your left."

I stepped inside and made my way down the hallway while he closed the door. His office was small, barely big enough for a desk and a filing cabinet, but it had a window with a view of a neat backyard. A grill and outdoor furniture were set up on the back patio.

Bert indicated for me to sit, and he took up the spot behind the desk. He pulled a blank notepad and a pen from his top drawer and scribbled the date on the top before glancing up at me. "You said on the phone that your friend is missing. How about you tell me a bit more about her?"

I nodded stiffly and spilled out all the basic facts about Fawn and everything we knew about Eddie and why she might have been taken. Bert diligently took notes while I talked, and when I was done, he slowly put down his pen and cleared his throat.

"Well, first of all, I want to say that I'm really sorry for everything you've been through. The fact none of this has been reported through the media is a tragedy. I've made some notes on aspects of the case that I can follow up with some friends of mine. I definitely think I can help you."

Relief spread through me. "That's great. Thanks."

The man nodded. "We'll get you a contract drawn up straightaway. Down payment is two-thousand dollars with weekly installments due after that—"

I choked on a cough. "Two thousand dollars?"

The man put down his pen. "Well, two thousand is my base rate, and then there's a per week charge after that, depending on how many hours per week I do."

"And how many weeks exactly do you think it would take you to find her?"

Bert shrugged. "It's truly impossible to say." He gave me a sharp look. "I'm sure you want to do everything in your power to find your friend, though, don't you?"

The judgment in his tone pissed me off in an instant.

I'd never been very patient with these assholes from Providence, who had no idea what it was like for the rest of us who hadn't been born with silver spoons in our mouths. "I spend hours every day asking every person I can find if they've seen her. I've made hundreds, if not thousands, of missing posters and plastered them to every pole I can find. I've visited every bar and strip club, checked every street corner searching for her. I want to find her more than I want to fucking breathe. I'm prepared to pay you something, obviously, but do I look like I have two thousand dollars?"

Bert pushed back in his chair and stood. "I guess we're done here, then. Nice meeting you, Augie. I hope you find your friend."

Anger pulsed through me, hot and fast. "That's it? You won't help me? You just said it was a tragedy!"

"Yeah, but so is not getting paid."

"You piece of fucking shit!" I balled my fingers up into fists.

I hated that Ophelia was right. That part of the reason I hadn't been able to find Fawn was because I didn't have the money to do so. The fucking guilt that swamped me was thick and real and felt all too familiar to every time I'd let my brother down.

Every time I hadn't been able to buy him new football boots.

Every time I'd been late picking him up from school because my car wouldn't start.

Every time he'd woken up to find some stranger in our house because I'd brought them home to fuck them for money.

The money I'd earned doing just that last night burned in my pocket. I needed it to pay my rent.

But I needed to find Fawn more. I pulled it out and put it down on the desk in front of him. "This is all I have right now. Give me a week to come up with the rest."

The man eyed me then let out a long sigh. "I'll take it because the case intrigues me. But if I'm letting you pay this off, then it's going to be with interest."

Relief settled over me. "Fine. Great. No problem. Where do I sign?" I would have told him anything. There was no way I was coming up with the rest of that money unless I found someone willing to buy a kidney. But this chump could suck a bag of dicks. Five hundred was more than fair for making a couple of calls.

I signed off on the contract, and Bert said he'd call me in a couple days with an update.

He walked me to the door while I profusely thanked him with fake sincerity and promised him a payment I knew I wouldn't deliver on.

At my car, I slid behind the wheel and turned the key, praying the engine would turn over.

The passenger-side door opened, a woman slipping into the seat beside me. "Hey, Augie."

My mouth dropped open. "Where the hell did you come from?"

I twisted and looked behind me, finally noticing her black car parked several houses away. "Were you following me?" I asked Ophelia.

She scoffed, "Please. Don't flatter yourself. I was in the neighborhood and saw your shit bucket of a car. How on earth is this thing still running? It's gotta be the same age as my dad."

I cocked my head at her. "You were absolutely fucking following me."

She ignored the accusation. "I was driving into town, saw your car parked outside a private investigator's house, and thought maybe I'd see what you were up to."

I raised an eyebrow. "And I would tell you because you've been so helpful and forthcoming with information?"

She grinned. "Exactly."

I rolled my eyes. "Get out of my car, Ophelia."

"You didn't hire that guy, did you?"

"So what if I did?"

She bit her bottom lip and slowly drew it through her teeth while I tried not to notice how hot that was. "Fire him," she said, voice full of defiance. "He has Mafia connections."

I snorted. "He lives in a posh house in Providence and drives a minivan. That man wouldn't know Mafia if one politely knocked on his door and asked for a cup of tea."

She shrugged. "Do I look like I have Mafia connections?"

I glanced over at her sleek dark hair, the formfitting jeans, and long-sleeved black T-shirt. She was almost as girl-next-door as Fawn was. "No," I admitted.

"And yet you know I carry a gun."

"Doesn't mean you're Mafia. A lot of women carry guns." Though generally not the sort of gun I'd seen in Ophelia's bag the other night. That had been a hard-core weapon.

She laughed, the sound tinkling through my car pleasantly. "Fine. I'm not Mafia."

"Too sweet and innocent?"

She smiled wryly and shook her head. "What if I told you I was worse?"

I squinted at her. She was tall but not exactly imposing. She definitely talked a lot of smack, but there was something behind her eyes that still reminded me so much of Fawn I could barely stand to notice it. "I'd probably say you were full of shit."

She laughed again, but this time it sounded a little bitter. "Yeah, I bet you would. Which is exactly why you're going to get yourself in trouble." She shifted, bringing one knee up slightly so we were facing each other. "Listen. I know we got off to a bad start, but it sounds like my sister cared about you. Which means she wouldn't want you wasting your money on men like Bert Leddith. Don't give him any money. It won't end well."

"Too late. I already did."

She groaned into her hands before finally glancing up at me again. "You aren't going to give this up, are you? You're just going to stick to it like a dog with a bone. Why?"

"Because I care about your sister."

"Are you in love with her?"

"No."

"You sure?"

I was. "I love her, but I'm not in love with her. She's twenty-two, Ophelia. She's soft and sweet and so fucking good." I swallowed hard. "She's everything I'm not."

"That's probably why she likes you," Ophelia mused. "She has a thing for bad boys."

I hated that. Hated the idea of her with a man like me. Someone who would ruin everything good inside her.

"It's why I'd destroy her. I love her enough to not want to do that to her."

Ophelia watched me then, quietly. The moment drew out as she studied me, then eventually shook her head. "Well then, Augie Mitchell. What do you know? We actually have something in common."

10

OPHELIA

I'd been avoiding my mother ever since Riddick and I had posted our proof-of-kill photos on the secure server she ran for the business. The online folders were locked down tight with more layers of software security than most government agencies had, but then she'd gone ahead and sent me two thumbs-up emojis, which was about as high as her praise got. So I knew she'd gotten the files.

Which meant her constant calls were now about something else.

I didn't need to answer the phone to know it was going to be about one of two things. Riddick. Or she had another job bag for me.

I didn't have nice things to say about either so I cancelled the call and turned my phone over on the tabletop.

"I saw that."

I gritted my teeth and looked over my shoulder at the

owner of the all-too-familiar voice. Like her phone calls also had conjuring powers, my mother stood there, in the middle of the café with a deep scowl etched across her face.

I turned back around. "Don't follow me if you don't want to see me avoiding your calls. We both know I don't want to talk to you."

She slid into the chair on the other side of the table and smiled brightly at the waitress. "Nora? Could I order, please?"

An older woman with faded blonde hair and skin so deeply brown I was sure she'd spent most of her life on a beach, came hurrying over, a notepad and pen clutched in her fingers.

"Your usual?" the woman asked.

"Yes, please."

I cocked my head in my mother's direction. "I wouldn't have come here if I'd known this was your place."

Mom shrugged out of her jacket and twisted to place it on the back of her seat. "If you were around more, maybe you would have known."

I sighed heavily into the remains of my coffee.

Mom's finger prodded against my forehead. "Stop frowning like that. Look at all those lines. Haven't you been getting your Botox injections?"

I didn't grace her shitty question with an answer. I wasn't in my twenties anymore. I had some fine lines. Who fucking cared? I never did, until I was around her for too long.

The older woman came back with my mother's coffee,

and Mom took it from her, taking a sip. She immediately handed the mug back.

"Nora, dear, this is really not hot enough. You know I like my coffee scalding. Could you try again?" She gave the lady an honest smile. The kind she could never seem to dredge up for me because I was clearly more disappointing than bad coffee.

Nora left to try again, poor old biddy, and I figured I may as well disappoint my mother a little more.

"Why did you tell Riddick I needed help doing the job I've been doing since I was fifteen?"

Mom folded her hands on the tabletop and gave me the same look she'd been giving me since I was a kid. The one that made it clear I was annoying to her because I couldn't read her mind.

"Why do you talk about it like it's a bad thing? You know Riddick is top of the game. You could learn a lot from him."

Yeah, a lot about things I was pretty sure I didn't want to know. While there was clearly some part of me that was messed up enough to enjoy taking people's lives for a living, I didn't torture people. I didn't put gunshots in places that wouldn't be fatal. My job was to kill quickly and cleanly and then move on. Maybe I took a minute, soaking in the scene and taking pride in my work.

But what Riddick did went beyond that. He was impulsive. Sloppy. He'd shot that woman in the throat, even though she had nothing to do with the job.

I'd seen the wild recklessness in his eyes.

Riddick was famous in our industry because he was ruthless and dangerous. But the small taste I'd had of his methods over the last few days had left me cold. I'd put on makeup that morning, gingerly dabbing thick foundation over the fading bruising on my chin from where he'd grabbed me in the storeroom of Jezebel's flower shop.

Riddick wasn't only dangerous to the targets in our job bags.

He was dangerous to everyone.

Including me.

"I know enough," I told my mother firmly. "I don't want him on my jobs."

She smiled at Nora again when a fresh cup of probably boiling coffee was placed in front of her.

It was tempting to throw it in my mother's face.

But I folded my hands in my lap instead while she took a sip and poor, hovering Nora could finally breathe a sigh of relief at getting it right. She scurried off.

Mom put her mug down with a clink of porcelain on the tabletop. "Well, I'm sorry you feel that way. You need to get to know him. Be seen a few places together. It'll make it more believable that this is a union of your choosing when we announce your engagement."

I raised an eyebrow. "My what?"

Mom frowned, and I wondered if I should point out that *her* Botox could probably use a top-up, too.

"Didn't Riddick discuss it with you?" she asked. "We ironed out all the details when I gave him the information about your last job."

I gaped at her. "You ironed out all the details about my engagement? Without even telling the bride?"

She huffed impatiently. "Stop being so dramatic. You're the one who argued with me about letting your brother love who he loved."

"What have Vincent and Scythe got to do with you marrying me off to Riddick?"

She reached beneath the table, pushing a bag in my direction. "Open it."

I already knew what it was. A new target.

"Why?" I could open it later when I was alone.

Mom shook her head like I was an imbecile for not understanding words she hadn't said. "You're so spoiled, and I blame myself for that. I've always just handed you everything. You've never had to do any of the hard work yourself."

I blinked and lowered my voice, straining toward her. "I don't do the hard work? Mom, last I checked, I was the one doing all the..." I darted a look around at the mostly empty coffee shop but didn't dare risk it. I made a face with my tongue hanging out and made a choking noise.

Mom didn't give me any praise for my acting abilities. "That is the second-to-last job we have on the roster. The work is drying up."

I shrugged. "So? Something else will come up."

Mom shook her head. "In over thirty years, we've never not been fully booked. Last year your brother was booked a solid twelve months in advance."

I rolled my eyes. "Good for Vincent."

Mom grabbed my hand from across the table, digging her fingernails in. "Stop being so flippant. The target in there is a small-time nothing job. So is the other one I have. They're jobs I had to take because there was literally nothing else. Do you know how embarrassing that is? Word has gotten around that Vincent and Scythe are out."

I prickled at the mention of my brother and the tone

in my mother's voice that made me think she would pull Vincent back in if she were given half the chance. It pissed me off more than anything else I'd heard come out of her mouth. She could pick at me. Tell me I was lazy, that I needed Botox, that I wasn't good enough. But when she said it about my siblings, it sent a red haze over my eyes. "So what if he's out? I'm still here, aren't I? People need to leave Vincent alone. He has a family. A baby due to be born soon. He's not coming back."

Her gaze turned dark. "Don't you think I know that? Don't you think I know that I'm stuck with you? That's why we have no work, Ophelia. People don't want you."

Her words stung, even though I should have been used to it. "Thanks, Mom. That's just great. If no one needs me here, I'll just go back to Spain and get a regular job where I never have to think about you and this life you dumped on me again."

I pushed back on my chair, the feet scraping against the tiled floor with a screech of protest that mirrored the one I wanted to let loose from somewhere deep inside me.

Mom grabbed my arm. "Stop acting like a child. You were the one who fought tooth and nail for me to let Fawn and Vincent go. You don't get to just leave now. You're the one ruining it. Now you're the one who'll fix it. What the hell are your father and I supposed to do if you just leave?"

I glanced over at old Nora, her wrinkled hands shaking as she ground up coffee beans. "I don't know, Mom. Maybe you could try working a regular job? Like everyone else does?"

Her mouth dropped open, like I'd just suggested

something as crazy as flying to the moon on her broomstick. "You ungrateful child. You'd leave us out on the streets, wouldn't you? After all we've done for you, buying you that apartment, funding your lifestyle. You know we aren't the only ones who have never worked a proper job. How are you going to get anyone to hire you to do anything when you're thirty-three years old and have no working history or college degree? Enjoy scrubbing toilets for a living, Ophelia. Because that's the only sort of job you're going to get if you walk away."

She was right. I hadn't worked a day in my life, other than for my parents.

The realization must have been written all over my face because my mother smiled smugly. "Sit down."

I did. While I was grateful for people who kept bathrooms clean, it would be a very different life from the one I'd always known. One that was full of hardships and trying to make ends meet. Living paycheck to paycheck. I doubted a janitor's wage would cover much of my monthly spend.

Mom knew she'd won. "Now here's what's going to happen. Since Scythe and Jezebel didn't work out, you and Riddick will announce your engagement. You've both been away, so we'll just say you met up overseas, fell in love, and the whole thing is just a beautiful combining of two powerful families."

I couldn't find the words to say anything.

Mom clearly didn't like the silence. "Ophelia, you said yourself that men didn't do it for you. That you found them and sex boring. You're so much like me at that age. I was the same. Why do you think I married your father?

Women like us, we marry for position. For power. Love is for sentimental fools like your brother."

The fact anyone could call Vincent and Scythe sentimental fools, and mean it, was ridiculous. They were cold-blooded killers at best, complete psychopaths at worst.

They'd just fallen in love.

And for the first time ever, I'd seen peace in my brother's eyes. Mom could call him a sentimental fool all she wanted, but I wasn't letting her force him back in. Because she would. If I left again, she'd find a way. My mother didn't know anything else other than this life. She wouldn't let anyone or anything stand in the way of her continuing the lifestyle she was used to. Not even her children's happiness.

She was right about me anyway. We were the same. I'd never even had an orgasm with a man. Never found them interesting or attractive.

Except for Augie.

The thought surprised me. As did the warming tingle I'd begun to associate with his name. My heart rate picked up every time I thought about the way he'd pulled his shirt off in that car, exposing tawny skin and muscles that had just begged for my fingertips. Then the way he'd run his fingers over my cheek and cupped the back of my neck while he'd stitched me up, those blue eyes so intent on his work he hadn't even noticed the way I'd practically melted beneath his touch.

I straightened my spine, shoving out those kinds of thoughts. They were distracting and, frankly, alarming. How much time had I spent in the last few days following Augie around? Enough that Riddick had caught me completely unaware and off guard and put me in a situation I couldn't control.

I changed the subject and picked up the job bag from my feet, praying it would be a target interesting enough to keep my mind off this entire web I seemed to be getting myself stuck in. I pulled the bag onto my lap and undid the zipper.

The blue folder that my father painstakingly created for each target was sitting on top. Without taking it out, I lifted the cover to take a peek at the front page of the documents. They always started with a photo of the target.

Augie's too handsome but perpetually pissed-off face stared back at me.

A gasp slipped from my lips, and my head jerked up, my gaze slamming into my mother's again.

"What?" she asked, leaning over the table to see what I was staring at. "Do you know him?"

I quickly shut the folder, like closing it might keep her away from him, even though it would take nothing for her to get another copy if she so desired. "No. Of course not. I just gave myself a paper cut."

Mom sat back, not caring I might have hurt myself. "Oh. Well, that job shouldn't take you long. When you're done with that one, there's one more. But after that, there's nothing. We need jobs from Riddick. We need to announce your engagement, and soon. His family isn't going to send any jobs our way until everything is legal and our companies merge." She frowned at me disapprovingly. "I can't blame them, with the way you're acting. You have to stop looking like you're going to run at any minute. That won't end well for any of us, Ophelia. Do not embarrass Riddick, and do not embarrass me. This family needs you to do your part."

I nodded absentmindedly, barely hearing her words.

I was too busy staring at the photo of Augie.

And the realization that I was going to have to kill him.

11

OPHELIA

With my focus split between poking around for information about Fawn, and finding out everything I could about Augie, my days became long and were often split into two. In the mornings, I tracked down all of Fawn's old friends and quizzed them. When did you last see Fawn? Have you had any contact with Eddie? Where were the places they liked to go when they were dating? Did she ever tell you anything that might help me find her?

Vincent or Scythe came with me when they weren't working at his club or taking care of his pregnant partner, but even their air of menace hadn't helped. The answers were all incredibly frustrating and led nowhere. When Fawn had left, she hadn't just left our family. She'd left her entire life behind and started a new one. The lack of information left me hollow, and I'd quickly realized I'd been too harsh on Augie. My dig about him not doing a good enough job in searching for Fawn because he didn't have the money or resources was proving to be bullshit. I had resources and more information about my sister's past than he did, and I still couldn't make any progress.

My afternoons and nights were spent doing surveillance on Augie, all with a growing ball of dread building in my stomach.

For days, ever since I'd gotten that job bag with his name on it, I'd sat in my car a little ways down his street and watched his house. I'd stress eaten bags of potato chips and soft drinks, waiting for something to happen, but things had been pretty quiet. He worked at the club until the early hours of the morning, then came home and slept until midafternoon, I guessed. At the very least, he never left his house during that time. One afternoon he'd gone out and put up new missing posters of Fawn, and I'd sadly trailed along behind him, while he replaced the old tattered ones with the new.

This man cared about my sister. They were obviously friends. He'd told me himself he loved her. I'd raided my sister's old home and seen the photos of him and Fawn and Eve with some of the other people I recognized from my visit to the club.

And I was going to have to kill him.

For the first time ever, what I'd been tasked to do didn't sit right. Normally, I couldn't care less about what people had done to find themselves the target of a hit. I did my job, and I did it well, without asking questions.

But I couldn't do that to someone my sister cared about. Not when he'd been the sole driving force behind trying to find her for all this time.

I leaned forward, peering through my binoculars at

Augie's house. If I was being generous, I would call it run-down. If I was being truthful, it was verging on derelict, though there were other houses on the street that were worse. At least Augie's place didn't have broken windows or grass so overgrown you didn't have a chance of reaching the porch without having to wade through it. The paint on the small house was peeling and flaking off. The roof was faded with years spent baking in warm Saint View summers. The driveway and a path that led to the front door were both cracked from use or tree roots growing beneath and destroying the concrete.

It was a sad little street from my point of view. But I'd hung around enough days to realize there was happiness here too. There were a couple of small girls who played together on one of their front lawns every day after school, doing handstands and cartwheels on the patchy grass. There were two older ladies who sat on a porch and played cards, only moving inside on particularly chilly afternoons. Augie had brought them groceries one afternoon, on his way home from doing his own shopping, and my stone-cold heart had thawed that little bit more.

I couldn't work out why someone would want him dead. Did that person know he brought these women food every week? Did they know how they stared up at him with adoration in their eyes and thanked him for his kindness?

Maybe they did and they didn't care.

I was trying so hard not to.

It really wasn't working.

It wasn't something that was allowed, and I knew

even before I hit the call button that it would go nowhere, but I rang my mom. The ringtone trilled in my ear, and I drummed my nails impatiently on the steering wheel, waiting for her to pick up.

"Is it done? Are you ready for your next job?"

I cleared my throat. "Hello to you too, Mother. How's your day?"

"Is. It. Done, Ophelia?"

I sighed. Clearly, she wasn't in the mood for pleasantries. She sounded stressed and impatient, and her mood wasn't likely to get any better when she heard my answer. "No. It's not. I have questions."

"Ophelia! It's been three days! What on earth is taking so long? I'm going to have to give someone else this other job if you don't hurry up! It's embarrassing how long you take to do one simple task. This is exactly why no one is giving us any work. You're getting a reputation, and it's not a good one!"

Irritation prickled up my spine. "I have a process. You know that. It takes some time, and this one is taking a bit longer than I expected."

Because I didn't want to do it and was finding any reason not to.

"Do I need to send Riddick down there to help you?"

I ground my molars at the insulting insinuation I couldn't handle my own jobs. "I warned you, Mom. Do not do that to me again. It will not end well. I'm not working with him."

It would have been weird to anyone not involved in this world, but working with him was worse than the idea of marrying him. Marriage was merely a formality. A contract between two parties to strengthen business relations. My mother and father led such separate lives they were almost strangers.

That's exactly how a marriage to Riddick would be.

But working with him was entirely different. I understood my mother's need for our families to merge. But he and I weren't about to become some sort of duo.

I was a solo act.

I always would be.

"Then what's the holdup?" Mom asked with an exasperated sigh. "This is a nothing job that should have taken twenty-four hours at most. I think Riddick is right about you. Maybe you've passed your peak."

My mouth dropped open. "Are you fucking serious? I'm thirty-three! Not eighty!"

She sniffed. "Well, prove us wrong. Get the job done."

"Not until you tell me who ordered it."

I could practically hear her rolling her eyes and I almost didn't blame her. This wasn't done. The only things I ever knew about a target were what was in the job bag. Anything more was a liability.

She clucked her tongue impatiently. "You know I can't tell you that. What if you were caught, Ophelia?"

"I wouldn't talk."

"You think that, but everyone has a tipping point where self-preservation kicks in. We can't have you just running your mouth because someone stuck pins beneath your fingernails. We promise our clients that level of security."

But I was desperate enough to beg. I just needed her to tell me Augie wasn't a good guy. That the way he cared about Fawn was irrelevant because he stole from charities or flashed families in parks. Just one thing that would make it easier to put a knife in his back. "Break the rules, Mom. Just this once. Please."

She paused, and for the tiniest of seconds, I thought she was going to do it. But then a deep voice came from her end, muffled but gruff, and Mom's breathing quickened.

"Mom?" I asked again.

"I have to go, Ophelia. Riddick is here. I'm giving him the other job bag. If you haven't finished yours by the time he finishes this one, he's coming to help you."

"Mom!" I snapped.

Her voice lowered. "No, don't 'Mom' me. You're embarrassing me. You're being as useless as Fawn right now."

She hung up.

"Fuck!" I slammed my fist down on the steering wheel. I needed to work out what was going on with Augie, and it needed to happen tonight.

His door opened, and he walked out onto the porch, another set of flyers in his arms. Early winter sun filtered through the handful of leaves still desperately clinging to their branches. It lit him up in golden hues, glinting in the highlights of his hair and kissing the chiseled slopes of his too-handsome face. His usual scowl was firmly in place, like he hated the world and everything in it, but it somehow only made him more attractive.

My insides clenched when he looked this way, but if he noticed my car, he didn't give any indication. I breathed a sigh of relief as he disappeared down the road in the opposite direction.

There was no time for messing around anymore. I

didn't even have the luxury of waiting for darkness. I reached across and pulled a couple of small electronic devices from the glove box, then got out of the car, locking it behind me because I'd learned enough about this neighborhood in the last few days to know it probably wouldn't be here when I got back if I didn't.

I didn't like the sunlight. I ached for the cover of darkness, but I had days at best before Riddick would be hovering over my shoulder again, and if he knew Augie was the target, then I might as well just put a bullet between Augie's eyes now.

It would be kinder than what Riddick would do if he caught Augie alone.

I strode down the street like I owned it, heels clicking over the cracked pavement. If I'd known I'd be doing this today, I might have opted for jeans and sneakers rather than heels I could break my ankle in. But I'd put on smart pants and a blazer this morning, with a top that cut low, showing off a healthy amount of cleavage.

I'd spent all morning trying to ignore the thought that I'd dressed this way for him. In case he noticed me sitting there, watching.

That was ridiculous. I didn't dress for men. Ever. These clothes made me feel like a boss bitch. That was more than enough reason to put them on in the morning.

My brain whispered that I was full of shit, but I refused to listen.

I raised a hand in greeting when the two old ladies playing cards stopped to stare at me. "Afternoon, ladies. Who's winning?"

Their suspicion melted away in an instant, both of

them claiming to be in the lead. I smiled and nodded, laughing at their bickering, even though my mind was on getting in and out of Augie's place before he returned.

"Well, I'll leave the two of you to carry on. I'm just headed over to Augie's place, so I'll catch the two of you later."

"Oh, he just left, sweetheart. You'll have to come back later."

I held up a shiny silver key. "It's okay. He gave me a key so I can get in. I'll just wait for him inside."

They smiled and waved, one of them telling me to "Go on then, dear," as I turned to walk across the road.

I imagined they'd spend the rest of the afternoon gossiping about the fact their handsome young neighbor had given a woman the key to his home.

Little did they know that key was actually to my front door, and I had zero intention of trying to use it at Augie's place.

I had a lock pick for that.

I got to the door and had it open in less than thirty seconds, the lock giving in with a few twists of the tool.

Honestly, his security was pathetic. I could have picked that lock at ten years of age, which probably meant half the neighborhood here could too. It was a wonder he had anything left to steal.

But when I opened the door, I realized he actually didn't. There was a TV in the living room, but it was tiny and ancient. An old leather couch sat facing it, but it was cracked, and one cushion had a tear that showed the stuffing inside. I wandered into the kitchen, opening a few cupboard doors that revealed clean glasses and plates, all mismatched and a few with chips taken out of them. It was clean but bare, much the same as the refrigerator when I opened it, just to be nosy. If anyone was breaking into this sad house, the most they were walking away with were two cans of beer from the bottom of the refrigerator. I placed an audio bug on the side of a cupboard and another behind the TV when a quick search through drawers and cupboards didn't produce anything of interest.

The stairs were the only other place to go. I took them slowly, hunting around for family photos or anything personal that might have given any insight to this man, but there was nothing but bare walls.

At the top of the staircase, I opened a door to my left. Shock punched through me at the turquoise walls and the room all neatly made up. A blue bedspread covered the mattress, and a TV sat in one corner, though both were a little dusty. On poking through the closet, I found a handful of clothes, including old football uniforms that ranged from teenage size to small boy. A surfboard stood in the corner, and the walls had photos of beaches and big waves.

Though I didn't even know him that well, I was instantly sure it wasn't Augie's room. The walls were too bright. The clothes too small for his broad shoulders. And there was a desolate air to the room that made me sure this wasn't where he lay down at night.

I was so convinced I didn't even put a bug in there.

I saved the last one I had for the bedroom across the hallway.

There was no doubt in my mind this was Augie's

room. An unmade bed sat in the center, silky black sheets a surprise beneath a dark-gray comforter. His pillows were strewn across the bed haphazardly, and I trailed my fingers over the place he slept. His blinds were open, with early afternoon sun streaming in over the dark-wood dresser that held his clothes. There was no closet, but that left room for a black armchair in one corner.

It was oddly placed, cutting off the flow of the room, and I found myself sitting, sinking back into the padded cushioning.

It was perfectly placed to watch the bed.

My breath quickened as my brain filled with the idea of watching him sleep. Of those silky sheets slipping down his hard body. Of them revealing the muscled planes of his back, his tattoos. Of them just barely covering the globes of his ass.

There was no doubt in my mind Augie slept naked. The man oozed sex appeal and confidence. There was no way he was slipping into a matching set of flannel pj's every night.

There was no stopping the flush of heat at the thought of sitting here, watching him do a whole lot more than sleep.

The feeling was so foreign it was almost alarming. Augie's scent permeated the air in the room so thickly it was like he was standing right in front of me. A rich mix of cologne and ocean, with a vague hint of smoke that I wanted to inhale deep so it could soak into my lungs.

"Get a fucking grip, Ophelia," I muttered to myself. My gaze drifted around the room as I stood again, seeking a place to plant the final bug. It was pea-sized, and I rubbed it between my fingers while I hunted around the bedroom for the best spot.

"Want to tell me what the fuck you're doing in my house?"

I spun around so quick I nearly dropped the bug, squeezing it at the last second so it didn't drop and go rolling away across the threadbare carpet.

Augie leaned on the doorway, his biceps popping from the way he had his arms folded across his chest. I couldn't help but stare at the way they strained at the thin, long-sleeved T-shirt, the material pulling tight.

By the time I dragged my eyes and my libido up to his face, he was smirking.

Shit. He knew very well I'd been checking him out. Which again, gave him the upper hand. I wanted to kick myself. I'd been so distracted thinking about the things he did in that damn bed I hadn't even heard the door open or him walking up the stairs.

"You going to answer me or you just going to stand there staring at my arms? If you want to open your wallet, I can take my shirt off for you. Give you a better look?"

I scowled at him. "No, thank you."

He raised one eyebrow. "No? You didn't come here for a private show?"

Damn that fucking heat flushing through me. Was thirty-three too early to be going through menopause? Maybe I could put the inferno inside me down to that instead of a reaction to the man standing in front of me.

But all I could think about was the sort of private show he did in here. That inferno engulfed me like a wildfire. "I was just leaving," I spluttered, striding for the door, my face burning. This was so embarrassing. I clearly needed some time alone with a vibrator.

Because I did not do this. I slept with men on occasion, just to try it out, but it was never satisfying so I always ended up taking care of myself.

I was never attracted to any of them. I barely knew what the feeling was.

Whatever was going on here with Augie was highly unsettling, and I needed a minute to recoup.

Augie wasn't giving it though.

He stepped in front of me, and I stopped just short of slamming into the solid wall of his chest.

Thank God, because with the way I was acting, I probably would have tried burrowing in there and inhaling him.

So fucking embarrassing.

"Get out of the way, Augie. Let me by."

He snorted, like I'd said something ridiculous. "Don't think so, sweetheart. You're the one who broke into my house. You're the one poking around my bedroom. You didn't seriously think I was going to let you just walk out without so much of a word as to why, did you?"

I blinked. In the overwhelming surprise of him catching me off guard, I'd actually forgotten I'd done any of that. The bug was still there, a reminder of my mother, and Riddick, and the job I came here to do.

Now would be the perfect time to kill him.

Except my gun was in my car, so if I killed him now, I'd have to do it with my bare hands.

That wasn't smart with a man Augie's size. I was a tall woman, but he was bigger than me in every way. If he saw me coming, he'd be able to overpower me.

Images of him grabbing my wrist and catching me around my waist popped into my head.

Him throwing me onto the bed.

I blinked hard.

Jesus fuck, there was something wrong with me.

The silence between us dragged on, and I realized he was waiting on me to answer him.

"Let me go, Augie." I tried to shove past him again.

Stupid move.

Stupid, stupid move.

In a second his fingers circled my wrist, hauling me back and then following up with his body. He crowded me, forcing me back into the room and to the wall, my spine meeting the drywall.

I sucked in a sharp breath when he pressed against me, pinning me in place.

His grip on my wrist was tight, but not painful as he dragged my hand up the wall, securing it above my head.

I breathed hard, curling my fingers around the bug so he wouldn't see it.

But he wasn't interested in what I was trying to conceal in my hand. His icy-blue eyes were fixed firmly on me.

"I said, what are you doing in my house, Ophelia?"

I was breathing too fast. My tits rose and fell while I sucked in breaths, trying to get enough oxygen, which felt impossible when I could feel every inch of his body tight on mine.

And I meant every inch.

Every sizable inch, pressed in places that were suddenly very interested in him.

Jesus Christ. I needed to make something up. Some

plausible excuse as to why I was here, but my brain was barely functioning amongst the hazy swirl of lust it was floating in. "I came to look for Fawn."

Augie recoiled, like I was a snake who'd just bitten him. "What the fuck? You came *looking* for her? Like I might be the sick fuck who's had her tied up in his basement all this time?"

I went to shake my head. It hadn't been what I meant. I'd meant to say I'd come looking for information on Fawn, but my damn hormones had my coherent thoughts held hostage, and it obviously hadn't come out that way.

But now that he'd mentioned it, I probably should be thinking of him as a suspect. All I had was his and Eve's word that Eddie was the one who'd taken Fawn. Yet nobody else I'd talked to had seen Eddie in months, if not years. He'd dropped off the face of the earth according to people he and Fawn had once hung out with.

Maybe Eddie was just a convenient excuse to cover up whatever Augie had done to her.

"Maybe I do," I said slowly. "You were one of the last people seen with her."

He released my wrist and took a sharp step back, any hint of emotion evaporating from his eyes and leaving only the bitter nothingness I'd come to expect from him.

Some deeply buried part of me was painfully disappointed to watch him shut down again.

"Get out."

He wasn't even going to argue with me.

I didn't move. "She's my sister—" I tried to explain.

"Get. The fuck. Out."

The frost rolling off him was so thick I could practically taste it. I didn't know how quickly someone could change. My body was still warm from where his had surrounded me.

And yet he was ice-cold.

With the tiniest of movements, I attached the bug to the side of Augie's dresser and then walked out.

I was halfway down the street before I could breathe again.

12

AUGIE

I was still seething when I got to the club, Ophelia's accusations ringing in my ears. I grunted a hello at Terry, who was probably used to my bad moods by this point and didn't seem too bothered by my sharp tone.

Lyric and Eve were sitting on the edge of the stage, their feet swinging, the two of them about as depressed as if they'd just been the ones accused of kidnapping and abusing Fawn.

I stopped short and stared at them. "Who pissed in your porridge?"

Lyric, in typical Lyric fashion, stuck her middle finger up at me. I flipped her one right back, because that was how she and I rolled.

Eve actually answered me though. "No one showed up for our dance class."

I winced at that. She and Lyric had spent days choreographing a new routine to teach during their first class. "Seriously? Not one person?"

"Not unless you count Terry."

I grimaced at the idea of Terry trying to swing his thick, unfit, middle-aged, too-many-donuts type of body around a stripper pole. It wasn't pretty.

"Nobody wants to see me in a G-string, kid," Terry called out from his usual stool by the door. "Not unless it's Halloween."

"Not even then," I murmured.

Eve shoved my arm as she got off the stage. "Do you have to always be such an asshole?"

"I honestly don't know any other way."

That at least gave her a small laugh. "I know."

We walked shoulder to shoulder into the changing room, with Lyric trailing behind us.

"I'm sorry about the dance class." I opened my locker, putting my bag inside. "That's really shit. I'm going out to put up more missing posters next week. I can put up some class posters too. I'm sure it's just because nobody knows about it yet."

"Or it's because nobody thinks a couple of strippers from the slums can actually teach a respectable dance class." Lyric's voice was sharp, the chip she'd always had on her shoulder on full display. "That posh class in the city that teaches pole is full every night of the week."

I wanted to disagree with her, but she was possibly right. I'd seen the dance studio she was talking about. It was all bright lights and mirrors where kids took ballet and tap classes during the day. The teachers were all perky cheerleader types, probably named Brittney or Chantelle.

It wasn't a scummy old strip joint with classes run by

two women who were amazing dancers but hadn't even finished high school.

"Fuck those rich assholes," I practically growled.

I wasn't only talking about the people who turned their noses up at those of us from the Saint View side of the border. Ophelia could go to fucking hell. She was exactly why I hated people with money. They were all so fucking privileged. Imagine being so full of yourself you thought you could just walk on into someone else's house and accuse them of the sorts of acts that made my stomach churn.

She was the one who'd come in here and told me to sit my ass down because my efforts at finding her sister weren't good enough. And yet *she* was wasting time looking in my direction when Eve and I had already told her it was Eddie who had Fawn.

Fuck her. Fuck her for not believing us. She was just another rich white person who thought she knew better than us broke-ass losers from Saint View.

I unzipped my gym bag so fucking viciously the zipper broke off in my fingers. But on top was a pink stuffed elephant, a little ballerina's tutu around its belly. My fingers hovered over it for a second, and I glanced over my shoulder. Lyric had moved out to the area off the change rooms that we used to warm up, leaving only me and Eve on the benches. I forced myself to pick up the elephant and thrust it in Eve's direction. "Here."

Eve glanced over, her eyes widening when she took in the little elephant. She reached for it, and I let her take it before burying my head in my locker again.

"What's this?" she asked.

I sneaked a peek in her direction. She turned the toy over with a small smile pulling at her lips.

I shrugged. "Nothing. I dunno. I walked past a market today while I was putting posters up and thought you could give it to the baby. You know. When you have one."

Her gaze snapped up to meet mine. "I'm not even pregnant yet."

I raised an eyebrow at the woman who had made no secret of the fact she and Boston were fucking at every given chance, on every available surface, trying to make a baby. "I don't think it's gonna take too long."

Eve chuckled as she leaned over and planted a kiss on my cheek. "I'm kind of old to be a first-time mom, so I really hope you're right. We're having fun trying though."

I wrinkled my nose and shoved her gently away. "For the five hundredth time, I don't want to know."

But I was happy for her. She'd spent too many nights caring for everyone but herself. It was her time.

Though I'd never tell anyone, I was sort of looking forward to having a baby around here. We needed something, anything, to bring some light back into our lives.

I wanted Fawn to be here to see Eve as a mother. Fawn would be the best aunty.

Unlike her older sister who probably ate babies for dinner.

I took off my clothes, trying not to think about the way Ophelia's gaze had wandered all over my body earlier. I was glad Eve had left because my dick gave a twitch of appreciation at the memory of Ophelia's body pressed beneath mine.

I had to force myself to think about everything that

had happened afterward in order to get my dick under control.

Not bothering with underwear, I pulled on a low-slung pair of jeans that showed off the V lines either side of my hips, and the dark-blond trail of hair that started beneath my belly button and disappeared beneath my fly. Women loved both, and these jeans always brought a lot of tips.

I fucking needed them tonight. It was the weekend, so it would be the biggest night of the week. I hadn't found anyone to go home with all week, and my wallet desperately needed the top-up. If I didn't make rent tonight, the odds of doing it any other night would be slim to none.

I wasn't scheduled to perform until later in the evening, so while Eve and Lyric did their thing on the main stage, and Phoenix did his in the smaller room, I played waiter. Though strolling around the club and handing out drinks didn't tip as well as dancing did, I still enjoyed it. It was a break from my norm, and getting to keep my pants on for a while was a nice bonus.

The stream of customers increased after the clock hit ten, and by eleven, the place actually had a bit of a buzz about it. Eve winked at me from the stage, her sultry performance face firmly in place, but the wink was a clear, 'Holy shit! We're actually busy.'

I grinned back at her.

Only for it to fall a second later when the baby eater herself walked through the doors.

"Fuck. Off," I muttered, putting down my drink tray and striding to the door where Ophelia stood gazing around at the place. I stopped in front of her and jerked my head toward the door she'd just walked through. "Out."

She rolled her eyes. "Do you still have your panties in a twist over this afternoon?" Her gaze dipped over my chest and stomach, following the line of hair that ran beneath my jeans with her eyes. "Or are you not wearing any?"

I shook my head. She thought she was so cool. So sophisticated and in control.

But I'd seen the effect my body had on her. I knew how to use that. I leaned in, my lips brushing the softest part of her neck, the bit right beneath her earlobe. "Care to find out?"

I didn't miss the sharp intake of breath before she shoved me away. "Don't do that."

I laughed. "You came to my club, Ophelia. You know I'm a stripper. You came for the show, just admit it."

Her cheeks went the prettiest shade of pink, but I pretended not to notice.

It took her a good thirty seconds to get herself under control before she came up with a reply. "Actually, I came to apologize."

I folded my arms across my chest and stared at her.

She stared back. Eventually, when I didn't fill the silence, she huffed out, "Well? Do you accept my apology?"

"I didn't actually hear one."

She glared at me. "You know what? This was a mistake."

She whirled around, but without any conscious thought, I instinctively grabbed her wrist and hauled her back. She stumbled on her heels, and I caught her arms, steadying her.

She was pissed. But some part of me liked it and couldn't help antagonizing her further. "I don't know where you grew up, but around here, when someone breaks into another person's house and accuses them of kidnapping and holding a woman hostage, with zero actual proof, an apology actually sounds something like, 'Augie. I'm really fucking sorry I was an uber asshole and broke into your home and accused you of shit you would never ever do. It's me. I'm the problem. I have no boundaries and I think the entire world revolves around me and what I want. I can't help it. I'm a spoiled little Providence princess and I know no better.'"

She tried to remove her wrist from my grip, but nah, I wasn't having that. She fucking owed me that apology. I wouldn't let her go. Of course, if she'd truly wanted me to, I would have, because contrary to her shitty ideas, I actually would never hold a woman against her will, not even this one who seemed hell-bent on insulting me at every turn.

But my gentle grip did the job, and I knew in an instant she didn't really want to get away from me.

I couldn't help the way that sent a spear of pleasure through me.

Fuck, she was pretty. Her brown eyes were so big, lined with dark makeup that made them seem black in the low light. Her lips were full and sweet, and when she bit the bottom one my dick kicked hard in response. Her hair was so long and glossy, falling down her back in waves that I just wanted to wrap around my fist and...

"Fuck," I swore beneath my breath, letting her go

before I ended up with a raging hard-on I couldn't dance with. "Whatever. Go."

The roles reversed so quickly I couldn't stop it. Her fingers clutching my arm, drawing me back toward her. Our gazes slammed together, and fuck if my breath didn't completely disintegrate with the sudden urge to drop my mouth down on hers so I didn't have to hear whatever she was about to sass me with.

But when she opened her mouth, her voice was softer than I'd ever heard it. "I really did come to apologize. I'm sorry about today. I was out of line with what I said. I know you love Fawn and you would never do anything to hurt her."

The reminder of her sister sent a stabbing hurt through me. I had no romantic feelings for Fawn. She was the little sister I'd never had, and I would do anything to have her back here right now.

Yet I was standing here, thinking about how it would feel to run my tongue along Ophelia's lips, to feel them part beneath mine and let me in.

I stepped back, putting distance between us. "Fine. Your apology is accepted. Whatever. See you around."

She refused to let me go. "Augie, stop. Wait. I meant it. I really am sorry. I know I made you uncomfortable."

Uncomfortable? Uncomfortable was noticing the swell of her tits beneath that low-cut shirt. Uncomfortable was the hint of a lace bra peeking out from beneath. Fuck! Why did I have to notice that? Now it was all I could see.

She trailed her fingernails across the back of my hand so lightly it sent shivers down my spine. "What can I do to make it up to you?"

I was going to Hell, because my very first instinct was to tell her to get on her knees and make it up to me like that. I almost groaned out loud at the very thought of those dark-brown eyes staring up at me, my dick in her hand, her pink tongue running over her lips as she prepared to take me in her mouth.

It was too fucking much.

I needed bleach for my brain.

And yet the words that came out only made things worse. "Eve and Lyric are running a pole class. Nobody showed up today."

Ophelia blinked. "Um, okay?"

"You're now their first student."

She barked out a laugh. "What?"

The idea hadn't been fully formed when I'd first opened my mouth, but it came together the longer I thought about it. "You said you wanted to make it up to me, didn't you? This is how you do it. I had to walk in here tonight and look at Eve's and Lyric's heartbroken faces because not one person had showed up for their class. They felt like shit, and when they feel like shit, so do I. I ain't got time for that. So you're now their first student." I eyed her. "And don't ask for a fucking discount because I know you can afford it, Miss I Drive a Porsche Around Saint View like Someone Ain't Gonna Try Stealing the Wheels."

Her mouth dropped open. "I don't dance."

"That's kind of the point of a class."

"It's a stripper class!"

I narrowed my eyes at her. "It's a pole class, not a lesson in taking your clothes off."

Fuck me if my damn traitorous gaze didn't roll down

her body at the very thought of what was beneath her outfit. "Bring a friend too."

"What? No!"

I shrugged. "Why? Because it's here, in Saint View, run by the people you think are the scum on the bottom of your three-hundred-dollar shoes?"

"I don't think that!"

I couldn't help antagonizing her. I was kinda enjoying it. "Your sister was one of us. Is that what you think of her?"

"Of course not! I love Fawn."

"Prove it then. Take the class. Support the people who supported her when your fucking family threw her out."

She narrowed her eyes at me and jabbed one sharp fingernail into the center of my chest. "I'll take the class, Augie. But don't you ever fucking say I threw her out. She wanted to leave, and I was the one who made it possible for her to do so. You know nothing about our family. Not one little thing. If you did, you wouldn't have said that."

I let her go because she was probably right.

And because, fuck, watching her walk away was so damn sweet.

13

AUGIE

"Take it off! Take it off!"

It was a rowdy group of women with pink cowboy hats who started up the chant, but the rest of the room quickly caught on and continued it.

Phoenix glanced over at me from his side of the stage where he rolled his hips in time with the beat. His single raised eyebrow questioned what the fuck I was doing.

He was already down to a tiny G-string that was half off his toned ass. We normally would have both been naked by now, but I was still firmly clad in my jeans.

Phoenix shifted over to me. "What's going on?" he asked, shaking his ass for the women in the front row who screamed in delight.

I couldn't get Ophelia off my mind, and my dick was proof of it. "If I take my jeans off right now this is gonna turn into a sex show real quick. My dick is hard as fuck."

Phoenix burst into laughter. "Seriously?"

"Seriously!" I grabbed my junk, and the women to the left side of the room let out another raucous cheer.

Phoenix and I both ignored them and kept on dancing.

"What's going on with you?" he asked. "You take a Viagra or something?"

"No! I swear, it's all natural. I just...I dunno."

"You need to get laid."

I so fucking did. I needed a pretty little brunette with big dark eyes who looked just like Ophe...

No, fuck that. Anyone but that. I scoured the room, searching for a blonde or a redhead. No brunettes.

My gaze landed on a sultry redhead who watched me with lust in her eyes.

That'd do.

I gave her a smug grin, and she sent me a flirtatious smile back.

She was so fucking up for it.

"Go," Phoenix said, noticing the interaction. "We're shutting in an hour anyway, so I can handle it until then. Happy to take the tips you would have attracted."

The relief was nearly instant at the thought of taking care of the problem that had plagued me all night, ever since Ophelia had walked out in a huff. My fucking dick just got harder every time I thought about her.

I clapped Phoenix on the shoulder and thanked him.

"Just don't do it here," Phoenix reminded me. "Eve will be pissed if you break her rules."

I groaned, really just wanting this to be over and done with, but he was right. I'd never broken Eve's rules before, and I wasn't about to start now.

I sauntered to the redhead's table, leaned down, and whispered my proposal in her ear.

She was on her feet, saying goodbye to her friends,

her fingers threaded between mine before I'd even completed the sentence. We were out in my car and then driving back to my house in minutes.

I didn't even ask her name. I didn't want to know it, and she seemed to feel much the same way. She stroked her fingers up and down my thigh, each pass inching closer to my aching dick.

Yet when she got there, I pulled her hands away and pushed them back toward her.

"You don't like it?" she asked with a pout.

I had no idea why I'd stopped her, but an excuse tumbled out of my mouth. "Can't concentrate on the road if you're touching me. Touch yourself. Get yourself wet for me."

She let out a little moan and slipped her fingers beneath the hem of her short skirt and hiked it up even farther, flashing me silky black panties. She moved them aside, showing off her hair-free mound before her fingers dove between her lips to rub her clit.

My dick reacted in exactly the way I expected it would, stiffening even further, and yet my brain kept blinding me with images and questions about Ophelia. Would she have gotten into the car and let me drive her back to my place tonight if I'd asked her? Would she have sat right there in that seat and fingered herself while I watched?

I groaned, and the woman on the seat beside me let out a sultry laugh. "Are we nearly there, baby? I need you inside me."

I cringed at her calling me baby. Bit back the bile at the pet name from a woman I didn't give a shit about. Thank fuck we were actually nearly there. I needed to get this over and done with as quickly as humanly possible, while still making it worth five hundred bucks for her.

I turned into my driveway and got out, avoiding the woman's outstretched hand under the guise of trying to get my house key out. I unlocked the door, glancing over my shoulder as a sleek black Porsche rolled past.

I paused, watching it, the expensive vehicle out of place in the middle of this shit neighborhood.

It was the exact same car Ophelia drove.

What were the odds of there being two cars the same as hers in the neighborhood tonight? Was she fucking watching me?

I froze, suddenly not wanting to let the redhead in, but she shoved her way past me, and I reminded myself I was working. Yeah, I was getting something out of it tonight as well, but this was my job. I needed money if I was going to live, and this woman was here, willing and waiting for me to give her what we both needed.

So instead of pushing her back out onto the street because it wasn't her my dick was actually craving, I let her in, leading her up the stairs to my bedroom and chose to forget Ophelia even existed.

"I'm Bec, by the way," she said from behind me.

It seemed weird to be finally introducing ourselves now that I'd watched her ride her fingers, but if she wanted names, then fine. "Simon," I lied to her, not wanting my name on her lips for some reason.

"Cute house," she said as I led her into my room and closed the door.

"No, it's not." The house was a fucking shit heap in dire need of repair. But whatever. We weren't here for interior decorating tips. We were here to fuck.

The second we got in that room; all I could think about was Ophelia standing in here just hours before. The way she'd smelled faintly of something fresh and flowery. The way her gaze had traveled over my body and the pure lust in her eyes before she'd tried to cover it up so I wouldn't see.

My cock had been so hard, pressed up against her soft belly.

It was her I'd craved ever since that moment, and no other woman was going to quell that ache inside me.

Fuck. I couldn't do this. I couldn't fuck this woman when it was really Ophelia I wanted beneath me.

I also didn't really have a choice.

Bec withdrew a small stack of bills out of her purse, some fifties, some hundreds, and placed them down on the top of the dresser.

Fuck, that was a lot of money. I could pay my rent and some. The internal battle waged inside me. Was Ophelia still outside? I couldn't help myself. I glanced out the open window, spotting her dark car parked a couple of houses down.

Bec thrust the money toward me. "You said five hundred, right?"

I swallowed. "I did."

"Then kiss me."

I forced myself to walk toward her. To put my hands gingerly on her hips, even though I didn't like the way they felt. Ophelia's hips were higher because she was tall. I'd liked it.

Bec laughed. "You don't have to be gentle with me. In fact, I don't want you to be. I like it rough."

I needed to give her what she wanted. This was my

business, and often it was word of mouth that brought women to my door at night. Women talked. They told their friends, and I'd always made an effort to be sure my reputation was that of a good time. I was the man women went to when they wanted to come. I was the man who knew how to coax an orgasm even from the most nervous of clients. I was good at this. I even liked it.

And yet no part of me wanted to kiss this woman.

"Get a fucking grip," I muttered to myself, Ophelia on my mind. "She's not your girlfriend."

"What did you say, baby?" Bec rubbed herself all over me like a cat.

Fuck, I needed that to stop. I pushed her up against the edge of the dresser, and she strained toward me, her fingers at the back of my neck, drawing my head down to kiss her.

I swerved and went for her neck instead. I opened my mouth and licked and sucked her skin but my heart wasn't in it. I couldn't do this.

I'd have to give her fucking money back and send her home.

"Oh, that feels so—ouch!"

I pulled back. "Ouch?" What the fuck? I hadn't even bitten her. There was no way what I was doing at her neck had caused her pain. I wasn't fucking fourteen with no experience.

But she twisted in the darkness and rubbed at a spot on the back of her hip. "There's something jutting out of the dresser there. See?"

I couldn't see very well because we hadn't turned the lights on, but I reached around her and felt the edge of the dresser where she was indicating.

Sure enough, there was a round lump that came off in my hand when I poked at it.

I flipped on the light and peered down at the little out-of-place object.

"What is it?" Bec asked.

It was another second or two before my brain figured out the answer.

A fucking bug.

And I knew exactly who'd planted it.

14

OPHELIA

The bugs I'd planted around Augie's house only worked if my end of the receiver was in range. Did I have to sit right outside his house in the dark? No. They worked over longer distances than that. I could have parked a street or two over, but I'd watched him leave the club with some woman. I'd watched her fall all over him on their way to his car, and him take her inside his home.

I wasn't jealous that he'd actually invited her in while I'd had to pick the lock.

I tried telling myself I was only sitting outside his house, listening to him take this woman to bed because it was my job. If I was going to work out how to keep him alive, I needed to know why he was the target in the first place. Maybe this woman had something to do with it.

Me listening to him kiss her was part of that.

The jealousy that churned in my stomach wasn't.

The feeling was so weirdly foreign I didn't even know what to do with it. So I sat there, like a fucking chump, staring at his bedroom window, knowing what he was doing on the other side.

Suddenly the light flickered on, and through the bug I heard the stupid, nasally woman say, "What is it?"

I froze, panic spearing through me at the thought they might have found the bug I'd hidden there. It wasn't hidden as well as the others had been. I'd been too distracted by Augie to hide it any better. Maybe it would have been smarter to not leave one in his room at all, since I hadn't had a chance to find the perfect spot for it like I normally would have.

But a deep-rooted part of me had desperately wanted to know what went on inside that bedroom. And it wasn't just the part of me that had been tasked with ending his life.

It was that very womanly part who had imagined all the things that went on his bed.

"It's just part of a bottle cap. Sorry, this room is a bit of a mess." Augie's voice sounded as neutral as it ever did.

I breathed a sigh of relief when there wasn't a sudden crackle of static, which would surely have happened if he'd found the bug. If I knew anything about this man, it's that he'd put his foot down on the tiny electronic device if he'd found it and my head-phones would have probably blown out my eardrums with the noise.

But all I heard was Bec's annoying laugh and the rustle of clothing. "I don't care, baby. Come here. I got myself all wet for you. I want you to feel it."

Ugh. Why did she have to talk? If it was just them breathing heavy, I could pretend they were doing sit-ups or something. Even with the light on, from this angle, the only way I could see them was if they went right to the window, so it would have been easy to pretend.

I wondered if he liked being called baby. It didn't suit him at all.

I rolled the word around silently on my tongue and all I could picture was him scowling at me.

But he must have liked it because he didn't tell her to stop it. His shadow crossed the window, and the next second his stupid handsome face stared out of it.

Right. At. Me.

Which was my own dumb fault for parking so close to his house.

And yet, when he opened his mouth, I was suddenly sure I didn't care.

"Take your panties off."

Bec tittered something in the background, but Augie wasn't looking at her. He was staring right at my car.

He had to know it was mine. Though it fit in just fine in Providence, it stuck out like a sore thumb in Saint View.

I knew he couldn't see inside. My windows were tinted almost black, which made seeing in impossible. I was safe from view in here.

Which was probably why I did the stupidest thing I'd ever done.

I took my panties off.

After all, I was sure that command was for me. Why else would he say it, standing there, staring at me instead of the woman he had inside?

"Are they off?" he asked.

"Yes, Daddy," Bec moaned.

I nearly vomited in my mouth. I was really going to need the woman to shut up.

Like he was thinking the same thing, he stopped asking questions and started making demands instead. "Spread your legs and slide your hand down your body."

Did I want to obey his commands? No. This was reckless. But the pulse between my legs and the way he stood there at that window gave me no other option. I hit the button on the side of my seat so I could tilt my chair back a bit, giving me better access, but made sure it didn't drop so low I couldn't see him.

I needed to see him. I hated that he was backlit so I couldn't see the details of his face.

But his voice was enough. It was deep and raspy. Growly and demanding. I slid my hand over the bare skin of my mound, my nerve endings awakening at the touch.

"Rub your clit. Slow. So fucking slow."

I pressed a finger to the little bundle of nerves that was yearning to be touched. The relief was almost instant and yet not nearly enough to be satisfying. I wanted more. If I'd been alone I would have gone hard and fast, just wanting to get to the finish line so I could go on with the rest of my evening. But I moved as slowly as Augie had commanded, teasing the bud to life with an agonizing touch that left me breathless and desperate for more.

"Slide one finger lower. Soak it inside yourself."

My head dropped back on the headrest. Fuck, I was wet. I slid my finger through the silky arousal and up inside myself without a hint of resistance. I instantly wanted to add another finger, to pump them in and out of myself while I rubbed my clit with the other hand.

Except he hadn't told me to.

So I didn't. I soaked my finger and went back to torturing my clit.

But fuck. I ached. There was an emptiness inside me that begged to be filled. Begged for his fingers or his tongue or his cock.

He was big. I'd felt him pressed up on me in that bedroom, and it was all I could think about now.

How there was no way he could disappoint me with a cock like that.

God, I fucking hoped not anyway.

"Fuck yourself with your fingers," he grit out harshly, almost breathlessly.

The tone in his voice had me watching him more closely, and I lit up inside when I realized he was stroking his cock. I couldn't see it, his waist was just below the windowsill, but his arm moved in a slow, back-and-forth motion that made me wish he was using that tempo on me.

I matched his pace, pushing my fingers up inside me while he pleasured himself.

It was two in the morning. There was nobody else out on the streets, and this little peep show felt like it was all between him and me. He jerked his hand faster, so I did too, fighting the urge to throw my head back and fall over the edge which was rapidly rising. My breaths became moans, and the windows around me fogged, but I wiped the windshield with the sleeve of my shirt so I could watch him.

The woman in his bed moaned loudly, and to drown her out, I rode my fingers harder, letting my own moans cover up the sound. I was so close. So achingly close, but he hadn't told me to come.

Fuck. I wanted him to give me permission.

"You're close. You're so fucking close," he murmured.

"Yes," I moaned, drowning out the woman answering the same.

"Do you know how it's going to feel when I let you come? How it'll spiral out from between your sweet thighs and spread through your entire body, inch by inch, second by second. How it will engulf you whole and leave your fingers soaked and your body trembling?"

"Yes!" It was practically a shout at this point, an incoherent groan because I just needed to come. My head spun; my thighs clenched. I was so on that edge it was the most painful pleasure I'd ever experienced.

And it was all because of the way he demanded those things from my body. From the way he stood there, his gaze burning through the darkness and the window tint, scorching me like he was on top of me, his body covering mine, his dick finding that wet, warm place that would blow both our minds.

I closed my eyes, waiting for the command to let go.

The woman's squeal cut through my headphones. It was so shrill and unpleasant it forced my eyes open.

Only to watch Augie press her against the window. Her head turned to one side, her naked breasts to the glass while he moved in behind her.

No.

No. No. No.

He wouldn't.

"Oh!" the woman screamed. "Oh, yes! Fuck! Just like

that! You're so deep, Daddy! Your cock is huge! I'm coming!"

I sat there, staring at the window, unable to look away while he fucked her hard, sending her spiraling into an orgasm that should have been mine.

Then he raised one hand in front of the light, so there was no way I could miss the fact it was only his middle finger that was up.

Confirming he'd found the bug.

He knew what I'd done.

None of this had been about pleasure. It was all about revenge.

Embarrassment flushed through my entire body, and I pulled my fingers from my pussy, hating that I had to wipe my arousal off on my panties before yanking them back up my legs. That was arousal he'd created with his dirty words that had been aimed at me.

But it was some other woman up there, taking his cock, screaming his name, coming as hard as the ache inside me begged for.

Fuck him.

Augie Mitchell could go to hell.

15

AUGIE

I ripped the sheets off my bed, gathering them up into a ball to shove into the washing machine. In the basement, I dumped in double the amount of detergent and set the longest wash time available before heading back upstairs to clean the rest of my room.

I wiped down every surface, vacuumed the shitty, worn-out carpet that was in dire need of replacement, and hunted high and low for any other bugs Ophelia might have planted.

I'd have to do the rest of the house as well. Who knew how many she'd left before I'd gotten home and found her.

The thought just pissed me off even further. This was not how I wanted to spend my day off.

I was in such a foul mood when my phone rang, I didn't even look at the display. Just picked it up and barked, "What?" down the line.

"Ah. Hello. Could I speak to Augie Mitchell, please?"

It was a surprised-sounding woman, one who definitely was not Ophelia.

Good thing, since I didn't want to hear another word from her. The fact she was so convinced I had something to do with Fawn's disappearance that she would bug my house made me want to scream. She was wasting her goddamn time focusing on me.

It wasn't the woman on the phone's fault Ophelia was a stubborn pain in my ass, but I snapped at her anyway. "Who wants to know?"

The woman cleared her throat. "I'm from *The City Daily*."

"Never heard of it. Not interested in subscribing. Bye."

I went to end the call, but the woman's voice cut through before I could get my thumb to the button. "No, wait! I'm not a salesperson. I'm a reporter. I saw the missing posters for your friend Fawn, and when I called the police information line, they gave me your name and number as the contact person for all media inquiries."

I frowned. "We haven't had any media inquiries."

The woman cleared her throat and spoke a little more calmly now she'd caught my attention and I wasn't hanging up on her. "Well, you do now."

A tiny kernel of excitement lit up inside me, but I wasn't exactly the most cheerful of people at the best of times, so I only replied with, "About time."

The woman, to her credit, ignored my blunt answer and carried on like I actually knew how to be pleasant. "I'd like to interview you, if possible. I want to run a story on Fawn and who she is. Does that sound good to you?"

I nodded quickly then corrected myself by answering. "Yeah, it does. When and where?"

"Are you local to the city?"

"Sure. I can afford those multimillion-dollar apartments on a stripper wage. No sweat."

The woman went silent on the other end, and I thumped my thigh with a closed fist, because fucking hell. My mouth had a mind of its own.

"Sorry. I mean, no. I'm out at Saint View."

"Saint View?"

I prickled at her tone. "Is there a problem with that?"

"No, of course not. I can meet you there if you tell me a time and a place. I'm afraid I'm not very familiar with the area."

I rolled my eyes. Lucky her. I wished I wasn't familiar with this shithole of a town either. "There's a diner on the main strip. Sally's at Saint View. I'll meet you there at midday."

I ended the call before she could agree or disagree and went back to cleaning every inch of my house, trying to erase the floral scent that reminded me of Ophelia. Had she rubbed her perfume all over the damn house, or was that scent just a figment of my imagination? Considering I'd gone through a packet of lemon-scented cleaning wipes, I was beginning to think it was the latter.

Just fucking great. A reminder of her I couldn't ever escape.

Fuck my life.

By the time midday rolled around, I was exhausted. I hadn't slept because all I could think about was fucking that woman while Ophelia watched from downstairs. The way she'd driven off with a squeal of tires had been satisfying for all of three seconds before I'd felt like shit.

I couldn't sleep after that. I knew exactly what I'd done.

So when I walked into Sally's I was already grouchy. But Sally's wide smile was hard to be mad about. She waved at me enthusiastically from behind the counter and told me she'd bring over my regular. I couldn't help but return the smile.

The woman was the only reason I ate most days. Her place, despite being right in the heart of the slums, was A plus. Those Michelin-star chefs could go fuck themselves with their fancy food. Sally's burgers and Eve's stew was where it was at if you asked me.

It was the middle of the lunchtime rush, and I glanced around the room, looking for a free booth to sit at. I loved this place, and some of my irritation with the world seeped away as the noise of the diner cocooned me.

Until my gaze came to a screeching halt on a dark-brown set of eyes staring at me from a booth in the back.

Hell. Fucking. No. This was my goddamn happy place. I had so few of them, she wasn't taking this one. She could go eat burgers on the Providence side of the border. I was pretty sure she was too stuck-up for greasy fries and burgers anyway. Surely, she was one of those assholes who preferred their food in tiny smears of puree across a plate with a smattering of something nobody could pronounce.

I stormed to the back of the restaurant. "Get out."

She studied a menu like my demands meant nothing to her. "Good morning to you too, Augie. Enjoy your fuckfest last night?"

I raised an eyebrow. Oh, we were going there, were

we? I slid into the opposite side of the booth. "Question is, did you? Since you were the creepy little perv sitting outside my house watching—*and listening*—to the entire fucking thing!"

The couple at the table next to us glanced over at us, but Ophelia and I both gave them a dirty look, and they quickly went back to staring at their menus.

Her gaze was full of fire when she turned it back in my direction. "Your girlfriend sounds like a D-rated porn star." She didn't even lower her voice when she started imitating Bec. "Oh, Daddy. Fuck me harder. You're so big." She stuck her tongue out and made gagging noises. "Did you pay her to say that just because you knew I was listening?"

I chuckled wryly. "I don't have to pay anyone to say good things about my dick, sweetheart. They always do though."

She narrowed her eyes at me again. "I told you. Don't call me sweetheart."

"Nah, I like that it pisses you off." I really did. She was hot when she was mad. Her eyes came alive, and her voice went deeper and kind of growly.

It made me want to put her on her knees, feed her my cock, and pull her hair until she used that growly hum to make me come.

My dick went instantly hard under the table, and I fought back the urge to groan. Not again. I'd only just dealt with this problem last night. I needed to get it under control. I couldn't walk around getting stiff as a board every time I saw her.

Which reminded me of the fact she was here in Saint View in the first place. "What are you doing here?"

"Free country, Augie. I go where I please."

I cocked my head at her. "So you came here in the hopes of seeing me then?"

She scowled at me. "What? No."

I huffed out a laugh. "Well, that's what I'm going to believe if you don't give me a reason. You don't seem like the type to eat at places like this."

"And why is that? I like…" She looked down at the menu, her eyes flickering side to side as she read the menu full of fried foods and plain flavors.

"You don't like a single thing on that menu, do you?" I let out a laugh of amusement.

She huffed out a sigh. "Would it hurt them to have something with a lettuce leaf?"

I sniggered, but it wasn't entirely at the fact I knew she was one of those fine-dining lovers.

I liked arguing with her.

Arguing with her was the only thing that made me feel alive lately, after weeks and weeks of feeling like some huge part of me was dead and rotting, the disease slowly spreading through my body until I couldn't come back from it.

That's what losing Fawn and not knowing where or how she was felt like. A slow, painful death I couldn't escape from.

Except when I was with Ophelia.

Fuck, she would be easy to get addicted to, with those pink lips and those dark eyes. Her skin was a warm brown that made me think of her lying out on a beach somewhere in a tiny bikini that would show every curve of her body.

That fucking hard-on wasn't getting any better. I

shifted uncomfortably at the tiny smile Ophelia tried to hide.

She was so damn pretty.

A woman stopped at our table, focusing on me. "Uh, hello. I'm Robyn Crestwood from *The City Times*. Are you Augie Mitchell?"

"So I'm told."

The woman's face flooded with relief. "Oh good. We're just waiting on one more interviewee to come."

I frowned. She hadn't said anything about this being a group date.

Ophelia pasted on a smile that was so fake I practically snorted with laugher.

"Ophelia Hanover. Fawn's sister. Thanks for doing your research and getting in contact with her *actual* family."

The woman did a double take. "Oh! I'm so sorry. I saw the way the two of you were looking at each other and just assumed you were Augie's girlfriend."

She smiled at me sweetly. "No. But he does like to fuck his girlfriend in front of me."

My mouth dropped open in unison with the reporter's.

"Excuse me?" the woman choked out.

Ophelia just carried on smiling like the complete and utter psychopath she was, zero fucks given that she was broadcasting our personal life to a random stranger.

The thought tripped me up. Since when did I share a personal life with this woman?

Since when did women throw me off my game the way she did? It was incredibly confusing. So much so I indicated for the reporter to take a seat just to distract myself. "Ignore her," I said stiffly. "Her doctor needs to change her medication."

Ophelia's fake-innocence smile went back to lips pressed into a thin line and daggers for eyes.

I settled back in my seat, much more comfortable now that I was back in control. I focused on the reporter. "What do you want to know about Fawn?"

The woman set her phone down on the table between us and opened a recorder app. She pressed another button to get it going then folded her hands in front of her. "Okay, so what I'd like to focus on first is who Fawn is, what she likes to do, and the relationships between the two of you."

"I have no relationship with him," Ophelia said quickly.

The reporter cleared her throat. "I meant your relationship with Fawn."

I smirked as Ophelia's cheeks went pink and she let out a little, "Oh."

"I worked with her," I volunteered, focusing on the reporter.

She nodded, jotting something down on a yellow legal pad. "Where at and for how long?"

I couldn't really remember when Fawn had first appeared on the doorstep of the club. "A year? Two? Maybe more? I can't remember. We work at Saint View Strip Club."

The woman glanced up from her notes. "And your roles there are..."

I frowned. "Well, as the name suggests, we aren't there to teach kindergarten."

The woman blushed. "Well, no, I mean, you're both..."

An irritation spread across the back of my neck. "You can say it. Strippers. We take our clothes off and dance. For money. That is generally what someone does when they say they work at a strip club."

Robyn ducked her head and scribbled something incoherent across her pad. "I'm sorry, I didn't realize your friend was involved in...the adult entertainment industry."

That slow spread of irritation turned into flat-out anger. I'd seen this before. Where I told someone I was a stripper and they automatically assumed I was a prostitute or a porn star as well. Which in my case, was true, minus the movie camera pointed at me, so whatever. But it pissed me off when people made assumptions. Especially when those assumptions were made about Fawn.

Fawn had struggled finding the self-confidence to even dance on stage in the beginning. It was only that Eve, Lyric, Phoenix, and I had spent countless hours with her, building her up, making sure she was comfortable, and teaching her everything we'd all learned the hard way.

She was so fucking likable, she just made you want to take care of her.

Even now when she wasn't here. Maybe now more than ever.

I opened my mouth to spit back a sharp response.

Ophelia beat me to it. "She's a stripper, Robyn. She's not running a child labor camp or trafficking women from third-world countries. You don't have to act so horrified."

I couldn't help the impulse to high-five her.

Or kiss her.

She had to stop getting pissed off around me 'cause it did nothing good for the urge to sit her up on this booth, spread her legs, and lick her pussy until she screamed my name.

Fuck.

Reporter Robyn didn't seem to share my same ideas about oral sex in public places. She huffed and edged away from Ophelia like she had some contagious illness. "That may be so, but strip clubs are what breeds men like that, aren't they? The traffickers and drug lords of the world."

"What the fuck?" I tightened my grip on the tabletop. "How do you figure that?"

Robyn's mask of politeness had disappeared entirely. "Taking part in those sorts of...acts...alters your brain chemistry. When women take their clothes off and dance for men, it just encourages the sex response in their brains." She looked at me. "It's not your fault. You can't control those basic human urges. But women can."

Ophelia stared at me, and for once, it was clear we were on the same page.

"Is this bitch for real?" Ophelia coughed out.

Robyn scoffed as she packed up her phone and papers. "This interview is over. We won't be running any stories about women who bring this sort of thing on themselves. *The City Daily* is for serious stories only."

I glared at her. "How is a missing woman who the police are doing nothing about not a serious story? Before you knew she was a stripper you were all for this fucking story, and now it's suddenly not of interest to your stupid elitist newspaper? Piss off then! Like we fucking need you!"

Ophelia reached across the table and put her hand over mine.

The warm touch of her skin was an instant balm to the storm raging inside me. I glanced over at her in surprise, waiting for her to tell me to calm down like Eve would have.

But Ophelia's eyes were just as fiery as mine. The ire behind them was aimed solely at the reporter who was so up her own fucking ass she wouldn't know a real-world problem if it bit her.

"Lady," Ophelia seethed. "I don't know what sort of patriarchal bullshit your mama fed you as a baby, and I don't care that you're too sheltered to have ever moved past that. But if you don't get your scrawny, fake-tanned ass out of my sight in the next three seconds, I will not be held accountable for what I do next."

Robyn froze at the threat, and frankly, I couldn't blame her.

Ophelia's voice had turned stone-cold. It was so low and deadly, I could practically feel the barbs on every syllable.

"Run, Robyn, run," I added quietly, playing along.

The woman did, slipping on the tiled floor in her high heels before skittering away down the aisle of booths.

I couldn't help laughing when she shot one terrified glance back at Ophelia, who snapped her teeth together like a rottweiler waiting to be told to attack.

The door closed behind her, and Ophelia finally looked back at me.

And then down at our hands.

She quickly pulled hers away and cleared her throat uncomfortably. "Um. Sorry. I didn't mean…"

I shrugged, taking my hand back to my side of the table as well. "Yeah, you did. I meant it too. Fuck her. Nobody gets to talk about Fawn like that."

"She was talking about you too."

I'd swallowed that bitter pill a long time ago. "Nothing new for me, sweetheart. People have been saying that shit about me for as long as I can remember."

"So why do it? The…"

"Whoring around for cash?"

If anyone else had asked me, I probably would have told them to go to hell the same way I had with Reporter Robyn just now. But Ophelia had asked in a way that wasn't full of judgment. Just curiosity.

She cleared her throat and turned away. "Sorry. You don't have to answer that. I just…" She shrugged. "I have money. She could have come to me. She didn't, and I hate that."

I didn't know what to say. All Fawn had told me was she didn't want anything to do with her family, and as far as I knew, that included her sister.

Something in the troubled depths of Ophelia's eyes told me she knew why, even if she didn't want to admit it.

I hated the way it hurt her though.

Which was stupid because I hated her too.

Isn't that what I'd convinced myself of while I'd been fucking that woman on the windowsill, knowing Ophelia was watching?

My phone buzzed on the table, and both Ophelia and I looked over at it.

The message preview showed Bert Leddith's name,

the private investigator sending a text beginning with, "Eddie is..."

I snatched up the phone, my heart rate increasing while I scrambled to get the message open. I hadn't heard a word from the man in the days since I'd hired him to search for Fawn.

"What does it say!" Ophelia demanded, leaning over the table to try to peek at the screen.

I jerked it back out of habit but then relented and put the phone back on the table between us. She had as much right as I did to see any information about Fawn.

And fuck. Maybe it would finally convince her I wasn't the bad guy here.

At least not this time.

That hadn't always been the case.

Ophelia craned her neck, twisting it into the most uncomfortable-looking position.

I stared at her. "Do you want to maybe just wait two seconds and I'll read it for you? Your neck is very ostrich-like right now."

She glared at me. "Get on with it then. You're so slow."

But there wasn't any real malice behind our verbal spars. For a minute, bonded over a common goal, it seemed we might have put that aside.

"Eddie's been spotted in Providence," I read from the message. "With a woman and a man."

"Fawn?" Ophelia asked hopefully.

I shook my head. "It says the woman was unable to be identified as Fawn from the photos I sent Bert. But he also couldn't say it wasn't her."

"How long ago was this?"

I stared down at the message, skimming over the

section where Bert reminded me I owed him more money, and found the bit where he gave the time and address of the sighting.

I glanced at my watch. "It was ten minutes ago. At a café in Providence."

Ophelia was already on her feet and shoving her purse strap up her shoulder. "I'll drive."

I blinked at her in surprise, easily catching her by the door with my longer strides. "Ah, no. I'll drive."

We strode out into the bright sunlight, both of us shielding our eyes from the glare.

"Your car is a piece of shit, Augie."

"True, but I'm the one who knows the address."

For some reason, neither of us pointed out that we had two cars here. We had no real need to drive together, even though we were going to the same place. I pretended not to notice, and she did the same, eventually following me to my car.

"Ugh, fine. God, you're annoying."

I grinned as I opened the passenger-side door for her. "I think you like my brand of annoying, sweetheart."

"I can open my own door, asshole. Get in and drive already."

I hadn't even noticed I'd opened it for her, but I waited until she got in and shut it for her anyway, before running around the other side, half expecting her to jump in the driver's seat and take off without me before I could get there.

She didn't though, and I got us on the road to Providence via a shortcut I took whenever I wandered that way to check on my brother.

I knew the address of the café Eddie and his crew had

been seen at because it was on the same street as Banjo's daughter's daycare. I took the turns easily, while Ophelia wrapped her arms around herself and stared out through the windshield stiffly.

"It wouldn't be her, right? Eddie wouldn't just have her walking around Providence like it's no big deal…"

"I have no idea," I admitted truthfully.

Except I could. Fawn wasn't outspoken. She didn't cause scenes or make a fuss. And if she was scared…

I could easily imagine a scenario where Eddie threatened someone or something Fawn loved to keep her quiet.

"He knows her. They spent years together," Ophelia said quietly. "He'll use all of her weaknesses against her."

I swallowed thickly. "The way she cares about other people…"

"Is her greatest weakness," Ophelia finished. "Shit." She turned and peered out the window. "All he has to do is threaten someone she loves, and she'll stay quiet."

There was nothing else to say. We drove the rest of the way in silence, and I parked the car right outside the café. Ophelia jumped out and ran inside, not waiting for me. I followed, stopping in the doorway, while she scanned the café.

I didn't know who I was looking for. I'd never even seen a photo of Eddie. All I could go off was Eve's description of the man who'd kidnapped both her and Fawn. But a big white guy with a beard and tattoos wasn't exactly helpful when that was probably half the population.

Oddly, though, not one person in that Providence café fit the description. There were only two men in the entire store. One was black and the other a scrawny man with glasses who had to be at least fifty.

I already knew before Ophelia even opened her mouth that Eddie and the woman weren't here.

The text I received a moment later confirmed it, Bert Leddith updating with a second message that said he'd followed the group until they'd become suspicious, driving in circles so Bert knew they were aware of him. He'd backed off and let them go before a confrontation could happen.

I typed back a furious response, telling the man he should have stayed on them.

His reply came back a second later, claiming I didn't pay him enough to put himself in danger.

I shoved the phone into my pocket angrily. "Forget it," I told Ophelia. "This is a dead end."

She spun around. "What do you mean? Where are they?"

"Gone."

She must have noticed the expression on my face because she didn't push it any further. She went to the counter where the twenty-something man behind the register was gawking at her like she'd just walked out of his teenage dreams.

Couldn't blame him.

Completely oblivious, she asked him for a caramel macchiato and then looked over at me. "What's your coffee order?"

"I'm fine."

She just waited.

I sighed. "Tea. English Breakfast, if they have it."

She let out a snort of laughter that should have been

so unattractive but was actually just fucking cute on her. "Seriously?"

"Fuck off. Just order my drink."

She turned back to the kid behind the counter. "An English tea for my very distinguished gentleman friend."

I rolled my eyes but sat my ass down in a chair facing the window anyway. She joined me, and a minute later they brought over two steaming mugs.

Ophelia chuckled quietly while I took a sip of mine.

"It's good," I told her. "Don't knock it 'til you've tried it. And better for you than that shit."

She scoffed, "Says the man who was willing to eat a grease-filled burger at that diner. It had four patties on it, Augie. Four. I want to have a heart attack just thinking about it. I can actually feel my arteries closing up as we speak."

She had a point. "I work out enough to not worry about clogged arteries."

She made a face at me. "Oh yes. I forgot. You're Mr. Muscles."

"Glad you noticed."

She took a sip of her sugar-drenched coffee, but I liked the little smile at the corner of her mouth.

I sipped my tea and stared out the window again. Luna's daycare was right across the road, and a bunch of toddler-sized kids ran around their fenced-in yard, playing in sand and riding little bikes that didn't have pedals.

Ophelia followed my line of sight and then cringed. "Ew. Children."

"You don't like them?" I asked her.

She held one finger up in my face like I'd just said the

most insulting thing ever. "If you're about to say, 'You're thirty-three, Ophelia, Isn't your biological clock ticking?' I will lean over this table and punch you right in the nose."

I grabbed her finger and lowered it to the table.

I didn't let go of it. "I don't give a shit whether you want kids of your own or not. I was just asking if you like them."

"Oh." The defensiveness fell out of her posture. "Sorry. I heard my mother in my head for a second there, and she makes me crazy."

I let go of her hand to cup my mug again. "Is she a nightmare?"

"In pretty much every way imaginable. Including wanting to marry me off so I can produce all the pretty babies her heart desires. Well, the babies her heart *would* want, if she had one."

I chuckled. "When other people talk about their nightmare parents it makes me glad mine aren't in the picture."

Ophelia sat back in her seat, studying me. "Poor little orphan, Augie, huh?"

I shook my head. "Something like that."

"So no family?"

"No parents. Not no family." I pointed across the road to the daycare. "One of those kids in there is probably my niece."

"Ah. So you have a sibling."

"A brother. He hates my guts though. With good reason. Doesn't talk to me. Won't let me see his kid. Can't blame him. I fucked up."

Ophelia toyed with the edge of a sugar packet. "Join

the club. Tell me how you fucked up and make me feel better for what I did to Fawn."

I'd never told anyone what I'd done to Banjo. At the time it had all made sense.

I'd thought I was saving him from himself.

But all I'd done was ruin my relationship with the only person, other than Fawn, who I gave a shit about.

Maybe it was about time I confessed my sins.

Seemed like Ophelia had a few of her own, so maybe she wouldn't judge me quite as harshly. Plus, I didn't have anyone else to tell. Phoenix and I didn't do deep and meaningfuls. I could have tried Eve but I already knew how disappointed she would have been in me.

I couldn't stand to have her look at me like that. Not when I was already rolling around in my own guilt.

But Ophelia was a virtual stranger.

I sighed heavily. "What didn't I do, might be the better question."

"Couldn't be that bad."

But it could.

"He met a girl. From Providence." I grinned wryly. "Lacey reminds me a bit of you, actually."

"So, she's a complete badass?" Ophelia winked at me.

I shook my head. "She's rich. Spoiled. At least, she was back then."

Ophelia seemed irritated, so I threw her a bone.

"Pretty."

Pink flushed her cheeks, but she rolled her eyes. "Whatever. Stop flirting with me and get on with it. What did you do to her?"

"Took a leaf out of your book and put a hidden

camera in Banjo's room. Filmed them having a threesome with Banjo's best friend, Rafe."

Ophelia's eyes practically bulged out of her head. "You did what? Jesus fuck, Augie."

"It gets worse. I then showed it to half their school at Lacey's birthday party."

Her mouth dropped open, but there was a hint of laughter in it too. "You didn't?"

It really wasn't funny. I still couldn't laugh about it. "I'm not proud of it."

"Then why did you do it?" she asked curiously.

I rubbed my hand over my face. "Because I was sure she was ruining his life. He was only eighteen, and she came in with a whole host of fucking baggage and problems that were weighing him down. Banjo's like Fawn. His weakness is the people he loves. He'd do anything for them, at the expense of his own happiness. It was a shitty thing to do, I can see that now. But at the time I thought I was doing him a favor."

Despite my claims, I didn't care what Ophelia thought, I couldn't meet her gaze. When she reached out and rubbed her thumb over the back of my hand, I pulled away.

Guilt swirled in my stomach. I fucking hated myself for that night. But I couldn't accept Ophelia's sympathy either because that wasn't even the worst thing I'd done. "I've done drug deals," I admitted. "Small-time, but I was a dealer, nonetheless."

"You live in Saint View. Doesn't everyone do that at some point?"

I lifted my head to find her smiling at me.

A genuine smile that was so fucking blinding it hit me

square in the gut. I was sure she'd never looked at me like that before. That every other smile had been sarcastic or snide.

They had nothing on how this one made me feel.

Fuck. When had I ever cared if a woman had more than one type of smile? When had I ever studied one long enough to notice? I'd never had a girlfriend. My life was one long string of one-night stands with women whose names I didn't know and faces I couldn't remember. I could probably blame my lack of healthy relationship role models for that. It's not like I'd ever seen a functional relationship while I was in foster care.

But Banjo was different. He'd known what he'd wanted all along, and he'd had the balls to go after it, even though his relationship with his two best friends and the girl they shared was far from conventional.

If anyone needed saving from anything, it was me. Which was why I'd stayed away from them ever since.

I sighed. "I wish dealing and the video were the worst of it."

Ophelia leaned back in her seat and folded her arms beneath her tits. That didn't help that little problem I seemed to develop whenever she was around. All the more reason to tell her the worst thing I'd ever done so she got up and left before my dick could get hard again.

"I tried to drag him into my business." I had to force the words out, the disgust for myself so strong I wanted to walk myself off the Saint View bluff. "We needed money, and fucked if I've ever had any idea how to make any. All I know is taking my clothes off."

Before this conversation, I wouldn't have guessed Ophelia had a sympathetic bone in her body, but she did.

I hated that it was all currently directed at me. "I don't deserve that." I pointed at her face and made a circular motion. "Stop."

"What?"

"Don't tell me what I did was okay."

She cocked her head to one side. "Why? Because you like living with the guilt of making a mistake?"

"It was a bit more than a mistake, Ophelia!"

"Maybe so, but you regret it, don't you?"

"Every fucking day. I cost myself the only family I ever knew. The only one I ever fucking wanted. So yeah. I fucking regret it."

"Did you apologize?"

I scoffed, "And say what? Oh, sorry I tried to drag you into prostitution because I thought that was all men like us were good for?"

She lifted one shoulder. "Not the most eloquent apology I've ever heard, but it's a start. I suspect it's one your brother and his partners might need to hear."

I shook my head and pushed back on the chair to stand. "Banjo has made it more than clear he doesn't want me near his family. I respect that."

I turned and walked away, heading toward the door.

"You're scared, Augie," Ophelia called. "Scared that if you try to reach out to him again, you'll get rejected."

I kept going, not wanting to hear her bullshit wannabe-therapist crap. I wasn't scared. I just didn't deserve Banjo's forgiveness and I knew it.

I stormed across the road to my car, rummaging through my pockets for my keys because my car was so damn old it didn't even have a central-locking remote. I shoved the key in the lock and got the door open before turning around for Ophelia.

My heart stopped when she was crouched at the fence line of the daycare center with a little dark-haired girl.

Who jumped up and down when she spotted me and shouted, "Uncle Augie!"

16

AUGIE

Those two tiny words hit me like a freight train. I couldn't describe the feeling any other way, other than it hurting so fucking bad I actually glanced down at my chest, expecting to see it ripped wide open, my internal organs all falling out onto the sidewalk.

Ophelia twisted around and smiled at me.

"Did you tell her to say that?" I snapped at her, my fingers trembling.

Ophelia's face fell. "What? Of course not. I just saw her watching you and..."

I knew she was telling the truth. Ophelia didn't even know what Luna looked like. She wouldn't have been able to pick the three-year-old out from the thirty other kids running around the center.

Like I was walking through fog, I edged around the car and onto the sidewalk, stopping a few feet away from the fence. "We shouldn't... We should go."

Banjo and Lacey wouldn't want me talking to their daughter. I knew that. Hell, at any minute, the daycare center staff would notice us standing there at the fence and probably call the cops to report us.

There was every reason to leave.

But one brown-eyed little girl staring up at me with the widest smile that forced me to stay.

"Uncle Augie!" she called again, reaching her pudgy hands toward me through the bars of the fence. "Hi, Uncle Augie!"

There was no walking away. She held a thread to my heart I hadn't even realized was loose, and every smile, every time she called me uncle, every reach of those small fingers drew me in until I was squatting beside Ophelia so all three of us were the same height.

"What's your name?" Luna asked Ophelia.

She smiled easily at the girl. "Ophelia."

Luna crinkled her nose. "Off...O-li... Your name is really hard."

Ophelia burst into laughter. "You know what? You're right. It is. You could call me something else. Maybe Lia?" Ophelia smiled softly. "My sister couldn't say my name when she was your age either, so she called me Lia."

Luna nodded enthusiastically and pointed at Ophelia's chest. "You be Lia. I'll be Luna." She turned to me and beamed. "And you'll be Uncle Augie!"

I couldn't move. Every time she said that it exploded my brain.

Ophelia reached over and took my hand, squeezing it encouragingly. "Talk to her."

I knew she was right. I probably only had a minute with her, and every part of me desperately wanted to form a connection with her. Something that would get me through the rest of her life that I had to watch from afar.

I cleared my throat. "Did your grandma tell you to call me Uncle Augie?" I asked her, sure that Willa next door was the only way this girl had recognized me and been able to put a name to my face.

But Luna proudly shook her head. "Nope! My daddy taught me."

I was so shocked a stiff breeze could have knocked me over.

I blamed that shock for not noticing the two people storming through the center until the woman's hands circled Luna's waist and yanked her up off the ground. "Get away from my daughter."

I stumbled back from the fence, Ophelia and I both pushing up to full height to go eye to eye with my brother and sister-in-law.

"Shit," Ophelia whispered, then spoke louder when I didn't say anything. "Sorry. We didn't..."

But Banjo's and Lacey's gazes were furious, and both directed squarely at me. Ophelia's words trailed away, and she stepped back, realizing this was my fight.

Lacey turned and gave Luna to one of the center staff who was hovering around nervously.

"Take Luna inside," she snapped at the woman.

"Of course. I'm so sorry. I didn't even see her over here. We'll phone the police."

"No need," I called to her. "We're leaving." I faced my brother and his partner. "Look, I'm sorry—"

"You're sorry?" Banjo barked at me. "What the hell is wrong with you, Augie? This is her daycare. You can't just come here and lurk around like some fucking child molester and talk to our daughter through the damn fence!"

I shook my head, wanting to explain that this wasn't why I'd come here. That I wouldn't have dared to go near Luna's daycare without their permission if she hadn't yelled out to me. What was I supposed to do?

Ophelia squeezed my hand again. "He wasn't—"

I cut her off. It was clear from the fury on Banjo's and Lacey's faces that no amount of explaining was going to make this situation better. I didn't want Ophelia defending me. I deserved every ounce of Lacey's wrath.

"We're leaving. I'm really sorry. It won't happen again."

Banjo's expression softened, but Lacey wasn't having any of it.

"Just stop it, Augie. Stop all of it. The showing up in places we'll be. The changing my flat tire. The leaving gifts. None of that will ever excuse the things you did to us. Do you understand me? Nothing excuses the fact that you're a piece of shit who never deserved to call Banjo brother. You sure as hell will never call my daughter your niece. When I say go to Hell, Augie, I mean it. Go to Hell and burn there."

She spun on her heel, hurrying through the center to where her daughter watched from behind glass windows, her chubby cheeks streaked with tears.

Tears that were my fault.

Every word Lacey had said was true.

Banjo just shook his head sadly. "I don't even know what to say to you right now."

"Nothing," I managed to get out, my voice so cracked

and broken it surprised me I could still form words. "She's right. Go be with your daughter."

Banjo gave a sad, short nod and walked away.

Just like he had years before.

Again, I only had myself to blame.

17

OPHELIA

etting my own apartment had been the first thing I'd done when I'd come back home from overseas. My mother had bitched and moaned about it, complaining about the fact I could just live with her and save my money.

Her house was beautiful. All her houses were. She owned many of them, and we'd moved around a lot when we were kids, going wherever the work took us.

But I would have slept in the gutter rather than sleeping in the luxury of her spare bedroom. So I'd rented an apartment on the Saint View-Providence border that wasn't particularly nice but wasn't the ghetto either.

Despite what Augie thought, I wasn't a pampered princess.

Not that much anyway. I did draw the line at living in Saint View.

I did really hate that my apartment had no elevator, though, and that when I came home with bags of groceries, I had to climb multiple flights of stairs to get to my top-floor apartment.

I gazed at the ground-floor apartment longingly as I passed it on my third trip, but no safety-conscious person in their right mind would rent a ground-floor apartment. Did people not realize exactly how easy they were to break into?

"Let me get that for you."

I spun at the deep voice behind me, my heart smashing against my rib cage because I instantly recognized the man's voice.

Riddick. Shit.

Without waiting for me to give him an answer, he took the bags from my arms and climbed the stairs, leaving me to trail along behind him.

Shit. Shit. Shit. I'd deliberately not told my mother where I was staying, because I'd wanted to avoid this entire situation. The only people who knew were my brother and Jezebel.

Scythe and Vincent would have stabbed someone before telling them anything about me. I was sure about that.

I pulled out my phone to call someone for help and found a message from my best friend.

JEZ

SOS! SOS! Riddick is on his way over! I'm so sorry! He threatened to decapitate my fucking cat if I didn't tell him where you lived. And you know he meant it.

I stared at the broad back of the man in front of me, and a shiver ran down my spine. I quickly texted Jez back a thumbs-up, letting her know it was all right. If she hadn't told him, Riddick would have found me another way. There was no point in poor, fluffy Midnight meeting his Maker before his time, just because Riddick was in a mood.

"Which apartment is it?" Riddick called.

God, I so didn't want to tell him. But what option did I have? My fingers twitched over the blade strapped to my thigh, but I also knew Riddick had reflexes as sharp as a cat and he'd see it coming, even with his back turned. All it would take was one swift push from him and I'd find myself with a broken neck at the bottom of three flights of stairs.

Not where I wanted to be tonight.

"Apartment twenty-five," I told him. "On your left."

He let himself in like he owned the place, which was my bad for leaving it unlocked after my last trip to the car. He added the shopping to the pile I'd already brought up earlier, while I looked back longingly at the door, wishing I'd bought more. Maybe I could pretend I had and then just get in the car and drive off.

The thought was appealing. Anything was better than dealing with whatever the hell Riddick wanted, which I already knew wouldn't be anything good.

But there was no point in running. No point in hiding.

He'd find me.

And the repercussions would be so much worse.

He leaned back on the counter and folded his arms across his broad chest. "How come you haven't finished your job bag?"

I froze, my fingers gripping tight around the plastic bag handle. "Have you done yours?"

He raised an eyebrow. "Why?"

I raised a shoulder. "Just wondering why you care about what I'm doing instead of doing your own job."

I cringed internally. The response was probably going to get me a backhand to the face.

But his response was worse. He went completely silent, only narrowing his eyes. A chill frosted the room as he pushed off the counter and crowded me against the refrigerator. "Here's what I think. I think your head isn't actually in the game and that your mother was right, asking me to get you back on track."

Irritation rose in my chest, lifting my chin defiantly. "I've been working this business my own way, in my own time, for over half my life, Riddick. I don't need you 'getting me back on track.'"

I went to duck under his beefy arm, but he blocked me.

"I disagree." Something flickered in his gaze. "A friend told me he saw you having coffee with some man in Providence today."

I glared at him. "So what if I was?"

"We're engaged to be married."

"We most certainly are not. I never once heard you ask, and I definitely didn't say yes."

"You know that's not how things work in our world."

I might have been scared of the man, but there was no way in hell I was being roped into the marriage without my consent. I'd literally rather be dead. "It's how things work with me. I'm not marrying someone I don't love."

Riddick scoffed, "So what? You want me to get down on one knee, tell you you're the most beautiful woman in the room, and promise to love and cherish you for the rest of my life?"

I shook my head. "No, Riddick. I don't want *you* to do that. *You* being the important word here."

The look in his eyes darkened. "Shame. Things would be so much easier if you were agreeable. It changes nothing, though, Ophelia. You know that."

I hated that I did.

I glared at him. "So you'll just force me into this, no matter the fact I've just told you I'm not interested?"

He shrugged. "It's a business arrangement."

Oh, fuck him. "This is my life!" I yelled at him. "My life is not a fucking business arrangement for you and my mother to orchestrate like I'm a piece of property."

He pressed his body against me in the exact same way Augie had a few days earlier.

When Augie had done it, even though he was angry at me for breaking into his house, I'd never felt scared.

Just turned on.

When Riddick did it, I couldn't breathe. His weight crushed my lungs and forced me to turn my head to one side and gasp for breath.

When I reached for the knife at my thigh, he grabbed my wrist sharply. "You are property, Ophelia. My pretty little piece of ass to do what I want with. You understand me?"

I couldn't move, my entire body pinned down with his. I couldn't get any air to make a sound.

"Do as I tell you and nod your head. Tell me you agree with me."

I nodded because I was going to pass out if I didn't.

He stepped back, not bothering to catch me when my

knees buckled and hit the kitchen linoleum. Pain radiated up through them as he walked away toward the door.

"I'll be finishing my job bag this week, Ophelia. Maybe even tonight. I expect yours to be done in the same time frame. Next week, we start our lives together. I don't need a marriage certificate to own you. I already fucking do."

He paused in the doorway to turn around and glare at me. "And so help me fucking God, if I hear again that you're slutting around with another man, I'll kill both of you."

I jumped when the door slammed behind him.

Seconds later, tremors racked my body, sending a chill through my limbs that I couldn't shake.

Sweat broke out across my skin, and a whimper escaped my lips. I pushed to my feet and ran to the door leading out onto a tiny balcony, but no amount of sucking in deep, cold breaths of night air could calm the terror inside me.

I couldn't go inside. The walls felt like they were closing in, the air too thick and sticky. It just reminded me of his weight on top of me, pinning me in place, refusing to let me move.

I hated to be stuck in small spaces.

It reminded me too much of being put in a cupboard as a child when I'd cried because I didn't want to help my mother clean up after one of her kills. Or the trunk she'd shoved me into once when I'd been so paralyzed with fear over a man's screams as she'd tortured him. Vincent had been in there with me, the two of us clutching at each other in the darkness while my mother shouted obscenities about how useless we were if we couldn't even clean up a job site for her.

I stared down at the road beneath my apartment, trying to calculate the distance and how badly I'd break my legs if I jumped.

The pain seemed preferable to spending the rest of the night in that apartment now that Riddick had been in there.

I forced myself inside long enough only to grab my purse and my keys. The front door closed behind me with a thud that sent a fresh wave of panic through my system, and I took the stairs two at a time in an effort to get away.

Riddick had brought a darkness to my door that crept down the stairs after me, chasing me out into the night. I paused at my car but then turned away, picking up pace until I was running into the night.

He would have bugged my car. Put a tracker on it somewhere. I was sure of it.

I ran and ran, until my lungs heaved, but that was still preferable to suffocating beneath Riddick's weight. I ran until the houses around me became smaller and unkept, and eventually, I realized exactly where I was running to.

Or maybe it wasn't a where, but a who.

Augie's street was quiet apart from the group of people outside his neighbor's house, a bright-red Jeep in the driveway. An older woman, three men in their twenties, and a woman with a little girl on her hip watched me run past.

It was only when I was banging on Augie's door hysterically that I realized they were Augie's brother and his family.

All of them staring at me like I was some sort of freak show.

Which I was. Barefoot. Running through Saint View in the middle of the night. Eyes probably possum-sized with panic.

I banged on his door again to avoid their stares.

They probably thought I was some sort of junkie, off her ass on a heroin bender. I bit down hard on my lip as Augie opened the door.

He stared at me. "Ophelia? What on earth?"

I didn't mean for it to happen, and I knew that in the morning I'd be mortified, but a sob burst out my throat.

In an instant, Augie's arms came around me, holding me tight to guide me into the house. There were murmurs from his family across the other side of the broken chain-link fence, but he cradled my head, protecting me from their stares and whispers.

"I'm sorry," I babbled while he closed the door behind us. "I'm so sorry. I didn't know where else to go."

He guided me to the couch, but I couldn't let him go. I clutched his soft gray T-shirt, burying my face in the fabric and inhaling the scent of him. He smelled like warmth and safety and just everything good.

He stopped trying to get me to sit down and just held me instead, his palm running up and down my back slowly and calmly, while he pressed his lips to my hair and murmured comforting words in a deep, gentle tone I'd never heard him use.

"Stop saying you're sorry. You have nothing to be sorry for."

But I did. I was sorry for Fawn. That she'd been taken by a man just like the one I'd run from. I was sorry for

Vincent and Scythe because I hadn't been here to protect them when they'd needed me.

And I was sorry I'd brought all of this to Augie's doorstep.

That Riddick would kill us both if he found out I was here.

That Augie was dead anyway, because by the end of the week, if I didn't kill him, Riddick would take my job bag and kill him himself.

"I'm sorry," I said again, not knowing what else to say.

He leaned back and put two fingers beneath my chin, tilting my face up so he could look in my eyes. "What's happened? Tell me."

I shook my head and tried to turn away.

But he wouldn't let me. His blue-eyed gaze held me tight, refusing to give in. "Tell me. Whatever it is, I'll take care of it." He put his lips to my forehead and breathed in deep. "I'll take care of *you*."

I was sure my heart stopped beating. That the world stopped turning. That everything ceased to exist except for him and me and a connection I'd never felt before and knew I'd never feel again.

Not now that Riddick had claimed me.

I lifted up on my toes and put my lips to Augie's.

He froze for the tiniest of seconds, and I let out a whimper, hauling him as close as I could get, the sound as desperate in my heart as it was to my ears.

"Lia," he murmured, a note of hesitation in his tone.

"Kiss me back," I whispered above his perfect mouth. "Please. Just kiss me back."

His restraint snapped.

In a second, he had me up in his arms, his tongue

running the seam of my lips and pushing into my mouth, hungry and desperate.

I wrapped my arms around his neck, holding him tight, fusing our mouths together as he climbed the stairs, kissing me with everything he had.

My head spun at the feel of him. At his taste. At his hold on my body and a new one that was slowly curling its way around my heart with something that felt scarily like feelings.

I kissed him harder, erasing the thought by sliding my tongue in time with his.

They weren't feelings. I just needed distraction. Something...someone...to remind me I was still alive. That I was still here even if Fawn wasn't. Someone to distract me from the fact I'd soon belong to a man I couldn't stand.

Augie strode into his bedroom, kicking open the door so hard it creaked in protest, but he didn't even bother trying to close it.

With the wall at my back, I whipped off my T-shirt, tossing it to the floor at our feet.

He groaned, holding me beneath my thighs, supporting my weight with a combination of his strength and leverage from where his hips pressed against my center. His mouth found my neck, and he sucked and kissed his way along the sensitive skin there, up to my ear where he mumbled words that sounded a lot like a promise to take care of me.

"What was that?" I asked between the breathy sighs his lips on my neck created.

He drew back, his eyes full of heat. "Let me go down on you."

I widened my eyes. "Um, what?"

He took the full brunt of my weight again, carrying me away from the wall and to his bed.

I braced myself to be dropped there, but he lowered me so carefully, his hand behind my head, that it almost brought tears to my eyes.

He grinned at me. "I'll be more specific. I want to take off your panties, run my tongue over your clit, and suck you until you come. Is that okay?"

"Does anyone actually ever say no to that?"

He shrugged, getting down on his knees and hooking his arms around my legs. With a sharp tug, he had my ass on the edge of the bed. He went for the button on my fly next, undoing it, and sliding down the zipper until my jeans were loose enough that he could get them down my thighs.

He groaned at the sight of my plain-black panties.

"I have nicer ones..." I explained. "I wasn't exactly expecting..."

He pulled my jeans all the way off and then ran his fingers beneath the elastic edges of my underwear. "Don't care. They're coming off anyway."

The panties went the same way as my jeans, and I flushed hot when his gaze rolled down my body, lingering on the swell of my tits, still in my bra, and then lower, between my widespread legs.

He moved in, mouth headed for the place I so desperately wanted him.

I put my hand on the top of his head, stopping him.

He looked up. "What's wrong?"

I squinted at him, the heat of embarrassment mingling with the fire of need. "I just want you to know that no man has ever made me come. It's…not something I do. So don't feel bad when it doesn't work. You can just fuck me. You don't have to worry about foreplay."

He raised one eyebrow. "As sexy as fucking you before you're ready sounds…" He made a face that made me sure it didn't sound sexy to him at all, "I think I'll make you come first. Sweet?"

I squirmed uncomfortably, shifting up onto my elbows so I could see him better. His mouth was literally inches from my pussy, and yet some part of me really needed him to understand. "Men just can't get me there. I've never been able to get off with one. It's honestly not worth your time. I'm a big girl, Augie, and I'm no virgin. Just fuck me. You don't need to feel—"

He put his mouth down on my clit and sucked hard.

I about bucked off the bed. "Oh!"

His tongue started up a leisurely pace, wandering its way from slow laps of my clit to licking up and down my slit. His beard stubble rasped over the soft skin of my inner thighs in a way I'd never thought would feel as good as it did. Little noises of pleasure escaped my lips.

He lifted his head and raised an eyebrow. "You're doing an awful lot of moaning for a woman who insists she didn't need her pussy sucked."

He slid a finger up inside me, and I nearly came on the spot. My moan of pleasure was so loud I really hoped his family next door hadn't heard. A second finger followed a moment later, and he licked and fucked me with his hand in perfect unison, taking me higher with each and every stroke.

I'd had men go down on me before, but it had never felt like this. I normally let them lick around for a minute or two, while they consistently missed my clit or poked at my insides on odd angles that made me cringe. And then I told them to fuck me.

None of them had ever argued.

They all got up like they'd been let out of Saturday detention and pulled their pants down, dick sticking out, ready to drive on home.

The really obnoxious ones spent thirty seconds down there, then expected me to reciprocate.

"You can stop," I told Augie, though it was honestly the last thing I wanted. "You don't have to—"

A third finger stopped my complaints with a shout of ecstasy. My orgasm built low in my belly, and I rolled my hips in time with his hand, taking his fingers deep while he tortured my clit in the best way possible.

I grabbed his head, holding him to me, digging my heels into the mattress, my legs opening so fucking wide for him it would have been embarrassing if I hadn't already thrown all caution to the wind. I rode his tongue and face, gasping at the pleasure so desperate to unleash inside me.

He stopped, disentangling himself from my grip.

I practically cried.

He chuckled softly. "What happened to the woman who was just telling me no man could make her come?"

I was sure my cheeks were red, but I ignored them. "She told the man between her legs to take his pants off so she could return the favor."

I sat up and reached for him, but he caught my wrists and pushed up onto his feet, guiding my body back down with his. He drew my hands up over my head, pinning my wrists to the mattress, and kissed my mouth.

He tasted of my arousal, his lips slick with it.

I'd never had a man make me wet like that. I probably should have been awkward, but it only made me want him more.

Augie drew back, gazing at me with his beautiful ocean-blue eyes. "While I love the idea of your pretty mouth around my cock, you didn't come. So lie still."

I frowned at him. "You were the one who stopped."

He shook his head at me, confusion written all over his expression. "Jesus, who the hell have you been sleeping with? I didn't stop. I was giving you a break. It's called edging, Lia. Heard of it? It's where I build you up but don't let you come until I've done that over and over and over again and you're fucking begging me for the release."

"I know what edging is, asshole," I complained.

I'd just never had it done to me.

Augie had an expression on his face that made me think he could read my mind.

It was ridiculous how hot he was. "If I let your hands go are you going to keep them there?"

"If that's what you want."

His voice took on a slightly growly tone as he let go of my hands and kissed his way down my body, over my lips, my cleavage, my belly, and finally getting back to where I was trying to control the quiver in my thighs.

He dragged his tongue along a path that cruised my inner thigh and the outside of my pussy before spearing through my folds again.

Instantly, with no thought from me, my hands flew down to his head, tangling in the dark-blond lengths while he thrust into me with his fingers. He alternated with his tongue, contrasting between the relative softness of his mouth and the stretching pleasure of three thick fingers.

He laughed into my most intimate parts, and I tugged his hair a little in protest of him laughing at me.

All it did was make him groan. "Fucking love when you do that."

My breaths came faster and quicker, him building me up, and I marveled at the fact this man had me literally writhing on the bed, and he hadn't even taken a stitch of clothing off.

I gazed down my body at him, watching him bring me to the edge, over and over, my orgasm creeping up, then falling back because Augie wouldn't set it free.

I twisted and turned, alternating between clutching his hair, scratching his shoulders, and digging my fingernails into the silky sheets on his bed. "Augie," I moaned, riding his face and his hand shamelessly. "Augie, fuck."

His mouth was a wicked delight. His fingers perfectly made to extract pleasure from my body.

And he did it all without a complaint, without so much of a hint of frustration or impatience, or with a hope that it might lead to the same for him.

Every time I gazed down at him, he was watching me. Those blue eyes locked on my face, watching to make sure everything he did had the desired effect.

"I need to come," I moaned, closing my eyes again, the orgasm building inside me in a swirl of pleasure that needed release.

He bit my inner thigh, not hard, but just enough I knew I'd have a hickey there tomorrow.

I was glad.

I wanted the reminder of how he'd made me feel tonight.

"Beg me, Lia. You want to come? Tell me how much."

I moaned. "Please," I whispered breathlessly, my hips moving faster, keeping time with his fingers that gave me more with every word I uttered. "I'm so wet. I need to come. Fuck me. Please."

"Not fucking you, Lia. Not tonight. But I am going to let you come."

To my shock, he flipped me onto my stomach and smacked my ass.

I screamed, a sound so hoarse and filled with pleasure I didn't even recognize it as my own. He lifted my hips, so my ass was in the air, and found my core again, this time licking me from behind while my knees trembled with the effort of holding my weight.

His fingers filled me, his tongue on my clit, but his voice still grumbled from behind me. "I want to touch you everywhere. It'll make this better for you, but you gotta tell me I can. Do you want that, sweetheart?"

I shivered at the pet name I'd hated only days ago.

In here, he could call me any damn thing he wanted.

"Yes," I groaned, not even thinking about exactly what I was agreeing to, just knowing this man made me want to give up complete control of my body. If he said it would make it better, then I believed him.

His thumb pressed to my ass, and it only took three rubs over the puckered star for me to fall apart completely.

"Oh! Augie!" I screamed his name, coming so hard my entire body locked up.

Pleasure spiraled out from between my thighs, my

internal walls clamping down on his fingers, my core dripping with how wet he'd made me. He held my hip, steadying me while he continued the onslaught, never letting me pull away, even though the sensation was overwhelming.

I buried my face in his sheets, my moans and cries and shouts muffled by the mattress, and thank God, because I was so loud there was no chance people couldn't hear me on the street.

The orgasm drew out, longer and harder and so much sweeter than any I'd ever given myself.

Eventually, Augie slowed down, licking me leisurely now, like he hadn't already spent...how long? Thirty minutes? An hour? Two? I had no freaking idea how much time had passed.

Only that Augie had done something to my body tonight that I hadn't even know it was capable of.

My knees slid out from beneath me until I was flat on my stomach, spread-eagled across his bed, too utterly exhausted to move.

He trailed his fingers up my spine.

I lifted a heavy hand and swatted at him. "No more. You broke me."

He laughed as he came to lie on the bed next to me, drawing the sheet up over my waist to cover my nakedness. He shifted onto his side, propping one hand up under his head so he could watch me. Slowly, with my pussy still thrumming in delight and my body as boneless as I'd ever felt it, I twisted my head so I could see him.

We stared at each other in silence for a long moment. I let my gaze wander over his beautiful face. He was definitely one of those men who aged well. The lines around his eyes and the fainter ones across his forehead proved he was no longer in his twenties. The dark sadness in his expression spoke to a life that had never been easy. I reached out and traced my fingertips along his stubbled jawline, somewhat surprised by my own actions, as well as the fact he let me.

Somehow, putting my fingers on his face felt a whole lot more intimate than him licking my pussy until I screamed.

"I don't feel right about coming over here and screaming your house down because you're an oral sex master." I gave him a sleepy smile. "I'm pretty good at blow jobs, if you want to find out."

He brushed a lock of hair behind my ear. "One day, I'll take you up on that. But not when you came to my house bawling your eyes out and clearly terrified."

I dropped my hand and looked away. "I wasn't bawling. Or terrified."

Except we both knew I was. He didn't need to say it. So I appreciated when he said, "Do you want to tell me what happened?" instead.

I did. I wanted to spill every secret I kept inside. I wanted to explain, except how could I? What was I going to say? That the psychopath I'm supposedly owned by would kill us both if he knew I was here? Oh, and PS, there's a target on your head and I'm the one who's supposed to kill you?

Yeah, that would go down well.

I forced myself to roll over. "I should go," I murmured, pushing myself up to sit.

But Augie's arms came around my waist, and he

pulled me back down to the mattress, tucking himself in behind me so his chest was to my back. "It's late. Just stay."

I could barely breathe. But unlike when Riddick held me and I couldn't breathe because he was trying to hurt me, with Augie it was because my heart beat too fast and my stomach fluttered with nerves. "I should—"

"Sleep," he mumbled into my hair. "You can run away again tomorrow. But for now, just go to fucking sleep, Lia."

For the first time ever, I let a man hold me while I closed my eyes.

18

AUGIE

I woke up in a mess of confusion, a woman's scent in my nose and a warm body nestled in against me. I blinked a few times, groaning because I never let women stay over, until I remembered it wasn't just any woman.

Ophelia.

Her almost black hair spilled across my sheets, her face relaxed in sleep and so fucking beautiful it did weird things to my chest.

She'd come here scared. Crying. So unlike the strong, badass woman I'd known 'til then.

Instantly, I'd known she wasn't leaving my house. Not until she told me what she was running from.

I peered around the dark room, looking toward the window that faced Willa's house. The sun rose over there, and my blinds were so old and broken that I could generally tell what time it was by how light the sky was.

I sat up fast when the sky outside was an eerie shade of orange.

Ophelia rolled over and blinked sleepily at me. "What's going on?"

It took a second for my brain to catch up with my eyes, but when it did, it sent a jolt of panic through my system. "Fire!"

"What?" Ophelia jerked up, twisting around only to see what I did.

But then I was gone, running down the stairs three at a time. "Call nine-one-one!" I shouted to Lia, slamming into a wall as I took the turn toward the front door too fast. Pain ricocheted through my body, but it didn't matter. I got out on the front lawn and stared up in horror at Willa's house, identical to mine in every way except for the plumes of smoke pouring from the second floor and the unearthly orange glow.

"Willa!" I hurdled the low fence that separated our properties, landing on the other side and sprinting up to her porch. I slammed my hand against the wooden door. "Willa!"

I tried the handle, and it gave way beneath my hand.

On the other side, Willa staggered through the smoky interior.

Horror filled me at the burns on her body. I ran to her, grabbing her arm to help her out, but she pushed me away frantically, coughing and spluttering, disoriented by the smoke.

"It's me!" I shouted at her over a roar of something I couldn't identify. I didn't know if it was blood in my ears, adrenaline, or if it came from the fire itself.

She pushed at me again. "No! Luna is upstairs!"

I was sure the blood drained from my face. Banjo's car was in her driveway. "What? Banjo and—"

Willa shook her head frantically. "Just Luna. The others took a limo to the city. Augie, please! She's in Colt's old bedroom."

I didn't think twice. I ran deeper into the smoke-riddled house.

Almost instantly I lost ninety percent of my visibility, the smoke permeating everything. My eyes. My ears. My mouth. My nose. I yanked my T-shirt up to try to filter some of it out, but it didn't help much. A racking cough seized my lungs, but I pushed on, each step taking me closer and closer to the invisible threat of a fire I knew lurked above.

The smoke only got worse as I made it onto the landing, the fire burning in the two front bedrooms, flames licking their way across the walls and up the carpets and dangerously close to the ceiling, fanned by a broken window that let in the cold night breeze. I pulled my shirt sleeve down over my hand and yanked the bedroom doors closed, hoping it would buy me a few more minutes.

Because fuck. I desperately needed them.

Luna's screams of terror cut through the roar in my ears, and I spun around, looking for where they came from before I remembered Willa saying she was in Colt's old room. I thanked the town planner who had been too lazy to come up with different designs for each house on this street. Willa's place was the exact same layout as mine, and I knew from years of Banjo and her son, Colt, being best friends that Colt's old room had been in the attic.

"Don't be up there," I murmured to the fire. "Please don't be in the fucking attic."

I thundered up the stairs, choking and coughing until I made it into the room.

The fire was beneath me, rapidly eating away at the ceiling of the bedrooms below us.

Burning through the support beams that kept the floor from giving way beneath my feet and sending me and Luna into the middle of the fire.

The floor groaned in complaint at my weight, but there was no time for thoughts. No time for concerns over the floor not holding me.

There was no other option when my brother's daughter was on the other side of the room, her arms outstretched, screaming for me to get to her.

I sprinted across the room, grabbing her from her bed and tucking her face into my neck. "It's okay, baby. I got you."

She clutched me with terrified little-girl fingers, her tiny nails pressing into the skin of my neck so hard it hurt, but I relished the pain.

While she was holding on, she was conscious. Breathing.

Which was becoming more difficult by the minute. I ran us both down the attic stairs to the landing, pausing for a second in horror at the flames that had eaten their way through the doors I'd closed and were attacking the hallway.

Outside, sirens wailed, but they weren't here. They weren't going to get here in time to help me. Or to help Luna.

Ash and debris fell around us, and Luna trembled violently in my arms.

The flames were too hot. Too close.

I couldn't fucking breathe.

Every lungful I sucked in was full of more and more smoke, my muscles shaking with the lack of oxygen and my brain fogging over, making it harder to move.

I was too slow.

I slumped against a wall, fighting the urge to lie down and sleep.

Luna lifted her head to look at me.

She didn't say a word.

She didn't need to.

The hopelessness was there in her big brown eyes.

Even at three, she knew.

We weren't getting out of here.

Fuck. That.

I didn't give a shit if I died. This world would be a better place without me in it.

But this tiny girl hadn't even had a chance to live.

Losing her would kill my brother and his family.

I wasn't doing that to them. I was already the cause of too much of their heartbreak. I wasn't taking their daughter to Hell with me.

I shoved myself off the wall and stumbled down the last few steps, dodging my way around flames and a fallen beam, straining for the open door and the two women I could see just beyond it.

Lia, her arms around Willa, trying to comfort her while she screamed at the burning house.

My gaze locked with Lia's, and she let out a shout, leaving Willa and rushing to the doorway. "Augie!"

She gripped my arm and guided me out, sweet, fresh night air filling my lungs, which burned like they'd erupted in a fire of their own. I didn't care. All I cared about was the little girl in my arms.

"Let me take her," Lia gasped. "You can barely stand up."

I tried to pass Luna over, but she clung to me like a koala, screaming when Lia put her hands on her.

I coughed and spluttered, staggering out onto the lawn while two fire trucks and an ambulance parked on the road.

Like seeing them gave me permission to stop, my knees hit the dirt, but I kept my grip on Luna, refusing to fall on her.

The paramedics rushed across the grass, but Ophelia took charge.

"The woman over there is severely burned. Please. Help her. I can't see any burns on these two, but they have smoke inhalation."

The paramedics assessed the scene in seconds and clearly decided Ophelia was right, one of them speaking into a communication device attached to his shoulder and ordering a second ambulance to be dispatched. The firefighters rushed in, hauling hoses and other equipment I didn't have names for, all while Luna clutched me tight, her coughs as terrifying to me as her screams.

Ophelia helped me shift to one side of the yard so we wouldn't be trampled by firefighters, and then she left, a moment later coming back with a portable oxygen tank and a mask. She tried to put it over my face, but I pushed it to Luna.

"She's okay, Aug. You're a lot worse."

I shook my head stubbornly. "I'm fine."

Ophelia frowned at me, but Luna's big eyes stared at me over the top of the mask, and she sucked in deep breaths that reassured me she was okay. They loaded Willa into the ambulance, sirens screaming, and Ophelia ran over to hold her hand, assuring the frantic older woman that her granddaughter was okay and all she needed to do was get in the ambulance and get herself taken care of.

The second ambulance arrived a minute later, two male paramedics rushing over to me.

"Hey, hero." One of them smiled at me kindly. "Heard you ran into a burning building to save this princess." He gave me a nod of respect. "Good on you. Mind if I take her now?"

I realized I had a grip on Luna as tight as the one she had on me. Again, I tried to hand her over, but she burst into tears, fighting to get back to me.

Instinctively, I put my arm around her, and her cries quieted.

"We're a package deal," I told the men. "We go together."

Neither of them argued, just dropped a stretcher down to the ground and helped me onto it. They propped the back up so I could sit with Luna on my lap, and I murmured comforting words to her as we bumped along while Willa's house burnt to the ground in front of us.

Ophelia ran alongside us, but they stopped her at the ambulance door. "You'll need to meet us there, Mom."

"Oh, I'm not..." But who Ophelia was or wasn't didn't matter tonight. Her gaze shifted to meet mine. "I'm going to go get you some things. Your wallet and phone and clothes, and then I'll meet you at the hospital, okay? I'll drive your car."

I went to say she didn't have to. That I barely knew her and she didn't have to come down to the shitty Saint View Hospital in the middle of the night when she probably just wanted to go home.

But the look in her expression said otherwise.

So I didn't argue.

I just held my niece to my chest and thanked all the fucking gods that she was still alive.

19

AUGIE

The ambulance took us straight into the emergency department at Saint View Hospital, though our paramedics had ditched the sirens halfway there when both Luna and I were breathing well, and our oxygen levels were apparently 'as good as could be expected.'

They wheeled us in, and a nurse tried again to take Luna from me, but by now, I had enough oxygen in my system that it wasn't just Luna clinging to me that made me say no. It was the fact her parents weren't here, and I wasn't letting her out of my sight for anything or anyone.

"She stays with me," I told the nurse.

The grumpy old woman who was probably at the tail end of her overnight shift scowled at me. "She needs to be seen in the pediatric department."

I didn't even bother trying to be polite. "Then treat me there too, or bring the pediatrician here. I don't care. But she's been through enough tonight. She's scared, and her parents haven't even been told what happened yet. Until they get here, we won't be separated."

The woman relented with a rude roll of her eyes and some muttering about this being the shift from Hell, but she pointed at a curtained-off treatment area, and the paramedics pushed us in that direction.

Luna and I shifted onto a bed, and I checked to make sure her oxygen mask was still fitted properly. It was, so I pulled the starched white hospital blanket up over her back and made slow, soothing motions up and down her spine.

From somewhere in the back of my mind, song lyrics appeared, and I found myself tunelessly mumbling the nursery rhyme. "Sing a song of sixpence, a pocket full of rye. Four and twenty black birds, baked in a pie..."

"Well, that's morbid. Someone call the ASPCA." Ophelia's tousled brown hair and ash-smudged cheeks popped around the curtain. Her gaze flickered over my face then fell to Luna. "How is she?" She cocked her head to get a better look. "She's asleep, by the way."

I relaxed a bit but didn't stop rubbing Luna's back. "She's okay, I think. We're just waiting on a doctor to come see her. But the paramedics said her oxygen levels weren't too bad and they probably would only hold us both overnight."

Lia sat in the seat next to the bed, and her shoulders slumped with relief. "Thank God for that. I was so worried driving over here. By the way, your car is horrible. It stalled at every set of traffic lights, so I just ran the last few. Sorry if you get a ticket."

I couldn't help but grin. "Did you grab my phone by any chance? I need to call my brother."

She nodded quickly and fished it out of the pile of things she'd brought with her. I eyed the clean clothes with longing, but there was no point putting those on until I'd had a shower. I reeked of smoke. It was in my clothes. My hair. Probably permanently etched into my skin.

But calling Luna's parents was the most important thing. I hit the number I had saved for my brother and hoped like hell he hadn't changed it in the few years since we'd last spoken.

It rang and rang until it eventually went to voicemail. I wasn't going to tell him what had happened like that though. I called again. And again. And eventually on the fourth try, he picked up the phone.

"For fuck's sake, Augie. What the hell do you want at four in the freaking morning? If you're on drugs or need me to bail your sorry ass out of prison, I—"

"There was a fire at Willa's place," I interrupted him, ignoring the jab of hurt that came from him assuming I was high or locked up.

Banjo went silent for a second, then he croaked out, "How bad? Luna—"

"Is okay," I promised him. "I got her out. We're at the hospital with her now, but Willa..."

There was a muffled shout on his end and the sound of other voices.

"She's hurt pretty bad, Banjo. You all need to come to the hospital. Now."

More questioning tones came from Banjo's end of the phone, and he relayed everything I'd told him to the rest of his family. Lacey's cry of pain cut through me, and I was instantly transported back to that hallway, feeling like I couldn't go on.

If I hadn't gotten up…

I tried to shove the insidious thought away. I *had* gotten up. And Luna was asleep on my lap and just fine because of it.

Lacey would get to hold her baby again tonight.

I didn't know if Colt would get to do the same with his mother.

Banjo's voice came back louder in my ear again. "We're leaving now. But we're an hour away. Stay with Luna, Augie. Please. Don't let her out of your sight."

I swallowed hard and nodded, even though he couldn't see it. "I've got her until you get here."

He hung up without another word, and I put the phone back down.

Lia smiled tightly at me. "You're going to get to see your brother again. Properly, I mean. He'll actually have to talk to you."

I nodded, closing my eyes.

The thought was fucking terrifying.

I wasn't aware of falling asleep, but when I woke, the sun was rising outside the window, and Ophelia was still slumped in the chair beside my bed, her head lolling to one side, her mouth open while she slept.

I chuckled. But even exhausted like she was, her hair a mess, and wearing my clothes which I hadn't even noticed before, she was still so beautiful.

In fact, I was pretty sure I liked this look on her better than when it seemed like she'd just stepped off a fashion runway in Milan, with her hair neatly combed and her expensive clothes all fitted and perfect.

Best of all, I liked her when she was naked in my bed, writhing around on the sheets.

My back was aching from being in one position so long. Or maybe it was all the stumbling around in the darkness of Willa's burning house, but I needed to get up and move. I tried to put Luna down on the bed beside me, but she woke up and shook her head hard. I smiled at her, praying she wouldn't freak out now that she wasn't quite as traumatized as she'd been earlier.

"Hey. Do you remember me?"

She nodded. "Uncle Augie."

"Yep. You know where we are?"

"Grandma's work."

I raised an eyebrow. "That's right. At the hospital where your grandma works. Lots of her friends are here too. They've been helping us feel better."

She just stared at me with those huge brown eyes.

I had no idea what to do. But my back was still aching, and I really needed to stretch. "I'm going to get up for a minute, okay? Do you want to just sit here on the bed?"

She shook her head.

Ophelia cleared her throat, though her eyes were still closed. "You can come sit on my lap if you want, Luna?"

The girl shook her head again.

I squinted at her. "Want me to hold you while I stretch?"

She nodded.

Ophelia hid a smile as I got off the bed with my niece.

Some tiny broken part of me fit itself back together with Luna's arms around me. If she didn't want to be put down, then I sure wasn't going to make her. I shifted to the edge of the bed and swung my feet down, wincing as they hit the floor.

"You okay?" Ophelia asked quietly, her hand hovering like my legs might give out and force her to catch me.

"Did a Mack truck hit me at some point? Because it feels like it."

"I can imagine. Augie, what you did…"

I winced. "I didn't do anything."

Ophelia looked like she wanted to argue, but I was grateful when she didn't. I didn't deserve praise for getting Luna out. Anyone would have done the same.

Someone yanked my cubicle curtain aside, and I turned around, expecting to see a doctor.

Instead, Lacey, Banjo, Colt, and their other partner, Rafe, stood at the end of the bed, all four of them haggard.

"Mommy!" Luna shouted, twisting in my arms to get to her mother.

Lacey burst into tears at the sight of her daughter, rushing forward and taking her from my arms. She sobbed into the little girl's hair while Luna happily chattered away about the fire and the ambulance, more animated than she'd been in hours, much to my relief.

Ophelia and I stepped back and let Lacey's men surround her and their daughter, the three of them engulfing their girls and putting their heads together, protecting them in the middle.

A lump rose in my throat watching the bond between them.

I'd never experienced anything like it. Didn't know what that sort of love felt like.

And yet I'd tried to ruin it for them. I'd been the one who'd tried to take away the very thing that held them together.

I fucking hated myself for it. If I'd succeeded, that kid who was so damn loved by everyone she met wouldn't even be here.

My brother pulled away and looked over at me.

I didn't even know what to say.

He held his hand out to me.

A handshake offered.

I took it, gripping his hand tightly.

"Thank you," he whispered, his voice clogged with emotion.

I nodded, waiting until his grip loosened before I let him go. "Come on," I said to Ophelia, taking out the nasal tubes delivering oxygen.

She covered my hand. "No. Wait. The doctors haven't even given you the all clear."

But I was fine. The longer I stayed in this hospital, the bigger my bill—that I couldn't afford—would be. "I'm good. I want to check on Willa, then I need to go home and have a shower."

Ophelia didn't seem like she agreed, but she followed me anyway. We edged around the group, trying to be as unobtrusive as possible and leave them to their reunion.

But Luna lifted her head before we made it out of sight. "Uncle Augie! Don't go!"

Like she had been ever since I'd plucked her from her bed, she reached her arms to me again.

I smiled at her. "Time for me to go. Your mom and dads are here now. They'll take care of you."

But she squirmed so hard Lacey had no choice but to put her down. She ran on her chubby-kid legs over to me and hurled herself at my shins.

Automatically, my hand cupped the back of her head.

Lacey's gaze lingered there, on her daughter hugging my leg and my fingers in her hair. Then her eyes rose to connect with mine.

I braced myself for it. The sharp tones she'd used with me when she'd caught me at Luna's daycare.

Instead, she stepped in and wrapped her arms around me tightly. "Thank you," she whispered against my chest.

I tried to swallow the lump in my throat that stopped me from spewing out all the apologies I'd owed my brother's girl for so long now. I wanted to tell her that saving her daughter was the least I owed her after the hell I'd put her through.

But by the time I'd dredged up the courage, she was stepping back, picking up her daughter and hugging her men again.

I took Ophelia's hand and silently led her away from my brother and his family, clinging to each other like they were in a stormy sea, but all they needed was each other to stay afloat.

20

OPHELIA

The nurses refused to tell us anything about Willa's condition, other than she was stable and having treatment. I could tell Augie wasn't happy about not being able to see her, but he didn't make a scene. Instead, he led me through the hospital, and I let him, marveling at the feel of his fingers between mine. We were both dirty with ash and sweat, but his hand around mine was nice.

Little sparks of pleasure at the simple touch radiated up my arm in the most peculiar way. I'd never felt like this with Nicholas the Noodle, as my brother had so affectionately dubbed my ex. I never really even remembered holding hands with him. Why would I? I wasn't a child who needed to be kept safe from oncoming traffic. I wasn't his property for him to claim ownership of.

When Augie held my hand, it made me understand why people did this.

I liked touching him.

I liked him touching me.

But this very simple act had the potential to get us both killed if the wrong person saw. Reluctantly, I withdrew my hand from his and tucked it into my pocket.

If he was bothered that I'd quit the public display of affection, he didn't comment. I watched him carefully, wondering if that expression on his face was actually relief? The longer we walked in silence without him saying anything, the more I convinced myself that's exactly what it was.

At his car, I dropped my gaze to my feet, so fucking awkward I wanted to die. I'd embarrassed myself with him last night. Thrown myself at him in desperation because I was scared.

Fucking terrified would be the better description.

In the cold light of the morning sun, I hated that woman I'd been.

I hated that I'd run to him in order to feel safe.

Hated that I'd been vulnerable.

My mother would be so bitterly ashamed of me, and frankly, so was I. If word got out that I went crying to a man every time I had a little hiccup, I'd be the subject of gossip for weeks. Even Jez would be embarrassed of my performance last night, and she was my best friend.

"Lia," he said sharply from the other side of the car.

I looked up, loving the way my nickname sounded on his lips and hating it all in the same moment. "Yes?"

"You have the keys."

"Oh!" I rummaged through my purse to find them. "Should I drive? You—"

"I'm fine. I'll drive."

I tossed him the keys and got in beside him when he unlocked my door for me. He drove out of the parking lot I'd haphazardly stopped in earlier when my heart had been pounding with worry over him and Luna.

God, what a difference a few hours made.

Augie drove us back to his place in a weary silence, neither of us attempting to make small talk. But when we pulled onto his street, he sucked in an audible breath, and I knew instantly why.

The street was chaos. There were people everywhere, and not just the swarm of police officers and firefighters. Onlookers crowded around on the pavement across the road, held back by police tape, but that didn't stop them gawking at the burned-out shell of a home that had once been Willa's.

"Fucking rubberneckers," Augie muttered, slowing the car right down to avoid the people who walked in front of us with their phones up, snapping photos.

I ducked in my seat, worried I might accidentally end up on a video that could be posted online.

Sitting in this car right now, with the man I was tasked to murder, was so incredibly stupid. When Augie disappeared, I would be questioned. Willa knew I was at his house. Lacey, Banjo, Colt, and Rafe had all seen me with him at the hospital.

This was exactly the situation you were supposed to avoid when it was your job to end a life.

And yet when Augie steered into his driveway and asked if I was coming in for a shower, all I wanted to do was say yes.

Not because I wanted to be clean, though that was definitely appealing, too.

But because my pussy throbbed at the memory of

everything we'd done together the night before, and I wanted a replay.

Fucking horny bitch. I'd had one mind-blowing orgasm from a man and now I wanted it all the time.

"I should go," I told Augie, getting out of the car and closing the door behind me.

He did the same on the other side. "Why? Do you have somewhere to be?"

But I didn't answer because our attention was caught by a fire crew traipsing out of the charred skeleton of the house next door. Their voices floated across the yard, easy for us to hear.

"No doubt in my mind, Chief. That fire was deliberately lit. Some sort of accelerant was thrown through the bedroom window, and these old houses are tinder boxes. So brittle and dry. They should have been ripped down a long time ago if you ask me."

Augie stiffened and took a few steps toward the fence line so he could hear better. "Excuse me," he called to the firefighter. "I'm the man who pulled the little girl from the building last night. But only her and her grandmother were home at the time."

The man glanced over at us, and his eyes flickered over Augie's soot-covered clothes and skin. "I heard the woman and child are both going to make it. You did good, son."

Augie shook his head, ignoring the man's praises. "There's no reason anyone would want to hurt either of them. Willa lives there alone since her son and daughter moved out. She's a nurse. She's practically a saint who walks on Earth. No one would want to hurt her."

The fire chief gave Augie a tight smile. "That's not

our job to determine. The police are here and will commence investigations once we give them our findings. It could just be random. But sometimes the people around us have secrets even those of us close to them don't know about. We don't know what your neighbor was up to."

Augie shook his head emphatically. "Not Willa. I've known her for forever."

"Like I said. Could be random." The chief rubbed a hand across the back of his neck as he pondered the situation. "But, son, right now, if I were you, I'd go get yourself cleaned up and get some rest. The police are very likely going to want to talk to you, and you'll want to have a fresh head for that."

Augie glanced over at the cops milling on the street. Two of them were watching us with interest, one writing something down on a notepad.

Augie swore low under his breath and turned away.

"What?" I asked him.

"Story of my life. I can already see them setting me up to take the fall for this."

I shook my head in confusion. "What? How? I'll tell them you were asleep next to me..." Shit. I already knew I couldn't do that. What if Riddick had insiders in the police force? If he found out I'd spent the night in Augie's bed...

I balked at the mental image of Riddick shooting that woman in the throat. The way she'd choked on her own blood in agony while Riddick had watched and laughed, zero remorse or care for the fact she was a complete innocent.

The urge to vomit came on strong when I thought

about what he would do to Augie. How it would be so much worse because of what I'd done.

A warning in the back of my mind cautioned that maybe he already knew.

That maybe the fire at Willa's house wasn't random.

Maybe Riddick just had the wrong house, and that Molotov cocktail or whatever it was that had been thrown through Willa's bedroom window was actually meant for Augie's. Their houses were nearly identical.

Augie, completely unaware of the questions forcing themselves into my brain, nodded toward the door. "Come inside. Have a shower."

But I couldn't. I shook my head hard.

Augie frowned and stepped in close, circling his perfect freaking fingers around my wrist and holding me tight. "Come on." His voice was low and gravelly. "Come inside. You're filthy and tired. Get clean. Let me lick your pussy again. Sleep. Then you can go."

His lips hovered over mine, and God, I just wanted him to lean in and kiss me. For him to remind me how good his mouth felt on mine, and how easily I could lose myself in him while my entire life imploded.

I'd been fooling myself, trying to convince my heart that his expression was because he didn't want me.

When he was standing right here in front of me, tired, dirty, exhausted, but still making it damn clear he didn't care about any of that.

All he wanted was for me to come inside.

I closed my eyes for the briefest of moments.

I didn't want to walk away.

I knew I had to.

I pulled my arm from his grasp. "Can't," I choked out.

"Thank you for last night, you were exactly what I needed, but—"

His expression changed in an instant, and this time I knew I wasn't mistaking the cold frost in those blue eyes. "Right. Cool. Forget I said anything. See you around." He turned to go inside.

This time it was me who grabbed him. "Augie, wait!"

He spun back around and glared at me. "For what, Ophelia? For you to tell me you had a nice time but now you have to go back to your real life in Providence? That all I'm good for is a quick screw to get your mind off whatever minor upset came over you last night? What was it? Your maid called in sick and you had to wipe your own fucking ass?"

I squinted at him. "What? That's...that's not why I came here."

He rolled his eyes. "Just go, Ophelia. You've made your position loud and clear. I served my purpose, now you're ready to move on. See ya."

He stepped inside and slammed the door behind him, leaving me on the porch, blinking at the door knocker in confusion.

It took a second for me to get pissed off.

For his accusations to sink through the bubble of warmth *he'd* created around me.

I wasn't a fucking Providence princess. I was so fucking far from it, it was laughable. But if that's what he wanted to believe, then so be it.

It was easier this way.

I didn't want to like him.

Hating him would make it a whole lot easier when I inevitably had to kill him anyway.

21

AUGIE

Water ran over my head and shoulders, the heat of it so pleasurable I wanted to sink down onto the tiles and stay there forever. But inevitably, the hot water ran out, and I dragged myself from the bathroom with a towel fitted around my waist. In my bedroom, I peered into the round mirror on the wall and shook my head at how bloodshot my eyes were still. My lungs ached, and I doubted I would be running a marathon anytime soon, but other than that, I was mostly unhurt.

A few scratches and a minor burn on one arm I hadn't told anyone about because it wasn't worth paying for medical treatment. I slapped some burn cream on it and wrapped it, not sure if that was the right protocol, but Willa wasn't home to ask so it was going to have to do.

My chest tightened at the thought of the woman next door and how badly she'd been hurt. I glanced at the clock on my phone and tried calling the hospital again to get information on how she was, but was told she was in treatment, and they didn't know anything yet.

I slammed my phone down on my dresser too hard, frustrated by the lack of information on the only mother figure I'd ever really had in my life. At least since the one who'd given birth to me had walked out all those years ago.

"Willa's not going to die," I muttered to my reflection. "Those burns weren't that bad. She'll have treatment, and scars, but she'll come home."

Except there was no home for her to come back to.

There would be no insurance that came in and built her some nice new place.

Shock punched me hard when I realized that even after she left the hospital, my time with Willa was over. If she didn't live next door, she would disappear from my life as easily as Banjo had.

The thought left me so cold and empty inside I could barely stand it.

This house was so fucking lonely.

It had only been bearable because Willa was next door.

Now she was gone, there was nothing here. Not for me. Not for anyone.

Fucking Saint View. I hated this place with everything I had. If I got on my board and paddled out into the ocean and just kept going, not a soul would care. They wouldn't even fucking notice.

I couldn't blame them.

My phone rang, and I picked it up without paying attention to the caller ID. "What?"

"Will there ever be a day when you just answer the

phone like a normal person? The words you were looking for are, 'Morning, Eve! How're you doing?'"

"How about, what do you want, Eve? I've had a shit of a night, and your positivity and optimism are making me stabby."

She ignored my grouchiness, well used to it by this point, and being her nosy self, she turned the conversation into an interrogation. "What happened last night?"

There was no point lying to her. In fact, it was surprising she didn't know already. Eve was not only the Queen of Saint View Strip; she was kind of the heart of the entire town. She knew everyone, and people liked her, especially after she'd saved the main street from developers who wanted to turn the town into some yuppie, vegan-eating, Pilates-attending sort of hip-ghetto-chic thing.

I still shuddered at the thought, though if I was being honest, maybe she should have let them. Couldn't be any worse than what it was now.

"There was a fire next door," I told her. "Everyone is okay, but I've been at the hospital—"

"Augie Mitchell! What the hell? Are you okay? Why didn't you call me?"

I shook my head silently. "Because you aren't my wife, my child, or my mother?"

I could practically hear the lasers shooting out of her eyes and destroying her house. "So what? Being your friend doesn't count for shit? Stop dodging the question. Are you okay?"

I didn't even know. All I could think about was getting on my board and paddling out, far away from land and letting the ocean do its thing.

"I'm coming over there," Eve announced when I didn't answer.

But I didn't want her here. *I* didn't even want to be here. "Don't. I'll be at work later. We can talk then."

She tried to protest, but I didn't want to hear it. "I'm tired, Eve. I'm going to bed. I'll see you later."

I hung up and put it on Do Not Disturb before collapsing onto my mattress.

Which was a mistake. The damn sheets smelled like Ophelia. Her shampoo. Her skin. Her sweet, slick arousal that had tasted better than any other woman I'd ever gone down on.

I closed my eyes, but it was all around me, thick and perfect, but torturous because she'd made it clear where she stood.

I just had to be okay with that.

I ripped the sheets off and threw them down the stairs, but I was too tired to find clean ones. I fell onto the bare mattress, not even bothering to get dressed.

It was cold, but I was too tired to care.

Sleep took me, and the darkness was comforting.

I woke to my 'get ready for work' alarm blaring and I groaned, my body protesting every movement, but at least my head felt a little clearer.

I rolled across the mattress and leaned down to pick up my phone from the floor, scrolling through the notifications that had come in while it had been on Do Not Disturb.

A spam email.

Two Instagram notifications for an account I hadn't posted on since Fawn had disappeared.

And a text from the private investigator I'd hired to look into Fawn's disappearance.

I opened it eagerly, praying he'd found something.

BERT

Working on something. Will let you know if it comes to fruition. Don't forget you owe me money. I don't work for free, Augie.

"Whatever, dickhead," I said to the empty room. "Give me something concrete, and maybe I'll pay you."

He'd been absolutely fucking useless so far. He could wait for his money.

Not like I had any anyway.

Which was only going to get worse if I didn't go to work. So as much as I would have liked to stay there on that bed for another forty-eight hours or so, I didn't. I got up, put on clean clothes, and went down to the club, early, like I always tried to be on a Sunday.

The club got trashed on Saturday nights, and Eve couldn't afford cleaners. I knew she would be there, scrubbing the place down, making sure it was as nice as possible for the rest of us to work in, and she shouldn't have to do that alone.

So when I pulled into the parking lot and her car wasn't there, I was a bit surprised. But I had a key and let myself in, locking the door behind me again. I winced at the sight of the place. It was bad, but I wasn't afraid of hard work. It was all I knew, and at least this sort of hard work didn't require me to take my clothes off or fuck anyone.

I nearly emptied the cleaning supply cupboard,

taking out the vacuum, mop, and a bucket of other supplies I'd need and got to work. Cranking up some tunes on Lucinda's DJ decks, I got to work.

I started at the back of the main area, where there were three private rooms we took clients who paid for a more personal experience. Lap dances or fully naked dances from the girls. Phoenix and I didn't give a shit about whipping it all out on the main stage, but the girls saved that for the men who paid more.

Each little room was set up like a living area, with couches and a bar fridge and their own individual speaker system so the client could choose what sort of music played while we danced. The only thing that reminded them they were in a club was the stripper pole.

I wiped each one down thoroughly, disinfecting them with wipes, while wondering where the hell Eve was. It was very unlike her to leave the club in this sort of state when we had to open again in a couple of hours.

I was just finishing up the third room and surveying how to best tackle the main stage when there was a thumping on the door. I rolled my eyes and went over to open it. "You forgot your keys, didn't you..."

Ophelia stood on the other side, her eyes widening when she realized it was me.

I went to shut the door, but she put her hand out, catching it with a glare that would have frozen most people to the spot.

But I was getting used to her moods and had no time for this one. "What are you doing here?" I demanded.

She pushed on the door, trying to open it. "Seriously? I'm here for my dance class. I assumed *you* would make yourself scarce."

"I assumed *you* wouldn't come." My voice came out sharp and harder than I'd truly meant, but goddammit. What was she doing? She couldn't just come down here and take Eve and Lyric's class after everything that had happened between us last night.

Especially not wearing that.

She tugged at the cropped black sports top, pulling it down over her belly self-consciously. "What?"

"Nothing."

"No, what? Was this the wrong thing to wear? I didn't know what to wear for a stripper class since you…"

"Since we what? Dance naked?"

"Well, yeah."

I shook my head. "It's a pole class. Not a fucking get-naked class. Wear what you want. Eve should be here any minute. Go wait over there. I've got things to do."

I left the door open for her and stalked back across the room to where the vacuum sat waiting for me. I stomped on the power button and shoved the stick across the room, cringing at the chunky sounds of food and dirt and glitter being sucked up through the head.

I was so aware of Ophelia's eyes on me. I didn't dare turn around for fear I wouldn't be able to control myself. It would be so easy to go storming across the other side of the room, pick her up from that chair, and carry her into one of the private rooms.

I wanted to taste her again.

Which was fucking stupid.

I should be charging her for that. Not craving her moans, her scent, the way her body felt beneath mine.

I shoved the vacuum harder and faster, pushing it

farther and farther away from the woman who seemed put on this earth just to distract me.

When I finally ran out of spaces to vacuum, I had no choice but to switch it off.

"Will Eve be here soon? The class should have started ten minutes ago."

I paused, frowning to peer over at the clock on the wall. "Eve's never late."

"Well, she is today. That clock isn't wrong. Unless I got the class time confused..."

But she hadn't. The class was at seven, and it was definitely past that now. "Give me a second."

I pulled my phone out, realizing there was a ton of missed calls I hadn't heard because I'd left the stupid thing on Do Not Disturb after my nap. "Shit," I muttered, hitting Eve's number and calling her back.

"Finally!" Eve answered, exasperation in her tone.

"Are you ever going to answer the phone like a normal person?" I parroted her words from earlier back at her. "The words you were looking for are, 'Hi, Augie, thanks for returning my call.' But whatever. Where are you?"

"Lyric and I are stuck in some sort of traffic jam in the city. We went shopping today, but there was an accident and they've closed the entire road back to the suburbs. We're all having to back up and get out another way, but it's taking forever. We aren't going to get there until right on opening, probably."

I glanced over at Ophelia, sitting on a chair watching me quietly. "Okay, well, that's all very well and good, but what about your dance class?"

"Did someone turn up?" Eve asked excitedly. "Really?"

She sounded so thrilled I didn't even have the heart to tell her it was only Ophelia, and she'd only come because I'd kind of guilted her into it a few days earlier. "Yeah, there's someone here."

"Someone came for dance class!" she squealed to Lyric, who let out a whoop from somewhere in Eve's car.

"I'll just tell her to come back next week then?" I asked.

"Wait, no! Don't do that. I don't want her to be disappointed. She might not come back at all. You take the class."

I blinked and stared over at the woman who'd had her thighs wrapped around my head not even twenty-four hours earlier. "What? Yeah, no. I'm not doing that."

"Augie, please! You have to!"

I twisted around and lowered my voice. "I don't even do pole! How am I supposed to teach Oph—" I slammed my lips shut.

"It's Ophelia?"

I groaned internally. "Yes."

Eve and Lyric went quiet.

"Shut up," I complained to them, even though they hadn't said a word.

"Aug, that woman is not there to learn how to dance. She's there for you. You'll be fine. Make sure she pays." Eve ended the call without letting me argue back.

I squeezed my eyes closed, cursing her in my head.

"She's not coming, is she?" Ophelia called.

"No."

"Great. See you then." She pushed to her feet and moved toward the door.

I screwed my face up and forced out the words. "I'll teach you."

Ophelia paused and then slowly turned around. "Why? You made it pretty clear you can't stand the sight of my face."

I choked out a laugh. That so wasn't the problem. It was more that I wanted to kiss her damn face. But I wasn't going to say that. "Eve needs the money. She'll kill me if I let you walk out."

Ophelia pulled the money from her purse and put it down on the table. "There. You've been paid. Tell her you taught me all your sexy moves and I went home and used them to lure men into my bed."

She flipped her hair when she walked away, and fuck if that sass didn't just spur me on.

Or maybe it was the thought of her dancing for other men.

Fuck that.

"Sit your ass down, Ophelia."

I expected more attitude, but to my surprise, she sat back down in a chair that rocked a little on its back legs with the force of her weight. I turned up the music and cursed Eve again for making me do this.

Sultry beats vibrated through the speakers, and I leaned over the bar on my way past, grabbing a bottle of vodka by the neck, and pouring a shot straight into my mouth as I stalked across the room to where Ophelia sat watching me.

The alcohol burned on the way down, but not as much as how bad I wanted her.

I pulled my shirt off and straddled her, one leg either side of her thighs, and she let out a yelp.

"What are you doing? This is supposed to be a pole dance class."

I clamped my hands onto the back of her chair and sank down, so I hovered over her lap, just inches away from touching her. "I'll teach you how to dance, but I don't do pole."

I waited for her to shove me away, and she started to, her hands coming up onto my chest. But then she stared up at me with those big brown eyes, and a spark of fire ignited behind them.

Fuck. Her hands on me felt so damn good. I rolled my hips, pushing them toward her and then back again, glaring at her the entire time, mad as fuck, and somehow turned on all at once.

"I somehow doubt that Eve teaches like this." She raised an eyebrow, playing the unimpressed role well.

But I saw the quick glance down my body that lingered on my abs.

I put my lips to her ear, letting my breath mist over her skin. "I'm not Eve. Now shut up and learn."

She bit her lip, like it was all that was keeping her from giving me the mouthful I deserved. Instead, that attitude lit up in her eyes, and she very slowly, very deliberately, dragged her fingers over my pecs and down my abs with a touch that was so personal it had me faltering.

The gleam in her eyes was a challenge.

Like she knew exactly how bad I wanted her and how, if she just touched me like that, I might shatter.

Two could play at that game.

I hauled her to her feet, wrapping my arms around

her, swaying in time to the music in a sensual slow dance that never failed to have every woman at one of my shows swooning. I felt more than heard her sharp intake of breath at how close I had her, every part of me pressing against every part of her.

She hadn't seen anything yet.

Normally I would have whispered in the woman's ear, asked her permission, but catching Ophelia off guard was way too much fun. And hell. I'd had my tongue buried in her pussy just hours ago. Unless she told me to stop, I wasn't going to.

I slid my hands from the small of her back over her ass and down to the backs of her thighs.

Without warning her, I picked her up, spreading her legs so she was forced to wrap them around me.

It put her core at my stomach height, and fuck if I didn't want to drop her lower to where I was rapidly getting hard.

I was always freaking hard around her. One look and I was a goner, but this was so much worse. Dancing with her like this. Touching her. Knowing how sweet her pussy tasted and how her arousal had coated my tongue so beautifully. It was torture.

"Augie! Put me down."

I looked up at her and smirked. "Sure thing, sweetheart." I slid one hand up her back, supporting her weight, and then lowered her to the freshly cleaned floor, laying her out on her back, hovering over her.

"Dammit, Augie! Not what I meant and you know it!"

When I did this with strangers in the club, I didn't put my weight on them. I kept a distance, always being careful not to touch them.

With Ophelia, I sank my hips down over hers, grinding my jeans at the seam of her workout pants. "You complain a lot for a woman who still has her legs firmly clamped around me."

Her eyes widened, and she stared down, like she was completely unaware of the way she was keeping me held to her.

Before she could complain, I rolled my hips against hers again, grinding on her in time to the music.

Her eyes flickered closed for a second as I put pressure on her clit, and a tiny moan slipped from between her soft, so pretty lips.

So I did it again. And again. Until her hips moved beneath me, her thrusting up to meet my downward strokes, her breaths coming in faster and shallower pants that matched mine.

I wanted to pretend it was the dance that was stealing my breath. That it was the physical exertion of what I was doing.

But it was her.

Beneath me. All dark hair and big eyes and a mouth so fuckable I wanted to pull her up by her ponytail and see how deep she could take me.

My dick wept with precum, desperate for me to do just that, right here, in the middle of the club where I'd promised Eve I would never.

My phone rang.

We both froze, staring over at it sitting on the edge of the stage.

I knew what would happen if I didn't get up and answer it. I was already on the verge of undoing my fly and slamming my cock into her.

"Fuck," I muttered, falling back to my knees, breathing hard, trying to get enough oxygen to my head to make a sensible decision. Eve was about the only person in the world who actually gave a fuck about me, and I'd just come very close to breaking the one rule she'd laid out for me.

I wouldn't do it.

But damn, I wanted to.

Ophelia let her legs fall away from around me, and I pushed back onto the balls of my feet to stand. I strode across the room and picked up the phone without looking at the caller ID.

All I wanted to do was look at her.

"This better be fucking good," I barked into the phone.

To my surprise, it was a man on the other end, not Eve calling in to see how her dance student was doing.

"The trail on Eddie and the woman he was seen with has gone cold," Bert Leddith said sharply into the phone. "But did you know he has a brother?"

"No. What's that got to do with anything?"

I was only half listening to the PI. I was too busy watching Ophelia get to her feet and brush herself off. She avoided looking at me, but her cheeks were pink, and damn that color was so good on her.

"From what I'm told, they're close. Everyone I spoke to said if Zane Sinclair doesn't know where Eddie is, then no one does."

I blinked and shook my head, trying to follow the conversation but doing a bad job of it because my dick was pounding with the need to follow Ophelia across the room and bend her over a table. "Wait, what? Zane who?"

Ophelia's head snapped in my direction. "Zane Sinclair?"

The PI repeated it in my ear, and I nodded at Ophelia.

She scurried over to me and frantically made motions for me to put the phone on speaker. I started to shake my head no, but she gave me a glare so deadly I quickly switched it over.

"Jesus," I muttered. "Settle down, psycho."

She glared at me, but Bert carried on, oblivious to me and Ophelia openly glaring daggers at each other.

I kinda liked her fire and attitude. Almost as much as having her placid and obedient beneath me. The fact she could be both blew my mind.

The PI kept going with his report. "I'm told Zane has a thing for sex clubs."

I scoffed at the phone. "Who doesn't?"

Ophelia rolled her eyes.

Bert chuckled. "Yes, well, apparently, he's a regular at a club called Psychos. It's in your neck of the woods."

"That's my brother's club," Ophelia hissed, at the same time I responded, "I know it."

We both stared at each other.

The man went on. "Great. Well, there's a party there tomorrow night. If I were you, I'd get yourselves on the invite list and see if you can talk to him. I think he's your best bet at finding your friend right now."

I cleared my throat. "Finding her is your job."

The man barked out a laugh. "Yeah, I don't think so, Augie. I'm a married man, and no job is worth me stepping foot in a sex club. My wife would end me."

"Pussy," I mumbled.

"Maybe so. But I don't get paid enough for a divorce.

So I've given you the info. What you do with it now is up to you. Use it. Don't. I don't give a shit."

"I'll go," Ophelia said, straightening. "Getting in is no problem, and I know Zane. Or at least, I've met him. I can ID him. If he's there, I'll get him to talk."

I cocked my head at her suddenly dark tone. Her voice had a sinister quality I hadn't heard from her. Despite the fact I'd just had her writhing on the floor beneath me, a shiver rolled down my spine that reminded me I barely knew this woman.

It didn't matter.

Because there was no way she was going into a sex club alone.

It wasn't just Zane Sinclair I was worried about.

It was the fact I'd just spent all that time getting us both riled up, only to walk away.

And that a sex club was the perfect place to take out some unwanted sexual frustrations.

22

OPHELIA

"*N*o. Hell no. Not even a tiny little chance of yes."

I glared at my younger brother and shoved away his outstretched hand that was currently preventing me from getting inside his club.

"You can glare at me all you want, sis, but I am not letting you inside. Do you even know what goes on during these parties?"

I widened my eyes and batted my eyelashes at him. "You sit around in your Sunday best and drink tea with your pinkies raised and eat cucumber sandwiches, right?"

Scythe nodded enthusiastically. "Yes! That's exactly what we do, and that is not your scene, so on your way." He flickered his fingers in a dismissive manner. "Skedaddle."

"Do I look like I'm dressed to skedaddle?" I went for the belt on my trench coat, knowing exactly what would happen before I could get it undone.

Scythe slammed his eyes closed and put his hands over ears. "La, la, la! Not listening! Not seeing! Could someone please bring me some bleach? I need to remove even the thought of what you were about to do. In fact, just give me a lobotomy right here, right now! Take my brains! Take them all!"

I rolled my eyes and strode past him and his theatrics, Augie following close behind me.

"He's so dramatic," I told Augie. "That would have never worked with Vincent."

By the time Scythe opened his eyes and realized what I'd done, a group of other people had done the same.

"I see what you did there, Ophelia!" he shouted over the crowd of people between us. "I'm not happy!"

I stuck my middle finger up in the air and kept walking. "Then stay outside tonight, brother. We'll both be happier for it!"

If he replied, I didn't hear it. I followed the people in front of me through a curtained-off doorway into a cloakroom. The sex club stretched out on the other side, a stark difference to the bar I was more familiar with.

By day, Psychos was a dive bar. A scummy hole-in-the-wall place that attracted locals from the biker club and no-hopers from the trailer park.

But a couple times a month, people came from both Saint View and Providence and even from as far as the city to attend the secret underground sex parties my brother and his partners threw in the adjoining rooms of the building.

On these nights, sultry music filled the air. People shed clothes at the door in favor of sexy outfits, lingerie, or nothing at all. The club became a den of iniquity. Women and men alike danced in gold gilded cages spread out around the warehouse-sized rooms. Others took it further, fingers wrapped around hard erections or rubbing over clits. A full-blown threesome took place in one cage, a small group of people standing around, watching.

"Holy shit," I whispered, standing in the doorway, watching it all unfold in front of me.

"Ophelia!" A curvy auburn-haired woman rushed over, her pregnant belly poking out between her lacy bra and panty lingerie set. She threw her arms around me, hugging me tight. "I didn't know you were coming!"

My sister-in-law, Bliss, was about the sweetest woman to ever walk the earth. She'd inherited the club when her brother had died, but it still kind of blew my mind that she'd continued to run it. She was so...nice. I'd never been able to picture her working here, and yet right now she was as comfortable about the orgy going on behind her as she was when she talked about the baby she was due to have in a few months.

"Scythe nearly didn't let me in," I admitted to her.

She laughed. "My brother never let me come here when he was alive either. Can't really blame him. Nobody wants to see their sibling...you know."

The fact she owned this club but still said, 'you know' instead of just saying 'fuck' was amusing. I couldn't help but like the woman. Not liking her would be like not liking puppies.

Only psychopaths didn't like puppies. My brother, for example, had an ongoing war with a little white dog he'd rescued.

"We aren't planning on...partaking," I told her. "So he doesn't have anything to worry about."

Bliss's gaze slid to Augie, who was standing a few inches behind me and a little to my right. She squinted at him, then must have realized she was being a bit awkward because she held her hand out to him. "Hi. Sorry. I was just staring at you like a massive creep, wasn't I?"

"He's used to women staring at him," I told her sarcastically.

Augie flicked his elbow out in protest, but I dodged the half-hearted rebuke.

I grinned at Bliss. "It's because he's so pretty."

Augie cleared his throat. "It's because I'm a stripper."

Bliss blinked in recognition. "Oh! You're Augie! I was trying to work out why you were so familiar. You look like Banjo!"

"You know my brother?" Augie asked. He shifted his weight side to side. "Does he...he comes here?"

Bliss laughed. "You look about as horrified as I'm sure Scythe was just a minute ago. They don't come here on party nights, but we've had them around for drinks. We did get stormed in once..."

Yeah, I didn't really want to know about my brother and sister-in-law getting stormed in at a sex club with a bunch of their friends. Lord only knew what had happened that night. I doubted it was PG.

Bliss clapped. "Anyway! Check in any coats or jackets here. You're probably a bit overdressed for the crowd inside, but everyone is welcome to wear whatever they're comfortable with in here, so when you're ready, just make your way on in. Everything is complimentary for the two of you. On us." She squeezed my hand. "I'm so glad you came. And that you're staying in town and not going back to Spain." She rubbed her hand over her belly. "This baby needs family around her."

I swallowed thickly at the unspoken words that echoed around my head. Fawn should be here. She'd be so thrilled if she knew Scythe and Vincent were having a baby. Bliss was so much like her. Soft and gentle with none of my hard edges. I couldn't imagine Bliss and I ever being really close, but her and Fawn? They could be besties.

I wasn't exactly sure how I felt about being at a sex party for hours in nothing but the lingerie I'd put on earlier that evening, but if this was where Eddie's brother hung out, then this was where I was going to be.

And this coat really was overkill. With so many bodies in one space, it was hot.

The sharp intake of breath from Augie when I dropped my coat and revealed the black lingerie beneath was just a bonus.

"You are not fucking walking around wearing that," he growled.

I glanced over my shoulder at him and grinned. "I don't believe I gave you a say in what I wear or where I wear it. If you don't like it, you can leave, you know. I didn't want you here in the first place."

He slipped his hand around mine possessively, a scowl on his face like a black thundercloud. I doubted any man would even glance in my direction.

The only one I wanted was him anyway.

Just the touch of his fingers wrapped around mine sent tingles through my entire body, that only increased when we moved into the club and wandered around the performance cages, stepping around women and men on their knees or people laid out on beds and couches.

I swallowed hard, watching one woman on all fours, howling in pleasure as men surrounded her, fucking her holes, tweaking her nipples, tonguing her skin.

Lucky bitch.

Wetness pooled at my core, my pussy starting up a dull throb I ignored because I was here to work. Not for pleasure.

But Bliss smiled at me as she passed and pressed something into my hand.

I stared down at the little gold key in my palm. "What's this?"

But she just winked at me. "You look like you might need it." Her gaze flickered to Augie and the desperate clutch he had on my fingers. "You both do."

I glanced over at him, ready to ask if he knew what the key was about, but his expression stopped me.

There was so much heat in his gaze it practically burned me alive.

He turned away and cleared his throat, shaking his head. "This was such a fucking bad idea."

"Because seeing me in lingerie is so awful?"

His gaze snapped up to meet mine. "Because seeing you in lingerie only makes me want to take it off you. Because being here in this room full of men who are all staring at you like you're a feast and they're starving is killing me. Because my dick is so fucking hard whenever you're around that all I can think about is sinking it inside your sweet, wet pussy and fucking you until you scream."

My mouth went dry at his words and the intention to carry them out in his expression.

I wanted it. Everything he'd said and so much more.

He crowded me in, desperate, blocking my view of the rest of the club. "Stop fucking looking at me like that, Lia, or I swear, you'll be naked and on my cock in front of every person in this room before you can blink."

Even holding his hand in this room, where Riddick might know people, was dangerous.

But a tiny moan slipped from my mouth. Heat flushed my skin, leaving a trail of fire that could only be put out by him.

No other man had ever made me feel like this.

Other men were barely even interesting. Tolerable at best but never something I actively sought out the way I did with him.

I didn't have to go to that dance class.

I had, because of him.

I didn't have to be here now. This was his lead, and I already knew it probably wouldn't take us anywhere. But I'd come because of him.

I'd sat in that fucking hospital for hours the other night, terrified and unable to calm the racing of my heart, all because of him.

He was dangerous.

I was going to get us both killed.

In that moment, I didn't care.

His lips came to my neck, kissing me there, sucking and licking and biting me in a way that somehow wasn't painful because I was so. Damn. Hot. I closed my eyes and let my head sink back against the wall, giving him better access to my neck while his hand slid inside my panties.

His big body blocked me from the rest of the room, giving the most miniscule amount of privacy, but it was reckless to let him do this here. Where Riddick's crew could be watching.

His finger slid inside me, and I cried out, clutching him, needing him to do it more.

"Faster," I urged him on, breathless and shaking.

He angled his hand, pushing a second finger inside and using his thumb to rub my clit.

I moved my leg to give him more room, opening myself up and letting the sweet, slick pleasure of a building orgasm wind its way through me.

Every muscle relaxed as he worked like he knew me better than I did. Every thrust of his fingers was so perfectly placed, hitting my G-spot and creating sparks behind my eyes. Every rub of my clit had me mewling for more and remembering the way he'd done this with his tongue while my legs had been wrapped around his head.

"Oh God," I moaned, my noises of pleasure mingling with others around me.

His head lowered, and he sucked my nipple through the lacy bra. I clutched his head to me, rocking my hips against his hand, searching for the finish line I so desperately needed to cross.

"Come for me, Lia. While everyone watches how beautiful you are."

It was too late to stop it, even if his words reminded me we were in a public place. I tried to put the brakes on. Tried to pull away, but he wouldn't let me. Like I was as light as a feather, he sent me over the edge, spiraling into the wind, soaring and tumbling while he held me tight. I pulsed and throbbed around his fingers, clutching his hair, the little key in my hand stabbing into my palm.

When I finally came down off the mountain, Augie stood and withdrew his fingers from inside me. With his gaze firmly on mine, he put his fingers to his mouth and sucked them clean.

It wasn't enough. He'd made me come twice, and I'd loved every second.

But for the longest time, I'd been well used to having to turn myself on.

Taking a man's cock into my mouth had come to be one of my favorites. On my knees, with his cock in my mouth, it didn't matter who the man was. I liked fingers in my hair. I liked groans of pleasure and words of affirmation.

Augie had been hell-bent on finding my 'on switches' for himself, but now I wanted to show him another.

23

AUGIE

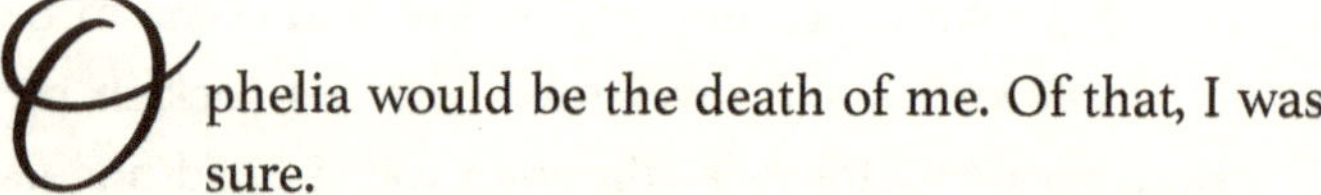phelia would be the death of me. Of that, I was sure.

But fuck. What a way to go.

I'd never been with anyone like her. Someone who drove me mad one minute but who I was desperate for in the next. When women touched me or talked in my ear, I generally wanted to turn and run in the opposite direction.

But when Ophelia did it, I just wanted more.

More of her words. Her lips. Her mouth.

Her sweet fucking juices on my tongue. God, I wanted to go down on her so bad it was a physical pain. Licking her off my fingers wasn't half as good, and when every asshole around me was getting sucked, fucked, or blown, it was hard not to get swept up in the moment.

Her rejections meant nothing when I had my fingers buried in her pussy and her moans in my ear.

Fuck, they just made me want her all the more. "Take your underwear off, Lia. I need you naked."

Her gaze darted around the club, landing on a darkened corridor. "Not here. Down there."

I didn't fucking care where. I just needed it to happen, and I needed it to happen now.

With her nipples and bra still wet from my mouth, her panties coated in her slick arousal, she led me out of the main room, leaving the sights and sounds of a sex party behind us.

But the corridor was no more private, though it was darker. Smaller groups had gathered, some sharing looks through peepholes, their hands around their cocks or buried in their pussies, most likely copying what was going on behind closed doors.

I grinned at Ophelia and raised an eyebrow at her. "This what you brought me down here for? Some peep show action?"

She grinned. "You want to have a look?"

"I want to watch you more."

I could practically see the way she melted. Her grip tightened around my fingers, and she dragged me deeper down the corridor, stepping around the salacious acts playing out in front of us.

"Where are we going?" I asked her.

She held up a golden key. "Honestly, I'm not exactly sure. But Bliss gave me this, and I assume the number eight engraved on it refers to a room..."

She stopped abruptly in front of a black door with a golden number eight in the center. The gold lock just begged for the little key in Ophelia's fingers.

She wriggled her eyebrows at me. "No peephole. So it's not *that* kind of room. What do you think is on the other side?"

I pulled her in, wrapping my arms around her bare waist, drawing her close so her barely covered tits were pressed against my chest. I dropped my head and put my lips to her mouth, kissing her deep and strong, stroking my tongue with hers, reminding myself what she tasted like.

She kissed me back, moaning into my mouth in that sweet way she had. Fuck, I was glad she was vocal. I loved hearing those little noises. Loved eliciting them from her body in ways I was beginning to not only understand but crave.

"I don't care what's on the other side," I whispered into her ear. "As long as you're in there with me."

All I fucking wanted was her.

She cupped my face with both hands, the metal of the key cold on my cheek as she took my mouth again.

The kiss was softer, slower than any we'd shared before.

It stole my breath in a way the others hadn't.

In a way that scared me so badly, I immediately knew it had to end.

I moved back and took the key from her fingers, leaning around her to fit it to the lock and turn it.

The door opened, and we stepped in, locking it again behind us.

I didn't want anyone else in here. It was one thing for them to look, for them to stroke themselves while they watched her come around my fingers. But I didn't want anyone touching her.

Because some voice in the back of my mind roared, "mine" every time I got near her.

And I didn't fucking share.

The room was dark, but two lamps cast a dim yellow glow that washed over our skin and clothing, making the space feel warm. A king-sized bed sat in the middle, covered in a black satin sheet.

No pillows. No comforter or blankets.

This room wasn't for sleeping.

Bondage points were attached to all four corners of the bed, but when I ran my fingers over one of the attached, soft cuffs, Ophelia shook her head.

"I don't want to be tied down. Not here. Not tonight."

I caught her wrists, pulling her in tight. "I'm never going to do anything you don't want. You say no to tying you up, I won't. Not my kink anyway."

She smiled up at me, suddenly interested. "What is?"

I chuckled. "What's yours?"

She shrugged, walking around, giving a sex swing in the corner a squinty glance before heading to a display of sex toys on a table. "Who says I have one?"

"Everyone has a kink, Ophelia."

I saw the shiver my words sent down her spine, and it only made me want to figure her out more. She'd been so insistent that men didn't do it for her. And yet I'd made her come twice now with no problem at all.

I didn't know which stupid rich pricks she'd been sleeping with over on the other side of the border, but maybe she should have tried the wrong side of the tracks earlier.

Her fingers lingered on the bejeweled ass plugs and nipple clamps, and I took mental note, storing that information away for future reference. Fuck, I'd like to use those on her. Every damn one, filling all her holes, clamping her tits, making sure every toy brought her the pleasure they were so specifically designed for.

"There is something that turns me on. Not a kink, as such. Just something I like."

"Tell me," I said eagerly. "Whatever it is, I'll do it."

I meant it. If I got to hear more of those noises, see more of her body, taste her pussy when her orgasm exploded, then I would do whatever she wanted.

No limits.

She came to stand in front of me.

Then dropped down on her knees, staring up at me through long lashes while she undid my belt. "Take your shirt off," she demanded.

That was easily done. I lifted it over my head and dropped it on the floor, but when she undid the button on my jeans, exposing the thick erection behind because I hadn't worn underwear, I stopped her. "Let me taste you."

But she shook her head hard. "You asked me what turns me on. This is it."

She wrapped her fingers around my cock, and I hissed at the cool touch of her fingers.

But still, I tried to pull away.

She squinted at me. "You don't like head?"

"Every guy likes blow jobs, Lia." I just couldn't remember the last time I'd had one. Fuck, it had probably been ten years, back before I'd started charging people to sleep with me. When people paid you for sex, it was all about them. I didn't kiss them, and I didn't like them touching me. I was there to do a job, not for pleasure.

"Your cock is huge," she whispered, gripping my

length with both hands and sliding them up and down my shaft.

That right there was the other reason I didn't push people for blow jobs. The size of me scared them, and it was an instant erection killer when someone looked up at you with stark fear in their eyes.

As such, I'd gotten really good at giving.

But I had little experience of receiving.

"You don't have to," I assured her. "The thought was nice, but get up on the bed. I want to make you come again…"

She rolled her eyes. It seemed to be becoming a habit. "You talk a lot of shit, Augie. Has anyone ever told you that?"

Most people didn't dare.

I kinda liked that she did.

Her mouth fit over the head of my cock, and I shouted at the soft, wet warmth that felt so fucking good I nearly came. On instinct, my fingers dove into the long strands of jet-black hair at the back of her head. I cringed at the pressure I put on her, thrusting my dick deep into her mouth.

I immediately pulled my hands away. "Shit. Sorry. I didn't mean to."

She reached up, taking one of my hands and put it back where it was. A second later, she switched hands, stroking my cock with one while sucking the end, her other hand reaching up and guiding me until I was back where I'd started.

She moved back for half a second to scowl at me. "It's only a turn-on if you aren't scared of hurting me. Hold my head. Pull my hair. Guide my mouth so it feels good for you."

I shook my head. "They're dangerous words, Lia."

There was a challenge in her eyes when she lowered her head again. One that screamed, "Try me."

I didn't want to hurt her. That had never gotten me off. I didn't want her choking and crying.

But she'd said this turned her on, and fuck if that didn't make me so hard I could explode at any minute.

As did staring down at her in underwear that left nothing to the imagination.

She ran her pink tongue cheekily along the underside of my dick, licking the thick vein. Her breaths were shallow, and she had her thighs clamped tight together, like she needed that pressure on her clit.

I grinned down at her. "Suck my cock, then, Lia. Show me how much it turns you on."

Her eyes fluttered closed, and she hummed around my dick like my words pleased her.

That pleased me. Way more than it should.

I held her head, fingers tight in her hair, guiding her pretty mouth up and down my shaft, shallow at first, giving her time to adjust.

But her moans were needy, and I loved them. I gave her more, pushing in a little deeper with each thrust, spurred on by the way her fingernails dug into my ass, encouraging me to fuck her harder and faster.

My mouth on her pussy, or hers on my cock, seemed to be the only times she truly let her guard down. Out on the streets she was hard and cold, full of sharp words, attitude, and sass.

But in here, on her knees, with her tongue wrapped

around my cock, there was a vulnerability to her. A softness that told me this was when she got to be herself.

Maybe the only time. When she was so preoccupied with how her body felt that she truly let go of every other thought in her head.

I thrust faster. Harder. Letting go of any concerns she couldn't take my size, when she'd proved she could.

When she'd proved she wanted to.

I'd never understood men who got off on taking women without their consent. Her wanting this? Her begging to get down on her knees and suck me was the hottest thing I'd ever seen.

Fuck, she felt amazing. "Need to come, sweetheart." I let go of her, giving her time to move away.

She didn't.

So fucking hot.

She moaned as the first drops of my cum hit her tongue. My balls drew up in a blissful agony and released, spraying hot liquid down her throat. She swallowed without a word, taking everything I had without jerking away.

I came until I had nothing left to give.

I brushed her hair off her face and tucked it behind her ear. "What are you doing?"

She hadn't moved. My cock in her mouth while the final tingles of my orgasm faded.

Nothing had ever felt as good. As sweet. As fucking perfect as coming down, staring at her, my dick warm and wet and barely deflating before it started getting hard again.

She noticed and sucked me harder, making me hiss.

"Nah, sweetheart," I said with a chuckle, pulling from

her mouth. "I see what you're doing there. But the next time I come it won't be down your throat."

Until that moment, I would have never imagined that Ophelia could pout. That wasn't her. She was strong and determined, and pouting just seemed...impossible.

But there was an expression of disappointment on her pretty face. "Call me a ho if you want, but I like it."

I kissed her mouth and shook my head, anger building up in me at the very thought someone might have made her feel less than for liking sex. "Fuck whoever put that idea in your head. Purist bullshit. You aren't bad or dirty for liking sex. Despite what one of my foster parents tried to tell me."

"Your foster homes weren't good?" she asked quietly.

I couldn't look at her. I turned away. "Depends on your definition. Some might think being used as a human ash tray is good. Or being too scared to sleep for fear of who might let themselves into your bed. Or being constantly hungry, belittled, or told you were a cheap piece of Saint View scum who would never amount to anything..." I caught her horrified expression in the mirror. "It's all relative. I met other kids who'd had it worse."

"Augie..." She stepped in and wrapped her arms around me from behind.

On instinct, I froze, those memories of my childhood too fresh in my head after dredging them up from the past where they should just stay buried.

She noticed how stiff I was and instantly tried to back away.

I caught her fingers, holding them to my chest. "Sorry. I didn't mean to do that. I'm just not used to..."

"Hugs?" she asked. "Me neither. Not that my childhood was as bad as yours… Well, not in the same way as yours anyway. But it wasn't exactly full of affection either. Trust me, this surprised me as much as it surprised you."

"Do you like it?" I trailed my fingers over hers.

There was a smile in her tone. "Don't tell anyone because it'll ruin my bad-bitch street cred, but yes."

I chuckled at her self-deprecating humor, enjoying the feel of her cheek resting between my shoulder blades. "Ophelia."

"Mmm?" she mused, sounding almost sleepy, despite the music that filtered through from outside the club.

"I never had any choices growing up. I had no power of my own. Everything was decided for me, from what—or if—I ate, to the clothes I wore, to the things I was forced to do, to where I slept at night."

"I'm so sorry," she said gently. "I hate that happened to you."

"So do I. I pushed my brother in the same way. I knew no different, and yet it took me doing it to him to realize how it was all connected." I let out a shuddering breath.

Her lips pressed to my back. "It's okay. You don't have to tell me this if it's too much."

I wanted to. There was an intimacy here, sparking in the air between us, unfamiliar but comforting.

These weren't things I could have ever told anyone else. Not Eve. Not Phoenix or Fawn.

Not Banjo.

In the darkness of a room with a woman who somehow felt safe, I was finally able to speak about it.

"I'm so fucking sorry for what I did to him. And I'm so damn sorry I wasn't there for Fawn either."

She moved around me, so she was looking up at me.

I didn't see our lack of clothes. Or hear the people talking outside our door.

All I saw was her and the understanding in her eyes.

It wasn't pity or shame or any of the other things I'd thought people would feel if I told them the truth about who I was.

She lifted up on her toes and cupped my face, touching her lips to mine softly.

I wrapped my arms around her, deepening the kiss, taking her lips and her mouth and her tongue and tasting every inch, savoring it, living in the moment because for once in my shitty fucking life, I had something good.

I had her.

"I need you to know something," I whispered, pulling back and rubbing my nose along the bridge of hers. "I need you to know that you always have a choice with me. That I never expect you to give me something you don't want to give. You never have to please me by doing something that makes you uncomfortable. I'm always going to ask, and all you have to do is say no. I never had a choice. But you do. Always."

She swallowed hard. "What do you want to do?"

I glanced over at the array of sex toys all laid out on the table to our left. The smile I gave her was suggestive, lightening the mood. "We're in a sex club. Seems a shame to only use this room for a deep and meaningful."

Her gaze flickered over and she grinned up at me. "All I have to do is say yes?"

I nodded.

She leaned in and brushed her sweet lips over mine. "Yes."

24

OPHELIA

ugie walked around me, switching our positions, so I faced the mirror and he stood behind me. With slow, deliberate fingers that brushed my skin, he unfastened the clasp of my bra and let it fall at my feet. He placed a kiss on my shoulder and then slid his hands down my arms, picking up my fingers and guiding them to the table of toys.

"Which one?" he whispered in my ear, breath tickling my neck.

I hesitated, casting an eye over the selection. Some of them I didn't even have names for. There was a selection of vibrators and dildos, but I was already good friends with my own, so they didn't seem terribly exciting.

The set of clamps sent a tremble through my body, though, and I picked them up, passing them back to him.

He groaned, his dick prodding the small of my back. Without lifting his lips from my neck, he watched me in the mirror as he attached them, my nipples singing out in pleasure.

"Fuck, they look good on you," he murmured. "You should never wear anything but these ever again."

I stared at my reflection in the mirror, my lipstick slightly smudged, though not an awful mess. I'd have to remember to give the brand a five-star review for holding up to both kissing and blow jobs. My hair was a tangled, wild birds' nest from having his hands in it for so long, but I loved the way it looked. Combined with the healthy flush beneath my skin, the tiny panties, and now the sex toy accessories, I'd never felt sexier.

Augie understood women in a way no other man I'd ever been with had. He'd understood the assignment without me even knowing there was one. I'd come with him multiple times now because he instinctively got how I thought, what I needed, and how that wasn't just a quick pump of a barely-there dick.

Augie took so much time with me it was almost maddening.

Even now, with his dick so hard, he could have just bent me over and taken me from behind. Yet he moved at a pace that made it clear this was the only place he wanted to be.

"Anything else?" He lowered his hands to my hips, dragging down the lace panties so I was as naked as he was. His palms groped my ass cheeks, kneading and massaging.

He bent his knees a little to press his dick between my thighs, stroking it back and forth through my arousal.

My gaze kept catching on the bejeweled ass plug. It wasn't big, and my memory was set on the way he'd touched me there before and how much I'd liked it. I wanted more.

I picked it up, turning it over in my hand.

"You done much of that?" Augie asked, his dick moving back to press against my asshole.

I gasped, liking the feel of how wet and warm he was.

But he was also freaking huge.

"Some," I admitted. "Never with someone as big as you though." I cringed in the mirror. "Sorry."

He bit down on my shoulder. "Don't apologize. You're a bad bitch, remember? Bad bitches don't apologize for needing prep work." He grinned at me in the mirror. "They demand it, Lia." He covered my hand again and steered it to a set of anal beads.

"I've never tried those," I admitted.

He let out a laugh. "You don't know what you're missing then. Can I?"

There was zero part of me that wanted to say no to this man. I was curious by his words, though. "Have you?"

"Yes."

"Fuck," I whispered. "That's so hot."

He laughed, picking up the beads and a tube of lubricant. "But this isn't about my ass. It's about yours, sweetheart. Your sweet, perfectly fuckable ass." He dipped a lubed-up bead between my cheeks, rubbing it slowly over my ass.

It was cold, and I jumped, but then he adjusted his position so he was slightly more to my side. One hand slid over my mound and found my clit, while the other played around with my ass.

"Take that clamp off. I want your tit in my mouth while I do this."

While I loved the feel of the clamps on, I also liked the tingle I got when they were released. And a moment later, Augie's hot, wet mouth covered one nipple, drawing it in, sucking on it hard.

It was such a different feeling to the clamp, one that only intensified the pleasure I'd found in wearing it. I took the other off, choosing to roll and tweak myself, needing that extra stimulation to match what he was doing with his mouth and hands.

My nipples sent pleasure right through my entire body, and I hummed with the need building inside me.

"Just the smallest one, Lia."

He waited for my nod and then pushed the first bead inside me, adding a new sensation. I closed my eyes, but he stroked my clit harder, until the insides of my thighs were coated in my juices.

"More," I begged, not knowing exactly what I needed more of, only that whatever he was doing felt good and I didn't want it to stop.

He switched things up, moving in behind me again, leaning me forward just a little so he had better access. His fingers thrust into my pussy, stretching me perfectly and rubbing against my internal walls, increasing the friction on the bead. In and out he worked me up, until I was easily taking three of his fingers and grinding back on him with abandon. I palmed my tits, squeezing my nipples, helping him push me toward the orgasm building deep inside me.

"More," I begged him again.

He gave me another bead, moving each one in and out a couple of times, stimulating my ass. Each bead was progressively bigger until I was panting with the need to come. The final ball was the biggest of them all, nowhere near his dick size, but big nonetheless.

"Tell me to stop," he groaned, testing my hole with the final one. "Tell me you don't want it."

"I want it," I swore. "I can take it. Please."

His hand groped my cheek, squeezing me there in approval. "I want to be fucking you when you take it, Lia."

I nodded so fast my head nearly fell off. I'd wanted this for weeks, been dreaming of riding his dick, sinking down deep, screaming his name. I hadn't picked this happening for the first time in a sex club, but hadn't this been exactly what I'd hoped for when we'd said we were coming here tonight?

Actually, this was so much more. Everything I did with him had been.

He hadn't even fucked me, and yet I was sure he'd already ruined me for any other man.

A crinkle of a condom wrapper came from behind me, and I practically mewled with impatience, desperate to fill the ache in my pussy that had been waiting for him ever since I'd first met him.

"Hurry," I moaned at him, pushing my ass back toward him.

He pulled my chin around and took my mouth, kissing me hard and deep. A kiss that spoke of experience and one that promised dirty, sinful things I was desperate for him to serve up. But like with everything else, Augie wouldn't be hurried. While I whined like a cat in heat for his cock, needing to be fucked hard and fast, Augie only gave me slow and steady.

He edged inside me, sliding in deep, angling himself so my orgasm came up so quick it took even me by surprise.

I cried out, coming hard around his cock, my internal

walls squeezing him and the beads. It only got better as he moved each one out then back in at varying speeds, using them at the entrance of my ass and then deeper to prolong the orgasm. It sent my eyes rolling back.

"I didn't..."

I didn't even know what I was trying to say. I didn't know I was going to come? I didn't know anal could feel like this? I didn't know how much a man who knew what he was doing would make a difference to how much I enjoyed sex?

I'd thought men didn't do it for me.

But this one...

This one *so* did.

"Stop being in such a rush to get to the finish line, Lia. I'm not even close to done with you."

I gasped when he pulled out and thrust back in, fucking me deep, getting me back to where I was so much quicker than he had the first two times. It was like my body knew now, and maybe even expected this man to deliver up multiple orgasms.

I tingled everywhere. My pussy. My nipples. My thighs and fingers. I let him slowly build steam, his fingers tight at the sides of my hips, holding me in place, watching me in the mirror so carefully it was like I was a work of art he couldn't stop staring at.

My mouth. My tits. My widespread legs and his hands on my skin. His roving gaze took it all in, his expression intent.

When Augie fucked you, he savored every inch, every moment. There was no other way to describe it.

"Take the last bead, Lia. Tell me you want it."

"Yes," I practically shouted, excitement coursing

through me. I ground back against him, another orgasm swelling inside me, one so powerful I was sure it would consume me if he didn't set it free. Pressure and pleasure all combined together, hitting every nerve ending between my pussy and the lubed-up ball in his fingers.

"Augie, please!" I shouted in frustration, needing him to fuck me hard and fuck me fast, bead inside me, my fingers alternating between my clit and my nipples. "Oh God. I need to come!"

Like he knew exactly what I was thinking, he drove into me faster, taking my body to a limit I didn't know existed. He gave me every inch of his cock, and every bead on the chain, all of it working together to push me to a high I would have never been able to reach alone.

"Come with me, Lia."

I already was, there was no holding it back. The orgasm exploded through my body, sending me down over the table when my legs wouldn't hold my weight. But Augie didn't ease up. Gone was the gentle, sensual screw from earlier, and in its place was the fast, hard fuck I'd been craving so bad.

My screams of ecstasy mingled with his groans, and there were noises outside our door, ones of excitement and need that made me think people out there were getting off just listening to what we were doing.

If only they could see it.

I could never fuck him in a peephole room.

Because he was the hottest man I'd ever seen both in and out of a bedroom.

And if he kept fucking me like this, around telling me his deepest, darkest secrets, I might find myself doing the same.

My secrets were so much darker than anything Augie had revealed.

He thought he was the messed-up kid from the Saint View gutter.

But I was the woman who'd taken over a hundred lives and hadn't felt guilt over any of them.

25

—————

OPHELIA

he party was in full swing by the time Augie and I emerged from our little sex den. A quick look at my phone told me the hours had flown by, and I was almost nervous the place might have emptied out by one in the morning.

It was quite the opposite.

There were nearly double the amount of people in the room than when we'd been out here earlier, Augie making me come with his fingers. A man looked me up and down, gaze lingering on my dark, probably swollen nipples.

"Pretty lady," he greeted with a wink.

Ew.

I opened my mouth to respond, but the low growl from behind me did all the talking required. The man took one glimpse of the possessive gleam in Augie's eye and hightailed it down the hallway toward the private rooms.

I looked over my shoulder at him. "You gonna growl

at every man who propositions me tonight? We're at a sex club. Your throat is going to get sore."

He tucked himself in tight behind me, palm grazing over my ass. "Not as sore as yours probably is from the way you sucked my cock in there."

I smiled to myself and at the memory of taking his dick so deep it had hit the back of my throat. "Not sore enough to not want to do it again."

He groaned, but we both knew I couldn't. It was getting late, and we'd come here for a reason.

"What does this Zane guy even look like?" Augie gazed around the club filled with men. "This is like searching for a needle in a haystack."

I didn't disagree, but we had such little information on Fawn and her whereabouts, I had to take any opportunity that came our way.

So yes, finding Zane here when I hadn't seen the man in years and only remembered him as a teenager wasn't going to be easy. But it had given me a night with Augie.

And it had taken my mind off the fact I was rapidly running out of days and excuses not to kill him.

"I searched for him online," I admitted, "but didn't get very far. He doesn't have a social media presence that I could find."

"Smart move if you're a piece of shit trafficking women," Augie muttered.

My heart sank. "Is that what you think they're doing?"

Augie shrugged. "I don't know. Maybe not. The fact she's Eddie's ex says maybe this is more personal for him. But I've heard rumors around town lately. Some hotshot businessmen went down for trafficking, so I know it's happening here."

My stomach turned to lead at the thought of my sister being sold to some creep who would just pump her full of drugs and use her until her body gave up.

I didn't want to think about the fact there was a very real possibility that Eddie, trafficker or not, was doing that to her right now.

While I had the time of my life, fucking one of her closest friends.

I looked away.

Augie reached out and took my chin, turning me back to face him. "What just happened? Where'd you go in your head just now?"

"We're awful people."

He squinted at me. "I'm no saint, but you're a sweetheart."

I choked on a laugh at how absurd that was. "You don't know me, Augie."

"I do."

I shook my head. "We fucked once. You made me come a couple of other times. But sex isn't intimacy. You know nothing about who I am or what I've done."

Embarrassingly, tears welled in my eyes. They were tears of frustration and anger more than anything else, but I hated them nonetheless.

"Tears are a sign of weakness," my mother's voice rang in my head. *"You never cry in front of a man, Ophelia. He will eat you alive if you just give away your weaknesses like that."*

I hated her voice. Hated that she was so often right and that I wore my weaknesses on my sleeve more than I should.

I couldn't cry in public. Not here.

Augie wouldn't let me turn away though.

So I took that anger inside me and spewed it all out onto him. "How do we even sleep at night, knowing that we're fucking behind Fawn's back?"

He blinked hard, recoiling. "Wait, what? That's what you're upset about? Fuck, Ophelia. Fawn and I weren't a couple."

"She had a crush on you. I heard the other women at your club say that."

"So what? The feelings weren't reciprocated. She never even told me, but if she had, I would have told her exactly what I'm reminding you of now. I'm ten years older than her. I'm all rough, sharp edges that would slice her to fucking pieces. I would have never gone there. She's like my little sister."

Everything he was saying was true. I'd only known him for a few weeks and yet I understood where he was coming from. It would be like me going after his brother. And while Banjo seemed like a nice kid, that's exactly what he was in my thirty-three-year-old mind.

A child.

I couldn't fault Augie for feeling the same way about Fawn. Fawn was a romantic at heart. She'd fallen in love so many times with boys who had just walked past her on the beach, only to find another infatuation by the time she'd washed off the sand. It was something that had always amused me because I was so the opposite.

He sighed. "What am I supposed to do, Lia? Pretend I don't want you just because of her crush?"

I sniffed and nodded once. "Maybe?"

I didn't sound convinced.

He took my arms, holding me so I couldn't look away. "I can't do that."

He stole my breath. He always fucking did. It was his eyes and the emotion in them that he reserved for me. I'd never seen him look at anyone else like that. With open honesty that showed who he really was on the inside.

He hadn't told Fawn about his childhood. The horrible things he'd seen. The horrific things he'd endured.

Only me.

My heart squeezed with a sudden rush of feelings that were too big to contain. My tongue burned with words it was too soon to say, and I bit down hard enough it hurt.

Out of the corner of my eye, a man caught my attention. I grabbed Augie's arm, digging my fingernails into his skin. "That's him."

He blinked. "What? Who? Eddie's brother?"

I nodded to the three men at a table in the corner. Much like Augie, they were dressed in jeans. Zane wore a white fitted shirt, half the buttons undone, his friends both shirtless. One had a woman on the floor, working his dick, but Zane and the third guy were both solo, watching performers in one of the cages.

"At least we aren't interrupting anything," I said through my teeth, storming in that direction, Augie close behind me. "If he was sitting over there getting his dick sucked this would have been a whole lot of awkward."

It was only his friend's gaze slow rolling over my body as we approached that reminded me I was wearing next to nothing.

Whatever. It didn't matter if he knew where Fawn was.

Zane finally glanced over when I stopped a few inches from him. He shook his head. "Not interested," he said and turned back to the entertainment.

I leaned down, making sure I was still a few inches higher than he was, so I had the appearance of having the upper hand. "Wasn't offering. Do you know who I am?"

His friend grinned. "Fucking hot, that's who you are. My friend here might be blind, but I am not. I'm definitely interested. Want to join this one here on your knees? I bet—"

Augie had him by the throat in a second. "Finish that sentence. I dare you."

Zane and the other guy both flew to their friend's defense, launching across the armchairs at Augie. Their chairs scraped along the floor, and people around us scuttled out of the way. The woman on her knees squealed, crawling out of the way.

On instinct, my fingers closed into fists, ready to defend Augie.

A sharp whistle split the room, and a guy in a flannel shirt came storming over, hauling Zane back into his seat and yanking his friend's arm back in a painful hold.

I recognized him as Nash, one of my brother's partners, and stopped him before he could get to Augie. I gave him my most charming smile. "Hey, brother-in-law. Long time no see."

Nash took in my face and then my outfit and winced, slapping a hand over his eyes. "Oh, Jesus, Ophelia! What are you doing here? Christ, I did not need to see you dressed in that. I have to spend Christmases with you, dammit. I can't unwrap presents if I know you hang out in places like this."

I rolled my eyes. "You do realize *you* hang out in places like this? Worse. You own the joint, and frankly I'm a bit insulted I haven't been invited to a party here before now. It's a lot different than the last time I was here."

Nash was still steadfastly trying not to look at me.

I sighed. "Honestly, you're as dramatic as my brother."

"Does he even know you're here?" Nash asked. "Christ, he's going to stab me just for being near you in your underwear. He'll actually put a knife into my intestines and leave me to bleed out. Do you want my shirt?"

I would have laughed at his horror, or perhaps told him I was just as capable as Vincent if I wanted a man gutted, but I had things to do. "No, but I need you to lay off Augie. He's with me."

Nash shot Augie a dirty look but softened a little at my request. "Tell him to keep his hands off my customers and I'll let it slide."

Augie backed up, his hands in the air in mock surrender. But that didn't stop him from staring down Zane's friend, who was rubbing his neck like someone had just tied a noose around it. "Fine. But if I told you what he just said about your sister-in-law..."

Nash's eyes darkened.

I shoved him away, exasperated. "Okay, that's enough with the protective bullshit from both of you, thank you very much. I just need a minute with these gentlemen."

I sat myself next to the man who had grown up a whole lot since I'd last seen him.

"You're Fawn's sister, aren't you?" Zane asked quietly. "We met once, when she was dating..."

"Your piece-of-shit brother. Yeah. We did. How about you tell me where he has her?"

One of his friends, the one with the apparently bruised throat from Augie's fingers, snorted. "Eddie ain't been around here for a long time," he drawled. "Word on the street is he owes big money so he's gone to ground."

I raised a questioning eyebrow at Zane, who darted a nervous look at his friends.

I noticed and got in his face. "Don't look at them. Look at me. I asked you a question. That true? Your brother not been around lately?"

"Eddie does what he pleases. Always has. I don't know anything."

Augie was almost vibrating with anger behind me. It was probably a good thing Nash was still hovering, because Augie this tightly wound wasn't a good thing. He was a loose cannon, likely to explode, and my sister and her whereabouts was definitely one of his triggers.

"See, here's the thing, Zane," I mused out loud. "I don't believe you. You seem nervous."

He swallowed hard and opened his mouth to answer, but his friend cut him off.

"He just can't talk to pretty women. It's you making him stutter."

Augie's low growl was a warning that the man was skirting the danger zone, and he turned away quickly. The third friend didn't seem to care though. He stared openly at me until something changed in his expression.

He pointed a finger at me. "Oh shit, I know you. You're Riddick's girl."

My blood ran cold.

Augie and Nash both turned to me, but it was Augie who asked, "Who the fuck is Riddick?"

Mission. Over.

"No one. I don't know anyone by that name." I grabbed Augie's arm, hauling him backward. "Come on. This is a waste of time. They don't know anything."

Nash watched me quietly, a concerned expression on his face when Zane's friend stood and pointed at me again.

"Yeah, it is you! He's been flashing around photos of you all over town. Damn. He know you're out here at a sex club with another man?" He let out a low whistle and shook his head at Augie. "You're brave, brother."

Augie's brows furrowed in confusion. "What is he talking about, Lia?"

But I couldn't speak. I needed to get Augie out of there before Zane and his friends could memorize his face.

I had no doubt Riddick would compensate them handsomely if they were smart enough to report back to him. Men like them, they were driven by money and greed and position and power.

There was no doubt in my mind they'd be spilling every detail to the one person I wished would just forget I existed.

Behind me, Nash shoved one of them back onto the couch. "Shut your mouth. She said she doesn't know the guy. You've got the wrong woman."

I appreciated my brother-in-law backing me up, and I could practically feel his concern following me out of the club. We grabbed our coats, and I shrugged mine on, hastily tying it at my waist.

Augie followed silently; his questions unspoken in the tension surrounding us.

I knew I owed him answers. Nobody was falling for my, "I don't know Riddick" act.

Not those guys inside. Not Augie.

Shit.

Scythe looked up when I shoved my way out of the club doors. He cocked his head to one side, taking in my expression.

In an instant, his fingers moved to the small of his back where I knew he always had a knife. One of probably three or four he carried religiously. I grabbed his hand before he could reach it and squeezed it.

"I'm fine. But we need to leave."

"Just tell me who I need to kill, Ophelia. You know I'll take care of it," he called after me.

I spun around and glared at him. There was nobody else out there in the empty parking lot, just me and Augie and my psychopathic brother, who hadn't at all sounded like he was joking when he'd made that threat.

Because he wasn't.

"He's joking," I assured Augie as we reached my car.

Augie glanced back over his shoulder at Scythe. "Didn't sound like it. You want to tell me what the hell just happened in there?"

My brain raced, trying to come up with a lie.

Because admitting to a man, even one as rough around the edges as Augie, that my family killed for a living was impossible. Augie might have been from the wrong side of the tracks. He might have seen things he shouldn't have.

But the man wasn't a killer.

His rough exterior hid how gentle he really was. There was no denying that. When he'd held Luna on his lap for hours at that hospital, soothing her with low words and comforting touches, that was all I'd been able to think about.

He was good inside.

I was anything but.

I opened my mouth, hating that I was going to have to lie to him but seeing no other way out.

"Ophelia!"

My head snapped up at my name shouted from the doorway.

Zane jogged across the parking lot toward me.

Scythe stood behind him, miming a stabbing motion then turning both palms skyward. His "Do I kill this one?" question silent but clear.

I shook my head hard.

Unsurprisingly, Scythe leaned back on the wall and crossed his arms over his chest, his disappointment clear.

Christ. Someone needed to let that man kill someone. He seemed to be desperate for any excuse. Was that how I'd feel if I removed myself from the game the way he had?

A couple of weeks ago I'd been sure I would. Sure I couldn't stop killing even if I wanted to.

But something about the sweetness inside Augie made me want to try. Want to be more like him.

He'd probably find it hilarious if I told him. He

couldn't see the good in himself. Only his mistakes and the people he'd hurt.

He wasn't the man he thought he was.

My heart squeezed at the thought of losing him when he realized who I truly was.

Because I would.

There was no possibility where I told him the truth and he let it slide.

Regular people didn't just accept killers.

Your brother's partners did, my brain argued.

But a second later, my mother's voice in my head fired back with the pure, honest truth.

Vincent was lovable. Scythe was special.

I wasn't either of those things.

Augie wasn't in love with me. I wasn't going to spill my secrets while he took me into his arms the way I wanted.

"Ophelia, wait," the man making his way across the parking lot said through heavy breaths from the exertion of running.

I snapped my attention back to Zane, giving myself a mental shake for being so fucking stupid and getting distracted. Zane could have pulled a gun or a knife, and that temporary distraction could have cost me my life.

Or Augie his.

My stomach swirled at the thought.

Jesus, what the fuck was I going to do? Riddick would kill Augie if he found out we were together at a strip club. If I didn't kill Augie, Riddick would take over my job and do it anyway. That fire at Willa's very well could have been him trying.

I wanted to get in the car with Augie and drive until I

didn't know the way back.

But I couldn't do that either because Zane's fucking brother had Fawn.

"What, Zane?" I snapped. "You're fucking useless to me if you know nothing about my sister."

He glanced over his shoulder and cringed at his friends leaving the club. They both stared at him intently.

He turned back to me. "Give me your phone."

"What? Why? You mug people now? I'm not giving you my phone."

Augie resembled a pit bull ready to attack, emerging from the interior of the car.

Zane stopped him with one sentence. "If you want to know anything about Fawn, then one of you give me a damn phone subtly enough they don't see."

I glanced at Augie, but I was already taking out my phone and handing it over.

Zane tapped his fingers across the screen. "They think I'm delivering a warning, so look fucking scared or something, would you?"

"Not exactly in my wheelhouse," I told him, dragging my defenses back up after a night of letting them down.

Zane raised an eyebrow. "You seemed pretty fucking scared when Sim mentioned Riddick. Channel that."

My mouth went dry, the fear sucking away any moisture instantly.

There was the shortest, tiniest electronic beep from Zane's pocket before he handed back the phone. "I called my phone from yours, so I have your number. I'll call you when I can."

"Wait," I hissed as he tried to walk away. I grabbed his arm. "What do you know?"

He lowered both his head and his voice. "Eddie is my Riddick."

I instantly let go of him, that fear at just the sound of Riddick's name echoing around my chest. An understanding passed between us. Zane's eyes burned in the darkness as he turned away and went back to his friends.

I finally slid into my car, clutching the steering wheel.

Augie and I both stared dead ahead at the men leaving the parking lot. Zane cast one final look over his shoulder at me, and his words echoed in my head.

Eddie is my Riddick.

He was scared of his brother.

Or maybe scared of what he'd do.

"Do we follow them?" Augie asked, leaning forward, fingers pressed to the dashboard. "They have to know where Eddie is, don't they?"

My heart squeezed at the hope in his eyes.

If Fawn was alive and well, Zane could have said that.

If she was dead, he would have just said that too.

I feared she was something in between.

And that still being alive might be worse than if he'd just killed her quickly.

I couldn't stand the glimmer of hope in Augie's eyes. I didn't want to jeopardize the only lead we had on Fawn.

"We wait for him to call," I said quietly.

Augie stared at me in disbelief. "If he doesn't?"

But Zane had gone out of his way to get my number. He'd risked the suspicion of his friends, which would no doubt be reported back to his evil fucking brother.

He wanted to help.

I let out a long breath and prayed I was making the right call. "He will."

26

AUGIE

The hospital reeked of antiseptic washes and misery. I held my breath and made my way along the corridors of the burn unit, trying my best not to look inside any windows, giving the patients the privacy the poor assholes deserved.

There was no happiness here. Only pain and suffering, and that feeling rode me hard while I searched for room eleven and knocked on the door.

A nurse poked her head out from the other side. "Yes?"

I cleared my throat, my fingers clammy with sweat. "I'm here to see Willa McCaffery. I was told this is her room."

The nurse frowned. "It is, but she's only allowed family—"

"Let him in, Penelope," Willa called with a croak in her voice I'd never heard before. "Can't you see he is family?"

I wanted to fucking cry, hearing her say that.

Penelope rolled her eyes and opened the door wider. "Honestly, if you were any other patient, we'd all be bitching about you in the staff room and you know it. You've had more visitors than the rest of the patients combined."

Willa chuckled as I entered. "They're my friends," she told me. "So you'd think they'd be a little more worried about my welfare, wouldn't you? Instead, all they give me is endless sass. Once I get back on the ward, they're all getting the night shift as punishment."

Penelope leaned on the doorway. "Just keep it down, would you? Your room is party central half the time, and the other patients are complaining about special treatment." But her complaints were half-assed, and it was clear she loved and was as worried about Willa as the rest of us.

Penelope turned to me. "Make sure she uses that pain relief. She can press the button every few minutes, but she's stubborn."

Willa lifted one hand weakly and shooed her friend out the door, which she closed quietly behind her.

I sank down into a chair at Willa's side, and my heart nearly broke in two, taking in how much of her body was wrapped in bandages. They covered her arms completely, and there were others peeking out of the neckline of her hospital gown. One side of her face was bandaged, the strips taped to shaved parts of her skull.

Willa tutted beneath her breath. "Don't gawk at me like that, Augie Mitchell. I'm just fine."

She wasn't.

"I should have got there earlier," I muttered. "I took too long."

She lifted one hand weakly like she wanted to swat at me but then she winced and placed it gingerly back down on the bed. Even still, her eyes burned into mine. "Rubbish. You got there exactly when you were supposed to. I'm really glad you came. I wanted to say thank you for what you did for Luna."

I shook my head. "You don't need to thank me for that."

"I do. You didn't have to run into that house for her. A lot of people wouldn't have."

I didn't feel right taking praise for something that hadn't been a choice. When Willa had said Luna was still inside, there was no question of would I run in or not.

I just did.

A knock came from the door, and Willa and I both glanced in that direction as it swung open.

Colt poked his head around the corner, his gaze searching for his mom and then landing on me.

Not all that long ago, every time Colt had looked in my direction, his gaze had been cold at best. Fiery with hate at worst. I couldn't blame him. He loved Lacey and my brother, and after what I'd done to them, I'd never blamed him for hating me.

There was none of that in his eyes now though. In fact, he gave me a half-smile. "Well, I guess this is good timing."

I didn't know what that meant, but he opened the door wider, revealing the rest of his family all crowded into the doorway.

Luna's eyes lit up when she noticed me sitting there, and her little-girl voice filled the room. "Uncle Augie!"

To my surprise, she broke away from her parents,

running across the room in pink boots with soles that lit up with every step. She threw herself at me, and I caught her with a soft laugh.

"Uh. Hi. How are you, squirt?"

She scrambled up into my lap and sat cross-legged like a tiny genie, peering up at me with big dark eyes. "Good! I went to school today and I told all my friends about how you saved me from being burned alive!"

I blanched at her choice of words, a jolt of fear that felt all too familiar reminding me both of us very nearly had.

Colt, Lacey, Banjo, and Rafe followed their daughter in. I expected one of them to pluck her from my lap, but they didn't.

Colt just ruffled her hair and smiled at her affectionately. "She's been terrorizing all the kids with stories of flames that eat ceilings and smoke that swirled like demons, haven't you, kiddo?"

I swallowed thickly, understanding exactly why she'd described it like that.

When she stared at me, she was searching for understanding. Validation. Someone who had experienced what she had.

"But we slayed those demons, didn't we, squirt? Luna and Uncle Augie ran through the building, jumping down stairs, spinning and turning, ducking and weaving, fighting our way through the flames, until poof! They were all gone!"

Luna nodded, bouncing excitedly on my legs. "And then we went in the ambulance." She turned to her mom. "They put the sirens on real loud, too!"

Lacey smiled fondly at her daughter. "I know, honey.

You told me. Pretty cool thing for you and Uncle Augie to experience, wasn't it?"

Luna nodded, her eyes shining with excitement, before she lost interest in me and scrambled down to go interrogate Willa about her injuries.

Banjo touched my shoulder. "Can I talk to you for a minute? Outside?"

I nodded quickly and stood, following Banjo out into the corridor. It was quiet out there, and the soft hum of nurses talking floated back from their station, but we weren't close enough to make out individual words. The hallways were otherwise quiet since it was outside of visiting hours and friends and relatives wouldn't be allowed in for another thirty minutes.

I closed the door to Willa's room behind us and mirrored Banjo's position, leaning on the wall opposite.

Nothing much had changed with him since he'd lived with me three years ago. His nose was still covered in freckles from the sun and too many days sitting out on a board in the ocean with me. I probably should have made him wear sunscreen more. His hair was shorter than it used to be but still long enough to flop into his eyes.

We were near identical heights, and though he'd always been a slimmer build than me when we'd lived together, age and three years of college football had filled him out.

He was no longer the boy I'd pulled from foster care. He was a man with a family who adored him and who he loved more than life itself. He scrubbed a hand over his eyes, suddenly looking so much older than his twenty-one years. "The firefighters told us she would have died in that fire if it hadn't been for you. They said by the time they got there, that top bedroom was fully alight."

I didn't know what to say.

Banjo didn't seem to need a reply. His eyes filled with a pain I'd never wanted to see in his face.

"I could have lost her, Aug."

Like he'd been holding it together way too long, his face crumpled and his head dropped.

I didn't know what to do. Banjo's shoulders shook with the grief and fear of where he might be right now if I hadn't been there that night. All I could do was what I'd done when he was a boy and he'd woken up screaming from a night terror.

I put my arms around him and pulled him in tight.

I waited for it. For him to shove me away.

But he didn't.

Without shame, he broke down.

Without judgment, I let him.

Eventually, he shifted back, wiping his eyes with the back of his hand and shaking his head, his cheeks pinking. "Go on, call me a fucking pansy for crying like a baby."

I shook my head. "I wouldn't do that. She's your daughter, Banjo."

He bit his lip and nodded, his eyes red. He sniffed and then nodded toward Willa's door. "All Luna has done since it happened is talk about you. Uncle Augie this, Uncle Augie that. It got so bad one day that we took her out and bought her the biggest ice cream sundae we could find just so we could have a break for a few minutes."

I couldn't help but smile. Fuck, that made my heart happy. "She's a great kid."

Pride took place of the fear and grief in Banjo's expression. "She is. And I'm glad we ran into you because I was going to call you anyway."

I blinked in surprise. "You were?"

He nodded. "I was wondering if you might want to come over for dinner on Sunday? I know it would mean a lot to Luna."

I swallowed hard. "Really? I don't want to make anyone uncomfortable..."

Banjo shook his head. "We all talked about it, and we all want you to come. Willa has been on us for years to sort our shit out, but..."

"You weren't ready."

His eyes held every truth. "You really fucking messed me up, Augie."

Guilt rushed in, even though I knew that wasn't his intention. "I know."

He just looked at me. Waiting for an answer.

I gave him a single nod. "I'd really love to come to dinner."

27

OPHELIA

aked in Augie's bed was turning out to be my favorite place to be. And not even only because of the wicked things he did to me there.

His shitty little house in the middle of Saint View had become some sort of safety zone in my head. Every time I went there I had to check to be sure I wasn't being followed, but when the coast was clear and I got to sneak in through his back door, everything felt good and right.

Until my phone buzzed, like it was doing right now.

Augie lifted his head from between my thighs and huffed out a sigh. "Can you please just deal with whoever is blowing up your phone? It's been going off for the past thirty minutes, and I cannot do my best work under these circumstances."

I pushed his head back down to where I liked it best. "I disagree. Do that thing with your tongue again and I'll deal with my phone."

He did as I requested, not asking me who was texting me.

He was good like that. He'd let the Riddick thing drop when I'd told him he was a colleague and a family friend. I had a feeling he knew there was a lot more to the story, but Augie wasn't one to pry.

Maybe because he didn't want people nosing their way around his secrets either.

Guilt plagued me though. He might have had his walls up with everyone else, but in here, Augie had spilled his truth. He'd told me all about the problems he'd created with his brother, his time in foster care, and what he remembered of his parents.

While I'd shared...exactly nothing.

"Harder," I urged Augie, wanting to bury the guilt inside me with an orgasm.

But my phone buzzed again, and Augie's annoyance was clear in his huff, even if he didn't say anything.

Fact was, my mother wasn't going away.

I twisted and grabbed my phone from the nightstand, opening her messages.

They poured in thick and fast.

MOM

Ophelia, where the hell are the proof-of-kill photos?

MOM

I need to get those posted.

MOM

Did the file upload fail or something?

MOM

You have actually done the job, haven't you?

MOM

> Oh my God, please tell me you have.
> Christ, if I have to admit to Riddick that
> you couldn't even get a job as simple as
> this one done, then I will die of
> embarrassment.

MOM

> Ophelia, honestly, this is a job your brother
> could have handled in an afternoon, and
> you've had weeks. I don't know why I
> expected more of you though. You have
> always been one endless disappointment
> after another. All my children are. I don't
> know what I did wrong. Cora and Gordon
> have Jezabel and Riddick so well trained.
> They are the perfect children. Yet here I am,
> with one daughter too weak for her own
> good, a son who is a pussy-whipped fool,
> and you, my eldest, too damn useless to
> get a single job done. What did I do wrong?

I ground my molars, reading that last sentence. "Narcissistic bitch," I muttered, my entire body tensing up with anger and resentment at the nagging feeling there was some truth to her words.

Augie rose from between my thighs and scowled at me. Without asking, he plucked the phone from my hands and hit the power button. "Changed my mind. We're just going to switch this off and pretend it doesn't exist, because you're suddenly so tense it's like going down on a stone."

"Sorry," I said unhappily, letting him turn the phone off and toss it across the room. "It's my mother. She makes me crazy."

He crawled up my body and laid himself out next to me, twisting onto his side and propping his head up with one hand. "Mothers are the worst."

I nodded in agreement. "The absolute worst."

He watched me carefully, then blew out a long, stuttering breath. "Hey, I was wondering something…"

I waited for him to say whatever was on his mind.

His gaze darted around anxiously, unable to fully rest on my face.

I poked him in the chest. "Are you nervous right now?"

"Yes, actually."

"Why? You gonna ask me to marry you? You got a ring hidden in these sheets somewhere?"

His mouth pulled up in a half-grin. "No. But I did want to ask if you wanted to come to a dinner with me."

I hesitated, knowing it would be dangerous to be seen with him in public.

He noticed and flopped onto his back. "Forget it. It was stupid of me to ask. I'll just go alone."

I hated the rejection in his expression and that it was me who'd put it there. I couldn't take it.

Plus, I wanted to go with him.

I always wanted to be with him lately.

He was all I could freaking think about.

I straddled him, digging my knees into the mattress either side, and hovering over his hips. "No, tell me. Where's the dinner? I want to come."

His eyes lit up like a little kid on Christmas morning. "Really?" Then he cleared his throat, trying to play it cool. "I mean, okay, awesome. That would be great."

I laughed at his poor job of being chill, and he

grinned, too, happily flipping us over so I was on my back and he was between my widespread thighs.

"It's just at my brother's house. Nothing fancy, I don't think. Though they do live in a big Providence mansion..." His eyes suddenly took on a look of despair. "Shit, do you think I need to get dressed up? I don't own a suit or anything like that."

I was still stuck on him inviting me to his brother's house. "This is a family dinner?"

He stopped his freak out and gazed down at me. "Yeah."

My head spun. "Just to be clear, you want to take me home to officially meet your family?"

He cocked his head to one side. "Well, yeah. If you want to? I mean, I know we aren't anything..."

I hated hearing him say that.

Every cell in my body revolted at the very idea of not being his.

Augie shook his head, irritation in his expression. "You know what? No. Fuck that." He took my hands, linked our fingers together, and slid them up the bed. "I don't know about you, but to me, we are something."

His face was fierce, angry almost, like he was daring me to argue with him.

All I wanted to do was kiss him.

I strained up, putting my lips to his.

He pulled back, staring down at me, out of reach.

"Don't kiss me to shut me up. I'm saying this whether you want to hear it or not." His expression softened. "I like you, Lia. I like having you in this bed and at my club and on my cock and in my shower. I want more than this though. I want to take you out. Show you off."

I couldn't help but grin at him, a slow warmth rolling through my body in a delicious way that had nothing to do with the fact his dick was rubbing over my clit and everything to do with his words. They were clumsy and unpracticed. As rough around the edges as he was.

They were everything I loved about him.

The thought stopped me dead.

But my heart wouldn't be denied.

"I like you too," I whispered back, the word 'like' so incredibly underwhelming to the way I actually felt. "I want to meet your family. Properly. At a dinner. Not just in a hospital hallway."

The smile he gave me was so magnificent, it damn near broke my heart in two.

Because in that moment, even though he hadn't said as such, it felt a whole lot like Augie was giving me his heart.

And I already knew I would be the one to break it.

28

ZANE

In the darkness of my bedroom, cold water hit me in the face, shock stealing my breath before I even had a chance to open my eyes.

But when I did, I wished I hadn't.

"Wakey, wakey, little brother. Time to rise and shine and tell me all about the fucking colossal mess you've made for me."

I swore beneath my breath, wiping the water off my face with the back of my hand. "Fuck off, Eddie. I didn't do shit."

My brother put his hands behind his back and paced the length of my room like he was some sort of aristocrat.

He was anything but. With his huge arms covered in tats, both of the professional and prison variety, Eddie had the appearance of a body builder. All thick biceps and chest and thighs.

But his face was ratlike. Cunning. Sharp.

He missed nothing.

"Get out of bed, Zane."

I desperately wished I could tell him to go to hell. But I didn't dare, even now. Getting mouthy with him wouldn't end well. I'd learned that lesson a million times over, both as a kid and then a teen, and then eventually, as an adult.

What Eddie wanted, Eddie got. No matter what it took. If he told you to get out of bed, then you did as you were fucking told.

Or there'd be a price to pay.

One I would have paid a thousand times over.

Except it was never me he went after.

Eddie was smarter than that. He knew I could take a beating. Fuck, between him and our old man, I'd come back from more injuries than I could count. Concussions. Broken bones. Cuts so deep I'd had to take myself to the hospital for stitches.

Until Eddie had worked out hurting me didn't get him what he wanted.

That was when he'd started hurting Mom instead.

And that was something I just couldn't bear.

Bile rose in my stomach at every memory of him hurting her, his fists slamming into her cheek, bruises on her frail arms and legs from him punishing her because his attacks on me had stopped being effective.

I got out of bed and hastily threw on some clothes. Following Eddie to his car, I got into the passenger seat silently, hating him with every ounce of my being while he revved the engine obnoxiously.

My gaze flickered up to the worried, age-lined face in the window, watching us from around the curtain.

"Wave goodbye to Mommy, then," Eddie taunted.

"You know she's up there worrying about her golden boy."

His voice reeked of childish jealousy, which was just baffling, considering the way he'd treated her for the past few years. He raised his middle finger at her through the windshield, and the curtain quickly fell back in place.

We drove in silence, Eddie's anger seeping into the air around us, charging it with aggression that soaked into me.

Fuck him.

Fuck this whole shitty life.

I hated all of it. Every. Last. Bit. If it weren't for Mom, I would have packed my shit long ago and left.

But there was no chance of leaving her behind. Not knowing what Eddie would do to her when he realized I'd run. He'd made that clear on the one occasion I'd tried.

My mom had been in the hospital for a month after that.

I'd learned my lesson.

Eddie made the rules. The rest of us just followed.

"Where are we going?" I questioned.

He didn't answer.

We drove until we were well out of town, on unfamiliar roads I was sure I'd never been down. The woods grew thicker the farther we went, and the roads became steeper until we were curving around bends and taking dirt tracks up a mountain.

Nerves suddenly picked up in my belly. It had been years since Eddie had last tried to kill me. I realized I'd somehow become relaxed about the possibility. He didn't hurt me anymore, not when he knew the bigger pain came from hurting someone I loved. All he had to do was threaten Mom and I did whatever he told me. Even if I didn't like it.

My heart rate picked up, thumping against my chest too hard, sending a surge of adrenaline through my body. I looked down at my phone, but there was no cell reception.

Fuck.

Getting in this car with him had been a mistake.

I tensed every muscle, waiting for some indication that this was it. The place he'd finally kill me.

It would happen sooner or later. There was no doubt in my mind about that.

The day I died; it would be at his hands.

I swallowed down the fear as the narrow dirt road opened into a clearing and a house came into view. "Whose place is this?"

Two other cars were parked in front, and Eddie parked right at the steps, his car in prime position. "Get out."

There was no point refusing.

I opened the door and stepped out, legs protesting my weight after sitting for so long.

Inside, Sim and Roman sat on a wide, brown leather couch, both of them ending their conversation when Eddie and I entered.

"Sit." Eddie indicated to the armchair to Sim's left.

I ground my teeth, every part of me wanting to tell him I wasn't a dog and he wasn't my master.

Except we both knew that's exactly what we were.

I sat.

Eddie's gaze swiveled to Sim and Roman. "You want to tell my brother here what you told me?"

Sim, weasel that he was, had no problem tattling like he was in kindergarten. "We ran into your bitch's sister at Psychos. She's been sniffing around town, asking questions about Fawn. Zane had a conversation with her. One we couldn't hear…"

My fingers flexed into fists. I hadn't been under any illusions that Sim and Roman were my friends. They weren't. I'd only been with them at that club because Eddie had demanded it. Even he didn't trust the weasel twins alone. They were loyal to him right now, but he was smart enough to know they'd turn if someone else dangled a sweeter carrot in front of their ugly faces.

It was why he always sent us out in groups. Nobody was ever solo. There was always someone ready to stab you in the fucking back.

Eddie glared at me. "What did you tell her?"

"Nothing."

Eddie laughed, wandering closer to clap me on the shoulder. "You're so full of shit. You never could lie. Remember that time when we were kids, and I killed that neighborhood stray? Mom straightaway asked you if I did it. You threw me under the bus so fast it was like it was doing two hundred miles an hour. You always were such an unbrotherly cunt." He bent down, resting his hands on his thighs so we were eye height. "So how about you do me a solid for the first time in your life, golden boy, and tell me exactly what you told Fawn's sister?"

I stubbornly refused to say a word.

"He told her we took the bitch! I'm sure of it!"

My fingers itched to punch the weasel asshole right in

his fucking nose, but reacting was exactly what Eddie was looking for. A tell. A weakness. Any little thing he could use against me.

Jumping up to throttle the piece of shit next to me was all of those things combined.

So I sat, reining in my anger, staring at the monster I shared DNA with.

Eddie pursed his lips and let out a slow, barely tuneless whistle. "Time is ticking, Zaney boy. Tick. Tick. Tick."

But what was he going to do out here in the middle of nowhere? Mom was hours away back at home. Eddie was all about instant gratification. If he took this out on anyone, it was going to be me.

Good.

I was so fucking sick of being his punching bag.

I already knew the second I swung a fist at him, Roman and Sim would come to his defense, and it would be three against one.

I was past the point of caring. It would be a kindness at this point to just end me.

I was sure Eddie had killed Fawn Hanover. He'd taken her and her friend then spent days with them tied up in our basement before finally letting the friend go when the heat got too much.

But Fawn's cries for me to help her still rang in my damn ears every fucking night.

I'd tried.

But that was my entire life's story. I tried and tried, but it was never fucking good enough.

He always won.

Anger boiled over, spilling from my veins, bubbling

up my throat and out my mouth. I shoved to my feet, angrily going eye to eye with the brother who'd made my life a living hell. "So what if I did? So what if I told her you were the one who killed her sister? What is she going to do, Eddie? Go to the cops? You know I already tried that, and you have them all on your fucking payroll so shit just slides right off you like you're made of goddamn Teflon."

Eddie raised an eyebrow, his breath hot across my face because we were so damn close together. "Ooh, what do we have here?" he mocked. "Little Zaney finally standing up for himself?" His gaze narrowed, and he laughed bitterly. "You're such an arrogant fuck. You always were. You think you know everything, but you know absolutely nothing. Not a single fucking thing." He shoved me toward the hallway. "Walk."

"Fuck off."

For a big guy, Eddie moved fast, his fingers wrapping around my throat, the force behind them crushing my windpipe. I had no choice but to stumble backward, fingers gripped around my brother's wrists, desperately trying to pry him off my neck.

Sim kicked out one of my knees, and a howl of pain lodged itself in my chest, nowhere else to go.

Eddie's expression lit up at the violence, and Sim purred in the glow of Eddie's approval.

I stopped fighting. What was the point? This was my life, just one run-in with my brother after the other and living with the consequences in between.

I let myself go limp.

Let him choke the oxygen from lungs until darkness

flickered at the corners of my eyes and blood rushed in my ears.

Eddie kicked open a door at the end of the hall, and a second later, a bright light flooded my eyes.

He let go of me.

Pure, sweet oxygen rushed in, and I doubled over, sucking in the deepest breaths I could, replenishing the air in my starving lungs. I coughed and choked, my throat burning, eyes watering.

A tiny noise came from the bottom of the basement stairs.

I wiped at my eyes with the back of my hand, my blood going cold at the thought of Eddie keeping some small defenseless animal down here.

The same way he'd done with that neighborhood cat before he'd finally put it out of his misery.

My vision cleared, my gaze locked on to dark-brown eyes, staring up at us in terror.

My heart squeezed so fucking hard I wished Eddie had killed me then and there.

"See?" Eddie practically fucking crowed. "You don't know shit, Zane. I've had her here this entire time and you had no idea."

Sim and Roman laughed behind me, like they'd been in on the secret, but all I could see was her.

Her hair was matted, blond on the ends but her dark, natural color at the top. Her clothes were barely more than rags, ripped and torn, still the same ones I remembered her wearing weeks ago when Eddie had first taken her. Weeks, or had the days turned into months? I couldn't even remember. Maybe it was longer than I'd thought because Fawn didn't seem well. She was gaunt, her cheeks hollowed out. She had her arms wrapped around herself, and she rocked back and forth, staring at us with what I could only describe as pure terror in her eyes.

"What have you done?" I said to Eddie, staring down at the woman who had once been so beautiful and vibrant my heart could barely stand it every time Eddie had laid a finger on her.

She still was beautiful, even beneath the dirt and the fear.

She still made my heart ache every time she glanced my way, even though she'd never seen me as anything other than her boyfriend's little brother.

Eddie looked past me to his goons behind me. "Get your cameras out, boys. You're going to want to film this. Zaney boy, being reunited with the woman he's spent his entire adult life jacking off over. Star-crossed lovers, these two!"

I stared at him in horror, and he laughed at my expression, slapping my cheek twice.

"What? You think I didn't hear you, tugging on your mushroom-sized dick, rubbing one out over my girl?"

I glared at him. "Fuck you, Eddie. I never did that."

That was the truth, but it had only been respect for her that had stopped me. Not because I didn't want her.

He wasn't wrong about that.

I'd wanted Fawn since I was fourteen fucking years old, and she'd walked in the door with my brother who was nearly twice her age.

"Get up here, peach," Eddie called.

His nickname for her had always made my skin crawl.

So slowly it looked painful, Fawn got to her feet, her

gaze glued to the floor. She limped from her hideout in the corner, across the room, reminding me so much of that wounded cat.

She took the steps, one at a time, each movement causing her to wince in pain.

"Are you okay?" I dared to whisper.

But it was clear she wasn't. It was clear she hadn't been for a really long time.

This entire situation was my fault.

When she'd disappeared from our basement, I'd assumed he'd killed her.

But now I realized that had been wishful thinking. I wasn't stupid enough to think he would have let her go, not after how long he'd spent searching for her.

So I'd convinced myself he'd killed her.

Because between that, and being Eddie's prisoner, death was certainly the better option.

A red haze dropped down over my eyes. I whirled on my brother, but he was quick to pin me to the wall with his meaty forearm, his gaze burning into mine.

He cocked his head to one side. "Do you understand yet, Zane, how actually stupid you are? How you know so little about the real world that it's embarrassing? You think because you turned twenty-one that you're some big man, but you have no idea. Now tell me what you told her sister. Every word so I can work out how to fucking fix it all."

For the first time since I'd entered the room, Fawn's gaze lit up with hope.

She gripped my hand, her fingers weak and cold, but her voice was strong. "Ophelia? You saw her? She's here?"

Eddie twisted her arm, wrenching it backward so

sharply Fawn let out a scream. He shoved her up against the railing, pushing her backward.

Her feet lifted off the floor, her hair dangling down, her one free arm reaching and scratching at Eddie, trying to get a hold on him to stop herself from falling backward and plunging to the solid concrete floor below.

I didn't think. Just acted on impulse, lunging for her.

My fingertips brushed her arm, just barely getting a touch before Eddie let her go.

Fawn fell over the edge of the railing, landing in a heap at the bottom, a tangled mess of arms and legs, blood, and dreams that ended the day she'd had the unfortunate luck of meeting him.

I stared at him in horror. "What have you done?"

He held a hand out toward Sim, who handed over the phone.

Eddie passed it back to me. "Send it."

I blinked, not understanding what he was saying.

He shoved the phone at me harder. "Send Ophelia fucking Hanover the video of her sister falling to her death."

I stared at him, the horror of what he was asking me to do too much.

"No." I couldn't do that to Fawn's sister.

"Do it or Mom can join her down there. The two of them rotting together. How does that sound?"

I stared at him with every ounce of disgust I could dredge up. "I hate you," I whispered. "One day, when I kill you, the world will be a better fucking place for it."

Eddie slung an arm around my shoulders, pulling me in as he added the video to a new message chat he'd started with the number I'd saved for Ophelia. He picked up my finger, forcing me to be the one to press 'send.'

He kissed my cheek, his lips as hard and chapped as he was. "You wouldn't have the balls, Zaney boy. You wouldn't fucking dare."

29
___

AUGIE

I didn't think I'd ever been as nervous as I was while holding Ophelia's hand, walking up the path to my brother's door. Sweat beaded on the back of my neck, despite the cold weather that should have had me shivering.

Lia squeezed my hand reassuringly. "Head up. Smile. You're okay."

But I wasn't. This felt like someone had offered me everything I'd ever wanted on a silver platter. I was either going to take it graciously, carry it carefully to a table, and place it down without a single thing going wrong.

Or I was going to flip the damn platter in the air and watch the entire thing rain down, each item smashing to pieces on the tiled floor.

The opportunity was there.

It was mine to ruin.

Which was exactly what I always did.

I held Lia's hand like she was a fucking life raft in a

stormy sea and forced my trembling finger to push the doorbell.

"You're a good man, Augie. The fact this means so much to you is proof you aren't the man you were the last time you were here. They'll see that if you let them."

Her words were soft and kind, and fuck, I so badly wanted to believe them.

The huge wooden door swung open, and Banjo stood on the other side, a white knitted sweater only accentuating the last of his summer tan. I did a quick check over my own outfit. Clean jeans, a button-down shirt with the sleeves rolled to my elbows because I couldn't handle how the little buttons made me feel like I was in handcuffs. And a black, smart casual jacket over the top.

Didn't seem terribly out of place with his outfit. At least there were no ties in sight. I was sure I would choke if I ever had to wear one.

Banjo stepped out of the way so Lia and I could come inside. Warmth hit me in the face pleasantly. There was no heating at my place, which only sucked for about one month of the year, since Saint View never got cold enough for snow. But the heat felt nice, and I shrugged out of my jacket.

Banjo took it, as well as Lia's coat, hanging them both in the closet to the right of the door, and then he grinned at me. "You good?"

I nodded. "Yeah. You?"

He laughed. "Yep." His gaze slid to Ophelia. "I'm Banjo. We never officially met." He stuck his hand out.

Ophelia took it, squeezing his fingers. "Ophelia. It's really nice to meet you outside of a hospital corridor. This house is amazing."

Banjo gestured around proudly. "It is pretty cool, isn't it? Still blows my mind that I get to live here and that my college tuition is all paid for."

I raised an eyebrow. "It is? But you didn't get a scholarship. I just assumed you had student loans…"

But that was probably a stupid assumption when you considered the house he lived in.

He shoved his hands in his pockets, almost guiltily. "Selina, Lacey's aunt, left me a college fund and a sum of money when she went to prison." He cringed, looking over at Ophelia. "I swear, that isn't actually as bad as it sounds. It's a long story and probably not one I should have been blabbing about during our first official hosting of family dinner."

Ophelia laughed, following Banjo through the rooms of the house. "It's fine. Every family has their skeletons, right?"

"I can't believe a Mitchell actually has money in the bank and will soon have a college degree," I said, a little in awe of my brother and the path his life had gone down. "I'm really happy for you, B."

I meant it. Every word. A few years ago, knowing this would have eaten me up inside with guilt and anger and jealousy. My head would have been full of questions about why money happened to other people but never to me.

But losing Banjo had changed something in my chemistry. Pulling Luna out of that house had cemented it.

All I actually needed was them.

As well as the woman whose fingers were threaded between mine. She and Banjo chatted so easily it was like they'd known each other for a lifetime, and later, when Luna ran down the stairs with a hairbrush and a bunch of clips, my heart nearly fucking beat out of my chest, watching Ophelia braid her hair and decorate it with the tiny butterflies.

Lacey and I were awkward, and I couldn't blame her for being standoffish. But when I offered to help with dinner, she agreed, pointing me toward the utensil drawer and then the saucepan of potatoes she'd already parboiled. We worked side by side in companionable silence, me mashing potatoes and watching the rest of her family while they went about various tasks. Rafe set the large dining room table, and Colt brought up a bottle of wine from the cellar.

When we all sat down, with Luna to my left and Ophelia on my right, I was sure no other moment in my life had ever felt this good.

Colt poured wine for all the adults, and Banjo found Luna some grape juice when she complained about her cup of water.

He kissed her chubby cheek before sitting down opposite her, his hand reaching for Lacey's leg beneath the table in the same way I had mine on Ophelia's.

"Well, we didn't cook all this food to just let it sit here and go to waste," Rafe announced. "Let's eat."

He leaned over, scooping some of the mashed potatoes onto Luna's plate, which she immediately stuck her finger in.

I chuckled and passed a bowl of peas to Ophelia when she requested them.

General chitchat flowed, without much input from me. Ophelia and Lacey got into a conversation about some new reality TV show they were both obsessed with, and Colt talked about his job at the prison and what was going on there.

I sat back and let it all wash over me.

It was the sort of family dinner I'd spent my teenage years dreaming of. There'd been so many nights where I'd gone to bed hungry, my foster parents not bothering to waste the money they got from the government on something as unimportant as feeding the kids in their care. With an empty stomach, I'd dreamed of giving Banjo a better life.

I hadn't succeeded.

But he had.

That was all that mattered.

It was hard not to remember the last time I'd sat at this table. It had been a Thanksgiving meal, and I'd come with one of my clients who had been a friend of Lacey's aunt.

That night had been the nail in the coffin for Banjo and me, and I hated that it was the elephant in the room now.

When Luna got sleepy and Colt carried her up to her bedroom, I knew I couldn't let the night pass without saying what I'd wanted to say for years.

I cleared my throat before I could chicken out, and everyone left at the table turned in my direction.

I wiped my sweaty palms on my pants. "I..." I coughed and tried again, this time focusing just on my sister-in-law.

She drew in a breath, like she knew what was coming and needed to steel herself for it.

"I'm sorry," I said to her quietly. "I know I owe you so

much more than just a shitty apology, but it's one I mean. I did some horrible things to you, and I know you don't have to forgive me. I'm grateful just to be here tonight, and if this is as far as it goes, then I understand. I wouldn't blame you at all. But I did want you to hear it. Because I do mean every word. Everything I did, I did it because I thought I was protecting him, or because I thought my way was his only chance at getting by." I swallowed hard. "Thank you for showing him and me, that there was...is...another way. That surviving isn't enough. That happiness trumps it all."

A tear welled in Lacey's eye and then dripped down her face. She opened her mouth to say something, but I was so scared of it being a rejection that I quickly focused on Banjo and everything I needed to say to him.

He just shook his head, cutting me off. "Stop torturing yourself. We know you're sorry."

"I need to say it."

"You've said it." He turned to Lacey with a questioning, raised eyebrow.

She nodded. There was a silent exchange between them, where neither needed to say a word but both clearly understood.

"We forgive you." Banjo's mouth turned up at the edges. "Can we go throw the football now?"

From the corner of my eye, Ophelia beamed, her fingers squeezing mine.

I couldn't believe his words. I shook my head, trying to remember all the apologies I'd practiced throughout the years, and yet none of them seemed enough. "Banjo, I..."

He just pointed at the football sitting by the back door.

God, it had been a long time since I'd thrown a football with my brother. "It's dark outside," I protested.

"Since when did that ever stop us?"

He was right. It never had. I grinned and followed him up from the table.

When he'd been a kid, there had been no money for cable TV or going to the movies or buying a PlayStation. To keep an energetic ten-year-old entertained, I'd spent hours out on our street, lit only by the one cracked lamp that worked, throwing balls at him while he ran to make touchdowns on a line we'd marked out in chalk a few houses down.

Often Colt and Rafe had joined us, me coaching all three of them, telling them off when they fucked up, cheering for them when they did good.

I hadn't even realized how much I'd missed it.

I paused at the back door and looked back at the mess. "We should clean up first."

But Lacey and Ophelia shooed us outside, Lacey with eyes that shined with unshed tears.

"I haven't seen Banjo this happy in ages. Go be brothers, Augie."

When I thanked her, it was the most heartfelt thank you I'd ever uttered in my life.

It was a thank you for her forgiveness.

A thank you for her taking care of my brother.

A thank you for giving him back to me, even though I would never deserve it.

The pigskin landed in my hands with a thump, and I raised an eyebrow at my little brother. "Nice." I tossed it back.

He caught it easily, cradling it to his chest. "College ball taught me some stuff."

"I hate that I never got to see you play."

Banjo sent the ball tornadoing through the night. "Still got a few games left after Christmas break, hopefully. Playoffs. Come to one of those."

"Let me know when and where and I'll be there."

He grinned, his white teeth shining in the moonlight. He'd turned on the outdoor lights, which were a lot better than the useless streetlamp we'd once thrown balls beneath. "Mom and Dad are coming to one on New Year's Day. Maybe you could come to that."

The ball fell at my feet. "What?"

Banjo cringed. "I'm guessing by the fact you just dropped that ball that the prospect of seeing Mom and Dad again doesn't fill you with excitement?"

"Mom and Dad? You mean the two assholes who abandoned us because having two kids in tow cramped their style?"

Banjo sighed, making his way over to a retaining wall that overlooked the sparkling blue pool.

I sat down heavily beside him. "I'm sorry. I shouldn't have said that. I had no idea you were back in contact with them."

He lifted a shoulder. "Mom reached out about a year ago. We've been taking it slow. She wanted to get to know Luna, and it seemed unfair to keep her away from her grandchild when she was trying to make amends."

I didn't believe that for a second. That she suddenly cared enough to be a grandparent when she'd been too damn selfish to be a mother. But then Banjo had always been a better man than me. He was kind and sweet. He'd proven tonight exactly how forgiving he was. It wasn't really much of a surprise that he was willing to forgive our parents when they'd come back into his life and started making demands.

He sighed. "You mad?"

I shook my head. "No. I get it. Just...I don't know, B. Just be careful."

"Mom's working at a café again. Dad is retired, but he's been making little wooden toys for Luna..."

"Isn't she a bit old for that?"

Banjo laughed. "Well, yes, she's much more into her Barbies at the moment. But it's nice of him to make an effort."

"It is. Shame he never did anything like that for us."

He side-eyed me. "People change as they get older. I think you can understand that."

He had a point. I'd never been able to say no to him when he used that hopeful face on me. I would have called it downright manipulative if Banjo had been capable of such a thing. But he wasn't.

"Fine. I'll come to the game they're going to."

"And you'll be nice?" he prompted with a laugh.

I frowned, but it was with the same good humor. "Don't push your luck."

He hid his smile by turning his face up to the night sky. "Glad to have you back, Aug. I fucking missed you."

I mirrored his position, so he didn't see the way my eyes suddenly got watery. "Me too."

The back door slid open, cutting through the quiet moment, and Lacey's voice rang out across the yard, "Augie!"

At the vague tone of panic in her voice, Banjo and I both stood.

"What's wrong?" he called out, already moving for the door. "Is it Luna?"

"No, she's fine." Lacey's gaze locked on mine. "Ophelia just got a text, and then she ran."

I shook my head in confusion. "What text? Ran where?"

Lacey wrung her hands as Banjo put his arm around her.

But her worried gaze stayed on me. "I don't know. But she's gone, Augie."

30

OPHELIA

Her scream.

Her fall.

Her body crumpled on the floor, limbs bent at wrong angles.

Blood.

I stumbled down the steps of the pretty Providence mansion, blindly groping for the car door handle and getting in behind the wheel.

My stomach churned, sick with the images that had played out silently on the little phone screen.

I couldn't breathe.

I slammed my foot down on the accelerator, the car lurching backward and spinning sideways, ripping up the perfectly manicured grass.

I would have to apologize to Lacey for ruining her lawn. For leaving without so much as saying goodbye.

Pushing the gearshift into drive, I got the car out onto the quiet Providence street, no idea where I was going, only knowing I needed to get out. Everything felt too small. The house. The street. The entire fucking town.

I put down the windows, letting the cold winter air blast the tears off my face. It did nothing for the aching burn in my chest and the constant loop my head played, showing me that video of my sister, over and over and over again, no matter how hard I tried to blink it away.

My mother's voice echoed in my head.

You didn't try hard enough.

You should have saved her.

You're the whole reason she's there in the first place. Wasn't it you she was trying to get away from when she left us?

I bit my lip, trying to fight the demons inside me, trying to argue back with logic.

But it was like a mouse trying to slay a dragon.

My mother's voice overruled everything else, and every word accused me of being the reason Fawn was dead in some basement.

In my rearview mirror, a set of headlights flashed.

I ignored them, barely able to keep myself on the twisting road that ran the length of both Providence and Saint View, the beach to one side and the bluffs rising ahead. Up there, high above this godforsaken town, maybe I could breathe again.

I just had to get there.

The car reared up behind me again, its lights too close to my bumper once more. "Fuck off!" I screamed into the emptiness of the car. But there was no anger in the cry, and it broke off in a desperate sob as another round of tears racked my body. I slammed my hand down on the steering wheel and cried. "Just leave me alone."

I couldn't stop. The tears came from some untapped

place inside me that had stored them up for weeks or maybe months.

Maybe even my entire life.

My mother had hit us every time she'd seen so much as a glimpse of weakness, and so I'd learned to hold back any sort of emotion that would set her off.

But now I couldn't stop. I gulped, trying to get myself under control, trying to pay attention to the danger warning going off inside me every time that car behind me got too close.

But my sister was dead.

And it was entirely my fault.

I'd done this. I was the one who'd gone to that club and stuck my nose where it didn't belong. That message had come from Zane's number. I'd pushed him, or Eddie, or both of them into doing this.

If I'd just stayed away. If I'd just never come home…

The road twisted and turned ahead of me, and the danger warning inside me increased from a squeak to a blaring siren.

My brother had once wrecked his car on this road.

And now there was someone behind me who seemed hell-bent on making me do the same.

The car's horn sounded, two short bleeps and then a long blare that cut through the roar of my engine and the sounds from the rough and windy sea below.

Oh, this guy was pissing me off.

I wasn't driving any faster. It was one lane each way, but fuck this guy, if he was so impatient, he could go around me on the wrong side.

I stuck my arm out the window and waved him on,

refusing to increase my speed on such a dangerous stretch of road.

The car pulled out, zooming up the left-hand side.

I stuck my middle finger up as he drew level with my vehicle.

Riddick stared back at me, his eyes dark as night, not a hint of a smile on his ugly face. He swerved the car an inch in my direction, herding me toward the guardrail that was the only thing separating me from the rocky cliff face and the ocean hundreds of feet below.

My tears dried up in an instant.

My heart slammed against my chest, but instead of creating panic inside me, it cleared my mind.

I slammed on the brakes.

Spun the wheel.

Planted my foot and took off back the way I'd come, thankful that my father, though good for little else, had at least taught me to drive well.

It would only take Riddick seconds to do the same, but those seconds were all I needed.

At the bottom of the bluffs, I took a side road. And then another. Cutting through the backwoods of Saint View that I'd learned well after the past few weeks of following Augie around. I pushed the car hard, and then harder, getting my foot as close to the floor as I dared. I spun around another corner, and then another, eyes alternating between the road ahead and the miles behind.

Searching for Riddick's headlights.

Listening for the roar of his engine, and his car closing in.

But there was nothing.

After twenty minutes of driving, burying myself in the heart of Saint View, I dared to pull over.

My breaths came in short, sharp pants, fear pulsing through my bloodstream.

I needed to get out of the car in case there was a tracking device. I retrieved my gun from the glove box, not needing to make sure it was loaded because it always was. I abandoned the car on the side of the road, taking off on foot through the darkness.

I shouldn't go there.

Everything inside me said I couldn't.

That I could be leading Riddick right to Augie's doorstep.

And yet I couldn't stop my feet from heading in that direction. From scurrying through the dark night with even deeper shadows. From turning down his street, and then his driveway, until I was standing on his doorstep, crying, desperate, and so fucking broken I was sure I would never be whole again.

I'd looked. I'd made sure he wasn't following me. I'd taken my ID and phone and a few other bits and pieces from my purse, but then dumped the rest while I'd been running. I'd checked everything still with me for trackers, as well as my clothes and my shoes.

Riddick knew nothing.

I was safe here.

I banged my fist against the broken screen door, rattling it on its hinges.

It opened.

Augie stared out from inside the house, his face instantly flushing with relief as he reached for me, hauling me inside. "Jesus fuck, Lia. Where the hell were you? What happened? I've been calling your phone and you didn't answer. I thought…"

I didn't know what he'd thought, but he held me closer, so tight I thought my bones might break.

But I welcomed it. Needed it.

He shut the door behind me and guided me into the living room, kissing the top of my head, cradling me close, not willing to let me go.

I clung to him. Dug my fingers into the back of his shirt. Inhaled his scent that I'd let myself get attached to. Breathed it deep, letting it soothe the ache in my lungs that was threatening to rip me in two.

A sob broke free, my eyes filling with tears that couldn't be contained. They spilled over onto his shirt, soaking the material and his skin beneath it.

"Tell me," he said into my hair. "Whatever it is, I'll fix it."

He'd said something similar before. The first time I'd shown up here on his doorstep, terrified by Riddick.

But this wasn't even about the psychopath who'd hunted me across town. He could chase me and threaten me all he wanted. It was only ever going to be a temporary distraction from the real pain that lay below, just waiting to destroy me.

There was no fixing this. No coming back from what we'd done.

Wordlessly, I handed Augie my phone, the horrific video I'd been sent still open on the screen.

It was cruel. I should have warned him. Should have prepared him so he didn't have to feel what I did.

But I didn't have it in me. Shock had control of my body in a very real way, and now that I was somewhere safe, everything inside me felt like it was shutting down. My fear and grief and overwhelm had me in its grips, and I had nothing left to give, even to this man who'd given me so much.

The sound he made when he watched my sister fall was one I would never be able to erase from my memory. It was deep. Guttural. A cry of pain from a parent who had just lost their child. Or a brother who had just lost his sister.

Like the entire world had slowed, Augie slid to the floor, taking me with him, the two of us wrapped around each other, bound in our grief, too wrecked to say a word.

Hope disappeared.

Nothing mattered.

Fawn was dead.

31

AUGIE

*N*umbness crept in slowly.

In the hours Ophelia and I sat there in the dark, it slid over my body, a serpent, winding its way up my legs, over my torso and arms, until it settled around my neck like a noose, pulling tighter and tighter until it was all I knew.

For the longest time, neither of us moved, the only sounds of our breathing, her occasional sob, and the pounding of blood inside my body.

It reminded me I was still alive.

And how much I fucking hated that.

Because without Fawn here, what was the point?

"I don't want to exist in a world she doesn't," I finally said into the quiet.

It was true. The darkness that had been creeping over me for months, ever since she'd disappeared, was a smothering fog now. It filled the room, squeezing out all the air, forcing its way into my throat and lungs in much the same way the smoke had.

Nothing good happened in Saint View. And I was part of why.

Darkness took everything I touched.

Everyone I loved.

Ophelia stared up at me with big, glassy eyes.

Whatever she saw in my expression changed hers. Determination came over her, and she crawled onto my lap, straddling me so we were eye to eye, cupping my face in her hands. "Yes, you do. You do want to be here, Aug. Because Banjo still exists in this world. And so does Luna." She brushed her lips over mine, her voice dropping to a whisper. "So do I."

She wiped her thumbs beneath my eyes, taking away tears I didn't even know I was crying. When she kissed me again, her lips were salty and wet.

But she was warm.

She was real.

And she was here, in my lap, in my arms, begging me to stay.

In all the other times I'd felt like this, there'd never been her. It didn't make the feeling go away. But it was nice to not be alone with it.

"I love you," I whispered against her mouth, my hand twisting up into her hair, cradling her head.

I didn't have pretty words. I didn't have some big pre-prepared speech, the kind I knew she deserved.

But I never said those words.

Not to Banjo. Not to Fawn.

I felt them. God, I fucking felt them so deep it had nearly destroyed me time and time again.

And yet, I was so screwed up in the head I'd never been able to voice it.

She made me want to. She made it possible.

She kissed my mouth again, slow and deep, stealing my thoughts, banishing the bad ones, at least for the time being. Her touch chased away the numbness. Every stroke of her fingers across my cheeks, every touch of her tongue on my lips, every part of her pressed against me.

The kiss deepened, her wrapping her arms around my neck, me pulling her in by the small of her back. We clutched at each other in the darkness, touching, feeling, clinging.

Without us saying a word, the bond between us cemented. It was there in the way our bodies moved together, in my heart beating in time with hers. It was in her grief meeting mine, combining but outside ourselves, in a place that didn't feel so much like being dragged beneath water.

It was still there, aching, threatening, but for a second, a minute, it felt a little less.

A tiny bit more bearable.

Like this wouldn't be the end.

Like it might just be a beginning.

"I love you too," she whispered between kisses. "So much. I'm so sorry."

I didn't know what for, but it didn't matter. Her 'I love you' was so sweet it was all I wanted to hear. I claimed her lips, tasting her mouth, grabbing her hips and hauling her in.

We both fell into it, letting the feeling wash away the darkness.

When she reached for the buttons on my shirt, undoing each one with nimble fingers and sliding the fabric off my shoulders, nothing felt more right than doing the same to her.

I found a tie on her top, tugging on the silky material which unraveled her shirt. My lips found her bare shoulder, kissing a path along her skin until I got to her bra strap.

She reached behind her back, unclasping it, and the lacy covering fell away, exposing her perfect tits, just waiting for my hands.

I stroked my thumbs over her nipples as I claimed her mouth again, joining us because I couldn't get enough of how she tasted and how kissing her felt.

I'd spent most of my adult life fucking around, screwing people I didn't care about, avoiding kissing because it felt too intimate when all I was getting paid for was sex.

But I couldn't get enough of kissing Ophelia. Of the way her lips were so perfectly made for mine.

Of how my heart beat when she touched me.

Something inside me desperately wanted this, and not just for now.

For forever.

She rocked her hips, my dick hardening beneath her core. She threw her head back when I ducked mine to take her nipple in my mouth, sucking and rolling the tight bud with my tongue, loving the feel of her hands in my hair.

I reached between us, undoing her fly and then yanking her pants and underwear down from behind. She lifted, scrambling to help me get her naked, and in a tangle of arms and legs, we managed to get her pants off completely and mine down enough to free my erection.

That was as much warning as she gave me before sinking down onto my cock.

I hissed at the wet warmth of her, engulfing me bare. I leaned into her neck, holding her still, desperately wanting to move but knowing we shouldn't. "No condom," I murmured.

She shook her head. "Don't stop me. Please. I'm on birth control."

That was the least of my worries. "I never fuck without a condom. Ever."

But I wanted to with her. She felt so good. I couldn't stop. I rocked her over my hips, and we both groaned.

"Me neither," she whispered, taking over the motion, impaling herself so deep on me my head spun.

That was all I needed to hear.

That we'd both been careful in the past, so now we didn't have to be. I thrust up inside her, mind blown at how different it felt to have a woman like this, no barriers between us.

She wrapped her legs around my waist, digging her heels into the carpet beneath us and using that leverage to rise and fall on my dick.

The single shitty light outside filtered through my broken blinds, and I was so grateful for every beam that kissed her skin. She writhed on top of me, meeting my thrusts with downward pressure that made us both gasp.

She was the most beautiful thing I'd ever seen, her high, perfect tits in my face, her rounded hips in my hands. I sought out her mouth, time and time again, needing her lips, my heart squeezing every time she whispered that she loved me.

Because fuck, I loved her.

Wanted her.

I rolled her onto her back, hovering over her, my weight on my forearms, but needing to see her face when she came.

She reached between us, her fingers finding that little bundle of nerves at the junction of her thighs.

"Rub, sweetheart," I said into her ear. "Like I would."

She moaned, starting up a gentle touch that mimicked the tempo I was thrusting into her with. Her eyes rolled back each time I ground my pubic bone against her, making sure that even though I gave it to her slow, I gave it to her hard.

"Oh!" she cried, the first flutters of her orgasm setting off something inside me too.

I wouldn't let them take hold, though, determined to fuck her slowly and for as long as I could.

We moved like that for as long as we could stand it. She came, her inner walls tightening in on me, but I managed to hold out until she came a second time, and then, there was no holding it back.

My balls ached with the desperate need to come inside her. To let my orgasm whip through my body, obliterating anything that wasn't lust and need for this woman who I'd never seen coming.

She cried out my name, her hair wild around her from thrashing through two orgasms, her fingernail marks in my skin, each one the perfect reminder of how much I fucking loved her.

She dragged me down so my weight was fully on top of her, her big eyes staring straight into mine.

Her name was a breathless sound of need on my lips when I finally let go. I drove myself inside her, her pussy clamping and spasming around me, drawing out every inch of pleasure.

I came hard, whispering that I loved her.

That I'd stay.

Forever for her.

Always fucking for her.

32

OPHELIA

I rolled over as quietly as possible, slipping out from beneath the blankets without disturbing them too much, and held my breath in the hopes the mattress wouldn't squeak.

Augie's warm fingers caught my bare hip, his eyes still closed. "Where exactly do you think you're going?" he asked, voice still groggy with sleep.

"I need food. And a shower. And clothes."

"I'll help you with the first two, but you do not need clothes." He tugged me back down onto the bed, his thick arm banded around my waist. His breathing almost instantly evened out into the steady, rhythmic breaths of sleep, and I marveled at the fact he could just drop off like that.

While I spent half the night worrying.

I lifted his arm. "I haven't worn clothes in almost two days, Aug. I need to go home."

"No," he mumbled into the back of my neck, like a tantrum-throwing child.

But damn, he was cute.

But there was no way around it. I had to go home eventually. I couldn't hide here in Augie's little love nest where we'd been holed up for days, ignoring the rest of the world and the horrible things that happened in it.

In here, it was just me and him.

I wanted to stay in it forever.

Augie's phone buzzed on the nightstand, and I took it as an opportunity to escape. I picked it up to toss it at him and paused, noticing the text message preview on the screen. I shook his arm. "Why is that private investigator saying you owe him two thousand dollars?"

Augie blinked open one eye and squinted at me in the morning sunlight. "Him again? Don't worry about it." He reached for the phone.

I held it out of his reach, worry erasing some of my happy glow. "Do you owe him money? Fuck, Augie! I told you he had connections. You have to pay him."

Augie flopped an arm over his eyes. "He's a low-level nothing and all talk with his 'Pay up or I'll take this further,' bullshit. He didn't even produce the information he was supposed to get, just sent us on a wild-goose chase. I'm not paying him."

Unease settled inside me, but I wasn't Augie's keeper. He was a full-grown man and could make his own decisions. We'd barely been a couple for forty-eight hours; I didn't want to start nagging him like a whiny girlfriend already.

I had enough problems of my own that needed dealing with anyway.

Riddick and my mother being the top two.

I loved Augie. I couldn't keep running in circles,

trying to keep both sides of my life from exploding into each other.

I had to get ahead of it.

Take back control over my own damn life.

I got dressed while the PI and Augie text argued. I kissed his lips, and he mumbled something about I better be coming straight back.

I smiled against his mouth. "Nowhere else I'd want to be."

I meant it.

We needed to stop hiding. I needed to tell my mother and my brother and Augie's friends about Fawn. I knew we'd never get her body back. Eddie would dispose of it so he couldn't be linked back to his crimes. But over the past two days, Augie and I had talked a little, making some plans for a memorial service.

We all needed closure.

And Fawn needed to be laid to rest.

It was all I could do for my sister now.

I pushed the thought away, unwilling to cry anymore. I didn't know how my body wasn't bone-dry after all the breakdowns I'd had in Augie's arms. It had left me with a raging headache and sore eyes, but there was something cathartic in the not wondering.

In knowing she was no longer suffering at Eddie's hands.

Revenge would come later.

Scythe and I would see to that.

But first our sister needed to be laid to rest.

"I've got to go to the club for a bit today anyway. Eve is going to fire me if I call in sick again, and she needs to know..." His voice was heavy.

I paused. "Do you want me to come with you? If you wait 'til I go home and get changed..." But I didn't want to. It was going to be hard enough to tell my brother. I'd barely pulled myself together, I wasn't sure I could take too many more hits in such a short space of time.

Augie seemed to know it. "I need to be the one to tell the others at the club. You go get what you need and then come back."

I kissed him one last time.

"Love you, Lia," he whispered, kissing me back.

"Love you too."

Walking away from him and this house and back out into the world was maybe the hardest steps I'd ever forced myself to take.

It was only when I got outside that I remembered I'd abandoned my car blocks away a few nights earlier.

"Shit," I muttered to myself. I could have just turned around and gone back inside but then I'd tumble back into bed with Augie, and I'd still have no clean underwear.

Besides, the morning sun was beautiful and warm, and it felt good to get out of bed, get some air, and move in a way that wasn't just thrusting my hips in time with Augie's.

For just a few minutes, I could come out here in the morning sun and enjoy it.

For a few minutes, I could pretend my heart didn't ache.

Despite my attempts at enjoying the stroll, the closer I got to my car, the shorter my breaths became. And it wasn't due to exercise.

The car sat on the road where I'd left it. To my

surprise, it still had all four wheels, though one of the back windows had been smashed out and the back passenger door was slightly ajar. Clearly someone had gone through it, searching it for anything of value, but they wouldn't have found anything other than the manual in the glove box. I never left anything in there worth stealing.

I surveyed the damage from the sidewalk, then inspected the car more closely, running my fingers beneath the wheel wells, around the mirrors, and beneath door handles. With the flashlight function on my phone switched on, I shined a beam of light around the inside, not caring too much about the shattered glass that glistened all over the back of the car but checking every nook and cranny for any sort of tracking device Riddick...or my mother...might have put on there.

I breathed a sigh of relief when the car came out clean.

Getting in behind the wheel, I drove through Saint View, across the border and back into Providence. On my street, I parked a way down the road, watching my building for a while, checking every car and person who came and went, searching for Riddick's face among them.

I couldn't get the memory of him out of my head. I'd used Augie's body to keep the fear at bay over the last few days, but now, without him to distract me, it was all I could see.

The plain, dark fury in Riddick's eyes as he'd tried to run me off the cliffside road.

It was a bluff, I was sure. He was angry because I'd been avoiding him. Or because he'd worked out I hadn't done my job. I doubted he actually wanted me dead.

And yet, if he knew about me and Augie, I would be.

"Can't sit here all freaking day, Ophelia. You gonna get yourself up and move?" I shifted off the seat and out of the car. I walked cautiously; my gun tucked into the back of my waistband.

When a young couple stepped out from one corner of the building, I very nearly put a bullet through them, my gut reaction to pull my gun and shoot.

It was only the fact I hesitated at the very last second that stopped me. They smiled, and the young woman waved politely as they passed. I let out a shaky breath.

The last thing I wanted to do was shoot someone.

"Get a fucking grip, Ophelia. It's the middle of the damn day and too early to be dealing with dead bodies."

I really hoped nobody was listening.

At the top of the stairs, I checked my door for any signs of forced entry, but there was nothing. It all looked completely normal, and I let out a little sigh of relief. Unless Riddick had come in with a fire ladder, or had somehow developed super Spider-Man wall-scaling abilities, there was no other way in.

I unlocked the door and stepped inside, putting my phone and gun down on the counter. I was suddenly starving, my stomach growling a reminder that while Augie was a sex god, a chef he was not. His refrigerator had been nearly bare by the time I'd left. I was definitely in the mood for some brunch.

I opened the refrigerator and grinned when there was a full carton of eggs there. I took out other ingredients, some ham and cheese, and then on impulse I grabbed a shopping bag and started filling it with as much food as I could fit.

Once I got back to Augie's place, this would get us through for a few more days. I was planning on packing enough clothes to last me at least a week because, frankly, the less I had to come back here, the better.

I was already itching to get back to him. But he'd be busy for a while, so food needed to happen first.

Fawn had always liked tomato, ham, and cheese omelets.

I shut the refrigerator.

Riddick was on the other side.

I jumped a mile, the eggs crashing to the floor and cracking open. A tomato rolled beneath the kitchen table.

Riddick raised an eyebrow. "You're cooking for two, I assume?"

We stared at each other.

My heart pounded.

We both lunged for the gun in the same instant.

He was taller and got there first, plucking it off the counter and holding it above his head liked some demented game of keep-away. He tutted under his breath. "Now, now, Ophelia. What would you need this for?"

I ground my teeth, fingers clenching into fists. "What are you doing here?"

He tucked the gun into his waistband, covering it with his jacket, and strolled around me in a circle, gaze creeping over every inch of my body. "See, it's funny you should ask me that. Because I was wondering the same about you."

I ignored the way this man sent terror through every inch of my body. For once, my mother's warnings about never letting a man see your weaknesses seemed like good advice. "My place, Riddick. Not yours."

He leaned on the fridge. "Now, that's what I thought too. But you haven't been here for days, have you, Little Ophelia?"

The 'little' taunt pissed me off. I was anything but, and talking to me like I was a child was a clear ploy at him attempting to take the upper hand. He was trying to get a rise out of me any way he knew how. I wouldn't give it to him.

"Where you been, Little Ophelia?"

I refused to say a word.

He leaned in, hot breath misting across my ear. "You going to answer, or have you forgotten?" He laughed. "Silly. How about I remind you then?"

He stopped his circle of taunts, halting right in front of me, his dangerous eyes so deadly dark I was sure evil lived behind them.

"I know you're sleeping with the target."

Every muscle in my body locked up, fear filling my throat and cutting off the air. With the last of it, I forced out words. "I don't know what you're talking about."

Riddick moved dangerously fast.

In a second, he had my ponytail in his hand, a fierce yank on it twisting me into an awkward position that sent fire burning through my skull. I bit down on a cry, unwilling to give him the satisfaction of knowing it hurt.

"You know," he hissed beneath his breath. "You're making a fool out of me."

I shook my head, hating that I winced when his grip on my hair tightened. "No, I'm not. I—"

"You think I care about your excuses? I don't want to hear them. You know why? Because they don't matter.

You're going to be my wife, Ophelia. That has already been arranged, and plans have been put in place."

Bile tried to choke me at the very idea of marrying this man.

Of any man.

Any man who wasn't Augie.

"No. I don't want that."

Riddick laughed in my face. "God, are you that stupid? Do you really think I care about whether you want this? Nobody fucking cares! You've been promised to me, and I intend to claim what's mine."

An anger rose in me so sharp and swift it almost knocked me on my ass. It was only the fact Riddick held me that kept me from falling. I glared at him, letting him see every ounce of hate in my heart. "I'll never marry you. I don't care what my family promised."

His eyes burned with rage, but his voice was deep and deliberate. He got in my face, making sure I saw every dark threat that spilled from his mouth. "You will, Ophelia. Because once I take lover boy out, you'll have no reason not to." He grinned. "You want me to do it nice and quick? Or should I take my time, slowly gutting him, watching his blood drain out while he screams in agony?"

My muscles locked in fear at the picture he painted. I shook my head hard, unable to keep the terror at bay when his malice wasn't directed at me but at the man I loved. I opened my mouth to argue, to agree, to say anything that would get him to change his mind.

But he pressed one thick finger to my lips with a smile so evil I knew I would remember it until the day I died.

"Shh, Little Ophelia. Let your husband take care of

everything. I'll kill him in just the way you were supposed to."

He whipped the pistol into the side of my head, and everything went black.

33

OPHELIA

hen I came to, it was dark. The apartment was silent, nothing but the steady hum of the refrigerator to make a sound, but even that felt too much for my aching head.

I groaned as I sat up and gingerly pushed at the sorest spot, wincing at the egg-shaped lump. My entire body hurt, not helped by the hard kitchen floor beneath me.

It took me a good thirty seconds to remember what had happened, panic spearing through the fog.

Riddick. Augie.

No.

I scrambled to my feet, ignoring the way the room spun in dizzying circles around me. My phone had disappeared from the kitchen counter. As had my gun. Shit.

I needed to warn Augie. There would be no fighting back against Riddick. His chilling threats replayed over and over in my head, adding to the building pressure behind my eyes that felt so thick it could explode at any minute. Through bleary eyes, I yanked open the door to my apartment and stumbled out onto the staircase. Down them, clutching at the rail for support, until fresh air hit me in the face.

That helped a little, and by the time I made it halfway down the road to where I'd left my car, my brain had cleared enough for me to remember Augie had been on his way to the club to tell the others about Fawn.

That was good. That wouldn't be the first place Riddick went, and even Riddick wasn't stupid enough to try to kill a man with a club full of witnesses.

Except a nagging voice inside me said he might just kill them all, no fucks given to whether he took one life or a dozen.

I'd worried about being like him. That I liked killing just for the sake of it.

Sometime over the past few weeks, I'd realized it wasn't true.

I didn't want to be like him.

I *wasn't* like him.

I sped through the streets of Saint View, driving erratically, knowing deep in my heart if I didn't get there in time, Augie didn't stand a chance.

The car bumped up the curb outside the strip club. The engine was barely off before I was out, running across the sidewalk to the front door, banging my fist against it and shouting his name desperately.

The door opened, and I practically fell through, Eve catching me before I could hit the floor.

"Holy shit, Ophelia? Are you okay?"

I shook my head and instantly regretted it. My headache more painful than any I'd ever experienced.

But I pushed past her, into the club, desperately searching the empty building for him. "Augie!"

A man at the bar turned around, and I did a double take. "Vincent?"

My brother grinned at me, a spoon halfway to his mouth filled with a thick, rich stew. "Scythe. Hey, sis."

I couldn't work out why he was here. My muddled brain tried to put it all together and only came to the conclusion that I had concussion and was seeing things.

Eve hurried over; her eyebrows knit together in worry. She winced when she noticed my head. "What happened there?"

I touched my lump again, remembering too late that it hurt like a motherfucker when I did that. "It doesn't matter. Where's Augie?" I blinked hard. "And is my brother here for a meal or am I seeing things?"

"Really here." He shoveled in another mouthful of stew, as happy as a pig in mud.

I still didn't understand, but Eve took pity on me and filled in the blanks with a quiet smile. "He's been dropping in every so often, checking to see if any of us have heard from Fawn."

"And because Eve always has this stew in the refrigerator and it's literally the best thing I've ever eaten in my life. She always feeds me. You want some?" He held up a chunk of dipping bread in my direction.

I couldn't even process him right now. I dragged my gaze back to Eve, who was still looking at me like a mother hen wanting to patch up my wounds.

"I've got a first aid kit..." she started.

I gripped her arm, cutting her off. "Is Augie here?"

"No. He called in sick again, which we all know is

code for he's in bed with you." Her tone was teasing, but there was happiness in it. She was clearly pleased about what was going on with him and me.

Scythe's spoon clattered against the bowl. "Ew. Can we not talk about my sister getting her groove thang on while I'm in the room? I really like this stew, Eve, but I don't want to find out what it tastes like on the way back up. And talking about Augie poking Ophelia with his pickle makes me want to hurl."

I squeezed my eyes shut, wishing I had a clearer head to be making sense of all this. I wobbled on my feet.

Eve steadied me again. "You need to sit down."

"I need to go find Augie."

But Eve's mother hen side had taken over. "Nope," she said determinedly, guiding me to a chair. "You're going to sit and let me look at your head—"

"No, Eve—"

"Fawn would never forgive me if I let you walk away without taking care of you first. Scythe," she called. "Tell your sister to behave.

"Sit yo ass down and do what she says. I won't be happy with you if she stops feeding me this stew. Seriously, Lia. Eat this." He brought his bowl over to where Eve was still towing me to the table. "You can't be swallowing down man meat on an empty stomach. Oh, ew. Now I'm grossing myself out..."

Their voices melded and swarmed around me, their hands reaching, touching, grabbing me. The room spun in nauseating circles, my headache increasing until a sudden urge to scream rocketed up my throat. I snatched my arm out of her grasp. "No! God, stop. Just stop! Fawn is dead!"

And so was Augie if they didn't let me leave.

"What?" Scythe asked, a chill in his tone.

I wanted to break down and cry at the way I'd just blurted it out. Eve stood stunned, not moving, her arms frozen in place as she waited for me to say more.

Or to take it back.

I couldn't.

I shook my head, deserving the ringing in my brain, but I had nothing left to give. "Eddie killed her."

"You can't be sure..." Eve whispered, but it was clear she knew I was.

"There's a video. I saw it."

Scythe stood slowly and walked away.

My shoulders sank. "Scythe!"

But he didn't respond. He didn't turn back. He just walked out of the club like the harbinger of death he'd once been.

There was no doubt in my mind he'd find Eddie and take care of what needed to be done. Even if it took the rest of his life to hunt him down.

I'd been trying to keep him out of this because this wasn't his life anymore. He had a family. A child due soon. People who needed him to be here, happy with them.

Not dead or in prison again.

Eve cried quietly; her heartbreak as ready to pull me under as my own had been.

I'd done this all wrong.

I couldn't stay to fix it.

"I'm sorry." It was all I could say as I backed out of the room. "I'm so fucking sorry."

Sorry that she'd lost Fawn.

Sorry that she'd probably lost Augie too.

Tears streamed down my face as I drove to Augie's house, not rushing now, knowing I was going to find his body. I'd been unconscious for hours. Riddick had been given all the time in the world when all he actually needed was minutes. If Augie hadn't gone to the club, and he'd stayed home, waiting for me, there was no chance he was still alive.

My mission to rescue him had become an inevitable body retrieval. Shock or maybe the concussion made me slow and sloppy, the tires hitting the gutter twice, though I couldn't bring myself to care.

There was no urgency anymore.

Just a sense of this was what I had to do.

My brain shut down, minute by minute, compartmentalizing the trauma and storing it away somewhere else so I could function.

Like a robot, I parked the car in his driveway. The front door was open. Had I done that when I'd left? Not locked it, just making it all the easier for Riddick to waltz on in and end the man I'd fallen so hard for, despite every reason not to.

I couldn't take it.

Losing Fawn. Losing him.

I didn't call out. With heavy feet, I forced myself to take the stairs to his second-floor bedroom. Forced myself to enter his room and stare down at his body, still on the bed.

He rolled over and gave me a sleepy, lazy grin. "Hey, sweetheart. You're back. Didn't even hear you come in."

I burst into tears, throwing myself onto the bed with him.

"Hey." He smoothed back my hair while I clutched at his arms, his skin, making sure he was as real and warm and alive as he seemed to be. "It's okay."

But it wasn't.

In an instant, everything changed. He might have still been alive, but that only meant Riddick hadn't gotten here yet.

I didn't know what had held him up, but I wouldn't look a gift horse in the mouth. I jerked myself out of his arms and opened his closet, yanking out T-shirts and sweatpants and anything else I could get my fingers on. Rummaging through the bottom of the closet, I found a bag and started shoving all his things inside.

He caught my wrists, spinning me around. "Hey. Stop. What's going on? Why are you emptying my closet?"

"We need to leave." I needed to tell him everything. Every ugly truth about who I was and the things I'd done and the danger I'd put him in. And I would. But it couldn't be here, where Riddick would find us. We were sitting ducks, and my heart thumped with the knowledge Riddick could be here at any moment. I spun around, eyes wide. "Do you have a gun?"

He blanched. "Lia, you're freaking me the fuck out. Talk to me."

"We need a gun," I muttered, giving up on the idea of packing his clothes and instead shoving at him to get up and put something on.

He wasn't moving.

Just staring at me with wide eyes.

Fuck, for all the bad shit he'd done, none of it came close to mine. He was so fucking innocent. I wasn't letting him die.

I couldn't survive losing him, too.

"Augie! For fuck's sake, get up!" My scream echoed around the room.

He flinched, but a determination fell down over his expression. "Not until you tell me what's going on. You're terrified, and that in itself is scaring me. What the hell happened while you were gone?"

A thump came from the front door, a heavy pounding that sent ice through my blood.

I was too late.

Riddick was here.

34

AUGIE

The thumping from downstairs was the only thing that could stop hurricane Ophelia.

She froze, staring up at me with huge eyes that made me want to kill whoever had put that expression of fear there. If I could just get her to stop and calm down enough to talk to me, I would.

"We're dead," she whispered.

I shook my head, moving around her to the bedroom door. "What? It's probably just one of the neighborhood kids playing ding-dong ditch."

But another round of thumping from downstairs had her shaking her head.

Until a familiar voice echoed up from outside. "Augie! You in there?"

The fight went out of Ophelia. She dropped her hands to her side, though I didn't miss the slight tremor that still plagued them.

I picked one up and squeezed it. "It's just Willa's son, Colt. I need to go see what he wants."

She nodded, the color returning to her face a little, but I was still worried about whatever was going on with her. "Stay here, and when I get back, we're going to talk, okay?"

"I'm coming with you."

I wasn't going to argue with her. I didn't like the idea of leaving her up here alone when I didn't know what was going on with her. I pulled on a pair of sweats and to the constant banging of Colt's fist, the two of us jogged down the stairs to open the door.

"Jesus fuck, Colt. You're buying me a new door if…"

Colt and Lacey stood on the porch, their faces white.

Lacey had clearly been crying.

I looked back at Lia who had worn a similar expression just minutes ago. "Does somebody want to tell me what the fuck is going on here?"

"Banjo's missing," Colt said bluntly.

My heart stopped.

All of us stared at each other.

Ophelia was the first to speak up. "Come inside. Quick. Please."

Colt pushed past me; his fingers wrapped tightly around Lacey's. I followed them into the living room, while Ophelia closed and locked the door, then peeped out of the broken blinds, watching the street outside.

Maybe she was just trying to give me privacy for a family matter.

But after the state she'd been in just moments earlier, I was pretty sure she was watching for something.

Or someone.

"What do you mean he's missing?" I asked Colt and Lacey distractedly.

Colt handed over his phone, and I had a sinking feeling of déjà vu. This was what Ophelia had done when she'd given me her phone with the video of Fawn's death playing out on it.

I wouldn't survive watching another video like that.

My fingers shook. "What is it?"

"Security footage from the front of our house," Lacey explained. "Banjo was out there playing football with Luna earlier. Luna came in crying, saying Banjo had been kidnapped."

Colt took over. "We thought she was playing a game at first. That it was part of some sort of hide-and-seek thing that she hadn't understood properly. But when we couldn't find him either, we checked the cameras..."

I hit 'play' on the video and watched in horror as a black truck stopped in front of the house. Banjo and Luna stopped playing, and Banjo walked over to the guy, who I'd bet anything had asked him a question. Maybe for directions.

In the next second, the back door opened and a masked figure pistol-whipped Banjo across the side of his head. He pulled my clearly disoriented brother inside the vehicle and the driver peeled out of the driveway.

Leaving my tiny three-year-old niece screaming in terror. Completely alone.

My hands shook.

"We've called the police. They came and took statements and a copy of the video. They said it might just be a prank, maybe his football friends or some sort of college hazing..." Colt's voice trailed off.

A tear rolled down Lacey's cheek. "I don't believe that. Not for a second. Those guys wouldn't do that. Not now.

Maybe back in freshman year, but—" She shook her head. "This doesn't feel like a prank." She stared at me desperately. "Do you know anything? Anyone who might want to hurt him? Surely this isn't some random thing. Luna was right there. She would have been the easy target. And yet they had no interest in her..."

I knew we were all silently thankful for that, and yet it didn't ease the horrifying truth that Banjo hadn't gotten in that car willingly.

I was pretty sure I knew who it was behind that mask.

Guilt hit me so hard it took my legs out, forcing me to sit hard on the couch. "This is my fault," I whispered. I looked over at Ophelia. "You told me not to get involved with Bert Leddith. You told me he had Mafia connections."

Colt and Lacey stared at me.

Colt's voice came out a growl. "What the fuck, Augie? What have you done?"

I stuttered over my words. "I don't know. I owe money..."

The silence was deafening.

Lacey let out a heartbreaking sob and flew across the small space, pummeling her fists against my chest. "What did you do, Augie? What did you do?"

I didn't know.

But I did.

The investigator had warned me he'd take things further if I didn't pay. Ophelia had warned me that the man had connections.

I'd ignored them both.

Thought I knew better.

I always fucking thought I knew best until it all exploded right in my face.

Like it was right now.

Lacey howled in agony, slumping down my chest with her fear. All I could do was catch her until Colt took her from my arms. His eyes were fire, burning me, his hatred right there in his expression.

Gone were the friendly smiles from the dinner we'd shared at his house, and the thank yous he'd given after I'd pulled his daughter from her grandmother's burning house. In one fell swoop, I'd undone everything I'd started fixing with them.

I deserved every ounce of the hate he threw my way.

And more.

Even if we could get him back, I knew this was it.

They'd never speak to me again.

Never forgive me.

Colt and Lacey moved to the doorway, but Ophelia stepped in front of them.

"It's not his fault."

Colt glared at her. "Do yourself a favor and stay away from him. He's a fucking disease. Every time we let him near us something like this happens." He glanced back over his shoulder at me, his lip curled in a snarl. "Save yourself before he drags you down, too, the same way he did to your sister and now Banjo."

I didn't retaliate.

There was nothing to say.

He was right.

But anger burned behind Ophelia's gaze, and she stood firmly in the doorway, not budging an inch when Colt tried to get past her. "It's not his fault. It's mine."

No way was I going to let her take the brunt of Colt's anger for something I'd done. "Ophelia, just let them go."

But she shook her head, and then her gaze switched to me. "It's not Bert Leddith who has your brother. At least I don't think so. I meant it when I said this is my fault." She bit down on her lip. "I'm so sorry. I was going to tell you."

Lacey glanced between us, her eyebrows furrowed in confusion, and then anger. "All I know right now is Banjo is missing, and somebody better tell me something I can give to the cops so they can find him."

Ophelia dragged her gaze away from mine and focused on Lacey. "The cops can't help him now. But I can." She came to stand in front of me and gave me the tiniest of smiles. With a trembling finger, she reached up and brushed my hair off my forehead.

Then told me everything.

How she'd been hired to kill me.

How she was promised to a man she didn't love. One who killed for business as well as for pleasure.

How that man had seen her leave Banjo's house the other night.

And how she believed that Riddick had either seen her leave Banjo's and assumed it was him she was having an affair with.

Or that Banjo was the second target. One that her mother had given to Riddick to take out when Ophelia hadn't killed me quickly enough.

"No, that doesn't make sense," I protested weakly. Thoughts swarmed my head. Questions pounded at my brain, trying to force it to make sense. "Who would put a hit out on Banjo?"

"Who would put a hit out on *you*?" she asked. "This job came in before you got messed up with the PI. There were two targets who came in at the same time. The one I was given was you. The one Riddick was given could very well have been Banjo. Who would want you *both* dead? It has to be connected."

But I had no idea. I couldn't think of anyone.

Ophelia brushed her lips over mine, but I flinched back, her words finally sinking in through the haze of confusion. I stared at her like she was brand-new. Like I'd never seen the way her brown eyes shone. Or the curve of her hips. Or breathed in the sweet scent of her skin.

I didn't know this woman.

This woman who lied.

Who killed.

She was a complete and utter stranger.

She was Ophelia.

But not Lia.

"This is what Fawn was running from, wasn't it?" I asked her stiffly. "From you?"

She swallowed hard, her eyes sparkling with tears. But her nod was absolute. It felt like the first truth she'd ever actually admitted.

I'd told her all my secrets. Every last one, from the insignificant to the ones that had ruined my life.

While she'd shared exactly nothing.

She didn't try to deny anything, and I was grateful because anger swirled around in my stomach. I didn't want to hear her excuses.

"Get out," I whispered.

She nodded. "I'll get him back, Aug. I promise."

But her words meant nothing. None of them had ever been true.

Not the promises.

Not the I love yous.

They were all lies and as fake as the woman who'd sold them to me.

35

OPHELIA

I'd promised Augie I'd get his brother back. I'd said the words with as much conviction as I could muster, trying to reassure him everything would be fine.

But like so many other lies I'd told him; this was yet another.

I'd seen how reckless Riddick was. How he didn't stop to think and plan things out. How he just acted on impulse.

Before he'd knocked me out, he'd accused me of sleeping with the target.

But it was Banjo he'd taken from his lawn, right in front of their little girl.

That was sick. Didn't he remember the childhood we'd had? Growing up with parents in this business meant I'd been subjected to one horrific event after another. It didn't matter how young I was at the time. Those memories were burned into my brain, never to be forgotten.

I never wanted to inflict that sort of pain on a child. How could he?

"Because he's a fucking psychopath," I muttered, getting into my car. "One with no humanity." Unlike my brother who was batshit crazy a lot of the time but would never hurt someone in front of a child.

Fuck. Scythe and Vincent were out there somewhere, hunting Eddie. I could have used their backup right now, but really, if Banjo was still alive, there was only one thing Riddick might accept in exchange.

I didn't need my brother for it.

I did need my best friend's help though.

Shit. No phone.

Her flower shop was just around the corner, though, on the Saint View-Providence border, not far from my place. It was late, but I knew she sometimes stayed until all hours of the night, making up new arrangements for the next day. I made the turn at the last second, earning myself a rude beep from the car behind me. There was a parking spot free right outside Jezebel's shop, and the lights were on. I thanked whichever lucky angel was shining over me.

I just hoped there was one watching out for Banjo too.

The bell above the door tinkled when I pushed my way in, and Jez looked up from behind the counter.

"We're closed—Hey!" But then her face fell as she took in my expression, the disheveled clothes, and the lump on my head. "Shit, come in. Sit down. What happened?"

"I want to tell you everything, but I don't have time. I need to know where your brother would take someone to torture them."

Jezebel's mouth flattened out into a hard line. "Shit. Not exactly what I was expecting you to say. Who?"

"Augie's brother."

She swore beneath her breath. She was the only person I'd talked to about Augie. She knew what he meant to me. I didn't need to explain his brother was important to me as well.

"Riddick will kill me if I tell you."

I grabbed her hand, understanding her turmoil. Riddick was the stuff of nightmares. The one person even people like she and I were scared of. Around anyone else, we were unbreakable.

But Riddick didn't play by the rules. He had no morals. No codes. He'd spent his entire life being trained to kill.

He was a weapon with no control.

I pressed my fingers into her palm. "Banjo has a daughter, Jez. She's only three. She needs him."

So does Augie, I mentally added.

I'd screwed that poor man over so many times in the last few weeks, the very least I could do was give him back the one person he loved most.

For a second there, I'd thought I could be another.

A tear slipped down my face. I didn't even have to fill Jez in on why I was crying. She knew. Because we were the same, me and her. She knew as well as I did there was no happiness in our futures.

Vincent and Scythe were an anomaly because they were special.

But for her and me there was no escape.

Fawn had known it. It was why she'd left the family. I wished I'd been half as smart and gone with her. Hiding out in Spain hadn't been enough. I was too tethered here. One tug on the string from my mother and I'd been right back here in the thick of it.

For all Fawn appeared to be weak, she was actually the strong one. The one who'd been able to stay away.

Jez rubbed my arm in sympathy. "I'm sorry it ended like this."

"So am I." She had no idea how much. My fucking heart felt like it had stopped beating. "But please, Jez. Just tell me where he'd go."

She thought it over for a moment and then made a face. "Do you know the old hockey rink in Providence?"

I squinted. "Old? I know the new one. That huge industrial thing on the road out to the city, right?"

"There's an older one behind it. One they haven't used in a lifetime. People have been campaigning to knock it down for years, but it has so much history attached to it they haven't been allowed. But it sits empty. Riddick used to take targets out there when we were in our teens. He'd force me to go with him and threaten me if I said I was telling Mom." She shrugged. "I don't know where else he'd go. Not his house. He doesn't like being outdoors when he puts someone to ground. I've noticed that. He almost always goes into their houses or work-places. If Banjo was removed from his house, then Riddick is probably holding him at the old rink. That would be my bet anyway."

I nodded and ran for the door, praying beneath my breath. "Please be playing with your catch."

The new ice rink parking lot had probably been filled with cars earlier in the day. Families towing their kids around with those stabilizers shaped like penguins. Teenagers hanging out with friends. Maybe groups of college-aged kids who played on hockey teams.

But when I pulled in, there wasn't a car in sight. The entire place was deserted, a quiet, desolate feeling to it, with the woods thick behind the two rectangular buildings.

The building in front was a huge monstrosity of a thing, with slick silver sides and a flashy "Providence Ice Facility" logo above black glass doors that marked the entrance. It was a multimillion-dollar venue the government had splashed a lot of money on to bring tourism to the area.

It was nothing like the dingy old building behind it. It had been abandoned for as long as I could remember, well before they'd built the new one in its place.

I steered my car in that direction. If there'd been a road here once, it had been demolished when they'd built the new building. The only way to get back to it was to walk across a lumpy field. Or drive your car over it.

I jolted up and down, praying I wouldn't get stuck in one of the ruts. My headlights lit up the decaying building, and a shiver ran down my spine. It was the sort of place people steered clear of because it might be haunted.

Of course, that's probably exactly what Riddick liked about it. If he was even here. I didn't see his car anywhere, but then he wouldn't be dumb enough to park it in view of the street where people would notice it.

Neither was I.

I rounded the back, and my heart hammered at the sight of Riddick's truck.

I'd thank Jez later for knowing her brother better than I did.

I got out, not bothering to shut the door quietly because my car engine would have given away my arrival anyway. With determined steps, I strode across the gravel and the knee-high weeds to the arena's back door.

The handle turned beneath my fingers, allowing me in.

Fucking cocky son of a bitch. He hadn't even bothered to lock it.

"Riddick!" I shouted into the darkness. My voice echoed around the old rink, bouncing off the high ceilings.

There was no reply. I moved farther in, running my finger along dust-covered bleacher-style seats and eyed the circular shape in the middle of the space that had once held ice. At one end, a tunnel mouth led to a deeper darkness I couldn't see beyond.

The cry of pain that came a second later came from that direction.

The sound speared through me, but it also brought hope.

He was alive.

"Banjo!" I shouted, running down the last few stairs and pushing up and over the banister that would have once stopped new skaters from completely hitting the decks. I headed for the tunnel, trying to work out what this would have been used for. The machine that smoothed the ice, maybe? The opening seemed too big to lead to the player locker rooms.

Another scream of pain had me both wincing and doubling down on speed. "Banjo!"

A light flickered on in front of me, bringing me to a screeching halt.

"Took you long enough." Riddick swung a camping lantern from his fingers. "Your boyfriend and I have been waiting for you for ages."

My gaze flickered to Banjo.

I had to bite down on my lip.

He was on a chair behind a desk. His dirty-blond hair stained red with blood that seeped down his temples and onto his cheeks. His hands were flat on the table, but I gasped at the sight of a knife embedded in each, pinning him in place, though neither seemed to be bleeding too profusely.

I shuddered at the thought his legs could be pinned in the same way.

Riddick chuckled. "You and lover boy are reunited! Say hello!"

Banjo didn't say anything.

I stared at Riddick, not wanting to give him more information about the truth of the situation but not wanting to make it worse either. He was a loose cannon. An explosion waiting to happen at any minute if I cut the wrong wire.

"Banjo was your target?" I needed to know if my assumption was right.

"Would you have been able to kill him if your mother

had given him to you?" he scoffed at me. "We both know you couldn't kill someone you had feelings for."

I shook my head. And this right here was why I took my time with a target. Why I did my research. Watched. Put some goddamn fucking thought into my kills.

So I didn't royally fuck up like Riddick just had, in assuming Banjo was the brother I was in love with.

But Riddick was cocky. Lazy. He thought he was so good he didn't need to put in the effort.

It was that very lack of preparation that had led us here.

It gave me the upper hand because he had gotten it so. Damn. Wrong.

"You're right," I told Riddick. "I wouldn't kill the man I love. But that's not him."

Riddick laughed. "I saw you coming out of his house in Providence. My contacts at Psychos told me you were in there, fucking him like the little whore I know you are. Your mom gave me this job because you can't do it. That's what she told me. It quickly became obvious to me why." He sneered at Banjo's silent form. "I thought you had better taste, Ophelia. This guy? Really? Is that why you don't want to marry me? Because you like them so young they could get you arrested?"

I blinked at Riddick's confession. He'd misunderstood my mother's words. He had no idea who Augie was or how I actually knew Banjo. All he'd seen was me coming out of Banjo's house that night he'd followed me up to the bluffs. Maybe his stupid friends who had been at Psychos had reported seeing me with a tall blond man who matched Banjo's description. Of course he fucking did.

He and Augie were brothers. They did look alike, especially in low lighting.

I eyed Banjo, waiting for him to tell Riddick he had
the wrong guy.

But he said nothing.

Protecting his brother.

They were good, these Mitchell boys. Despite everything they'd been through, despite their shit upbringings
and lives that had dealt them harsh blows and cruel
turns, they were good.

Even if they couldn't see it.

I could.

"He's not the man I was with at Psychos, Riddick. For
Christ's sake. He's probably not even old enough to get
into Psychos! You said yourself how young he is." It was a
bluff. I knew Banjo was a college senior and had likely
already turned twenty-one, even if he did look younger.

Riddick cocked his head and then yanked Banjo up
by his hair. "You twenty-one yet, kid?"

Fuck me. All our job bags were the same. They all
started with a target bio. If he'd even read it, he would
have known Banjo's true age. My mother had wanted me
to work with this man? It was a wonder he'd managed as
many kills as he had without getting caught.

Riddick was damn sloppy.

Vincent would have been disgusted.

I silently willed Banjo to be coherent enough to lie.

He didn't answer. Just groaned in pain.

As much as I didn't like it, that was probably a
blessing in disguise. Better he not be able to talk than
him talk and say too much.

Riddick might have been unprepared, but he wasn't

stupid. One wrong step, and both Banjo and I would be dead.

Riddick stared at me, trying to work out if I was lying or not.

It was now or never.

I'd come here knowing there was probably only one thing that would get him to leave Banjo alone. I stepped into Riddick, picking up his hand and threading my fingers through it.

He stared down and then back up at me. A corner of his mouth lifted. "What's this about? You've made it pretty clear you can't stand me, Ophelia."

"Maybe so, but the feeling isn't mutual, is it?"

Riddick's lips pressed into a line. He didn't answer.

That was enough to tell me I was on the right track. Riddick was never silent. He ran his mouth constantly, making sure everyone around him knew he was the alpha dog.

But I'd never seen him with a woman. Never heard Jezebel talk about him with a girlfriend.

I might have once been willing to let my mother set me up because I'd been with so many men who just didn't do it for me.

But I suspected Riddick needed it because he couldn't get a woman by himself.

"Women run the other way when they see you, don't they?" I asked him.

His breath came in short, angry pants through his nose, telling me I was on the right track.

"They take one look at you and something inside them screams to run, don't they?" I rubbed my thumb over the back of his hand. "You a virgin, Riddick?"

"No," he huffed out.

It had been a bluff. I didn't really think a man like him in his thirties, despite his off-putting appearance and the way he couldn't hide that there was something abnormal about him, would actually still be a virgin.

But the way he'd said no...

Fuck. I remembered the way he'd pushed up against me in my apartment.

He'd wanted me, but he hadn't forced me.

When he so easily could have.

He could have forced any woman if he wanted to.

Maybe that was the one moral line Riddick had held on to. Maybe he did just want someone who actually wanted him.

I could relate to that. I almost felt sorry for him.

Until Banjo let out a whimper of pain and I knew this couldn't go on any longer.

"Let him go, Riddick," I said softly, stepping in so the heat of my body seeped into his. "I'm not in love with him. I'm promised to you, so any other man I've been with is inconsequential anyway."

Riddick leaned into my touch, lowering his head to my neck and inhaling my scent. "You always smell so good."

"So do you." I tried not to choke on the words.

"I don't want you with other men."

I shook my head. "We'll get married. You and me. There'll be no other men."

He inhaled sharply. "I want you to want me, Ophelia. I don't like having to force you."

I rubbed myself against him. "I do want you," I lied, hating every touch but knowing it was all I had to give. If this didn't work, there was no backup plan. I didn't even have a gun anymore.

"Prove it," he demanded.

My mind raced. I had no idea. Other than...

"Tomorrow," I said with conviction. "No more waiting. We get married tomorrow."

He raised an eyebrow. "Tomorrow?"

I nodded quickly. Hell. What did it matter anymore anyway? This was always going to be my life. Augie had been the sweetest of reprieves. A time I would look back on for the rest of my life and silently thank him for, because it would be those memories that got me through endless days with a man I despised.

"Tomorrow," I confirmed again, though the word was starting to sound strange to my ears. "We'll do it at my mom's place. It's nice in her yard. All your friends. Our siblings and parents. Invite whoever you want. Our families will be merged, and so will our businesses. My parents will be pleased. You'll have a wife. Everyone will be happy."

Everyone except me.

That didn't matter if I could get Banjo out alive.

I pressed onto my toes and kissed Riddick's cheek. "But let him go. That's all I ask."

Riddick's eyes narrowed in suspicion. "He's a target. I was given a job to do, and I need to do it."

"My mom won't care if there's a wedding to distract her. If our business is merging with yours, she doesn't have to worry about our reputation anymore." I smiled stiffly and forced out the words. "We can just rely on yours."

The sentence tasted sour. But it had the desired effect of making Riddick preen with pride.

"I'll take care of you," he promised. "And when you have my children, you'll take care of them."

Nothing had ever sounded quite so reprehensible.

And yet one look at Banjo with his damn hands knifed to the fucking table, and the memory of his little girl in the back of my mind, had me nodding like wiping asses and snotty noses was all I'd ever wanted.

With Augie, the idea of kids seemed kind of fun and sweet. I might have even been persuaded to have one, with time.

With Riddick, even the idea felt like a life sentence.

"Whatever you want." I was willing to agree to anything. "Just let him go."

Riddick shrugged. "Fine. He can go."

I wasn't waiting for him to change his mind. I rushed to Banjo's side, my back to Riddick, trying to keep his eyes off Augie's brother.

He lifted his head. "What are you doing?" he whispered, more coherent than he'd led Riddick to believe though his voice was still laced with pain.

I wrapped my fingers around the first blade. "This is going to hurt." I yanked the knife out from his skin, his scream of pain echoing around the room.

Riddick whistled. "Hurry up, Ophelia. If we're getting married tomorrow, I have a lot to do."

Banjo stared up at me with huge eyes. "You can't marry him."

I swallowed hard, gripping the handle on the other knife.

Banjo braced himself.

I yanked it out.

Under the cover of his screams, I whispered a final plea.

"Tell your brother I'm sorry." I swallowed hard. "And that I'll always love him."

Banjo got up and staggered toward the door, his fingertips dripping with crimson blood. But at least his legs seemed unaffected. He would be able to make it back to the main road.

But this was the end of one for me.

When Riddick put his hand to the back of my neck and steered me toward the door, I let him.

36

AUGIE

Police swarmed around Banjo's home, their lights flashing red and blue through the windows, while Colt, Rafe, Lacey, and I all sat in the living room, none of us speaking.

Lacey seemed tiny, squished onto the couch between two of her men, her eyes red from crying. "Do you think Luna's okay with my mom?" she asked Rafe.

He rubbed her hand briskly. "She didn't even stir when I dropped her over there. When she wakes up in the morning, April is going to take her out for pancakes."

"She'll love that. Sugar and ice cream and syrup for breakfast," Colt added, but his voice was devoid of emotion.

I listened. It was impossible not to. But I didn't dare say a word.

After Ophelia had dropped her bomb of truth, Lacey and Colt had allowed me to come back here with them, since for once, this entire thing wasn't my fault.

But all I could think was that there was a hit on me and my brother.

And I had no idea who had ordered it.

Or why.

I could understand someone wanting to take me out. I pissed people off at the drop of a hat. I made no effort to spare anyone's feelings. I'd slept with so many women it was probably inevitable that eventually I'd pick the wrong one, and her jealous boyfriend or husband would come after me.

Or have the connections to pay someone to do it.

But there was no reason to kill a college senior who had never been in any trouble and spent most of his time with his family.

It didn't make sense.

An officer from the Providence Police Department walked in like he owned the place and stared at the four of us, his gaze lingering on me and then Lacey. He scowled at her. "Good to see you're finally sitting here like I told you to. Just so I understand, is this man here part of your...foursome?"

She stared up at him, anger blazing in her eyes. "Sergeant, you know very well I've already explained our relationship to you."

He shrugged, jotting down something on his notepad. "Just making sure you didn't forget one of your lovers. You seem to have quite a few."

Colt and Rafe both shoved to their feet, ready to throw down with the ignorant prick of a cop, but I stood up, too, putting myself in between them.

"Sit down," I said calmly. "He's not worth it."

Lacey had it anyway. She pushed me out of the way.

"You're not going to find Banjo standing here questioning me about our sex life, Sergeant. I suggest you do your damn job, and do it out of my sight. Get out of my house."

The man put his hands up in mock surrender and walked away.

Lacey sank back down. "They're unbelievable," she seethed. "Nothing changes with them! They're so fucking useless I could scream. Why aren't they out there searching for him?"

None of us had ever had good experiences with the Providence Police department. Few people did. They were mostly old-school, corrupt bastards who got their rocks off picking on people who lived in Saint View and taking money under the table from those who lived across the border in Providence.

"I don't know, Princess," Rafe soothed. "As soon as the sun comes up, I'm going out there to find him. I don't care that they want us to stay put and not get in their way. Fuck that."

Colt and I nodded in agreement. Dawn was only an hour away. I had no idea where we'd go or what we could do to find him, but anything had to be better than sitting here.

Shouts came from outside, and all of us twisted in the direction of the windows.

Officers who had been congregated at various points on the lawn suddenly took off running, a group of them stopping just a way down the street.

"What is it?" Lacey asked.

I shook my head, squinting through the darkness. "No idea, but they're real interested in it. I'm going out there. Fuck the cops."

The others trailed me, and I strode across the lawn, arguing with the officers who again tried to tell us to go back inside and sit down.

An officer moved to one side, and I caught a flash of dark-blond hair, matted with blood, lit up beneath a streetlight.

"Banjo!" Lacey's scream ripped straight from her heart. She sprinted across the lawn, throwing herself at him, wrapping her arms around his chest and hugging him like she couldn't quite believe he was real.

Rafe followed in a second later, sandwiching her between them and holding them with a fierceness that no smart person would mess with.

Colt's relief was evident in the slump of his body and the way he doubled over, pressing his elbows to his knees.

I rubbed a hand over his back. "You okay?"

"No," he choked out, shaking his head, his voice croaky with emotion.

I knew what he meant because I wasn't either.

Somebody pulled a first aid kit from the back of a cop car and found some gauze to press to the wounds in Banjo's hands that were deep and nasty.

Anger boiled in my system.

At Riddick who was nothing more than a faceless name to me, but who had inflicted injuries on my brother that turned my stomach.

At Ophelia, because every mark on his body could have been prevented if she'd just told me who she really was.

But she hadn't trusted me. Hadn't loved me enough to try.

And this was the fucking outcome.

Banjo took the gauze from the cops but refused their offers of help. Lacey and Rafe tried to argue with him, but he insistently stepped away from them and made his way over to me.

He stopped in front of me, his face dirty, beaten, covered in blood.

My heart broke in two, shattering right down the middle. I shook my head. "I'm so fucking sorry."

"You should be. What the fuck are you doing here?"

I recoiled at the anger in his words, even though I knew I deserved them. "I'll go." It was enough that he was alive. "After everything I did...and everything with Ophelia..."

He grabbed me by the shirt and then swore, dropping his hands and cradling his injuries to his chest. "Fuck, that hurts." But then his gaze focused through the pain. "Ophelia was the one who found me. Augie, she promised to marry Riddick. *Tomorrow*."

The words were a sucker punch. It suddenly felt like it was my face that was broken and bleeding. I swallowed hard. "She moves quick."

Banjo eyes filled with anger. "Don't be a dick. You always fucking do this. Something gets hard and you just walk the fuck away. You love her."

I couldn't deny it. I did. "What does that matter? When has loving someone ever been enough to make them stay? I loved our parents. They left. I loved you, and you fucking left as well." I grimaced and shook my head. "I didn't mean that. I know you had a reason to walk away and that it was my fault—"

"She loves you too."

I sighed. "She lied. I don't even know who she is."

That only seemed to piss Banjo off more. "Then fucking learn, Augie! That woman just found me in the middle of nowhere and agreed to marry a complete psychopath in order to save me. Why the hell would she do that if she doesn't love you? You think she loves me? I've met her all of two or three times!"

"You're worth saving. No matter the cost."

"Not to her I'm not! I'm fucking nothing to her, other than what I mean to you." He got right up in my face, his blue eyes blazing. "That guy, Riddick? If you let her marry him, Augie, she's as good as dead. Even if he lets her live, a life with him wouldn't be one worth surviving. I know that just from spending a few hours with him."

I hated everything he was saying.

But I also couldn't stand the injuries on his face. His hands. The torture he'd suffered.

That was what Ophelia did for a living.

She was a stone-cold killer. One who didn't understand remorse.

"Look down at your hands, Banjo. What Riddick did to you? That could have just as easily been Ophelia. You want that sort of person in your life? In Luna's?"

He went silent. But it was only for a second before he shook his head. "I don't know what she's done in the past, Aug. But you've done some pretty messed-up shit too."

His eyes were so fucking earnest. When I stared into them, there was no doubt as to who Banjo was at his very core.

"I've forgiven you. Maybe you could show her the same kindness."

We stared at each other, him holding my gaze until I eventually turned away.

He could forgive.

But he and I weren't the same.

We never had been.

And that hadn't changed.

37

———

OPHELIA

I had nothing to wear to a wedding.

Riddick had escorted me straight from the old ice arena to my mother, who had gotten out of bed at his insistent pounding on the door and come downstairs in a nightgown that looked like she'd just stepped out of some movie set. Her dark hair fell softly around her shoulders, her perfectly painted toenails peeping out from her open-toed slippers.

The only thing that gave away that she was rattled was the way she kept her face ducked because she wasn't wearing makeup.

Riddick pushed me through the doorway, none too gently. "We're getting married tomorrow," he'd announced to her.

Mom's head had snapped up, her eyes suddenly bright. "You are? Tomorrow?"

"Your daughter's idea. I'll be back around three for the ceremony?"

Mom had nodded like I wasn't even in the room.

"Wonderful! Of course. I'll arrange everything. Thank you!"

Riddick had leaned in and kissed my cheek, then dropped his voice to a low whisper. "I really hope you don't change your mind, Little Ophelia."

"I won't," I'd said about as enthusiastically as if I was being forced to crawl through mud. "I'll be the one in white."

Except I probably wasn't going to be in white, because who had a wedding dress just lying around in storage at their mother's house? What did it matter anyway? I could wear these same clothes I'd been wearing for days. Maybe I wouldn't even shower. If I got to the top of the aisle and I smelled like a sewer rat, maybe Riddick would change *his* mind.

I stared at the ceiling in the guest room, contemplating a future with a man like Riddick.

It didn't paint a pretty picture.

It would be a continuation of my childhood. Only worse because I'd be bringing children into this life.

Children I wouldn't be able to protect from the horrors of what their parents were.

I didn't cry. There was no point. I was just resigned to the fate I'd always known was coming.

My bedroom door opened and then closed.

I didn't bother looking over, not caring who it was, until Jezebel hovered over me, studying me with a worried expression. She was pretty, her blond hair curled around her oval face. Her dress was a deep purple, and it hugged her curves sweetly. She wore a fresh flower pinned above her heart.

Neither of us said anything. She just lifted the covers

and got in beside me, not caring she was probably destroying her corsage in the process. "You can't marry him," she whispered.

I sighed heavily. "We both know I have to."

She twisted onto her side and punched my arm. Hard.

I rubbed at it. "What was that for?"

"Because I know you don't want this. Who would? My brother would make any woman miserable for the rest of their lives."

I shrugged. I'd be miserable anyway. Augie hated my guts, and rightly so. No other man had ever made me feel the way he did, so the odds of finding another seemed pretty small. Marrying Riddick didn't sound like a walk in the park.

But I didn't care.

None of it mattered anymore. "My parents need this to happen, Jez. I've known all along I'd have to marry someone they chose for me. Does it really matter who?"

"Yes! You don't love him! Vincent is with someone he loves."

"All the more reason for me to take one for the team. If I do this, she'll have no reason to try to ruin his happiness."

Jez fell silent at that. "I don't want this life," she said into the silent room.

But neither of us had a choice in it.

We never had. I'd tried to pull away, but there was always something that drew me back.

It was time to just give in.

ow my mother had managed to get a violinist with less than twenty-four hours' notice, I had no idea. But one stood at the bottom of the stairs when I emerged from my bedroom. Mom had waltzed in an hour earlier, found Jez and I curled up in bed, and promptly kicked her out, claiming it was mom and daughter time.

She'd dragged me out of bed and practically shoved me in a shower, hovering around like I might jump out of the tiny second-story window if she left me alone too long.

When I'd finally got out, smelling of rose-scented bodywash, she'd thrust a white dress at me.

It was one from the back of her closet and was half a size too small so it pinched every time I moved.

Seemed fitting that I would be in pain throughout the wedding I didn't want to be a part of.

Using the railing for balance, I came down the stairs slowly, not missing the way my mother and father, dressed to the nines, talked and laughed with Jezebel's parents.

"For fuck's sake," I muttered. "Could you kiss their asses any more? Isn't it enough that you're selling your firstborn to them?"

But I plastered on a fake smile when Mom waved me over to say hello to them.

Jez's mom, Mira, took in my outfit and gave a nod of satisfaction, like I was the fattest pig at the county fair, and she'd just won a blue ribbon.

Mira clucked her tongue. "Well, I can say your ugly duckling did turn into a bit of a swan, didn't she?"

Mom gave a peal of laughter, like it was the funniest thing she'd ever heard and not a plain fucking insult.

Jez's father looked me up and down with barely withheld disgust. "She'll do. I would have preferred someone with lighter skin and hair. But if this is what Riddick wants, then so be it."

Oh goodie. I got the parent-in-law tick of approval.

Mom beamed at them, like she'd needed their okay before this wedding could go ahead. She clapped her hands together. "Right. Well, if everyone could go outside and take a seat, we'll get this show on the road!"

She was practically giddy with excitement.

I just wanted the floor to open and swallow me whole.

The handful of people in the room filed out, and the violinist started up a different song.

The wedding entrance song.

Might as well have been the *Star Wars* death march.

My mom took one arm, and my father took the other. The two of them escorted me outside, to a red carpet that had been laid on top of the synthetic grass. I stared at the small group of people. There wasn't anyone I knew. Nobody sat on the bride's side. Not one person.

Every face on the groom's side was a stranger, other than Jez's, who didn't even glance my way as she was too busy with her phone.

My heart sank. "Where's Vincent?" I whispered to mom as we started down the aisle. I wanted my brother.

And my sister.

"He couldn't make it," she whispered back. "Now pay attention. There's your groom."

I squeezed my eyes tight, not wanting to see Riddick

waiting for me at the other end. That would only make it all too real.

I hated that Vincent hadn't come. I knew he didn't agree with any of this and he would have wanted me to fight this marriage, but we were past that point now.

I just wanted my brother by my side.

I walked slowly, moving robotically down the aisle, my mother's nails digging into my arm so hard it was like she thought she was single-handedly stopping me from running away.

My father said nothing, as usual. As completely checked out of reality as he always was. I wished I could do the same.

When we reached the officiant, she smiled at my parents. "Who here gives this woman to this man?"

I ground my teeth at the old-fashioned line. Like I was a piece of property that could be transferred from one man to another.

"We do," my mother answered loudly and clearly. "Wholeheartedly with our full blessing."

God, I couldn't stand her.

I was grateful when she released her grip on my arm and her and dad stepped back to fill two of the empty seats on my side of the congregation.

A chilly wind blew across the lawn, raising goose-bumps on my arms.

Or maybe that was just the dread sitting like lead in the bottom of my stomach because Riddick took my hand.

I wanted to shrink away.

I should probably get used to it, since that's what would happen now. I'd become smaller and smaller, married to a man like him. Until I was just like my father, barely a shell, not saying a word because of how Riddick dominated me.

I missed Augie. Missed the way his touch felt. Missed the way his voice rumbled in my ear.

If I closed my eyes, I could be back in his little house, naked in his sheets, his strong arms keeping out the world.

"Ophelia," Riddick snapped.

I shook my head and opened my eyes. "Sorry, what?" I looked between him and the officiant, trying to catch up on what I'd missed.

"It's time for you to say your vows, sweetheart," the lady said kindly.

Sweetheart.

Augie called me that.

My heart squeezed.

So did Riddick's fingers around mine. So hard I let out a tiny yelp of pain that had the officiant staring at me with concern and Riddick's expression morphing into something that appeared satisfied.

Like my pain pleased him.

Jez caught my eye from the front row, in the seat next to her parents.

She gave the tiniest shake of her head, a desperate plea in her eyes for me to not do this.

I turned away, back to the officiant. "I'm ready."

She nodded, clearly not one-hundred-percent sure what was going on here and uncomfortable because of it, but I tried to smile reassuringly at her. The last thing I needed was her refusing to marry us because she thought I wasn't here under my own free will.

She raised her voice so it would carry across the garden. "Before we begin the vows, I'm obliged to ask. Does anyone in attendance disagree with the marriage of Ophelia and Riddick? If you know of any reason these two souls should not be joined in sacred matrimony today, speak now or forever hold your peace."

I darted another glance at Jez.

Who looked very much like she wanted to stand up and object. Despite her mother's grasp on her arm, I suspected one tiny nod from me might have given her the courage to do it.

I wouldn't.

Riddick would probably snap her neck right here and now.

Quickly followed by my own.

Jez saw the expression in my eye and sat back, resigned.

I turned in my mother's direction, stupidly hopeful she might see how much I didn't want this and let it go at the last second.

The woman had her phone up, recording the ceremony with a huge smile plastered across her over-Botoxed face.

Of course she'd want proof our families had joined. She'd probably send the video out on the dark web just so everyone knew our family had a new connection. A dangerous one that should be feared and respected.

I sighed heavily. "Just get on with it," I told the officiant.

With a pitying expression, she began, "Riddick. Do you take Ophelia to be your lawful wedded wife, in sickness and in health, 'til death do you part?"

"I do," Riddick said proudly. His voice dropped, so only the officiant and I would hear. "'Til death, Little Ophelia."

A shiver ran down my spine.

"Do you, Ophelia, take Riddick to be your lawful wedded husband, in sickness and health, 'til death do you part?"

I opened my mouth, but nothing came out.

Riddick's fingers tightened around mine, but all I could see was me and Augie wrapped around each other in his little house.

Dirt-fucking-poor.

But happy.

I couldn't give that up.

Even if Augie didn't want me, I'd had a taste of what that kind of love felt like. How could I go the rest of my life, never feeling that again?

"Don't embarrass me, Ophelia," Riddick said, low and dangerous. "We made a deal."

Banjo. I squeezed my eyes shut. My happiness. Or Banjo's life.

There was no contest. I had to go through with it. "I d—"

The back door swung open so hard the glass cracked and splintered, falling to the paved ground in spears.

My brother walked in, gun raised, and without a second of hesitation, let off a single shot.

It whistled past me so quick I didn't even register it was a bullet.

Riddick let out a grunt, drawing my attention to the crimson pool of red spreading across his white jacket.

Screams and shouts erupted around us. Another gunshot pierced the air.

"And you get a bullet," Scythe said above the chaos, taking down one of Riddick's guests who'd pulled a weapon. "And you get a bullet," he cried, sending another shot into a man who lunged for him. He shot another two rounds into the sky, looking like the full-on psychopath I knew he could be.

With his hands raised like he was summoning a demon from the skies, he yelled, "You can all get fucking bullets if you want to keep this bullshit up!"

A hush fell over the crowd. All of us staring at the scene my brother had created.

He strode up the red carpet, stepping by the one man he'd killed and another who was on the ground writhing.

Riddick had stumbled back, unable to hold his weight with all the blood he was losing. But it wasn't enough to stop him from shouting at his sister. "Do something!"

Scythe scoffed, kneeling at Riddick's side and cocking his head. "Why are you hoping she'll help you? She's the one who called me to let me know about this little party I wasn't even invited to." He glared over at our mom, who was still recording everything with a frighteningly exuberant expression on her face. "I'm real fucking hurt, Ma. Real hurt."

Riddick's father made a move toward Scythe, but Scythe just laughed in his face.

"Sit down, old man. We both know I could take you out in an instant. Don't piss me off. I'm not in the fucking mood. I already lost one sister. I'm not losing another." He glared at Riddick, leaning down and tracing the bullet hole in his jacket with the nose of his gun. "There's only one alpha dog around here, Riddick, and it's never been you. I might be out of the game, but I'm not out of the family. You'll stay away from my sister, or I will make your life a living hell." He dug the nose of the gun into the wound while Riddick howled.

Scythe shook his head, stood back, and added three new bullet holes to Riddick's body. One in his gut. One through his heart. The last one through his brain. "Oops," he laughed. "Changed my mind. You're dead."

Covered in blood, he glanced at the officiant, who was cowering by the fence with her hands above her head. "By the way, I object."

Everyone stared at Scythe. No one moved. Not to scream and run away. Not to try to help Riddick, though he was clearly past that point.

Scythe had made his mark.

And with my mother's video still rolling, it was one nobody would forget anytime soon.

Scythe stared at me, eyes wide, face smeared with Riddick's blood. He held out his hand, his expression gentling. "Come on. There's someone who wants to see you. Jez wasn't the only one who called me." He jerked his head toward the end of the aisle where Augie stood, deathly still.

Shit.

He'd seen every inch of my dirty laundry. It was all right here in front of him.

The real truth of who my family was. Who I was.

I walked slowly, on wobbly legs, back down the aisle to stand in front of him.

I could only imagine what he saw when he looked at me.

A killer. Danger. The woman who'd put his whole family at risk.

And yet his gaze searched my body urgently, flicking over every inch of my skin. "You're okay?"

I swallowed hard. "Physically, yes." But I shook my head, my eyes filling with tears. "In every other way, no." I couldn't help it. I reached for his hand, taking it and rubbing his cold fingers through mine. "I'm so sorry I lied. I don't want to make excuses, so I won't, but, Augie..." I spread my hand out, indicating the carnage behind me. "This is who I am. I don't want it to be, but this is my truth. You know it all now."

My heart thundered behind my chest as I drank in the sight of him. It had been barely twenty-four hours since I'd left his home, and yet I felt like I had to memorize every plane and angle of his too-handsome face. Commit it all to memory so when he walked away, I would still have it burned there. "I love you. I know I don't have much to offer other than that. I come with baggage. So much fucking baggage, and a family who is batshit crazy..."

"I hope you're talking about Vincent," Scythe said grumpily. "I'm just fine. No need for medication here!" He toed Riddick's dead body absentmindedly.

We both ignored him, and I gave Augie a sad smile.

"I know apologies and I love yous aren't enough to change what I did. But I'm glad you know. I can walk away now, knowing that at least I gave you that."

We stared at each other, but there was nothing left for me to say.

"Excuse me." I moved around him, unable to stand

there any longer for fear I'd do something stupid. Like throw myself at his feet and beg.

I wouldn't do that. I had to be able to stand on my own two feet and look myself in the mirror at night. Riddick had already tried to take so much from me. I couldn't give it away to another man.

Augie caught my wrist. "Lia," he whispered.

A tremble raced down my spine at the nickname I loved hearing on his lips. A ball of emotion rose up my throat at how bad I wanted him. At how bad I needed his touch. His words. His heart.

I turned around, sure all of that was written on my face.

He cupped both my cheeks, drawing me in, our breaths mingling while we breathed together. He brought his forehead to mine, and a tear slipped down my cheek.

I couldn't stand it. Being this close to him but not being his. "If this is goodbye," I whispered. "Please. Just do it fast. I can't take it."

He shook his head, lifting my face so I had to look him in the eye.

"I love you," he whispered. "I don't know how not to."

The sob burst out of my mouth as he pressed his lips to mine.

He didn't say anything about the fact I was sprayed in drying blood that wasn't mine. He wrapped his arms around me, lifting me off the ground and claiming my mouth in a kiss that stole my breath.

Our mouths moved, tongues stroking, but it was more than just something physical. Something inside me connected to him. It joined and coiled, spinning my head, taking my heart with it, and cementing the fact no man would ever make me feel the way Augie Mitchell did.

"I love you, Lia," he said again. "Every part of you. Everything you've done. Everything you'll do in the future. It doesn't matter. You've seen me at my worst, and you love me anyway. Let me in. Let me do the same thing for you that you did for me. All you have to do is say yes." He sucked in a breath. "Say you'll be mine."

Earlier, when the officiant had asked me something similar about taking Riddick, the words had dried in my mouth. Like a ball of lead, I hadn't been able to get them out.

But with Augie they rolled off my tongue without hesitation. I kissed his sweet mouth and said words I'd never thought I'd want to say to a man. "Yours. Always."

A marriage hadn't happened here in this garden.

But a commitment had. A declaration of love. A silent promise that for better or worse, we'd keep choosing each other.

"This is great!" My mother's voice broke through my bubble of happiness. She practically skipped over to my brother and kissed his cheek. "I got the entire thing on video. Once I get this up online, everyone will know we're number one again. My son, taking out a key player like Riddick! Wow. When you shacked up with that woman, I was sure she had you so pussy-whipped I'd never see this day, but you're back! And back with a bang! Thank you!"

She beamed with pride at the bodies on the ground. Riddick's parents and the other guests had disappeared while I'd been having my moment with Augie. My father had already gone into cleanup mode, dealing with the officiant, who would be paid and threatened enough to keep quiet. If anyone reported the gunshots, that was nothing a wad of cash to the police chief wouldn't fix.

Mom was on cloud nine. Like she'd planned the entire thing and it had gone off without a hitch. "We don't need their family. This changes everything. With them only having Jezebel and us having the two of you, we'll be drowning in jobs again. You should both go home and get changed and have some sleep, because it will be busy! We'll be able to buy you a big new house, Ophelia. There's actually one for sale just down the road. Won't that be perfect?"

I stared at the woman in complete and utter disbelief.

Scythe picked up her hand from his shoulder and shoved it away.

"Go to hell, Mom," I said for both of us, knowing we shared the same sentiment. "He's out. I'm out. Fawn is dead, not that you took even a second to grieve. We're all done, do you hear me?" I strode across the lawn so I was eye to eye with the woman who'd tormented me my entire life.

Her mouth dropped open. "You can't! Not now, after all of this!"

I glared at her. "We can. We are. Don't call us. Don't contact us. To you, we don't exist."

"You live in properties we own! You can't just say you won't work for us anymore while we're supporting you! This is what families do, Ophelia! Stop being such a princess."

I gave a hard laugh. "I'll be gone by nightfall. You can take your damn properties and burn them to the ground, along with the entire business."

Rage consumed her. "So, what? You're just going to leave your father and me on the streets to starve?"

I whirled around and gave her a look that shut her evil mouth right up. "I'm sure it will feel a whole lot like all the times you locked us in cupboards and didn't feed us for days. I think you called it 'toughening us up.'" I shook my head at her in disgust. "Your turn to toughen up, Mom. I don't care what you do or where you live. You can both rot in hell for all I care."

Mom turned to Scythe, clearly hoping he'd disagree.

Scythe jerked his head in my direction. "Killing people makes me hungry, so I was kind of only half listening while I planned out what I was going to get to eat on my way home, but ditto to everything she said. I'm team Ophelia."

My mother just gaped at the two of us, but her real ire focused in on me. Just like it always had.

This woman had never loved me. Never even tolerated me. I was an asset. Until I wasn't.

"So, what?" she screamed, gaze sliding past me to land on Augie. "You're just going to go live in some shack in Saint View with him?"

On instinct, I stepped in front of him, blocking her view.

Augie wouldn't have it. He stepped back to my side, standing tall, facing off against my mother.

Side by side.

His hand in mine.

His support silent but strong, his face stony with anger on my behalf.

She laughed bitterly. "Go then. Go live in Saint View with your slut of a boyfriend. See how quick you get sick of slumming it. Or do you think you can live off his brother's money too? That didn't work out too well for his parents, did it?"

I blinked in confusion. I didn't understand what that meant.

But Augie stepped forward, a low growl in his voice. "What?"

My mother, every ounce of her nasty black heart rising to the surface was more than happy to fill Augie in. "Such a good thing you're handsome because you clearly aren't smart. Your parents were the ones who put the hit out on you and Banjo. I suggested that killing Banjo would be enough for them to make a claim on the money and other assets his wife's aunt left him when she went to jail. But your mom insisted that Banjo loved you and if he had a will, it was you he would have taken care of in it."

Augie frowned. "You're wrong. He would have taken care of his daughter."

Mom rolled her eyes. "If she'd been a threat, she would have been on the hit list too. Your brother's family is already taken care of through Lacey's assets. We checked into it. The only person in Banjo's will is you. If something happened to him, you'd be in the money. If something happened to both of you, however, especially because you don't have a will or a wife or any dependents..."

"His parents might have had a case," I concluded, sick to my stomach for Augie. I knew his family history was rocky at best and that he'd been estranged from their parents for most of his adult life. But this still had to hurt.

Augie shook his head. "They have no money to hire someone. Or even the contacts..."

Mom shrugged. "Your mom is my favorite waitress at my favorite café. And I looked stupid when Riddick came to me and said he wanted to start doing jobs with Ophelia. I didn't want to say I had none. So I took the job, no cash up front. We would have claimed it back once they got their payout."

Which meant she could still make money from Augie's death.

Scythe seemed to have the same idea.

His fingers shot out and grasped my mother's neck, tilting her head to one side so dangerously far it seemed it might snap at any second. "You already ruined Fawn's life," he said deathly quietly, the complete blackness of his dark side unleashed. "You will not ruin Ophelia's. Or mine. You touch so much as a hair on Banjo, Augie, or any of my family, you'll be sorry."

Mom, despite the surely uncomfortable position she was in, tapped my brother on the hand.

He released his hold enough that she could talk.

She swallowed hard. "You've made your point clear, Son. You can keep your house. You're the alpha."

Scythe switched back to his playful smart-assy. "Should I get a nametag for my collar? Should I start howling at full moons? Awoooo!"

We all ignored him, well used to his brand of crazy. I stared at my mother. I needed to hear her say it. To hear her let me go.

She didn't say anything. But eventually, she sighed and gave me the tiniest of nods.

It was the least she could do after a lifetime of torture.

A part of me suspected I'd never truly be free, but for

now, it felt like a release. A burden of weight lifted from my shoulders, disappearing into the sunset.

Augie wrapped his arm around mine and drew me in, his lips to my ear. "Let's go home."

Home might have been cheap housing in the worst area of Saint View, but words had never sounded sweeter.

38

AUGIE

anjo walked slowly across the park, his hands in the pockets of his hoodie. He had a beanie pulled low, which I suspected probably hid the bandages he would have needed after his run-in with Riddick.

He stopped in front of me, practically reeking of sadness.

"Show me," I demanded.

He didn't have to ask what I was talking about. He took his hands from his pockets. Both were fat with bandages.

I grimaced. "What did your surgeon say?"

He shrugged. "It's a bit of a wait-and-see game."

"You going to be able to use them?"

Banjo rubbed one across the back of his neck. "I mean, yeah. He said I should heal nicely, with time."

"You don't have time. You're in the middle of the college football season."

He waved his hands at me. "Not anymore."

My heart fell. "You can't miss this last part of your senior year. It'll ruin all your chances of going pro."

Banjo smiled at me fondly. "You were the only one who thought I was going pro, Aug."

I hadn't dared show up at his recent games, but I'd been at all his high school ones. I'd kept up with his college highlights on YouTube. "You're good!" I insisted.

"Decent," he admitted. "Not pro-level good. I probably should have given it up a while ago, but I love it. And I'll continue loving it, playing with Colt and Rafe and Luna in the backyard. Or on weekends with friends. But I was never going pro, even before this." He nudged me with his elbow. "I appreciate the blind support though."

I smiled back, finally relenting in the face of his sensible argument. "Always."

We both stared across the road at the little café. Through the big glass window at the front, our mother could be seen moving around, serving coffee.

Looking all sweet and innocent as she delivered food to tables.

All while knowing she'd tried to have both of us killed for a couple hundred thousand dollars.

"I'm so stupid for letting her back into my life," Banjo said, regret heavy in his tone. "I brought this on myself by telling her about Selina leaving me money before she went into jail."

I shook my head. "You couldn't have known they were capable of this. You didn't even know them. I remember them from when we were kids, and even though they were shitty parents, I would have never picked them to be this desperate."

"You sure you want to go in there?" Banjo asked.

I didn't. But I knew Banjo did, and I wasn't letting him go in alone.

We were brothers. It was a relationship I was never going to take for granted again.

We both set off across the street. I opened the door for him, since his hands weren't much help to him right now, and he entered the little shop, me close behind him.

"Take a seat anywhere," Mom called without lifting her head. "I'll be right with you."

"Mom," Banjo said quietly.

She turned around, a smile stretching across her face. "Banjo! Sweetie, I wasn't expecting you."

Her gaze slid to me, and her eyes widened. "Augie!"

Neither of us replied. Second by second, her smile fell away. "Take a seat. I'm due for a break. I'll join you in just a moment."

Banjo and I took a booth in the back, away from all the other customers. I was glad. What I had to say to this woman didn't need to be heard by anyone else.

She slid into the other side of the booth a moment later, her apron twisted in her aged hands.

She seemed so much older than I remembered. Smaller. Frailer.

Still not a parent.

"You know, don't you?" she asked softly.

"Yes," Banjo replied.

Her shoulders slumped, but then she steeled her expression, ignoring me, a pleading tone in her voice when she spoke to her youngest son. "I never meant for it to go this far. I'm sorry, I don't know what I was thinking. I tried to stop it all back when they threw that Molotov cocktail through Willa's window and—"

"What?" Banjo and I snapped in unison.

She stared at him with big eyes, and then looked to me, and then back to him. "They said your car was there and so they assumed you were too."

I remembered Banjo, Colt, Lacey, and Rafe taking a limo to the city that night, celebrating an anniversary. They'd been picked up from Willa's after dropping Luna there for babysitting. Leaving Banjo's car in the driveway.

Mom gave him the most pathetic, pleading look. "I didn't know they'd be so reckless. That they'd try to...do it while Luna was there..."

A rage so hot I was sure I'd never felt anything like it coursed through me. I couldn't contain it. "I know you don't give a shit about me, but you nearly killed an innocent, three-year-old girl. Not to mention Willa! She was the closest thing we had to a mother, and you damn near ended her. Fuck. You sit over there, acting all small and innocent, playing the 'I'm sorry' card like we could ever fucking forgive you. But you're as sick and twisted as the people you associate with."

Banjo shook with a rage I'd never seen from him before. But while mine came out in a rush of words and a storm of anger, his came out in a chilling threat.

"Stay away from my family. Leave town. Run away, like you did all those years ago. But this time, stay gone. Because if I ever see you here again, you'll find out you aren't the only one who has connections."

He didn't have to say another word.

I stood, and he followed me out.

It wasn't until we were outside in the bright sunlight, away from the building, that he turned to me.

In an instant, he was the boy I'd rescued from foster

care. The one I loved so much it fucking killed me. I put my arms around him and held him, neither of us saying anything.

His shoulders shook silently, but after a while he pulled back, sniffing once and dashing tears off his face with his bandaged-up hands. He laughed. "Wanna go to the beach?"

I grinned at the abrupt change of subject. "You can watch me surf."

"I can watch you wipe out; I think you mean."

"Ooh, big words from a little grommet."

He shoved his shoulder into me, jostling me off the sidewalk. "I'm nearly twenty-two! I hardly count as a grommet anymore."

"You'll always be a grommet to me, little brother."

He grinned, and I soaked it in, finally feeling whole.

* * *

I'd taken exactly three steps inside my house before I realized something was different. There was a pretty floral scent in the air, coming from two candles on the entryway table that had most definitely not been there when I'd left.

In the living room, my old, threadbare couch had acquired two new cushions that were a girly pink color. My battered coffee table gleamed with...I swiped a finger across it. Was that some sort of wood polish?

"Lia!" I called out. "What happened while I was gone?"

She stuck her head around the corner from the

kitchen, a nervous smile on her pretty face. "Do you like it?"

I walked over to her, putting my arms around her waist. "You bringing your things into my house and making it ours?" I dropped a kiss on her lips. "Yeah, Lia. I love it."

She beamed at me, then kissed me back. Our tongues tangled for a second before she drew back sharply.

"How did it go with your mom?"

I shrugged. "As well as can be expected. She'll leave town if she knows what's good for her."

"I'm glad. Hopefully your parents and mine are both holed up in Hell. Or at least somewhere far, far away where we never have to deal with them again." She frowned and swiped at my wet hair. "Did you go surfing? It's freezing!"

It had been, but it had made me feel alive. "I want to teach you. You'd be so hot out there on a board." My dick got hard just thinking about it. I rubbed it against her.

"Mmm?" she asked, smiling at me. "You aren't worried about me trying to drown one of your friends? Or stabbing that guy who runs the juice stand?"

I sniggered, breathing in her clean, feminine scent. "If you tell me you're done with that game, then I believe you."

She pressed up onto her toes, bringing her up to the same height I was. "I'm done. I have no idea what I'm doing next." She cocked her head to one side. "If I take some more of Eve and Lyric's dance classes, maybe I can come work with you."

The groan I let out at the idea of her swinging around a

pole naked quickly turned to a growl at the thought of other men seeing her like that. I lifted her into my arms, wrapping her legs around my waist. "Dance for me, Lia. Just me."

I sank down onto the couch with her on my lap, and she laughed between kisses, her happiness so damn sweet because there was so much sadness and misery around us it would have been easier to linger in that.

But we'd made an effort for this house to be our safe haven. Where it was just me and her and nothing else.

I took my phone out of my pocket and put some music on, the phone connecting to the Bluetooth speakers automatically so sultry beats filled the room.

"I have no rhythm," Ophelia complained.

"Liar," I whispered into her neck. "You have plenty of rhythm when you're riding my cock."

She shivered, and I grabbed her hips, rocking her over me in time to the beat. She took over a second later, grinding on me, her pussy writhing over my dick that grew harder by the second.

I tugged at her shirt.

But she grinned, slapping my hands away. "No touching. Isn't that the rule?"

I slid my hands up beneath the fabric, palms flat to the warm skin of her back. "Not in my club. My club is a lot more like Psychos. All touching is allowed. Encouraged even."

Her laugh was throaty and sexy and had me thrusting up to meet her movements.

"That so?" She leaned back to take her top off, and it took me all of three seconds to unclip her bra.

Her tits fell into my hands, and I immediately sat forward, putting my face to her pretty nipples, licking and sucking each of them in an alternating pattern, cupping her and using my thumbs for friction when my mouth was otherwise occupied.

God, she tasted good. Her mouth. Her skin. The arousal I knew had to be building between her legs. The way she rubbed herself against me had us both hot and bothered, her breaths quickening, the sounds she made coming out more like moans.

She pulled away to stand and I frowned at her. "Where are you going?"

She shimmied out of her pants, leaving her in nothing but a pair of panties. I lapped up the sight of her, all long limbs, curvy hips, a sweet handful of tits, and a coy smile that was only for me.

I glanced at the broken window coverings. "Half the street can probably see you right now, Lia. Get back down here."

She shook her head, swaying her hips side to side and then lowering her panties to reveal her smooth snatch. "Let them watch. Let them see exactly what you do to me."

She plunged her fingers between her pussy lips, drawing them out as wet and glistening as I knew they'd be.

I nearly fucking came when she bent forward, giving me her fingers to taste.

At her flavor, I grabbed for her thighs, desperate to get them open and on my face.

But she danced out of the way, finding the beat again, moving so damn seductively I knew I'd be replaying this in my head for a lifetime.

I pulled off my shirt and my shorts, glad I'd had a

shower at the beach so I didn't have to waste time now. I palmed my cock, stroking the hard length while she danced, one hand between her legs, rubbing her clit. The other sliding up and down her body, gliding over her stomach and tits, up behind her neck and into her hair.

The growl I let out was so fucking possessive it shocked even me. I caught her hips, holding her tight, and shoved my face between her folds, tongue-fucking her viciously, earning every gasp from her mouth.

Two fingers up inside her was all it took to have her coming. I knew her body well by now, knew exactly where her G-spot was and how she liked it worked. Knew exactly how to lick and suck and play with her until she came again.

I drew her down onto my cock, hard and fast, taking her roughly because I knew she was so wet it wouldn't hurt her. She screamed my name, and I loved the way it sounded on her tongue. Loved the way we moved together, each of us giving the other what we needed. She ground down, meeting my upward strokes. I sucked her nipples, grazed my teeth over the pink ridges that drove me mad for wanting her. She bounced on my cock, over-sensitive from her first orgasm and so easy to fall into a second when I worked her clit.

She squeezed and clenched around me, and I had to grit my fucking teeth not to come inside her hot wetness. But I couldn't. Not yet. I wasn't done.

I was never going to be done with her.

I stood and dropped her down onto her feet, walking her backward to a wall and then flipping her around until she faced it. I followed her in close, pushing her tits into the wall, forcing her head to turn to one side. She gasped when I palmed the sweet curves of her ass, grabbing two indecent handfuls and stroking my wet cock in between.

I glanced over her tight rear hole.

"Yes," she groaned. "Augie, please."

The urge to fuck her ass was so damn strong, but I refused to be a man who took her there before she was ready. Instead, I thrust hard into her pussy, bottoming out inside until we were both breathless.

"You want me to fuck your ass, sweetheart?" I whispered into her ear, taking her slow from behind.

"Yes," she moaned.

"Take my finger first."

I pushed the tip inside her. Her body tensed then adjusted to the intrusion, taking me deeper until my finger, and then two, were pressing against her internal walls, my dick on the other side, making her so fucking tight I could barely stand it.

My balls drew up, desperate to come, but I refused to let it happen. I sank my mouth down on her shoulder, loving she was tall enough to do that without pulling out of her. I breathed through my nose, trying to get myself under control while the perfect feeling that came from the two of us together tried to fry my brain.

"More, Augie," she begged.

It was music to my ears. Her permission to take her there was hot, knowing she wanted it as much as I did.

"Rub your clit, sweetheart. Nice and slow."

She twisted, moving her arm and getting her hand down between her legs. Her hips rolled some more, settling into a new rhythm as I pulled out of her and notched my cock at her rear entrance.

Her breathy gasps of pleasure had my cock leaking, coating her ass in my arousal and hers.

The urge to slam into her was there, but this needed to be her show today. It had to be on her terms. I refused to have it any other way.

I stared down, watching while she worked her ass back onto my dick, her tight entrance opening for me so fucking beautifully my balls ached.

She stroked her clit harder, sliding back on my cock that I fought so hard to keep still.

She took every inch, until my cock was swallowed up, encased in her, so warm and beautiful.

"Fuck me, Augie," she demanded, sliding forward and then back again, taking over, letting me watch and learn what tempo she liked. She arched her back, taking me deep, groaning my name and demanding to make her come again.

That was all I needed to take over. I reached around, covering her fingers with my own, setting a new pace on her clit while I fucked her ass. I started slow, gradually working her up, until she stopped making demands because I was already meeting every one.

"I can't wait to do this with a vibrator in your pussy," I told her between kisses.

She shuddered in pleasure at the idea, just like I knew she would. So I kept going, filling her ear with every dirty thing I wanted to do to her body.

She slammed her hips back against me, her body insisting I finish, even if I had managed to fuck her into the sweetest sort of silence.

The kind where it was only our moans, our breaths,

the indecent sounds of sex so hot I wished we were recording it.

I gripped her hips, my fingertips digging into her flesh as my balls drew up tight, my orgasm refusing to be held at bay a second longer. I shouted her name, deep and guttural and so fucking mine.

Forever.

39

OPHELIA

There could be no official funeral because there was no body to bury. Scythe and I had spent weeks searching for Eddie and Zane. We'd scoured Saint View and Providence and every surrounding neighborhood, hoping to find anything that resembled the house we'd seen in the video of Fawn's death.

But it was like looking for a needle in a haystack.

Eddie and Zane were gone. The only link left behind was their mother, who hadn't been helpful. The woman was barely there, staring out the window, rocking back and forth, muttering nonsense beneath her breath.

She was broken, and every instinct in me said her sons were the reason.

All I could think when I looked at her was that it was better Fawn be dead than be like that.

We all needed closure though. I'd called Eve and asked if we could use the club to have a memorial service. Even if there was no body, Fawn deserved a proper send-off.

It was the least we could do after failing her so badly.

Augie lifted my chin and dipped his head. "Stop it."

I both loved and hated that he knew me well enough to know what I was thinking. It was new, sharing that sort of intimacy with someone. Having a man who watched out for you, and knew when you needed a pep talk, because he understood your expressions.

"None of this is your fault," he reminded me for maybe the hundredth time.

I was slowly starting to believe it. I wasn't there one-hundred-percent, but with him, and the therapist I now saw twice a week, maybe I would be eventually.

Banjo came over with Luna on his hip, Lacey, Rafe, and Colt behind them. They hadn't known Fawn, but they'd come for Augie.

And for me.

Lacey took my fingers and squeezed them, the shorter woman staring up at me with her eyes glistening in sympathy. "How are you doing?"

"I'm fine," I lied.

I could feel Augie's frown, but it disappeared when Luna reached for me.

"Aunty Lia, can I have a sleepover at your place?"

I took her, even though my fingers trembled at the 'Aunty' tag. I looked to Banjo. "Did you...?"

He grinned and shook his head. "That's all her. Do you mind?"

I gazed into Luna's sweet, heart-shaped face. She wriggled in my arms, patting my cheek excitedly, no idea she'd just rocked my world with a single word.

"Can I?" she asked. "Mom said it was okay if it was okay with you and Uncle Augie."

I kissed her forehead. "Absolutely. We'll stay up until midnight, and we'll eat all the candy and we'll watch sca..." I glanced at Lacey. "PG-rated movies?"

Lacey nodded with a smile. "Good choice if you don't want her sleeping in between the two of you."

Except that sounded quite nice. I was ninety-nine-percent sure Augie and I both had too much childhood trauma to ever want one of our own.

But damn if I wasn't going to be the best aunty to this little girl. I could give her that.

Banjo cleared his throat, catching Augie's attention. "Listen, I know this is not the time or place to get into in depth, but I've been doing some thinking." He held up his hands, both still bandaged to the hilt while his bones and tendons healed. "Not much else to do when you're sitting on the sidelines, watching your team practice."

Guilt stabbed at me, and again, without even looking at me, Augie squeezed my fingers. It was a silent reminder that this also was not my fault. I was not the one who'd put knives through his brother's hands.

Banjo continued, not noticing the silent war I was having with myself. "After graduation, I want to start a not-for-profit."

Augie squinted at him. "That does what, exactly?"

Banjo already had a pitch prepared. "I want to go around to the underprivileged schools in the area, starting with Saint View elementary, but with the aim to expand to the middle and high school as well. I want to run after-school football clinics. And maybe other sports too." He stared at his older brother. "I want to keep these kids busy and active and out of trouble and gangs, the way you did for me and Colt and Rafe."

Augie froze. "What? I never did that. You three were just good kids."

Colt shook his head. "After my dad died, it would have been easy for me to get myself in trouble. I had such a chip on my shoulder. The whole reason I didn't was because you and Banjo were out on the street every night, tossing that ball around and expecting me to show up as well."

Rafe nodded. "Your place was where I went when I couldn't stand my father a second longer. If I hadn't had you guys, I probably would have been doing a whole lot worse than smoking a bit of pot behind the school buildings." He glanced over at Luna. "You didn't hear that."

"What's pot?" she asked curiously.

Lacey quickly distracted her with a candy, so no one had to answer that.

Augie opened his mouth to argue with them again, but this time it was me who squeezed his hand. A reminder that though he'd screwed up some things, he hadn't gotten everything wrong.

Banjo waited for him to settle and then looked him in the eye. "Lacey, Rafe, Colt, and I talked it over. We have the money to get this off the ground and we want you to help me run it."

Augie's was quick to shake his head. "I can't. I don't know how."

Banjo laughed. "You don't know how to throw a football with some kids? You haven't walked in their shoes and come out the other side? You can't relate to them at all, in any way? Is that seriously what you're telling me?"

Augie opened his mouth but then closed it when he realized Banjo was right.

I whispered something in Luna's ear, and she giggled then tapped her uncle on the shoulder.

"Say yes," she told him with all her three-year-old sass. "You have to!"

He relaxed, his shoulders dipping as he smiled at her. "Do I now? Says who? You? You're a pipsqueak. Can you even throw a ball yet?"

Luna screwed up her face at him in outrage. "I can so, too!" She scrambled to get down from my arms. "Where's a ball? I'll show you right now!"

Banjo smoothed her hair out and gave Augie a knowing look. "See? You'll be just fine."

Augie nodded and stuck his hand out for Banjo to shake.

Banjo frowned down at his banged-up hands and raised an eyebrow at his brother. "Really?"

Augie slung an arm around his shoulders and laughed instead. "Fine. No handshake. But I'm in. If you truly want me."

"We do, Aug."

We all did. Banjo. Luna.

Me.

At the front of the room, up on the stage, Eve clapped her hands together, drawing everyone's attention. My brother stood with his family. Lyric and her partner, Zeph, and their little girl were at the back of the room with Phoenix and Eve's brother, Dylan. Terry, the bouncer, had his arm around his wife, their teenage kids nearby. There were others I didn't know, but Eve commanded all of the attention.

"I think we all hate that we're here today. But we need this. She deserves it. So the mic is free. I know I personally would love it if you all came up and said something about her. I want to know the Fawn you all knew, and I want you to know the one I did." Her bottom lip trembled. "Because she was beautiful. Smart. And one of the best things to ever happen to both me and to this club. Fawn was kind and her heart was big. I'm a better person for knowing her, and I know you all feel the same way." She wiped her tears away on the backs of her hands then held up her glass. "To you, sweet woman. For reminding me that goodness exists in this world."

The rest of us raised our glasses in a toast to my sister, and then one by one, we all got up on stage and told our memories of her. Some were sad. Some were funny. Some made my brother groan and cover his ears because he just didn't need that sort of information about his sibling.

We all left sad, but somehow lighter.

Afterward, when Augie closed our front door behind us, and that sense of safety enveloped me once more, I knew I could finally let my sister go.

She was laid to rest.

And I was home.

EPILOGUE – FIVE YEARS LATER
OTIS

*D*ad groaned, staring at the damage to the front of his car. "Piece of shit fucking shit! This is so much worse than I thought it was in the dark last night. Motherfucking deer are so stupid."

He slammed the crinkled hood down and stomped around the other side, complaining as he lowered himself onto a board that rolled beneath the jacked-up car. There was still animal fur and blood stuck in the grill. The windshield was shattered, and I didn't know what was broken beneath, but I guessed that was the deer's fault too.

I hated that deer. I hated it for being in the way and for making my dad angry.

I hated when he yelled.

The metal clanging and his shouting hurt my ears. I tucked my arms around my legs, wriggling away but not daring to go too far because he'd told me I had to help.

"Pass me that wrench," he snapped.

I jumped up, staring at the pile of tools in front of me,

but I couldn't identify any of them. Fear trickled in, my hand hovering over them all, while I desperately tried to remember which one was which.

"Hurry up, kid!"

Closing my eyes and hoping for the best, I grabbed one and held it out to my dad. "Here you go."

He took it without looking at it and went to fit to something beneath the car.

"What the hell is this? I said a wrench!"

A second later, the tool came hurtling back through the air, smashing into my shin bone.

Pain exploded through my leg, and a scream erupted from inside of me as I collapsed onto the grass. I howled into the late afternoon sun, no chance of holding back the tears that fell down my cheeks. I curled into a ball, clutching my leg, and sobbed in pain.

Dad didn't care. "Shut up and pass me the actual fucking wrench. What's wrong with you? Are you stupid?"

I couldn't stop crying. It hurt so much. More than when I'd fallen off the monkey bars. More than when I'd sliced my finger on the sharp knife in the kitchen. More than when I broke my arm last summer.

I tried to reach for a different tool, but I couldn't move. Every time I tried; pain splintered through my whole body. Darkness flickered at the corners of my eyes, and my stomach churned like I wanted to puke.

Dad slid out from beneath the car and sat up, his belly sticking out from underneath a dirty blue shirt. "Stop fucking crying."

I couldn't.

He sighed, leaning over and grabbing the tool he

actually needed. "Go inside and cry to your mama, then. I don't want to hear it. Fucking sissy."

Relief poured through me, even though my leg throbbed so bad I couldn't put weight on it. I crawled away, still crying but trying to keep it quiet enough he wouldn't hear and get distracted.

The door to our house was such a long way away from the car though. I dragged myself through the long grass, hating how it made my bare arms and legs itchy. "Mommy," I whispered beneath my breath. "I want my mommy."

I shouldn't have said it.

Even when I whispered, he always seemed to hear me.

Dad stormed across the yard, catching me by the back of my shirt and lifting me like I was a shopping bag. "I can't stand your fucking sniveling, kid."

The screen door crashed back against the wall, and Dad tossed me inside.

I landed hard on the kitchen floor at my mother's feet.

In a heartbeat, she knelt, smoothing back my hair from my face. "What happened?" she whispered, running her soft hands all over me and stopping at my leg that had swollen up with a huge lump. "You're hurt!"

"What happened?" Dad asked. "What happened is your son is a useless crybaby who needs to toughen the fuck up." He moved around the kitchen, opening and slamming doors as my mom took me into her arms.

Instantly some of the pain went away. She hummed softly beneath her breath, holding me close.

I liked the sound of her heart beating, even though it was going really fast.

The pantry door slammed; Dad too angry to close it softly. "Why don't we have any fucking food? I bought all that shit for you to bake with and none of it's done!"

"I did bake," Mom said quietly. "I baked a dozen cookies two days ago. You already ate them all."

Dad dropped down on his haunches, going eye to eye with her, his voice that mean one I hated the most. "Then get your fat, lazy ass up, and bake some more."

I didn't want her to. She baked things all the time, but he never said thank you.

"Don't go," I whispered, clutching her dress.

But we both knew she had to.

That we both had to do whatever Dad wanted.

Mom stood, the shackles around her ankles and wrists jangling when she moved around the kitchen.

I hated them.

I hated how they hurt her skin. How they left her with sores. How she could never come outside into the sunshine to watch me kick the ball, even though I was getting really good at it.

Mom took down some flour and sugar and then opened the refrigerator. She added several eggs on top, carrying them to the counter above my head. She put them all down and turned to pick up the mixing bowl.

One of the eggs rolled off, cracking open and making a mess on the kitchen floor.

My dad stared at it. "Now look what you've done," he snapped at her.

"I'll clean it," Mom told his quietly. Her chains rattled as she tugged them out of the way of the mess.

Dad looked over at me, his lips twisted into a snarl. "Your mother is as stupid as the animal she was named after. And as pathetic as the one I mowed down last night." He shook his head, his words coming out with bits of spit forming at the sides of his mouth. "Just a useless little fawn."

THE END...for now. The series continues with Fawn's story in Saint View Strip #4. See www.ellethorpe.com for details on the rest of the series and free bonus scenes.

SAINT VIEW READING ORDER

EACH TRILOGY CAN STAND ALONE, BUT IF YOU WANT TO BINGE...

SAINT VIEW HIGH
REVERSE HAREM

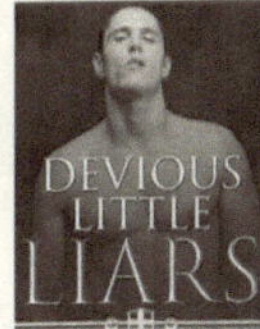

SAINT VIEW PRISON
REVERSE HAREM

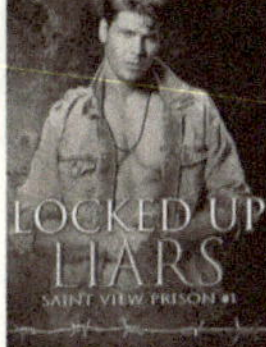

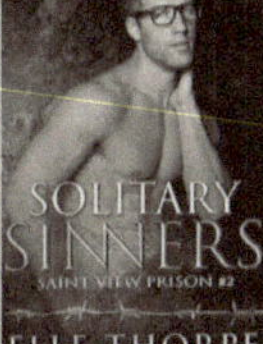

SAINT VIEW PSYCHOS
REVERSE HAREM

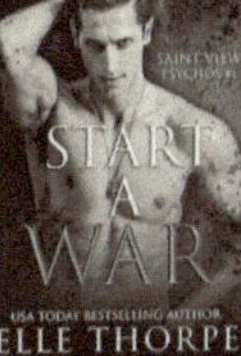

SAINT VIEW REBELS
REVERSE HAREM

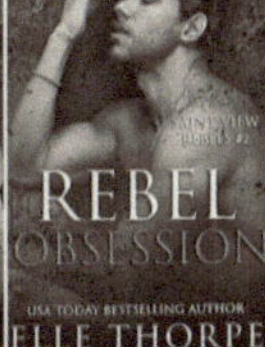

SAINT VIEW STRIP
MALE/FEMALE
(BEST READ ANY TIME AFTER PSYCHOS)

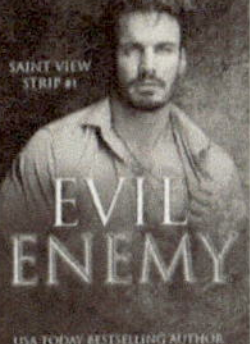

PLUS SHORT STORIES AND BONUS SCENES AT
WWW.ELLETHORPE.COM

**WANT SIGNED PAPERBACKS,
SPECIAL EDITION COVERS, OR
SAINT VIEW MERCH?**

Check out Elle's new website store at
https://www.ellethorpe.com/store

ALSO BY ELLE THORPE

Saint View High series (Reverse Harem, Bully Romance. Complete)

*Devious Little Liars (Saint View High, #1)

*Dangerous Little Secrets (Saint View High, #2)

*Twisted Little Truths (Saint View High, #3)

Saint View Prison series (Reverse harem, romantic suspense. Complete.)

*Locked Up Liars (Saint View Prison, #1)

*Solitary Sinners (Saint View Prison, #2)

*Fatal Felons (Saint View Prison, #3)

Saint View Psychos series (Reverse harem, romantic suspense. Complete.)

*Start a War (Saint View Psychos, #1)

*Half the Battle (Saint View Psychos, #2)

*It Ends With Violence (Saint View Psychos, #3)

Saint View Rebels (Reverse harem, romantic suspense)

*Rebel Revenge (Saint View Rebels, #1)

*Rebel Obsession (Saint View Rebels, #2)

*Rebel Heart (Saint View Rebels, #3)

Saint View Strip (Male/Female, romantic suspense standalones. Ongoing.)

*Evil Enemy (Saint View Strip, #1)

*Unholy Sins (Saint View Strip, #2)

*Killer Kiss (Saint View Strip, #3)

Dirty Cowboy series (complete)

*Talk Dirty, Cowboy (Dirty Cowboy, #1)

*Ride Dirty, Cowboy (Dirty Cowboy, #2)

*Sexy Dirty Cowboy (Dirty Cowboy, #3)

*Dirty Cowboy boxset (books 1-3)

*25 Reasons to Hate Christmas and Cowboys (a Dirty Cowboy bonus novella, set before Talk Dirty, Cowboy but can be read as a standalone, holiday romance)

Buck Cowboys series (Spin off from the Dirty Cowboy series. Complete.)

*Buck Cowboys (Buck Cowboys, #1)

*Buck You! (Buck Cowboys, #2)

*Can't Bucking Wait (Buck Cowboys, #3)

*Mother Bucker (Buck Cowboys, $#4)

The Only You series (Contemporary romance. Complete)

*Only the Positive (Only You, #1) - Reese and Low.

*Only the Perfect (Only You, #2) - Jamison.

*Only the Truth - (Only You, bonus novella) - Bree.

*Only the Negatives (Only You, #3) - Gemma.

*Only the Beginning (Only You, #4) - Bianca and Riley.

*Only You boxset

Add your email address here to be the first to know when new books are available!

www.ellethorpe.com/newsletter

Join Elle Thorpe's readers group on Facebook!

www.facebook.com/groups/ellethorpesdramallamas

ACKNOWLEDGMENTS

I've been waiting four years to write this book.

Augie was one of the very first Saint View characters, first appearing in book one of the world, Devious Little Liars. He was an asshole from page one. He was most definitely one of the 'bad guys' in the Saint View High series, and he did some despicable things that earned him a lot of haters. He deserved that hate.

But when I finished that series, I couldn't shake a nagging feeling that I had done Banjo dirty. That I hadn't actually given him a happily ever after, because although he was happy with Lacey and Colt and Rafe, he didn't have his mom, dad, or his brother.

Banjo is one of the sweetest characters I've ever written and while some characters would be just fine without their family, I knew Banjo wasn't.

Something also kept saying that while other characters do bad things for evil or selfish reasons, Augie did them because of how he loves his brother. He made mistakes. But I knew they were mistakes that Banjo would eventually forgive after Augie had grown up enough to own them.

I hope I managed to redeem him in your eyes too.

As always, there's an ever growing group of people who make these books possible.

Thank you to the Drama Llamas. You guys make my days fun. If you aren't already a member, it's a free reader group on Facebook where I share all sorts of stuff. Come join us, everyone is welcome. www.facebook.com/groups/ellethorpesdramallamas

Thank you to Montana Ash/Darcy Halifax for writing with me every day.

Thank you to Sara Massery, Jolie Vines, and Zoe Ashwood for the constant support, friendship, and book advice.

Thank you to the cover team:

Emily Wittig for the discreet covers and Wander Aguiar for the photography.

Thank you to my editing team:

Emmy at Studio ENP and Karen at Barren Acres Editing.

Dana, Louise, Sam, and Shellie for beta reading. Plus my ARC team for the early reviews.

Thank you to the audio team:

Kathleen and Troy at Dark Star Romance for producing this series. Thank you to Corvin and Michelle for being the voices of Augie and Ophelia.

And of course, thank you to the team who organize me and the home front:

To Donna and Ari, for taking on all the jobs I don't have time for. Best PA's ever.

To my mum, for working for us one day a week, and always being willing to have our kids when we go to signings.

To Jira, for running the online store, doing all the accounting, and dealing with all the 'people-ing.' Not to mention, being the best stay at home dad ever.

To Flick and Heidi, for helping pack swag, and to Thomas, who refuses to work for us, but will proudly tell everyone he knows that his mum is an author.

From the bottom of my heart, thank you.

Elle x